SKYWALKER:
A FAMILY AT WAR

SKYWALKER: A FAMILY AT WAR

Written by
Kristin Baver

Senior Editor Alastair Dougall
Designer Jon Hall
Senior Production Controller Louise Minihane
Production Editor Marc Staples
Managing Editor Sarah Harland
Managing Art Editor Vicky Short
Publishing Director Mark Searle

For Lucasfilm
Senior Editor Brett Rector
Creative Director of Publishing Michael Siglain
Art Director Troy Alders
Story Group Pablo Hidalgo, Emily Shkoukani,
Creative Art Manager Phil Szostak
Asset Management Shahana Alam, Chris Argyropoulos,
Nicole LaCoursiere, Gabrielle Levenson, Sarah Williams

Cover artwork: Matthew Ferguson
All images: © LucasFilm
With thanks to Megan Douglass for proofreading.

First American Edition, 2021
Published in the United States by DK Publishing
1450 Broadway, Suite 801, New York, NY 10018

A catalog record for this book is available from the Library of Congress.
ISBN: 978-0-7440-2731-0

DK books are available at special discounts when purchased in bulk for
sales promotions, premiums, fund-raising, or educational use. For details, contact:
DK Publishing Special Markets, 1450 Broadway, Suite 801, New York, NY 10018
SpecialSales@dk.com

Set in 10.6/16pt Minion Pro
Typeset by Jouve (UK), Milton Keynes
Printed and bound in Great Britain by Clays Ltd, Elcograf S.p.A.

For the Curious

www.dk.com

This book is made from
Forest Stewardship Council™
certified paper—one small
step in DK's commitment
to a sustainable future.

For Haley and Ian, the next generation.

Contents

Contents

Part Two: The Twins

Part Three: The Dyad

Prologue

The mask of Darth Vader looms over the Skywalker family like a shadow stretching over three generations.

For Anakin Skywalker, it came to be seen as a symbol of his power as a Sith Lord and Imperial loyalist. Privately, the mask was a life-supporting element of his cybernetic suit, a means of concealing his personal suffering and scarred features.

For Anakin's son, Luke, the mask symbolized the potential for evil and cruelty inside the young Jedi's own heart. It was the frozen face of a man who murdered his father and his mentor. And ultimately, it was the last piece of the Imperial machine Luke helped to dismantle in his quest for freedom from his personal demons.

For Anakin's daughter, Leia, the mask and its unseeing eyes were emblematic of the Empire's stifling regime. It was the epitome of everything she and the rebels gave their lives to fight against in their quest to break free from the shackles of Imperial regulation and despotic rule.

After Anakin's demise and the fall of the Empire, the mask was melted and deformed by the flames of his funeral pyre. That should have been the end of its story. Yet nearly 30 years later, the warped visage of the Sith Lord continued to seduce the Skywalker line with its promise of unfettered strength and supreme authority.

When Anakin's grandson Ben Solo, son of Leia, came into possession of the mask, he viewed it not as a symbol of evil, but a family heirloom, a beloved relic from a bygone era. It is said that after adopting the persona of First Order enforcer Kylo Ren, the last of the Skywalkers worshipped the mask and spoke to it with reverence, as if it were the image of an absent god or a sacred talisman.

Kylo Ren wore his own mask. This was a helmet that concealed his unscarred features, a tool for intimidation as much as a means to conceal his identity, his face, and his fear. Yet it could not compare with the metaphorical weight of Darth Vader's doomed disguise.

Darth Vader's mask was a more significant and formidable emblem of the Empire than the regime's seal or the Emperor himself. Long after the man who had worn it was gone, it retained the power to topple governments and seduce a new generation of the Skywalker line with the promise of absolute power, of total control.

Part One

THE FATHER

Chapter 1

The Force, Anakin, and Shmi

The man who would one day become the ruthless Sith Lord Darth Vader was once a boy of courage and compassion. Anakin Skywalker grew up in utter obscurity—enslaved, forced to work for food and shelter, only to have his life gambled away like chips in a game of sabacc at the whim of his master. Fortunately, he was sheltered from many of the harshest realities of life and an unjust galaxy by the tender care of his mother, Shmi Skywalker.

In her own youth, Shmi had once known freedom, but that was before she and her parents were captured by a roving band of pirates. As is typical of such a nefarious, motley lot, pirates are rarely interested in having extra mouths to feed, unless their prisoners can provide an essential service for the gang. And even then all they really care about is ready money. Shmi never spoke of what became of her parents, if she knew at all. She alone was sold in a slave market to the gangster Gardulla the Hutt. Shmi recalled the marketplace smelling like herd animals and waste matter, a dank place where the slavers who ran the auctions specialized in breaking the spirit of their captives while coming perilously close to breaking their bodies. Even after she had left the threat of the marketplace behind and relegated it to her memory, the sound of a cracking electro-whip would cause Shmi to instinctively wince in fear.

Despite these dire circumstances, Shmi Skywalker possessed seemingly boundless reserves of resilience and fortitude. While in Gardulla's service, Shmi mysteriously became pregnant with her son. There was no father to share her burden or her joy. Although she could not find the words to explain it, she dared to believe that the child was special and deserved a better life than she could give him. The Jedi Qui-Gon Jinn, when he came to know the boy, was convinced that Anakin was the one foretold in an ancient Jedi prophecy, in which the Force itself—the galaxy's all-embracing metaphysical power—and the microscopic midi-chlorians teeming inside and around all forms of life had conceived the boy.

For years, Shmi and Anakin endured a harsh existence on Tatooine, an arid and sparsely inhabited planet in the Outer Rim, where slavery was prevalent, many parsecs outside the jurisdiction of the Republic. This largely barren world was a haven for those wishing not to be found for one reason or another. Given Tatooine's pitiless desert climate and impoverished economy, those who made their home there—whether seeking solitude, forced into servitude, or slave-owning gangsters—had to be tough to survive.

While in Gardulla's custody, Shmi and Anakin were forced to live among other slaves and families in communal quarters. The young mother and child shared space with six other serfs: privacy was a dream, solitude a myth. Nevertheless, Shmi made the best of her misfortune, raising her son to care for these strangers as if they were family.

Gardulla's penchant for gambling led her to devise creative ways of settling her debts. When Anakin was still quite young, the Hutt lost Shmi and the child in an ill-advised podracing wager with another gambling obsessive, the Toydarian junk dealer Watto. This turn of events proved to be the start of better fortunes for the small Skywalker family. As Shmi and Anakin were the only slaves Watto had in his service, they were permitted to reside in a home of their own on the outskirts of Mos Espa spaceport. The building was a meager hovel in Slave Quarters Row, originally built by mining conglomerates as temporary housing for migrant workers. Constructed with neither longevity nor care in mind, it was assumed that these densely packed slums would, in time, be pulverized into nothingness by Tatooine's frequent sandstorms. Still, Shmi was content; to her, it may as well have been a palace.

Despite a more agreeable living situation, Watto was not a particularly kind master. He did, however, sometimes show flashes of compassion. If Anakin finished all his tasks he was allowed to go home early, while Shmi could perform certain quieter duties at the comfort of her private work station.

As Watto dreamed of amassing enough wealth to purchase a veritable army of laborers, Shmi focused on creating a loving home for her son. Mother and child alike worked long hours cleaning and repairing the various items and parts that came through Watto's junk shop. Anakin exhibited a remarkable aptitude for mechanical engineering; he became an expert in repairing broken droids, enabling his master to recoup far more wupiupi, one of the only forms of money the Hutt clan seemed to recognize, than any mixed bag of old components would fetch on the market. Anakin's technical prowess was the key to his survival; his skill made him a valuable servant to Watto as he turned the greedy trader's junk into profits. In his spare time, the boy was also an avid inventor, using his ingenuity to build and race podracers.

He even cobbled together a protocol droid from scraps, which he called C-3PO, that served as a physical manifestation of Anakin's deepest hopes and desires. The boy longed for a life far from Tatooine, free to explore the galaxy and fulfill his dreams of becoming something far greater than a Toydarian's property. The droid he constructed was capable of millions of forms of communication. Anakin daydreamed that, one day, with C-3PO as his faithful traveling companion, he and his mother would be able to venture anywhere in the galaxy and be understood and be able to understand the natives, whatever their language. In the meantime, Anakin hoped the droid could help his mother simply by easing her workload. What greater gift could he give the woman who had, for so long, been forced to do the bidding of more masters than he knew? A mechanical servant of her own would take some of the weight of her tedious work cleaning endless computer parts and keeping Watto's messy shop in some semblance of order.

Tucked into bed late at night, Anakin would listen with rapt attention as Shmi told him fantastical tales of the Jedi Knights and of brave young people who managed to rise above their dull lives to become heroes in their own time. Sometimes, when Shmi was too exhausted by her day's labor, Anakin would regale his mother with a favorite fable she had told him. If he was in a mischievous mood, he might instead rattle off stories of angels from far-off moons and other tales he'd heard passed between deep-space pilots when they stopped at the shop to trade or sell their wares. None of these stories involved a life on Tatooine. For why dream of what you know to be true when you can turn your mind outward, toward the great unknown among the stars?

* * *

The year Anakin turned nine years old, the course of his life was forever altered when three strangers and a sturdy-looking astromech droid entered Watto's shop. The travelers were in desperate need of parts to repair their ship, a gleaming silver craft from the planet Naboo, but soon found their only method of payment, Republic credits, was no good so far from the Core Worlds.

At first sight, the trio seemed as mismatched as one of Anakin's most cobbled-together inventions. Inside Watto's shop stood a gangly Gungan with floppy ears and a jaunty gait, soon introduced as Jar Jar Binks. This alien was accompanied by a tall man, his tied-back long hair framing kind but cautious eyes. He was clad in rough-hewn garments that were little better than the rags with which Shmi clothed her son. Anakin would come to know him as Jedi Master Qui-Gon Jinn. Between these two intriguing individuals stood the most beautiful girl the boy had ever seen.

The way the young lady carried herself suggested that she had never been forced to endure hard labor or the clawed backhand of a displeased master. In fact, it was unimaginable that she would have to answer to—well—anyone. As Anakin later learned, Padmé was really the 14-year-old Queen Amidala of Naboo in disguise; however, her humble handmaiden garb could not conceal her regal nature, or her dazzling smile and thoughtful eyes. Compared to the young boy, his face smeared with grease and engine oil, dirt beneath his fingernails, his mop of hair and ragged clothes trapping pockets of sand that he would be shaking out for hours after his day was done—Padmé was perfection personified. She seemed to hold all the promise of the galaxy in her eyes, creating a painful awareness in Anakin of how far out of reach all of his dreams really were.

All of his dreams but one: Anakin fancied himself a pilot. This ability not only afforded him a remote chance of one day escaping Tatooine—if he could get his hands on a ship powerful enough to travel beyond the planet's atmosphere—it was the only time he felt free. At the helm of almost any craft, Anakin was the master of his own destiny. Inside a cockpit or pod, he could imagine that he was far away from Watto's tumbledown shop and the unforgiving world he called home. In those rare moments, he could control whether his craft came to an abrupt halt or soared faster than he'd ever dared before. He alone could decide if he wanted to swoop left or bank right, duck beneath a rocky outcrop or climb ever higher. Anakin longed to feel just as free outside of a protective cockpit's shell, a servant to no one but himself, answering his own wishes and desires.

When thoughts of flight took him far away, his mother's careworn face brought him back to reality with a jolt. She had been a slave so long—and Anakin hated to think of leaving her to a life of solitude and servitude. Furthermore, both himself and Shmi were fitted with a transmitter to ensure their compliance, a device rigged to detonate at the first sign of escape. For a slave, thoughts of freedom were entwined with fears of certain death, although sometimes Anakin dared to wonder if the transmitter was anything more than an empty threat intended to quell the seeds of rebellion. Hoping to conquer the specter of death looming over them both, Anakin had tried to build a gadget that would locate and help him remove their transmitters, but without success.

By happenstance, or the will of the Force, Anakin came across the three offworlders he had encountered at Watto's shop a second time as they meandered through Mos Espa, no closer to procuring the parts to fix their ship. As the winds of Tatooine threatened to whip the sands into a vicious storm, Anakin invited his new exotic friends to take shelter in his humble home.

If Shmi ever allowed herself a moment of pride, it always centered on the son she had managed to raise, in the face of cruelty and carelessness, into a bright and kindhearted young man. Anakin gave freely without thought of reward by inviting the travelers to enjoy the safety and relative comforts of his home. While Watto and so many others on Tatooine were driven by greed, the Skywalkers had very little to call their own. But Shmi was adamant that her son should not grow up to be jealous of those who had more, or stingy about sharing what they could spare. Slaves they may have been, but there were still many others in the galaxy poorer than they. Shmi often reminded Anakin, as he fretted over some setback, that the biggest problem in the universe was that nobody helped one another. Then they would see about tackling the problem together. What they lacked in material wealth, they made up for in emotional riches and the ingenuity to make something useful from the bits and pieces abandoned by those who squandered their fortunes. The sufferings Shmi had endured in her own childhood—separated from her parents at such a young age, sold into a life of labor—were soothed by her boy's enthusiasm for his own creations and willingness to help others. Despite so many privileges being far beyond their reach, the Skywalkers learned to become self-reliant survivors.

When they sat down to dinner that evening, Anakin glimpsed what he believed to be the hilt of a Jedi lightsaber hidden beneath Qui-Gon's cloak and eagerly questioned him about it. In the marvelous stories Shmi had told him, just the sight of this wonderful weapon could induce whole armies to surrender; and the Jedi were so powerful they were even able to vanquish death itself . . .

Eager to impress the offworlders, and the young woman Padmé in particular, Anakin diverted them with stories of his technical skill and sharp reflexes, boasting of abilities that would surely make him the first-ever human champion of one of Tatooine's few forms of entertainment, the dangerous podracing sport. Anakin failed to mention that, though he had competed before, he never actually finished a single race. His pride was so injured by this truth that he worried that revealing his previous failures would inspire more pity than praise among his new friends.

Without much business or industry, much of Mos Espa's economy and leisure-time activity revolved around the podracing track. The featured contests involved more than a dozen racers in a variety of custom-built crafts—little more than cockpits tethered to a pair of roaring, oversized engines. These vehicles blazed around a dusty track, soaring at speeds exceeding 700 kph, slamming into one another, and dodging rocky outcrops as well as a host of other dangers and pitfalls. The most successful racers were local celebrities, openly cheating to maintain their grip on fame and the prize money afforded to winners. Spectators attended races out of curiosity, vicarious thrills, or for profit. Podraces drew high-rolling gamblers, gangsters, and would-be gangsters, who looked on from private viewing boxes. Ordinary citizens could watch from the stands or rent viewscreens to get a closer look at the fast-flying vehicles as they hurtled by tracking holocams.

Before each event, Shmi felt a creeping sense of dread close around her like a heavy cloak. She was well aware of her son's skill at the controls of a podracer, but also powerless to deny the whims of their master Watto when he forced the boy to race. There was some solace in knowing that Anakin loved the sport, but not enough to comfort a scared mother watching her only child circling a track at breakneck speed, potentially seconds away from death.

Not long after entertaining the travelers with his podracing exploits, Anakin Skywalker got his first taste of fame as a competitor in the prestigious Boonta Eve Classic. As the single largest annual podrace on Tatooine, originally conceived to commemorate the Boonta Eve holiday, the race was hosted by the notorious Hutt crime lords and drew more than one hundred thousand spectators. Jedi Qui-Gon persuaded Watto to bet that if Anakin won the race, Watto would keep the winnings, but give Qui-Gon the parts he needed to repair his ship and grant Anakin his freedom. If Anakin lost, Qui-Gon promised to give the Toydarian the Queen of Naboo's starship, leaving himself and his friends stranded. The bet was too tantalizing for Watto to resist.

To racegoers, Anakin was a decidedly risky gamble. In the previous contests Watto had forced Anakin to enter in the past, the Toydarian had never once bet on him to win. However, Qui-Gon believed the boy's luck was about to change, knowing something that no one else looking on that day was aware of. In a quiet moment, Shmi had revealed to him her most private and personal secret. Watching from the stands, only Qui-Gon and Shmi knew of Anakin's mysterious conception, and what his mother could only describe as a special power, almost a second sight, that allowed her son to perceive events before they happened. This was the reason behind Anakin's incredibly fast reflexes—a huge asset when podracing. While cleaning a superficial cut Anakin had suffered while preparing his podracer the night before, Qui-Gon had taken a small sample of the boy's blood. The Jedi Master said it was to test for infections, but he surreptitiously had the sample analyzed for midi-chlorians, the microscopic organisms that indicated a level of Force-sensitivity that could, in time, be honed and trained by the Jedi Order. The analysis revealed that Anakin possessed more midi-chlorians than the test could measure, an off-the-charts reading that surpassed that of the greatest living Jedi of the time—Master Yoda, who had trained Jedi for centuries. The results afforded the first quantifiable proof of what Shmi had long suspected—her son was special. Different. Destined for something far greater than the life of a slave.

During the race, Anakin remained calm and trusted his instincts, overcoming engine problems and evading the flaming debris of crashed vehicles. Finally, foiling a vicious attempt to force him off the track, he sailed across the finish line to glory.

Long after his victory, tales of Anakin overcoming tremendous odds to emerge Boonta Eve champion circulated throughout the region. It was obvious that Anakin Skywalker was no ordinary boy. While his podracing skills won him his freedom, they also brought hope to the hopeless: If a young human—and a slave no less—could pilot a podracer and not only survive but win, what other daring feats might those watching in the stands or at home accomplish in their own lives? What obstacles could *they* overcome?

However, as the thrill of his triumph began to fade, Anakin was forced to confront the biggest decision of his young life. Freed from slavery as part of Qui-Gon's cunning wager, the Jedi offered the young boy the chance, not only to realize his dream of leaving Tatooine, but to one day become a Jedi Knight.

Anakin knew he had a life-changing decision to make and looked to his mother for guidance. Escaping Tatooine would give him the opportunity to explore the galaxy as he'd always dreamed. Leaving opened up exciting possibilities—yet, at the same time, Anakin could not deny that part of him longed to remain. Accepting Qui-Gon's kind offer meant Anakin would have to renounce the comforts, scant as they were, of everything he had known. Worst of all, he would have to leave his mother. He would be leaping into a metaphorical abyss, untethered, and forced to explore who he might become without her strength or guidance. Everything would change.

However, a Jedi does not believe in luck or in accidents. Anakin and Qui-Gon's paths seemed destined to cross. And Shmi, wise as any Jedi, knew how to help her son make the best choice for himself, the first choice he would make as a free individual.

Allowing her young son the ability to choose his own path and pushing for him to accept the gift of change was Shmi's ultimate sacrifice. Would she have wanted anything different? Above all else, Shmi's instincts were to keep her son safe. For her, Anakin was the sole bright spot in a life of drudgery, during which she had fought hard to find a balance between cautious optimism and the dark realities of slavery. And when she was called upon, she did exactly what her son would, years later, *fail* to do. She let go.

That is not to say that Anakin made the choice with confidence. Shmi told her son to be brave—a simple and final piece of advice for him to carry into the future. She also told him not to look back. Embarking on the path to his destiny in the care of Qui-Gon Jinn aboard Queen Amidala's Royal Naboo starship, Anakin first made the acquaintance of Obi-Wan Kenobi, his future master and friend.

In time, Anakin would be hailed for his courage. But the only way he could walk away with a clear conscience was to make a promise, a solemn oath to one day return to Tatooine and free his mother. He would never stop looking back.

Chapter 2

Qui-Gon's Promise

Anakin Skywalker was not the first slave Qui-Gon Jinn had resolved to set free. He was fiercely opposed to the odious practice of slavery, which occurred throughout the galaxy—sometimes right under the nose of the Republic, even though the bondage of sentient life was officially outlawed.

Qui-Gon was regarded as something of a maverick among the Jedi Order. He was known to challenge his Padawan, Obi-Wan Kenobi, with penetrating questions like, "What use are ideals if we cannot fit them to the universe as we find it?" Qui-Gon was so fearless, he wasn't even afraid to question the Jedi Order's rules or the Jedi Council itself when he felt it was acting upon the *letter* rather than the *spirit* of the Jedi Code.

Eight years earlier, on a mission to the planet Pijal—when Anakin was still just a babe in arms unknown to the Jedi—Master Qui-Gon Jinn had an epiphany when a Republic representative was sent to ensure an important treaty be signed to open a new hyperspace route. Qui-Gon realized the pact essentially supported the use of slave labor by one of the conglomerates involved, the powerful Czerka Corporation, ensuring it could operate in perpetuity while continuing to utilize an illegal work force of droids and sentient captives. His conscience deeply troubled, Qui-Gon attempted to free a young woman, Rahara Wick, who had helped him to surreptitiously investigate a terrorist cell opposing the treaty. Sadly, she was soon recaptured by the cruel Czerka organization, but the Jedi was successful in ensuring the treaty was not signed without revisions that allowed for further review.

Qui-Gon's moral discomfort increased when, by means of the Force, he experienced a series of dark and disturbing visions of the future—visons that converted the formerly pragmatic Jedi into a true believer in the literal meanings of some of the Jedi Order's most ancient prophecies. In his youth, Qui-Gon was unsure whether these ancient prophets were foretelling events to come, or whether their writings were simply metaphors that could be applied to things that had already transpired. As he grew older, Qui-Gon retained a youthful curiosity for these prophecies, which he attempted to share through his teaching of his Padawan, sometimes to the younger man's irritation.

On Pijal, the Force showed Qui-Gon glimpses of a bloody battle erupting at the coronation of the planet's new queen, Fanry. Although both his apprentice Obi-Wan and, more importantly, the Jedi Council doubted that Qui-Gon's visions were anything more than dreams—or possibly, fragments of a future in perpetual flux—Qui-Gon's nightmarish visions turned out to be true. From this point on, he developed a deeper respect and understanding of the Force's cosmic powers.

After Qui-Gon returned to the galactic capital of Coruscant, he was unable to shake the feeling that the Jedi Order itself was starting down a dark path. Master Jinn was not alone in his concerns, but all those who suggested interference by the ancient order of the Sith or a coming war, including the Jedi Master Sifo-Dyas who once held a seat on the Jedi Council, were summarily ignored. Many of Qui-Gon's worries centered around political gambits. It seemed to Qui-Gon that the Jedi had become more attuned to acting as secret police and enforcers for the highest-ranking politicians rather than fulfilling their oath as peacekeepers of the galaxy. Too often, the Jedi were wielded as a weapon of the Republic, a threat to bring systems in line with the Galactic

Senate's authority. Through the lens of history, it was clear that the democratic Republic was indeed entering a dark time, bedeviled by greedy delegates inside the Senate and beset by allegations of corruption that went all the way to the Supreme Chancellor's office. Civility had given way to ruthless politicking.

Around this time, Qui-Gon received a coveted offer to join the Jedi Council and thus become one of the 12 Jedi steering the Order and offering guidance to Jedi Masters in the field. To the other members' astonishment, Qui-Gon rejected their proposal, certain that his true path was still unspooling before him. And so it was that, just a few years later, Jedi Master Qui-Gon came to be traveling the galaxy with his Padawan Obi-Wan Kenobi when he happened upon young Anakin, the child whom Qui-Gon came to believe was the individual mentioned in an ancient Jedi prophecy: *"A Chosen One shall come, born of no father, and through him will ultimate balance in the Force be restored."*

As a teacher, Master Qui-Gon Jinn was unorthodox, but he was calm in battle, a steady guide in the mysteries of the Force, and humble in his study of the future. He sought to understand rather than control, recognizing through his education that to see the future was to accept the will of fate, not to recklessly attempt to change it. Certainty could only breed arrogance, another portal to the darkness. Qui-Gon had once been the student of Jedi Master Dooku, who subsequently fell to the dark side and took the name Darth Tyranus and the nobility of his birthright as the Count of Serenno. However, there was nothing in Master Qui-Gon's character to suggest any burning embers of the same thirst for power. Quite the opposite; there was something about his calm demeanor, serene blue eyes, and even tone that made people instinctively trust him.

As Anakin embarked on his lonely journey among the stars, his mother's face receding into memory, Qui-Gon became the closest thing Anakin had to a family. For a boy who had only ever known a mother's love, the Jedi was something of a father figure. However, Qui-Gon was preordained to keep Anakin at an emotional distance. Compassion was encouraged in a Jedi Knight, but not love, and certainly not fatherhood.

Qui-Gon was nevertheless ready to defend the boy against danger, and with the Queen of Naboo in tow, danger came calling before the crew could even leave Tatooine.

On the sand dunes at the outskirts of Mos Espa, Qui-Gon and the child encountered a Zabrak menace called Darth Maul. While the Jedi Master and Sith Lord clashed lightsabers, Anakin alerted the others to Qui-Gon's plight, and he escaped Maul by leaping aboard the vessel as it hovered nearby.

***

Following this harrowing encounter, as they approached Coruscant, the capital of the Republic Anakin had his first hint of how different his life would be far from home. The vast metropolis stretched as far as the eye could see, level by level, reaching toward the sky. Coruscant was about as far removed from his origins as any world could be.

Gazing down at the magnificent, urbanized heart of the Republic gave Anakin a chance to wonder what his life might have been like had he not been enslaved. If his grandparents had never been captured by pirates, and his mother never sold into slavery, he might have been born on a prosperous world under Republic rule. Whether his family would have still been poor or reclining among riches was impossible to say. However, had his life begun on a more civilized world, his unrivalled connection to the Force may have been discovered much sooner. The Jedi would have sought him out as a youngling with the raw, untapped gift of Force-sensitivity and patiently helped him reach his full potential.

When Qui-Gon brought Anakin before the Jedi Council, Anakin was much older than most who typically walk such a path. The oldest initiates into the Order were typically no more than five years old, and even those raised some eyebrows. The Force was strong with him, of that there could be no dispute. But even under the watchful gaze of the

Jedi Council, Anakin could not fully reconcile the opportunity to become a Jedi with the harsh reality of missing his mother. That emotional pull, coupled with his age, gave the wisest Jedi pause. Padawans were not expressly forbidden from communicating with their birth parents or siblings, but most who were brought to the Jedi Temple as younglings felt little connection to their biological families, having been inducted into the Order as infants. After nearly a decade with his mother, Anakin could never forget Shmi in this manner. Nor could he reach her. With no way to tell her that he was safe and thriving, or to know for sure how she was faring, anxiety lurked beneath the surface of his outwardly controlled demeanor.

For the first time, Anakin felt the weight of a predetermined future when, standing before the Jedi Council, he was hailed as the Chosen One. His pride swelled at the notion, the first seeds of an arrogance that would fully bloom when he reached adulthood. Qui-Gon maintained that finding Anakin was the will of the Force. Even those Jedi who scoffed at Qui-Gon's fervent belief in prophecy could not argue against the vergence in the Force that surrounded the boy, a cosmic supernova that seemed to dwell deep inside him.

However, despite Anakin's predisposition and strength in the Force, his training would require him to overcome both emotional and physical obstacles. Even at the age of nine, he was already far behind other Padawans and younglings in basic lightsaber skills. He had often unwittingly called upon his strong connection to the Force while at the controls of a hurtling podracer, but actually harnessing the power of the Force was a very different matter. Anakin had no real understanding and therefore little respect for the Force as a spiritual guide through life. He could not wrap his young mind around the idea that he was a part of some all-powerful energy at work in the galaxy when he had endured so many individual hardships. If he were truly as strong as they said, he wondered why he had been enslaved his whole life. And why couldn't he have freed his mother with a flick of his Force-wielding hand?

As the Jedi Council gazed upon Anakin for the first time, wise, diminutive Master Yoda sensed that Anakin was gripped by fear. And fear was a *dangerous* ally. For the Jedi, fear was a path to the dark side of the Force, an entry point to misgivings that could be nursed into anger and hate. Nevertheless, Anakin's emotional response to his situation, including his fears, was a very human reaction to the sudden upheaval he had experienced in his life; Qui-Gon believed that, with the proper guidance, Anakin's natural anxieties would subside and be replaced by a Jedi's clarity of vision. If Jinn was correct, the boy would bring balance to the Force, defeating the creeping darkness that was already beginning to cloud both the Force itself and the Jedi Order's abilities to perceive the threat to it.

However, where Qui-Gon saw promise, Obi-Wan Kenobi and many on the Jedi Council sensed trouble. Obi-Wan did not hide his concern, even from Anakin himself. The boy's raw power in the Force was something to be wary of. He was malleable, and in the wrong hands, such explosive potential could be turned to evil.

Few were surprised that Qui-Gon defied the Council's initial adverse reaction to his request to make good on his promise and train the child. With Obi-Wan almost ready to become a Jedi Knight himself, Qui-Gon was free to take on a new Padawan, and he was determined that Padawan should be Anakin—once the Council came around to the idea, at least.

Qui-Gon began to gently coax Anakin toward a greater understanding in the ways of the Force. If questioned, Qui-Gon would have argued that he was not training the boy, merely providing guidance as a mentor and guardian in his absent mother's stead. Just as he had done while helping Anakin into his podracer before the Boonta Eve Classic, Qui-Gon offered the boy the benefit of his wisdom: "Always remember, your focus determines your reality," he told him. "Stay close to me and you'll be safe." Those words would resound in Anakin's subconscious for years to come, an echo of wisdom—and false hope—forming the basis of his doubts that anyone could truly protect him. And if no one could, his young mind reasoned, he would have to become the strongest Jedi who had ever lived in order to protect those around him instead. If he focused hard enough, he could make it come true.

At this time, the unscrupulous Trade Federation was implementing a blockade on the planet of Naboo, stopping all shipments to the peaceful planet in protest over the taxation of trade routes. However, this boycott was merely a clever cover for a plot to invade. While the Galactic Senate sat idly by, Qui-Gon, Anakin, Obi-Wan Kenobi, and the faithful astromech droid R2-D2 embarked upon a mission to protect Queen Amidala and disrupt the Trade Federation's invasion of her planet. Once on Naboo, Padmé revealed herself to be Queen Amidala and forged an alliance with the Gungan army to mount a counterattack against the Trade Federation invaders. In the midst of their success, Qui-Gon and Obi-Wan once more encountered the beastly Darth Maul.

This warrior was strong in the Force and carried a double-bladed lightsaber that burned blood red, betraying his allegiance to the dark side. With his appearance, came irrefutable proof: the Sith, an ancient order of Force-wielders devoted to the dark side, deception, and greed, long thought defeated and destroyed, had returned. Beneath a cloak of secrecy, a new Sith Lord, Darth Sidious, and his apprentice Darth Maul, had risen up, secretly orchestrating the Trade Federation's invasion of Naboo as their first act in a scheme that would ultimately lead to the last days of the Republic and give rise to the Galactic Empire. In a duel that pitted the light against the darkness, Qui-Gon and Obi-Wan fought Darth Maul, unaware of the true malignant deceit of the Sith at work inside the Galactic Senate. As the Jedi would learn too late, Darth Sidious was really Sheev Palpatine, a placid-looking senator from Naboo who was willing to sacrifice his homeworld to push the peaceful Republic to the brink of war.

As the battle raged, Qui-Gon was pierced by Darth Maul's blade. Determined to avenge his master, Obi-Wan attacked Maul, but in his anger and despair lost his own lightsaber and nearly his life. Summoning the last of his strength, and empowered by the Force, Obi-Wan called Qui-Gon's lightsaber to his hand to cleave Maul in two. Thus the apprentice and the sacred weapon came together to avenge the fallen Jinn.

It was too late for medical intervention; no amount of bacta could heal Qui-Gon's mortal wound. All Obi-Wan could do was cradle his master's head and heed the Jedi's dying wish: To train Anakin Skywalker, despite his own deep misgivings.

***

Had Anakin been more attuned to the Force, he might have felt the tremor as Master Jinn's life was extinguished. As it was, the boy was doing what he did best: flying. Finding himself thrust into the battle, Anakin and R2-D2 sought shelter inside a Naboo starfighter. Through a combination of smashing buttons and switches to override the autopilot and R2-D2's navigational skill, the pair managed to take off. Whether by luck or the will of the Force, Anakin piloted his fighter toward the Trade Federation's Droid Control Ship, which was commanding a legion of mechanical troops on the ground. Landing right inside the vessel, Anakin fired his laser cannons at a handful of B1 battle droids. Just as Qui-Gon had advised, Anakin relied upon his instincts and lightning reflexes—and a lucky shot ignited the enemy ship's main reactor, effectively ending the battle on the planet's surface below. To Anakin, the experience of battle was more intense and exhilarating, more thrilling and terrifying than any podrace.

Once back on the ground, Anakin's thrill of victory was immediately tempered by the crushing news of Qui-Gon's death. In a few short days, Anakin's life was completely altered and reimagined by the guidance and teachings of this mysterious Jedi. With his swift demise, all Anakin could think was: "What will happen to me now?" In the darkest corners of his mind, fear sent him spiralling into hypothetical scenarios where he was forced back into servitude, never to see his mother again.

Although no one realized what was at stake at the time, Anakin's very future hung in the balance. Had Qui-Gon survived and Maul been vanquished, Anakin would have been raised under the watchful, calm tutelage of a seasoned teacher. Although the two would likely have had their disagreements, Qui-Gon's compassion for the former slave might well have brought about a very different outcome. Perhaps Qui-Gon himself would have helped his Padawan return to Tatooine and free the slaves. At the very least, he would have empathized with Anakin's restlessness with the strict Jedi Code, offering solutions beyond the scope of Obi-Wan Kenobi's regulation-driven mind. Perhaps Shmi Skywalker would have been saved. In either case, the predatory Sith Master Darth Sidious may well have had a more difficult time manipulating young Anakin's future and twisting his many natural gifts into perverse, unrecognizable versions of themselves.

As it was, almost as quickly as he'd found it, Anakin lost the closest thing he had ever had to a paternal presence, a willing guide with an unshakable belief in his abilities. For those precious few days, Qui-Gon was a calm advisor, a much-needed buoy for the stormy passions of the young, Force-sensitive boy. Qui-Gon had perfected the art of meditation in combat, focusing his energy for the most skilled defense in his quest to maintain peace in the galaxy. According to the Jedi Code, even in conflict, a Jedi could stay true to the Order's teachings by accessing its connection to knowledge, serenity, and harmony instead of giving into emotion, passion, and chaos, using the Force and even their lightsabers only for defense.

The specter of Qui-Gon would loom large in Anakin's thoughts as he embarked on his quest to become a Jedi and the trauma of losing his master would haunt Anakin in a very different way than the separation from his mother. While Shmi held the assurance of the comforts he knew, Qui-Gon had given him the promise of a meaningful future. The patient Jedi represented a bridge between Anakin's former enslaved self and the vast unknown, a future of infinite possibilities the boy was only beginning to grasp.

The sole remaining constant in Anakin's life was the Force itself. The soon-to-be-trained Jedi Padawan could feel the thrum of energy binding the galaxy together. Watching the Jedi Master's body turn to ash on a sacred funeral pyre, Anakin felt a profound sense of loss. In light of the prophecy, Anakin wondered if his very existence had somehow brought danger upon his kind friend. With Obi-Wan's help, Anakin hoped to prove Qui-Gon Jinn's most earnest and heartfelt belief—that he was, truly, the Chosen One.

Chapter 3

Two Mentors

A passionate nature predisposed to internal and external conflict characterizes the Skywalker bloodline. However some of the blame for Anakin's all-too-human, troubled temperament also rested with the challenging circumstances he found himself in and those who nurtured him in his formative years. When the calm, caring, guiding influence of Shmi and Qui-Gon Jinn was gone, two very different individuals stepped into the breach to fill the emotional void in Anakin's life. The first was his new Jedi Master, Obi-Wan Kenobi; the second was Sheev Palpatine.

As Anakin grew up, he idealized his memory of Qui-Gon, especially in the moments when he found himself at odds with Obi-Wan. The Jedi Knight made good on his promise to Qui-Gon, fulfilling his dying wish with the blessing of the Jedi Council to take Anakin as his Padawan. Master Yoda was a lone dissenting voice, concerned by the danger he felt inherent in the boy's training.

In their first years together, Anakin came to see Obi-Wan in much the same reverent light he held Qui-Gon's memory, looking up to his master with awe and unwavering belief. But in his mind's darkest corners, Anakin's perception of his master was gradually colored by doubts he had overheard Obi-Wan express when Anakin was just a boy. Kenobi had called Skywalker "dangerous." No matter how he tried to shake this from his mind, the remark embedded itself in the boy's subconscious. In moments of despair, Anakin's deepest fears appeared to him as an ugly truth: Because Qui-Gon Jinn had died, Obi-Wan was stuck with an apprentice he didn't want or ask for, and one whom he believed would do more harm than good.

From Obi-Wan's perspective, it was Anakin who had got the raw deal of being saddled with a master who was barely beyond the Jedi trials himself, and who was still grieving the death of Qui-Gon. If Obi-Wan was powerless to help his master at the moment he needed it most, after being struck down by Darth Maul's blade, how could he be sure he could set Anakin on the right path?

For centuries, the Jedi Order had acted as moral guides to those who wandered, teachers strong in the Force helping those in need to learn the skills to help themselves. In this manner, the Jedi maintained peace in the galaxy—or at least on the planets under Republic control. At the height of its power, the Jedi Order had close to 10,000 members. Nevertheless, the Jedi were so intertwined with the politicians in the Galactic Senate it was virtually impossible for them to act without the Republic's consent. As a result, their particular form of guidance and hard-won wisdom was reserved only for systems that ideologically aligned themselves with democracy.

Young Anakin Skywalker had great difficulty understanding the rules that governed the scope of the Jedi's activities. To his mind, their reticence to intervene and help systems outside the Republic's jurisdiction seemed to go against the Order's very principles. Already, at the age of 12, and only a few years into his training under Obi-Wan Kenobi, Anakin began to doubt his path as a Jedi Knight, and even considered leaving the Order altogether. Obi-Wan, for his part, also had doubts about Anakin's future. But, like his master before him, Obi-Wan was reluctant to blame Anakin. Instead, he tended to blame himself for the boy's troubles.

On a mission to Carnelion IV to answer a distress beacon, Kenobi attempted to teach his young charge about the necessary limitations of the Republic and the Jedi's sphere of influence. The icy planet's civilization had been nearly destroyed by civil war. Standing amid the ruins, Anakin found it hard to comprehend how the Jedi and the Republic could have amassed such power, superior capabilities honed to intervene in just such a situation, and sit idly by and do nothing.

During the mission, the pair encountered members of the warring native tribes. Anakin employed his deft skill at fixing tech to aid the cause of a group known as the Open. For a moment, he relished being hailed as the savior of the planet, but he had been deceived, manipulated into aiding one side of the conflict against the other, while Obi-Wan became involved on the opposite side. They were ultimately saved when a Republic fleet intervened, but their quest foreshadowed things to come for master and apprentice.

Despite Obi-Wan's initial misgivings about Anakin and their near-20-year age gap, Kenobi came to see Skywalker as a brother, an equal, a partner. As Kenobi entered his thirties he could see that Anakin still required his tutoring and guidance but was on his way to becoming a Jedi Knight in his own right. However, that bond never seemed to be enough for the troubled young man who, above all, craved a parent's love and guidance.

Anakin presented many difficulties to the Jedi shepherding his care. He was headstrong and given to challenging his master openly in front of others, when he should have been following Obi-Wan's lead. Kenobi could entertain a spirited debate behind closed doors in the name of education, but Anakin's unabashed defiance sometimes made the master feel as if he was losing control of his apprentice. Anakin's late entry into the Order meant years of lost training; to try to make up for that time, Anakin's teachers put him in classes with other Jedi learners who were far younger than him. Anakin felt out of place while also behind those in his age group. Early on it became clear that Anakin could not follow the well-trodden path of an ordinary Padawan; his life experiences and genetic makeup set him apart, making the shelter of the Jedi Temple feel more like a cage than a sanctuary.

Among the other Padawans, Anakin was thus something of an outcast. He was naturally curious, often asking questions about Qui-Gon Jinn's fatal duel, and once used his acumen with droids to alter a training program to battle a holo creation that looked disturbingly like Darth Maul. He seemed to be transfixed by the past. Whisperings that he was the Chosen One certainly didn't help when he tried to blend in and convince the other young Jedi that he was just like them. But it was more than this prophecy that set him apart from the others. Acceptance in the Order does not dull the sharp tongue of a child, and Anakin's impoverished upbringing as a slave made him an easy target for ridicule.

Fueled by jealousy of his abilities, the other students would murmur to each other that, skilled with a lightsaber though he was, Anakin Skywalker would never be a great Jedi. He was still too much of a *slave* to his emotions, they laughed. Just a slave. The words infuriated Anakin, igniting the combination fear and fury that so often threatened to boil over in the young man. In one instance, he turned to meet the gaze of his attackers, hatred for them coursing through his body. Reaching through the Force, he snatched their lightsabers from their belts, flipped the weapons and ignited them in the air, an emphatic challenge to their arrogance.

It was not the Jedi way to use the Force for attack, nor to cut down mindless creatures merely following their nature. A well-trained Knight should be able to send even the most threatening beast safely on its way without bloodshed simply by bending its will. However, this skill often eluded young Anakin. When seeking to calm a vicious creature, his own doubts and trepidations would get in the way. At those moments, hacking at the danger before him with his lightsaber was the only solution that presented itself. Anakin's deep well of unfettered rage made calming another creature's aggression virtually impossible.

At these times, his master Obi-Wan would intervene, rebuking his Padawan for losing control of his emotions. For his part, Anakin seemed to accept that he still had much work to do to contain his repressed feelings of anger and fear.

Obi-Wan convinced himself that, with enough training, Anakin's barely suppressed rage was simply an instability that, with patience, he would overcome in time. However, it was patience, with himself and the system, that Anakin found the most elusive of all the Jedi teachings.

Anakin's curiosity and dissatisfaction with the status quo were natural for a boy of his age, Obi-Wan realized. However, while Anakin had respect for his master as an individual, he was far less impressed by the teachings they were sworn to follow. Obi-Wan wondered whether he was the best teacher for such a challenging and extraordinary student. He longed for Qui-Gon's guidance, even just a moment to commune with his former master and seek his counsel. As it was, he could only rely on the years he had spent with his mentor and the lessons acquired during their partnership in life.

Anakin's rebellious ways reminded Obi-Wan of Qui-Gon's unorthodox methods—at times it almost seemed to Obi-Wan that Anakin could have been Qui-Gon's son, no matter how unlikely the idea seemed. As it was, Obi-Wan was the closest thing Anakin had to a father, and, just like many children across the galaxy, Anakin chafed when Obi-Wan showed disappointment in him and his actions. The young man convinced himself that his master failed to see his true strength and that he was being stifled by his criticism. In time, according to the Jedi prophecy, Anakin would rival some of the greatest Jedi alive, including the legendary Masters Yoda and Mace Windu, champions of the Jedi Order and its guardianship of the galaxy. Knowing that his future held such possibilities fueled Anakin's resentment against his master. This resentment fostered another perilous character trait for a future Jedi Knight: hubris.

***

Meanwhile, Sheev Palpatine, having moved up from Senator for Naboo to become the Supreme Chancellor of the Galactic Republic, watched

Anakin's journey with detached attentiveness. His exalted position gave Palpatine almost unrestricted political power and unlimited access to the Jedi Masters and their abilities. With a benevolent smile plastered across his wrinkled face, Palpatine could walk into the Jedi Temple at any time and turn a kindly offer of helping to shape Anakin's future into a command that not even Master Windu could refuse.

Unbeknown to the Galactic Republic and everyone else, Palpatine was secretly a Sith Lord. A cloud of the dark side's making concealed this fact from even the most experienced Jedi Masters, who sensed something nefarious at work but could not trace its source. Thus Palpatine enjoyed the protection of the Jedi instead of their enmity. Well aware that Anakin had helped end the Trade Federation's blockade and invasion of Naboo, the Chancellor's home world, the devious Sith used this knowledge to insert himself into Anakin's life just as the young Padawan was questioning his place among the Jedi.

Because no one within the Order—not even Obi-Wan—sensed his true intentions, Palpatine prepared Anakin for a dark future as his Sith apprentice with impunity. Skywalker's skill with a lightsaber and volatile personality made him the ideal candidate, Palpatine knew. While becoming one of Anakin's closest confidants, the calculating politician schemed to instill a dangerous sense of ambition in the already arrogant boy.

As Anakin neared his teenage years, his roiling emotions called for the steady calm of Qui-Gon Jinn or the acceptance of his mother; Sheev Palpatine was a willing and welcoming substitute for both. When he called Anakin "son," the boy felt that he would do anything for him, just for the chance to feel part of a family again.

Using the seedy underworld of Coruscant as his classroom, Palpatine opened the young man's eyes to the suffering of those dwelling on the planet's lowest levels, far below the glittering cities where Palpatine ruled over the Galactic Senate and Anakin studied in the sacred Jedi Temple. Many residents of these gloomy sub-surface levels had never even seen sunlight, a tragedy that a boy raised beneath the twin suns of Tatooine couldn't even imagine.

Palpatine claimed these expeditions were a way of understanding some of the less-fortunate inhabitants of the Republic's core world. In truth, they were ploys—tests—to not only see if Anakin was pliant, but to expose Anakin to the hypocrisies inherent in the Republic that, Palpatine confidently expected, would one day lead him to reject the Jedi Code.

Right under the nose of Republic officials, sentient beings were being bought and sold as slaves in this hopeless district, a disturbing reminder of Anakin's own past. Although the young man claimed to rarely think about his childhood enslavement after his induction into the Order, Palpatine saw through the lie and into Anakin's heart, where he still hoped to help his mother and free other slaves, not only on Tatooine, but all across the galaxy.

With a benevolent sigh, Palpatine deftly probed Anakin's insecurities while praising the boy in the ways he craved. This was the first, but certainly not the last, time that Palpatine would feed Anakin's ego. Palpatine frequently hailed the young man as the most gifted Jedi he had ever met. To Anakin, Palpatine's praise, pointed questions, and insightful observations seemed to forge a strong connection, a bond that he rarely enjoyed with his fellow Jedi.

Bit by bit, Palpatine cunningly stoked the young man's disillusion with the status quo on Coruscant's surface, where prosperity reigned, without a thought to the less fortunate souls below. This fresh way of thinking validated and mirrored many of Anakin's own concerns; he never suspected that Palpatine was quietly clawing at his emotional wounds. In this way, Palpatine forged the first link in the bond between himself and the young man he genially referred to as his boy. He made Anakin promise that he would not disclose what he had seen or learned on the sub-levels when he returned to the Temple. It would be their secret.

Knowing Anakin's doubts and fears enabled Palpatine to more easily expose the cracks in the boy's will, allowing the darkness in. Palpatine would sometimes confess to being wistfully envious of the predetermined life of a Jedi—and at such a young age, too!—when all of his own life had been made up of tough choices. Though Palpatine's words were seemingly kindly meant, to Anakin, the ability to choose his destiny was a freedom he was reluctant to relinquish. He had chosen to walk the Jedi path, but, since his acceptance in the Order, every decision had been made for him. And in hindsight, even that first step seemed like a childish choice, made on a whim by an uneducated young slave because a magical man with a weapon made of light had offered him the chance to be free. Intellectually, Anakin knew that he was no prisoner; he could leave the Order at any time. But Palpatine's words struck home—the course of Anakin's life would indeed be predetermined if he remained on the path to become a Jedi Master. While Obi-Wan earnestly believed that being a part of the Jedi Order made him stronger than being an individual on his own, Anakin felt more at ease being one half of a whole, even with all of his skills and talents. Always two. No more. No less.

Anakin was quickly learning that the life of a peacekeeper was not free. A Jedi was devoted to the Order, and as such had to obey the Jedi Council even when an individual's personal convictions clashed with their guidance. Far below the surface of Coruscant, Palpatine had surreptitiously exposed a different ideological path to the insecure Jedi. Under the sway of the Supreme Chancellor, skilled in the art of suggestion, Anakin was a more than willing recipient of the older man's insinuations. Watching a senator with a pronounced gambling addiction bet everything on a roll of the dice, Palpatine speculated that an unfavorable result might be enough to drive him to a level of greed that could finally be exposed by the Chancellor's office. Palpatine wondered if the Jedi's mastery of the Force might allow them to manipulate the dice, and drive the corrupt senator toward certain ruin and exposure. It was easy enough for Anakin to rationalize that it was the spirit of the

Jedi Code, if not the letter of their law, not to intervene in this way. Anakin loved to fix things to his liking and began to nurse a misplaced belief that, like the broken bits of junk in Watto's shop, with enough time he could mend anything. Even the galaxy. By using his abilities for good, shaping future events, he began to see himself as a savior once more.

Qui-Gon Jinn, too, had enjoyed fixing things. The Jedi had once manipulated a chance cube to win a bet against Watto, when the smug Toydarian had offered that one of his slaves could be freed through a gamble—Anakin or his mother. Although Anakin was unaware of Qui-Gon's own manipulations of fate—and Anakin's future—in that case, he was no stranger to Qui-Gon's line of thinking that the Jedi ideals were useless if they did not serve the interests of the flesh and blood individuals living in the galaxy.

The teenaged Jedi, with Obi-Wan's guidance, ultimately resolved to continue on the path toward becoming a Knight. But most importantly to young Anakin, Palpatine had offered him a place by his side, once his training was complete. An alternate future, a door to be opened, if Anakin desired, after he had mastered all the Jedi had to offer. On the surface, Palpatine seemed to be promising the young man the sense of belonging that he longed for. In reality, Palpatine saw Anakin as a powerful tool for his masterplan: a new Galactic Empire with himself as supreme ruler.

Chapter 4

Love and Loss

By the time Anakin Skywalker reached adulthood, he was at war with himself. Influenced by Supreme Chancellor Sheev Palpatine's promptings, the Jedi apprentice was torn between the self-sacrifice required by the Jedi Order, and his own burning desires to go his own way, and fulfill his destiny. Just as the Force created a bright vergence in the young man, his longing for a future he could control centered around the radiant Padmé Amidala.

It is not uncommon for a young Jedi to feel love and affection, just as every Jedi must contend with their own demons beckoning them toward the darkness. However, in every case, a Padawan must choose who they will become and whether they will be ruled by their emotions or learn to control those feelings. They alone must decide to remain connected to the larger balance of the Force or allow themselves to be skewed toward more egocentric pursuits. The path of control and kinship with the Force can lead to a selfless life within the Jedi Order; while powerful emotional attachment to another person is likely to result in a life of self-centered ambitions and feelings. Anakin liked to think he could resolve this dichotomy; all he needed to do was to find the right approach to bypass the seemingly stringent Jedi Code.

When Anakin and Padmé had first met, their circumstances could not have been more dissimilar—she was used to living in well-appointed, palatial apartments. However, she had grown up on Naboo in a simple stone house that had been built by the roughened hands of her father, Ruwee. Padmé always felt a sense of calm and serenity when she crossed the threshold and breathed in the familiar odors of her ancestral home. For Padmé and her older sister, Sola, the humble abode was warmed by the love Ruwee and their mother, Jobal, had for each other and their children. Both Padmé's parents instilled compassion for others in their young daughters, taking them off-world for relief work to give them a greater understanding of the cooperation and community that helped build a truly great civilization.

By the age of 14, the brilliant young woman was already an accomplished politician, having secured election as Queen of Naboo. In the midst of the first of her two two-year terms, when her ship was forced to land on Tatooine, she chanced to meet the nine-year-old slave who would become the Jedi Anakin Skywalker. For both of them, this encounter was significant for very different reasons.

For Padmé, the desolate planet exposed the young ruler to the stark realities of the greater galaxy, where slavery was still prevalent, despite the Republic's rules forbidding it. Subsequently, Anakin and the Jedi Qui-Gon and Obi-Wan had helped to free her planet in the Battle of Naboo when the world she loved was oppressed by the Trade Federation—a debt neither she nor her planet could ever repay.

When her second term as ruler was complete and a new queen was elected, Padmé planned to return to Tatooine to begin humanitarian efforts there, inspired by the memory of Shmi Skywalker and the countless faceless servants she represented. However, when Padmé was offered the chance to continue her political career as Senator of Naboo, she dispatched one of her handmaidens, Sabé, to Anakin's homeworld instead and chose to serve as her planet's key ambassador in the Galactic Senate. Neither project seemed to impress her friend and former Senator of Naboo, Sheev Palpatine, but Padmé was not to be swayed even by the Supreme Chancellor on matters that she felt were fundamental to the

Republic's democratic values. She adamantly believed that the protections inherent in a working democracy should be extended to every citizen in the galaxy, not only to those who inhabited planets where the Republic found valuable resources. Padmé was regarded as a woman who was not afraid to stare evil in the face, one who refused to back down out of fear or cowardice.

As she neared adulthood, Padmé's outspoken nature made her a target for detractors, chief among them the Trade Federation leaders she had clashed with when she sat on the throne. The galaxy at large was becoming fractured at this time, and unrest in the Galactic Senate was also increasing, with thousands of solar systems prepared to leave the Republic as part of the Separatist movement led by the political idealist and former Jedi, Count Dooku.

In time, as Anakin Skywalker—five years Padmé's junior—neared his twenties, the Separatist regime made it more and more difficult for the Jedi Order to maintain peace. In response, the Galactic Senate began to consider creating an army of the Republic, a military unit unlike any the peaceful democracy had required in centuries—in fact, not since the founding of the modern Republic itself.

The mere consideration of creating a military wing to wage war against the Separatist regime turned Padmé's stomach. She had famously declared in the Naboo throne room, while still Naboo's queen, that she would never condone a course of action that would lead to war. By the age of 24, Padmé had become a leader of the peace-loving Loyalist Committee and a friend and ally of prominent lawmakers, such as Senator Bail Organa of Alderaan. Her political leanings made her unpopular with the Trade Federation and others Separatist supporters, but she remained steadfast, despite death threats and assassination attempts. In public, Padmé made sure never to show a trace of weakness or fear for her own safety.

Resolved to cast her vote against the Military Creation Act, Padmé was touching down on Coruscant when one of her decoys, Cordé, was murdered by a bomb blast. This terrorist act spurred Palpatine to suggest that the imperilled young senator should be placed in the care of the Jedi, who would be more skilled as bodyguards than her usual security detail. And so it came to pass that, nearly a decade after their first fateful meeting, Obi-Wan Kenobi and his 19-year-old Padawan Anakin were called on to guard Padmé.

The last time Padmé had seen Anakin, shortly after Qui-Gon Jinn's funeral, the boy was preparing to embark on a life of service as a Jedi. In the ensuing years, if Padmé gave Anakin a thought, she simply recalled a scared young boy who had made her a charming but childish gift—a handcarved japor snippet necklace, for luck—and the plight of his poor mother, Shmi, left behind the day they departed Tatooine. Shmi had reminded Padmé of her own mother, Jobal Naberrie, who was a calming presence at home in the mountains of Naboo. Like Shmi, Jobal was often consumed with worry for her children's safety. She longed for her daughter to turn away from public service, at least for a time, and think of her own needs. Jobal feared that taking on such onerous responsibilities at such a young age—Padmé was, after all, just eight years old when she joined the Apprentice Legislature—had robbed her ambitious child of the simple, carefree joys of youth. Too young, Padmé had become focused on the greater good only to ignore her own passions and desires.

Anakin's admiration for the queen's beauty was the stuff of pre-teen infatuation, but it was her magnanimity that stayed with him in the years they were apart. Not only did she care deeply for the plight of the people suffering on her world and on planets far from Naboo, she had regarded him—a common slave—as a person of value, despite her regal status. For someone so used to being overlooked, that feeling of being truly seen and appreciated was intoxicating. When they were apart, Padmé—or at least the idea of her from a nine-year-old's point of view—was never far from his mind. Padmé's kindness made him feel as if he could achieve anything he set his mind to. At the same time, it was impossible to forget that they were from very different worlds. Despite the distance separating them, Anakin's fantasies were fueled by news holos of Padmé's political exploits and her dazzling smile. During his waking hours, when he felt most alone, his thoughts would wander until, often unbidden, her face came into focus. The only other person Anakin longed to see and called to mind as frequently—although in an altogether different manner—was his mother, Shmi.

By the time Anakin and Padmé became reacquainted on Coruscant, much had changed. Padmé was a senator, her very public life increasingly threatened by Separatists seeking to break from the Galactic Republic and prepared to silence her by any means necessary. Anakin was well on his way to becoming a Jedi Knight, no longer a silly little boy with a mop of sandy blond hair. He was also totally smitten by her. Exercising the diplomacy that had already gotten her so far in her career, Padmé politely ignored the potential awkwardness of the situation. Obi-Wan was intent on protecting Padmé, as the Jedi Council had mandated, but Anakin took the matter personally. He declared that he would not rest until he found the person or persons trying to kill her. His outspokenness surprised his usually unflappable master. Cracks in Anakin and Obi-Wan's relationship were starting to show. The Padawan was less content to play the role of dutiful student and more liable to push back on Kenobi's teachings with a petulant scowl. To Obi-Wan, Anakin showed troubling signs of headstrong aggression, and a disturbing tendency to charge into situations that required a sensitive, diplomatic hand.

On Coruscant, Obi-Wan and Anakin heroically foiled a second assassination attempt when a pair of venomous kouhuns were let loose by Clawdite bounty hunter Zam Wesell in Padmé's private apartment while she slept. Anakin and Obi-Wan pursued the shape-shifter and caught up with her in the Outlander Club. Before Wesell could reveal the name of the thug who had hired her, a poisoned dart pierced her throat and she died.

This incident forced master and apprentice to part ways. While Obi-Wan Kenobi investigated the assassination attempt further, in hopes of finding who had masterminded the plot, Padmé retreated at once to the safety of her home world with Anakin, on his first solo mission, as her protector. This executive order, issued by Palpatine, was a cunning move to eliminate Padmé's influence—a stumbling block to the creation of the Republic's army—from the Senate. At the same time, Palpatine suspected that being alone with Padmé was likely to fuel the discord and dissatisfaction brewing in young Anakin's heart.

Even the simplest creature could see how Anakin's feelings for Padmé permeated his every glance, smile, and act whenever she was in the room. The senator kept her emotions in check, reminding Anakin that he would never be anything more to her but the little boy she had met on Tatooine. As much as this apparent rejection stung, Anakin found the thrill of the chase enticing, coupled with the forbidden nature of his love. True to his character, Anakin was convinced that he could fix the situation. He was sure the problem wasn't that Padmé didn't return his feelings: She was just allowing their respective obligations to the Senate and to the Jedi dissuade her from loving him.

The Jedi Code was strict about forming attachments. The wisest masters recognized that personal feelings and obligations could influence even the most dedicated Jedi's actions, and that love would quickly warp a Jedi's carefully honed impartial judgement. But while possession of another was not permitted for a Jedi, Anakin reasoned that *feelings of compassion*—the very definition of unconditional love—were essential to a Jedi's life, and he did nothing to try to contain or restrain them. Beyond the giddiness he felt in Padmé's presence, Anakin's infatuation also provided a welcome distraction from nightmares about his mother's plight on Tatooine. These had begun to encroach upon his sleep, leaving him exhausted, his nerves frayed with worry.

With the Gungan Jar Jar Binks left in charge of her political duties, Padmé, her identity concealed by simpler clothes, boarded a freighter. Anakin and her loyal droid, R2-D2, were her sole companions. The trip would have been arduous, if not for the pleasant company. Although uneasy—someone was out to kill her, after all—Padmé felt a certain freedom to traveling incognito, which she only ever enjoyed when impersonating one of her own handmaidens during a decoy maneuver. Anakin felt freer, too. Although troubled by the threats against her, the assignment gave him a sense of adventure and independence apart from his usual responsibilities as a Padawan. As the sole Jedi aboard, he eagerly took charge of the situation, despite Obi-Wan's stern reminder that no significant actions should be taken without first consulting a higher authority. Using public transport, the three easily hid in plain sight, perched on crates and hunched over their rations in a nondescript star freighter's crowded mess hall, lost among the emigrants headed for the promise of prosperity on Naboo.

The feeling of liberation, coupled with Padmé's carefree laugh, brought something at the edge of Anakin's consciousness into sharp focus once more. Suddenly he was 12 years old again, battling the darkness in his heart that cried out for release from the Jedi's rules, a consideration, however fleeting, that he could walk away from the Jedi Order and forge a new path. As his eyes rested on Padmé's exquisite features, unadorned by a queen's ceremonial makeup or formal senatorial dress, he felt a pang of grief knowing that if he continued to work toward becoming a Jedi Knight, he could never love this, or any, woman. Not in the way he wanted, at least.

Once safely tucked away in the seclusion of the Lake Country, Padmé seemed to become more receptive to Anakin's feelings. Their days were filled with bucolic picnics, and the free exchange of ideas, secrets, and insecurities. Far away from the Temple and assassins, Anakin entertained Padmé with stories of his most daring exploits and beguiled her by showing off his skill with the Force, something Obi-Wan Kenobi would have surely admonished him for.

With no distractions of duty or trappings of finery, Anakin and Padmé were just two old friends on a journey together, learning to understand and getting to know one another anew. Their time together exposed their differences and cemented their bond. Padmé's upbringing on Naboo had included lazy vacations basking in the sun on idyllic sandy beaches or swimming in sparkling waters, but, thanks to Anakin's harsh childhood on Tatooine, sand had very different associations for him. His sad life up to that point opened a well of compassion in Padmé's heart, while her tales of joy-filled youth made him feel the tug of desire for a similar future of careless delight.

To Padmé's surprise, she found she had more in common with Anakin than she thought. When they butted heads planning the safest route to avoid exposing her to another assassination attempt, it was simply because each of them wanted to take the lead. It was also comforting to spend time with another soul who felt misunderstood and underestimated. However, Padmé embraced people's misconceptions of her character as opportunities to surpass their expectations and emerge victorious. Anakin wrestled with similar issues like a man thrashing in a nest of gundarks.

One of the things eating away at Anakin, no doubt fueled by his status as the Chosen One, was his belief that he was outpacing Obi-Wan in mastering the skills of the Jedi. He was impatient to leap forward, conquer more trials and become a Jedi Knight in his own right. Padmé's reappearance in his life only served to complicate his feelings further. Her world, and everything she represented, was the complete opposite of Anakin's reality, a bittersweet temptation luring him away from his ordained path.

Anakin resolved to free his mind from torment and discover once and for all if Padmé felt the same way he did. Privately, Padmé had begun to care for Anakin deeply. However, on this occasion, her clearer head prevailed, laying out the kind of rational, firm rebuttal that had won her admiration among her more experienced senatorial colleagues. Anakin claimed that he was willing to give up everything to be with Padmé. However, she replied that she could not, in good conscience, allow him to disrupt his Jedi studies, nor allow herself to be distracted from her political work. To be together would be to love in secret and to live a lie, entering a relationship built on a foundation of deception. Intellectually, it was a terrible idea.

***

The night Anakin confessed his feelings for Padmé, his slumber was interrupted by yet another horrifying vision of Shmi in agony. Although he thought of her often, and sometimes, in a meditative trance, could even feel her warmth through the Force, Anakin had had no contact with his mother since the day he left their home in Mos Espa. If the continuing nightmares proved to be omens of events yet to be, the future seen through the Force, he knew he was running out of time to keep his promise to save her.

Having been so moved by the plight of the slaves on the barren planet during her first visit to Tatooine, Padmé agreed to accompany Anakin back to his home world to put his mind to rest. This enabled Anakin to simultaneously fulfill his Jedi duty—to protect the senator from harm—and rush to his mother's aid, fulfilling his duty as her only son.

Unbeknownst to Anakin, during their years apart, Shmi had escaped the yoke of slavery without his help. Watto's business had become far less lucrative without young Anakin toiling away at his workbench, so the Toydarian had sold his last remaining servant—Shmi—to a moisture-farmer named Cliegg Lars who lived on the outskirts of Mos Eisley. For reasons that mystified Watto, Cliegg had freed Shmi, having fallen in love with the handsome woman, and *married* her. As she had in the slums of Mos Espa, Shmi settled into the Lars homestead and adapted to her new life, treating her stepson, Owen, as if he were her own. When she thought of Anakin, she imagined a life of happiness, traveling among the stars, and helping those in need. Although she missed him greatly and longed to see the man he would have become, she knew he was better off far from Tatooine.

Around the same time that the nightmarish visions began invading Anakin's dreams, Shmi was abducted by a tribe of nomads known as the Tusken Raiders. Regarded by settlers as territorial savages of the Jundland Wastes, these so-called Sand People posed a threat to colonists who wandered too far from their communities. Shmi had not let fears of these mysterious hunters keep her tethered to her new home. In the early morning light, she had relished the privilege of wandering—no longer governed by the whims of a slave master—foraging for mushrooms on the moisture vaporators that dotted the Lars farmland. That was where they found her—a hunting party of Tusken men who regarded the lone woman as a prize. At that moment, the fleeting freedoms Shmi had enjoyed vanished forever.

By the time Anakin made his way to Cliegg's door, his mother had been gone a month. Thirty locals had mounted a rescue mission, only to have the majority of their party wiped out. Cliegg, although he still loved her, was ready to accept that his wife was probably dead.

The stark details of her kidnapping were Anakin's worst nightmares come to life. But no amount of farmers compared to one well-trained Jedi, Anakin reasoned. He was not willing to give up so easily.

As Tatooine's twin suns drifted below the horizon, Anakin sped off on Owen's rusty speeder bike. Anakin's training in the Force and knowledge of the region he had once called home soon brought him to the Tusken Raider camp. Inside one of the circular huts, he found Shmi Skywalker slumped against her bindings, bruised and beaten. She was too weak to stand or tell her son of the horrors she had endured, her voice little more than a soft rasp. Anakin moved swiftly to release her bonds, searching for words of comfort.

In her weakened state, Shmi was not sure whether her son had really come to her rescue or if she was dreaming. She cupped his face gently in her hands and tried to muster the energy to tell Anakin that she loved him. The effort was too much: The life suddenly drained from her body and she fell back into Anakin's arms, her eyes wide but unseeing. Anakin's years of Jedi teachings, learning to control powerful emotions, were undone in an instant. He cursed himself for ever leaving Tatooine without her. Shame morphed into rampant fury and blazing, blind rage. Laying Shmi's body gently on the cool ground, he stepped into the moonlight and ignited his lightsaber.

With no regard for their cries, Anakin slaughtered the entire Tusken encampment—the hunters responsible for kidnapping and torturing his mother, and all the women and children, too. Cliegg Lars believed the Tuskens were vicious, mindless monsters, and Anakin treated them as such, dispatching them like a butcher, devoid of all emotion. Somewhere, still conscious in the cosmic Force, Qui-Gon Jinn cried out in anguish, as Anakin took his first steps toward the dark side. The ramifications of this brutal event would be felt for years to come, a trauma passed down in two generations of Skywalkers not yet born.

When Anakin returned to the Lars homestead, he was a changed man. The shock of losing his mother immediately after finding her again, and the horrible truth of what he had done in his anger, made him physically ill. He found that Jedi teachings were useless in helping him regain the control he so desperately craved, so instead he focused on something insignificant that could be fixed. With Shmi's body recovered for proper burial, he retreated to a shed and started tinkering with the broken shifter on Owen's speeder bike transmission. Everything seemed simpler when he was repairing a machine, an activity that had helped ease his frenetic mind as a child. Engrossed in the intricate task, a sense of calm and clarity took hold for the first time since he had heard Cliegg's story of Shmi's abduction.

Anakin would later reveal the atrocities he had committed to only two people—Padmé and Palpatine—although the tremor that rippled through the Force that day was felt by some of the most prescient Force-wielders in the Jedi Temple. If he thought he could hide the darkness from the masters, he was mistaken.

Padmé treated Anakin's admission with compassion and sympathy— it is easier to excuse misdeeds perpetrated by the ones we love, after all.

Troubled as she was by the massacre of the Tusken Raiders, she could see that this act did not define Anakin's character, but was the result of immense grief and justifiable anger, a serious but momentary lapse in judgment. To be angered—even to the point of losing control—was human, she reasoned, and although the Jedi aimed to have the utmost restraint, some sorrows were just too great to ignore.

However, Anakin himself remained racked with guilt and regret for leaving his mother to her fate, for failing to act faster to save her, and for stooping to retribution instead of seeking justice. In his shame, he vowed to become the most powerful Jedi that ever lived—one who could even stop people from dying. Padmé believed his words were nothing more than a young man expressing fantastical wishes to soothe his searing pain, but Sheev Palpatine saw an opportunity.

Chapter 5

The First Battle of Geonosis

Shmi Skywalker's grave was still fresh when Anakin got word from Padmé's loyal astromech R2-D2 that Obi-Wan Kenobi was in trouble. With no time to process his grief, Anakin was thrust into the crucible of war.

In their time apart, Kenobi's circuitous search for Padmé's would-be killer had taken a strange turn on the remote planet of Kamino, beyond the Outer Rim. He had discovered that, a decade prior, the Jedi Master Sifo-Dyas, who had been plagued by visions of a coming war, secretly ordered the creation of a massive clone army without the approval of the Jedi Council. Obi-Wan's investigations subsequently led to the bounty hunter Jango Fett—the DNA template for the clone troops—who was connected to the Trade Federation. Its leader, Nute Gunray, still harbored a grudge against Padmé, the young ruler who had staved off his invasion of Naboo, and the Federation was among the factions pledging their military might to the growing Separatist movement. Obi-Wan followed Fett to a Separatist base on the planet of Geonosis. There, he discovered the Separatists were building droid soldiers, similar to those employed in Gunray's invasion army of Naboo ten years prior. Through the machinations of the dark side, two armies were simultaneously ready to do battle for control of the galaxy.

Anakin relayed his master's message to the Jedi Council, which gave him strict orders to stay the course on his vital assignment to protect Senator Amidala at all costs. However, Padmé could see that having just lost his mother, Anakin would not be able to sit idly by while his master, mentor, and friend risked a similar fate. Just as she had helped Anakin on his quest to return to Tatooine and save Shmi, Padmé made the call to plot a course to Geonosis and help Obi-Wan if they could. Thus, in order to follow the Jedi Council's command, Anakin had no choice but to join her.

On the harsh and rocky planet, only half a parsec away from Tatooine, the rescue mission was cut short when they were attacked and captured by a squad of insectoid Geonosians and their droids. Anakin and Padmé were shackled to two stone pillars in Geonosis' imposing Petranaki execution arena with Obi-Wan similarly restrained nearby. According to Geonosian custom, all three were to be killed in front of a cheering crowd by a trio of vicious predators: an acklay, a reek, and a nexu.

The arena became the first battlefield of the coming conflict, signaling the end of Anakin's youth. Just before they were delivered to be slaughtered for entertainment, Padmé declared her love for the Jedi and the two shared another kiss. In contrast to Padmé's refusal to give in to her emotions during their tryst on Naboo, this time her confession was one of quiet desperation; she was certain their luck had run out. However, her acknowledgement, and the realization that his love was not unrequited as he had feared, only made Anakin more determined to find some way out of their predicament.

Padmé broke free from her bonds using one of the hairpins that held braids together; at the same time, Obi-Wan redirected the acklay's attack to use the creature's sharp claws to slice through his own restraints. Unable to free himself from his chains, Anakin clambered onto the back of the horned reek, his manacles creating a makeshift collar preventing the beast from bucking him off. Soothing the reek by means of the Force, Anakin guided the half-tame creature as skillfully as he once had a podracer, and Padmé and Obi-Wan jumped on behind him. Despite these daring feats, Count Dooku's droid army closed in and they were surrounded by a squad of droidekas, trapped with no weapons and no way out.

To their surprise, dozens of lightsabers, like beacons of hope, ignited amid the bloodthirsty crowd and more than two hundred Jedi peace-keepers leaped from the stands to defend the Republic and their own, as the Jedi Order made one final, desperate attempt to stem the impending chaos of inevitable war. Many Jedi lost their lives that day, and even the most esteemed members of the Jedi High Council struggled to control their emotions as so many brave and noble protectors were slain.

Overwhelmed by Dooku's mindless machines, in no time barely a handful of Jedi were left, including Anakin and Obi-Wan, to make a final stand. At that critical moment, the Republic deployed its army of clone troopers, led by prominent Jedi masters, including Master Yoda.

In what would come to be known as the First Battle of Geonosis, loy-alists and pacifists buried their ideals. The Republic's unity had been eroding for many years, not helped by a Jedi Order blinded by loyalty to their mission and reluctant to evolve in changing times beyond their sacred, ancient Code. Far away from the tranquility of the Jedi Temple and the spirited debates of the Galactic Senate, the populations of entire planetary systems felt devalued, overlooked, and forgotten. In time, diverse species banded together to oppose what had become, in their eyes, a depraved government only benefitting the Republic's wealthiest citizens.

Up until that point, Count Dooku was simply thought to be a peaceful idealist who disagreed with the direction of the Republic's government. However, in ordering the murder of so many Jedi, it was clear Dooku was no longer the man who had been trained by Yoda or who had taught the peace-loving Qui-Gon Jinn. After Obi-Wan had defeated Darth Maul, Sheev Palpatine, Sith Lord Darth Sidious, had secretly taken Dooku as his new apprentice.

The threats to Padmé's life were but a single manifestation of the massive, interplanetary movement, a vendetta against an outspoken, seemingly untouchable politician, whose assassination would make a statement that not even the elites on Coruscant could ignore. While Padmé was in hiding on Naboo with Anakin, events in the wider galaxy moved remorselessly toward war. In response to the Separatist threat, Jar Jar Binks, deputizing for Padmé in the Galactic Senate, had proposed a radical motion giving the Supreme Chancellor emergency powers. Once passed, Palpatine easily overruled any debate surrounding the Military Creation Act, thus erasing any progress Padmé had made toward a peaceful, diplomatic solution to the Separatists' concerns. And without the checks and balances of the senators representing their people, Palpatine's first action was to activate the secret clone army, a declaration of war.

The battle between the Republic's forces and the Separatists' droids spilled over into the desert beyond the arena, resulting in heavy losses on both sides. Yet even in the wake of that first skirmish, safely aboard a newly procured Republic gunship and armed with borrowed lightsabers, Obi-Wan and Anakin pursued Dooku, still hoping to end the conflict as quickly as it had begun.

The encounter tested Anakin's strength both as a Jedi and as an individual. Shaken by the sight of their brothers and sisters in the Force lying dead on the battlefield, the usually controlled Obi-Wan convinced himself that he and his apprentice could take Dooku alone, failing to see that Anakin, impatient at the best of times, had lost all restraint. When enemy blaster fire had sent Padmé tumbling out of their gunship, to lie, possibly injured, on the sands, Anakin had snapped. A terrible sense of loss threatened to overwhelm him as he realized the fall could have killed or mortally wounded the woman he loved. Anakin loudly voiced his intentions of abandoning all notions of duty to rush to Padmé's side, ready to renounce, not only the Jedi, but their newfound role in the fight. Only Obi-Wan's sternest admonishments pulled his Padawan back from the brink.

Anakin fought to settle his mind on the task at hand. With Dooku in his sights, he entertained thoughts of bravely rising up against the evil threatening the Republic and singlehandedly striking it down. He would become a living legend, extolled for the quick thinking and superior skill that had kept a single planetary battle turning into an all-consuming galactic war.

But Anakin's feelings for Padmé, and his fears over losing her, fueled his every move that day. Inside a dimly lit hangar bay, Anakin charged Dooku alone, perhaps the most egregious in a list of failures to heed his master's commands. Instead of engaging in a typical lightsaber duel, lightning crackled from Dooku's fingertips, and Anakin was slammed into a stone wall. While Anakin lay injured on the ground, jolted and exhausted, Obi-Wan regained some clear-headedness in battle, using his lightsaber to deflect Dooku's lightning. But the white-haired Sith dodged Obi-Wan's attacks with the speed of a much younger man, and soon gained the upper hand. As Dooku raised his weapon to deliver the killing blow on his wounded opponent, Anakin summoned all his strength and the power of the Force to come to his surrogate father's aid once more. Anakin and Dooku dueled with lightsabers until one elegant weapon was cleaved in two and, the other clattered to the floor along with Anakin's right arm, the lifeless limb severed at the elbow by Dooku's blade.

Anakin's years of Jedi training and lightsaber form exercises had proven insignificant when pitted against the ferocity of a real-life foe, aiming to maim or kill rather than simply win an honorable clash of sabers. Coupled with his frayed emotions and clouded judgment, he was no match for Dooku's abilities or his focus. Anakin would bear the emotional and physical scars of their encounter throughout the war and the rest of his life.

Master and apprentice would have perished that day along with the countless others dead on Geonosis if not for the swift interference of Jedi Master Yoda. For hundreds of years, the Force-attuned Yoda had been using his wisdom as a teacher and a guide to shepherd thousands of eager young Jedi through the Temple. At that moment, on Geonosis, Yoda was forced to face the monster his lost student had become, and resolved to atone for the evil Dooku had helped bring forth. With patience and skill that surpassed most other living Jedi, Yoda deflected Dooku's malicious lightning. The two briefly clashed lightsabers, but Dooku could see he would always be an inferior student to Yoda's superior skill. In desperation, he reached out through the Force to move a massive column toward the crumpled forms of Obi-Wan and Anakin, knowing Yoda's conscience would not permit him to sacrifice the Jedi even for a chance to eliminate the threat before him. With Yoda distracted by saving Obi-Wan and Anakin from certain death, Dooku fled for Coruscant with vital plans for his master's ultimate coup—a superweapon that could lay entire planets to waste.

The Separatists were eventually outmatched and outnumbered that day. The battle was remembered as both a military victory for the Republic and a moral defeat for the Jedi and their peaceful ways. The shroud of the dark side had fallen over the galaxy and everything the Jedi held dear was soon to be betrayed. And for Anakin Skywalker, the skirmish, Padmé's declaration, and Shmi's death combined to mark the end of his innocence, and the start of his betrayal of the Jedi ways. With the peacekeepers morphed into generals in the conflict, the values that had upheld generations of Jedi were beginning to crumble, shattering Anakin's moral compass.

Chapter 6

The Jedi General

Following the clash on Geonosis, war between the Republic and Separatist forces raged for three years. Subsequently known as the Clone Wars, this would prove a time of tumultuous upheaval for the Republic, the Jedi Order, and Anakin Skywalker, a young man just barely into his twenties. In the new reality brought on by the conflict, the Jedi were forced to reevaluate their place as peacekeepers and instead turn their attentions to commanding legions of clone troopers on the frontlines. For Anakin specifically, his time as a soldier on the battlefronts challenged the Jedi teachings, turning the harsher aspects of his personality—which the Jedi sought to subdue—into attributes that allowed him to excel in a strange new galaxy besieged by military strife. His passionate nature and fiery temper made him a formidable warrior.

Anakin enthusiastically embraced his new role as a Jedi general and quickly came to trust his clone troopers like the loyal, invaluable Captain Rex as much as he did his fellow Jedi. While most struggled with their new role, Anakin was a success by any measure. From his roots as a slave, he had risen to win the heart of a queen, and a place among the legendary Jedi. Before long, he was sure, he would become famed for his selfless deeds on the battlefield, a giant among men, a charismatic leader marked for high office in the Republic.

As Anakin's old lightsaber was damaged beyond repair on Geonosis, he resolved to construct a new one—with a gleaming hilt encasing a stunning blue blade—using the craftsmanship that had made him such a valuable commodity on Tatooine years before. This weapon—created not for defense or sparring, but for battle—was heavier than his first and able to withstand the rigors of war.

On Coruscant, the best medical droids in the galaxy fabricated a gleaming prosthetic limb to replace the right arm he had lost during the duel with Dooku. Although at first this mechno-hand produced a strange sensation, to his satisfaction the trade-off for losing his real hand was a more powerful appendage giving greater grip and range of motion. Over time, Anakin added armored shielding to enhance his cybernetic replacement. While not overly concerned with the cosmetic appeal of the arm, he often covered the skeletal fingers with a customized, autoseal glove. The recognition that Anakin himself was now part machine added a level of complexity to his place in the fight, commanding the soldiers who battled a Separatist army almost entirely comprised of droid soldiers. The naked technology of his arm and hand was a gruesome reminder of his potential for defeat. He tried his best to ignore this evidence of his vulnerability, focusing instead on the power his mechno-limb gave him to bolster his confidence and give himself renewed purpose.

Anakin Skywalker emerged as a heroic figure on the battlefield just as he had predicted. He shed the Padawan braid that marked him as a student. His close-cropped, sandy hair grew a darker brown and as long as he pleased, in acknowledgement of his new status as a Jedi Knight with more freedoms and responsibilities. He did not adopt a beard, allowing his youthful looks to contrast with his powerful physique. The lean muscle he had built up through years of Jedi training exercises filled out his new Jedi robes, which no longer appeared ill-fitting and oversized. Standing at 1.88 meters, the young boy who had been so eager to join the Jedi's monastic ranks was all-but erased. His blue eyes, how-ever, remained the same, as much the source of his boyish charm as his impish grin.

The same characteristics that made Anakin a difficult Padawan ensured he excelled as a Jedi general and came to be known as a great warrior—although Master Yoda would later argue that wars did not make anyone great. While others in the Order wrestled with the moral dilemmas war posed, trying to find ways to remain righteous while fighting the enemy, Anakin's natural imprudence and inflexibility made him a decisive leader. He quickly realized that when his anger flared in the arena of battle, he did not have to shrink from it, but could instead allow it to fuel attacks on the enemy. When he gave in to his wrath, he could force even the most reticent prisoner of war to give him any information he desired. He never spoke of this to Obi-Wan or anyone else, of course. He knew that his master would have quickly reminded him that the Jedi way was to move past anger to a place of calm clarity. In the thrill of combat, Anakin found that he could annihilate virtually any opposition with a combination of intelligence, strategy, and instinct. Like the heroes of the stories his mother had told him as a child, Anakin Skywalker's name tumbled from the mouths of pirates and smugglers, spreading tales of his triumphs across the stars.

His newfound military rank gave him power over hundreds of clone troopers, yet he struggled to comply with the chain of command. When duty took him to familiar places, such as Tatooine, or when facing the collateral destruction of innocents or the enslaved, Anakin's actions were strongly influenced by his personal feelings.

In the Corvair sector, Anakin clashed with Republic Admiral Wulff Yularen during an attack on a Separatist droid foundry, in what at the time appeared to be a key operation to ensure eventual victory in the conflict. Anakin realized that hundreds of Kudon slaves were running the lines inside the factory, which had not yet been fully automated when war broke out. Yularen ordered Anakin to destroy the facility, but instead he launched his own mission to liberate the slaves first. Try as he might to shake the feeling, every slave reminded him of his mother and the child he once was. By ignoring Yularen's orders, freeing the slaves and inspiring them to fight the Separatists' battle droids, Anakin saved their lives. There was also a concomitant benefit of Anakin's insubordination: If the factory had been destroyed and the slaves killed, the Separatists would have used the brutal Republic attack as propaganda for recruiting neutral worlds to their cause.

In the wake of another Republic success in the Battle of Christophsis, a strategic mission on behalf of a member of the Hutt clan that had formerly enslaved the Skywalkers required Anakin to put duty before his personal feelings. On Anakin's homeworld of Tatooine, wandering the sand dunes so soon after burying his mother, he aided the notorious crime boss Jabba the Hutt—a sluglike alien whose influence on Coruscant extended from the prestigious political circles to the criminal underworld—by rescuing his kidnapped son, Rotta. If the Republic and the Jedi had not agreed, the Hutt clan would have made it difficult for Republic troops to pass through its territory, thereby ensuring a Separatist triumph in some sectors. Although Anakin tried to maintain an air of compliance, he hated the Hutts; the strategic importance of the mission didn't make it any less unsavory for him.

The ramifications of war slowly spread; its widespread devastation gradually pushed Anakin closer to the brink of an unknown future. When the war took Anakin back to Geonosis, the place where it had begun, he struggled to overcome the trauma he had endured in the arena and the loss of his limb during his fateful duel with Count Dooku. Everything about the planet reminded him of his humiliating defeat. During the Second Battle of Geonosis against Separatist forces, the imprisoned leader of the Geonosians, Poggle the Lesser, was reluctant to talk, until Anakin reached out through the Force to choke him into submission and brutally secure the information he required. Anakin never spoke of this incident to Obi-Wan, who would have surely chastised him for this loss of control.

The violence of war undoubtedly eroded Anakin's conscience, yet more nefarious factors were at play. The Sith were gaining strength, while the Jedi's principles were becoming more compromised with each battle. Nothing was sacred to the Republic's foes; the Separatists engaged them on all fronts, employing bounty hunters for clandestine attacks, such as breaking into the sacred Jedi Archives to retrieve the names of Force-sensitive children identified throughout the galaxy but too young to train. As months of combat stretched into years, the Republic slouched toward victory of a sort, but the Jedi were powerless to see how this victory would manifest itself . . .and at what cost. Too often, instead of merely defending against an attacker, the Jedi found themselves on the offensive.

The Separatists—with Darth Sidious pulling strings behind the scenes—were cunning and calculating opponents, unconcerned with fighting fair. They infiltrated Republic ranks with spy droids and kidnapped key operatives, including Anakin's faithful blue-and-white astromech R2-D2, a gift from Padmé and a tangible token of their love. Anakin rescued R2-D2 from Skytop Station, ensuring the droid did not give up important Republic military secrets. Always one to flout the rules, Anakin was not prepared to erase his droid's memory banks after a mission according to protocol; unfortunately, this made the astromech a valuable prize for the enemy. R2-D2 was much more than a mere copilot and mechanical companion for Anakin. Possessing a unique personality and resourcefulness that seemed to go beyond his programming, R2-D2 rose in the military ranks to command his own reprogrammed battle droids and lead other missions.

The conflict made Anakin and Obi-Wan brothers in arms, but Anakin's friendship with Supreme Chancellor Palpatine also continued to grow, the younger man readily sharing secrets with the politician he was too ashamed to tell another Jedi, from his massacre of the Tusken Raider camp to the more aggressive forms of interrogation he had employed during the course of the war. In every case, his confessions were met with sympathetic support. Anakin, a master of self-justification, began to buy into the idea that he genuinely *was* the Chosen One, capable of becoming the galaxy's savior. In this way, he allayed his secret fears and feelings of shame.

With increasing frequency, Anakin's intentions—to help the galaxy find the peace it found so elusive—were being unconsciously thwarted by the dark side. Palpatine's influence helped persuade Anakin that the Jedi's ideals effectively made them incapable of the ruthlessness required for ultimate victory. The wrongs Anakin perpetrated—which he had come to see as essential to the Republic's war effort—would not be enough to win the war if the other Jedi Knights refused to play their part. As far as he was concerned, almost any means was justified to return the galaxy to a peaceful state that the Jedi could once again protect. To achieve this goal, moral compromises were inevitable.

On one diplomatic mission to protect the pacifistic Duchess Satine Kryze of Mandalore, Anakin and Obi-Wan were called upon to defend her against would-be assassins as she traveled to Coruscant. When it was discovered that the traitorous senator Tal Merrik intended to blow up Satine's glittering starship with everyone aboard, Satine and Obi-Wan faced a dilemma. To kill or maim Merrik was against their sworn ideals. Anakin, however, had no such scruples. He ran his lightsaber blade through the would-be bomber.

As the months passed and the war showed no signs of abating, Anakin found it easier to justify his behavior to himself. Even as he slipped further and further away from Jedi ideals, drawing ever closer to the dark side, he allowed himself to believe that he was doing what was right and just for the Republic cause. Anakin was not alone in that view. It was fully endorsed by Palpatine and other key members of the Republic's military, such as Wilhuff Tarkin.

All the while, the conflict swung wildly this way and that in a wrenching series of victories and defeats. The Republic seemed about to turn the tide of the war when Jedi Master Even Piell acquired the coordinates for the Nexus Route, a hyperspace corridor that would be a tactical boon for whichever side possessed the intel. However, before

Piell could relay the information to the Jedi Council, he was captured and imprisoned in the Citadel on the sulfurous planet of Lola Sayu, along with his soldiers and Captain Tarkin. This fortress had been especially constructed 500 years before to hold rogue Jedi in the unlikely event that a Knight would ever turn against the Republic. Earlier in the war, the Citadel had fallen into Separatist control. It was thus the ideal place for Separatist leaders to interrogate a Jedi prisoner. Anakin mounted a daring rescue mission and the coordinates were recovered, but, sadly, Piell himself was killed.

As the seemingly never-ending war entered its third and final year, taking a toll on clones and Jedi generals alike, the true depth of the Separatists' depravity was exposed. The Republics' foes had dabbled in devastating and grotesque weapons of biological warfare throughout the conflict. An early example of this was the Separatists' plot to release the Blue Shadow Virus, which had been secretly concocted in an underground lab on Naboo, Padmé Amidala's beloved homeworld.

As Anakin turned 22, he found solace in the cacophony of battle and the unwavering loyalty of his troopers. The clones were quite literally born to be soldiers, dedicated to serving Anakin and the other Jedi. And among their ranks it was understood and celebrated that General Anakin Skywalker never asked his men to endure a risk he wasn't willing to take on himself, nor sent them to unknown corners of the Outer Rim while he remained protected from harm on the safety of a ship's bridge. He never treated them as dispensable; this was a point of pride for him and his clone troopers alike.

During the Citadel escape, the Separatists had gained a valuable prize: a clone trooper. Echo was a dedicated soldier who would never have consciously betrayed the Republic. But in the hands of the enemy, he became a tool for carnage. This sinister indicator of the Separatists' growing strength—and the lengths to which they were willing to go to win—was revealed during the Battle of Anaxes, when one of the Republic's largest shipyards came under attack. With Anakin leading a counterattack from the air and Jedi Master Mace Windu commanding troops on the ground, the Republic should have been able to swiftly vanquish the Separatist forces. Instead, the battle dragged on for weeks, an agonizing descent toward probable defeat marked by mounting casualties and demoralized soldiers. The Republic's tacticians believed that the Separatists' droid army had gained access to valuable battle strategies devised by Captain Rex and Echo, his fallen brother, whom the Republic believed was dead. This intel was incorporated into their analytics to predict every move the Republic made.

Despite being genetically engineered to become one of the Republic's finest soldiers, Rex was still human, the same as Anakin. He had endured the loss of many of his closest brothers in arms and Anakin was painfully aware how fragile even the strongest soldier truly was beneath his armor and behind his stoic stare. Many clones came to detest the conflict—even though the war was the reason they had been conceived.

Anakin resolved to repay Rex's loyalty with whatever encouragement and assistance he could. On an unsanctioned mission to Skako Minor, Anakin showed newfound restraint as he led the experimental unit Clone Force 99. Known as the Bad Batch, they were a team of so-called defective clone troopers, whose mutations the Republic used to advantage on the battlefield. In their company, Anakin's own attributes that defied the common Jedi could be recast in his mind as benefits to the cause.

Anakin was undoubtedly aware that he was acting against the Jedi Council's wishes on the stealth mission to infiltrate the Separatist base run by the neutral Techno Union and pinpoint the mysterious signal purporting to come from Echo. In truth, by that point in the conflict, he no longer cared, as long as he was doing what he believed was right, even if that meant that he and his men were on their own.

Behind enemy lines, Anakin came face to face with a physical manifestation of his own mental anguish and a future reality he could not yet comprehend. Echo's damaged body was preserved in stasis so that his mind, plugged into a complex series of wires, could be utilized to bring down his own brothers in battle.

The war was making fools of the Knights. Anakin was sick and tired of trying to play by Jedi rules of engagement against enemies who so often ruthlessly circumvented them and then sought to exploit the Order's scruples against exacting retribution. After Echo's rescue, the Republic discovered the Separatist Admiral Trench had developed his own personal strategy for victory—total annihilation of the enemy—by planting a bomb in the fusion reactor at Anaxes. It was so powerful that it would have blown up most of the planet and made Separatist victory inevitable.

Anakin confronted Trench on the bridge of his ship and demanded the means to disarm the bomb. Assuming that the Jedi Code would prevent Anakin from killing him, the ruthless Harch tactician refused. But Anakin's patience was exhausted. Slicing off Trench's cybernetic arms with his lightsaber, Anakin made it crystal clear that he would not permit the nobility of the Jedi Code to hold him back. Yet even after Trench revealed the all-important information, he made one final desperate strike, giving Skywalker a powerful electric shock with his cane—and paid with his life. Anakin stabbed the admiral through the chest.

The death of Trench was a serious setback for the Separatists. However, sieges of a growing number of Outer Rim planets were seriously stretching the Republic's forces. Jedi generals and their clone soldiers were scrambling to defend dozens of planets against major offensives and struggling to deploy reinforcements to those most beset by the enemy. To Anakin, it was becoming clear that, to bring an end to the war, the Republic would have to eliminate the rest of the Separatist leaders or face an endless parade of droid soldiers and eventually succumb to defeat.

Chapter 7

Teachers of the Force

To the galaxy at large, the Clone Wars were a series of planetary skirmishes between the Separatists and the Republic. Most citizens remained unaware of even deeper troubles brewing, orchestrated by the Sith. At the same time, the Jedi were gradually losing their standing in the eyes of the galaxy. No longer revered as peacekeepers, they were gradually becoming despised and feared as warmongers.

For Anakin in particular, the war was analogous to the paradoxical nature of his very soul, where his desires were locked in battle with his longing to overcome what the Jedi held were debasing emotions. He tried desperately to find the key to controlling both. The prophetic weight of being heralded as the Chosen One, a mortal man on whose shoulders the fate of the entire galaxy rested, only added to his inner conflict. His future was thrown into uncertainty as he struggled to meet the expectations of the Jedi Order and its ideals amid the chaos of war. His desire for control ran counter to the core beliefs of the Order. Anakin clung to those he held dear even as it became clear that his power to keep anyone completely safe, including himself, was limited. His formidable strength in the Force could not compensate for his very human frailties.

Despite the Jedi's beliefs that anger and fear served the dark side, Anakin—and all the Jedi on the frontlines—inevitably experienced these emotions in combat. Anakin in particular was in thrall to them. In the midst of the Battle of Christophsis at the start of the war, Jedi Master Yoda sent the newly appointed Jedi Knight Skywalker a Padawan to teach: a Togruta named Ahsoka Tano. Yoda hoped that the responsibility of guiding a young and powerful apprentice would help Anakin quell his turbulent nature. It was obvious that the young man still yearned for parental acceptance and support. By taking on a Padawan, Anakin could fulfill the nurturing role of a paternal presence himself—and emerge the powerful Jedi the prophecy foretold. As the war threatened the peace and prosperity Yoda had seen flourish for more than 800 years, he hoped that Qui-Gon Jinn had been right and that Anakin would bring balance to the Force. But first Anakin had to find his own internal equilibrium, and teaching Ahsoka would make a fine test.

Anakin had often felt responsible for matters outside of his control, but until he became Padawan Tano's teacher, he had never truly been accountable for another's fate beyond the clones he commanded in battle. To inhabit the new role, Anakin had to confront his deepest fears and resentments, or allow both himself and his charge to suffer the consequences.

Even in a time of peace, Anakin and Ahsoka's partnership would not have been an easy one. The Jedi Council chose her as Anakin's Padawan precisely because she was as headstrong as he had been in his youth. While they could not ignore that the young general still exhibited these traits under duress, the Jedi believed that seeing these failings mirrored back at him by his charge might *just* be the push Anakin needed to shake off his own childish behavioral quirks.

Mentoring Ahsoka certainly forced Anakin to contend with some of his own most abrasive traits. The young Padawan, just 14 years old at the time of their introduction, was rough in her speech, overeager to show her master her strengths, reckless and arrogant in the excellence of her skills, and actually *thrilled* to be catapulted into battle. In short, she was just as exasperating as Anakin had been when he became Obi-Wan Kenobi's Padawan. Ahsoka was also unfailingly brave, like her master.

In time, Anakin realized that he could not save Ahsoka from herself—a valuable lesson he failed to appreciate fully when it came to facing his own demons. At the Battle of Ryloth, Ahsoka disobeyed his direct command and lost most of her squadron, a crushing blow for the young leader. Instead of allowing Ahsoka to wallow in her shame, Anakin thrust her back into combat with a new mission, a vote of confidence that forced Ahsoka to swiftly regain the clarity to learn from her mistakes. Yet Anakin still foolishly believed he could save Ahsoka from external perils.

One of the clearest examples of the repercussions of the paradoxical nature of Anakin's role as warrior and peacekeeper, and the lengths to which he would go to protect his Padawan, occurred deep in the Crelythiumn system, far beyond the Outer Rim. A 2,000-year-old Jedi distress code lured the Jedi Knight to the realm of Mortis. Obi-Wan and Ahsoka joined him on the mission. A holy confluence of the Force, mystical, dreamlike Mortis reflected Anakin's personal turmoil back at him like a dark mirror. Ironically, when he returned from the brink, Anakin would be hard-pressed to recall what had occurred there, or explain what he had seen. It was as if the Force itself had been in some way testing the Chosen One.

The Force kept many secrets, but the Jedi had divined that it could be both a neutral entity binding the galaxy together and responsive to sentient beings, whose choices determined their individual destinies. At the same time, the Force was an all-powerful energy, capable of directing a user's actions as well as granting them powerful abilities. The Force had a peculiar and unknowable will of its own.

Mortis appeared to Anakin like a crystalized moment of eternity that transcended the rules of time and space. Seasons shifted with the hour; plant life thrived during daylight only to be destroyed when darkness fell, consumed by acidic rains. Life met death, as nature demanded, only to be rapidly reborn, die, and be reborn anew, in an endless cycle . . .

News of the Chosen One's possible existence had reached the three beings ruling Mortis: the benevolent being, the Daughter; her malevolent brother, the Son, who was allied with the darkness; and the Father, who attempted to keep order between his two endlessly bickering children. In a spiritual sense, the Daughter and the Son represented the opposites of Anakin Skywalker's nature, while the Father encapsulated the wise, measured man he would have to become to contain his warring emotions.

In that ethereal region, Anakin endured trials of physical, emotional, and spiritual strength, testing his capability to bring balance to the light and the dark, in himself and the galaxy.

During one fateful "encounter," he was visited by a specter with his mother's face. Anakin knew it was a trick of the mind, but for a moment, he let himself speak to the vision as if it were his mother. He was briefly soothed by her presence, then tortured by the same question that had haunted his waking hours: If he truly was the Chosen One, wouldn't he have had the power to save her life?

In another "encounter," the spirit of Qui-Gon Jinn also appeared to Anakin, his warm smile as encouraging as it had been when Anakin was a young boy. Nothing could shake the Jedi Master's conviction that Anakin was the Chosen One, but he cautioned that the Jedi would have to enter the heart of darkness and overcome his deepest fears to fulfill the prophecy.

In yet another "encounter," Anakin watched, horrified, as Ahsoka was kidnapped from his care and infected by the dark side. With sickly, yellow eyes, her body ravaged by the darkness flowing through her, Ahsoka challenged her master to a lightsaber duel and was executed by the Son before his eyes. Using himself as a conduit, he drained the last bit of life from the dying Daughter to revive Ahsoka rather than allow her to be lost—to the dark side or to death itself—while the world collapsed around them.

Anakin's Mortis experience was an abstract representation of the polarity between Anakin's conscious and unconscious mind. Internal strife was a natural, and indeed necessary, part of what made Anakin and every living sentient being whole—for light cannot exist without darkness. The Jedi preached that virtuous deeds and decisions could shape a destiny able to withstand the dark side encroaching from outside, but only if Anakin first conquered the darkness within himself.

As Ahsoka grew up, it was natural for her to test the boundaries of her place as an apprentice. Anakin watched over her anxiously, like a worried parent. He was unaware that his fervent desire to keep her safe from harm was a manifestation of a secret desire to control the lives of those close to him and in doing so control his own destiny.

When Ahsoka was 16, during a battle in the jungles of the planet Felucia, she was captured by Trandoshan hunters. Anakin blamed himself, and obsessively scoured the same ground over and over for signs of his lost charge, barking orders at the clones he commanded. It was clear that he took the loss of his Padawan personally, an admirable trait for a leader who was nonetheless in opposition to the teachings of the Jedi.

In contrast, Jedi Master Plo Koon, as fond of "little 'Soka" as her master, viewed the situation with cool detachment; he was saddened by Ahsoka's plight, but resolved to play his part in the larger cause and adhere to the Jedi Code. Leaving Felucia felt to Anakin as if he were abandoning his apprentice and all hope of finding her. But Master Plo reminded Anakin that saving Ahsoka was beyond his reach. If he truly believed in Ahsoka's skills and abilities—and his own as her teacher—he would trust in the Force and his Padawan. Ultimately, thanks to her training, Ahsoka managed to rescue a band of youngling captives and, with help from the towering Wookiee warrior Chewbacca, find her way back to Coruscant. Yet, despite her success, Anakin could not shake the feeling that he had let her down.

***

As the war dragged on, the Jedi Order was corrupted by the inevitable atrocities of the sprawling conflict, which stretched supply-chains and soldiers to breaking point. The machines of war quickly turned thriving planets into war-torn graveyards. Innocent populations, caught between Republic and Separatist forces, grew disgusted with both sides and disillusioned by their promises of a brighter future. And the galactic war did not prevent planet-based civil conflicts, greedy opportunists, and other social blights from creating greater ruin on a smaller yet no less damaging scale. In time, the demands of battle called for the Jedi to become spies, scoundrels, and slavers all in the name of victory.

Beyond the battlefield, Anakin and his brethren conducted secret Republic missions to stave off Separatist attacks, engaging in duplicity to prevail. Once invigorating for their theatrics, these clandestine operations began to fill Anakin with dread. On one occasion he was forced to go undercover as a slaver inside the heart of the galaxy's most notorious slave empire on the planet Zygerria in order to free 50,000 Togruta colonists. In the course of the assignment, Anakin had to infiltrate a slave auction—much like the one in which his mother had been sold as a child—and Ahsoka was forced to wear the shameful flowing teal robes of his servant. His duty to the cause obliged him to work his way into the good graces of the planet's queen, Miraj Scintel, and even act as her bodyguard. Anakin found that return to servitude, however brief, utterly humiliating.

His faith in the Jedi and their ideals was undeniably damaged when his own master, Obi-Wan, was gunned down by a sniper on Coruscant before his eyes. Anakin was stunned, unable to comprehend how his friend and mentor, who had survived so many battles, could be murdered so suddenly and senselessly. He swiftly located the perpetrator, a bounty hunter named Rako Hardeen, and honored what he knew would have been his master's wishes sending the assassin to a Republic prison rather than following his own instincts to kill him in revenge.

Eventually, forced to expose their deception or risk the death of one of their own, the Jedi revealed to Anakin that the man he'd apprehended—and nearly murdered—was in fact Obi-Wan. Working deep undercover to untangle a Separatist plot to kidnap Supreme Chancellor Palpatine, Obi-Wan had undergone various medical procedures and swallowed a vocal emulator to take on the appearance of his supposed assassin. The Jedi Council did not foresee the effects Obi-Wan's ruse would have on Anakin's conflicted psyche, or anticipate the lengths Anakin would go to avenge his fallen master. When "Hardeen" subsequently escaped from prison, Anakin was beside himself. He turned for guidance to his friend Palpatine, who seized the opportunity to further alienate Anakin from the Jedi by sending him to hunt down Rako. He gave the floundering young Jedi permission to use violence, while also imbuing him with the self-confidence and support that was sorely lacking from his supposed Jedi comrades.

Blind to Anakin's thoughts and feelings on the matter, the Jedi Council stuck to their cunning plan and removed the bounty on Hardeen's head. This only added to Anakin's confusion and rage. He could not understand why the Jedi would not want Obi-Wan's killer caught and punished. How could the very symbol of peace and justice in the galaxy allow one of their own to be murdered with apparent impunity? The effects of these questions lingered long after the nature of Obi-Wan's secret mission had finally been revealed to Anakin. Thus his initial angry confusion festered into dismay that the Jedi—even Obi-Wan himself—had failed to put their trust in him.

For much of the war, Anakin had believed that the Jedi were unwilling to go far enough to actually win. After this perceived betrayal, he had to face the fact that the Jedi *were* prepared to use underhanded tactics. Anakin realized that the ethics of the Jedi had been compromised by the war. It was no longer the same Jedi Order he had romanticized as a child. He grappled with the conflicting ideas that he could be the Chosen One of Jedi lore, a storied Jedi general at the forefront of so many Republic victories, yet still be denied the Jedi's full confidence.

By contrast, Palpatine was showing more trust in Anakin than ever, treating him as a partner in their avowed pursuit of a fairer and more just galaxy. Their relationship blossomed. Instead of Palpatine acting as mentor and protector, Anakin was honored to act as Palpatine's bodyguard, the roles somewhat reversed. His pride swelled in the knowledge that the Supreme Chancellor only needed him to feel secure. Where the Jedi failed to appreciate and utilize Anakin's astonishing abilities, Palpatine—his advanced age and frail physique making him vulnerable in Anakin's eyes—showed how much he needed Skywalker by his side.

Although his faith in the Jedi and his own master had been shaken, Anakin's trust in Ahsoka was absolute. Inspired to avoid engendering the same feelings of betrayal he felt with his own teacher, Anakin strived to be a better and more open adviser, and a fierce protector. Ahsoka was almost always by Anakin's side during his adventures. By the age of 17, Ahsoka had grown into an impressive commander and teacher in her own right. Master and apprentice were an almost unstoppable team on and off the battlefield, moving as one, two halves of a whole, both vital to the other.

During a firefight in the skies above Cato Neimodia, Anakin was knocked unconscious in his starfighter. His ship was covered by buzz droids, their whirring saws sending his craft hurtling toward the ground. Ahsoka, seeing the danger Anakin was in from her cockpit, leaped to his rescue, and, with the help of R2-D2's rapid calculations, saved him from a fiery demise.

It was during that fateful rescue, carried out over the jeweled cities of the colony world inhabited by Trade Federation barons, that the unthinkable took place on Coruscant: a terrorist bomb attack on the Jedi Temple. Because they were off-world at the time and thus had solid alibis, Anakin and Ahsoka were called upon to investigate. Master Yoda and the other elders were aware that the dark side had clouded their perception of the Force for far too long, making even the current ranks of the Jedi possible suspects. The fact that the war had come to the Republic's capital was not surprising, and the Jedi should have understood that their role as generals of the Republic made them prime targets. However, they were caught completely off guard by the bombing, shaken that their enemies would stoop so low as to attack their sacred home.

The Jedi Temple was more than the headquarters of the commanders of the Clone Wars; it was the place where younglings, freshly claimed by Jedi seekers, took their first lessons in understanding the Force, learning the art of meditation and practicing lightsaber forms with Master Yoda. It was a center of contemplation, where Master Mace Windu and the rest of the Jedi Council—which by then included Obi-Wan—considered the ramifications of every decision facing the Order as a whole, and of every Jedi in the field. The Temple was a solemn oasis in the bustling metropolis of the capital, a place of justice and serenity in a climate of political uncertainty. Most importantly for Anakin, it was his home. As much as Anakin chafed at the restrictive rules imposed by the Order, and at times questioned the direction of the council and its faith in him, he found it hard to comprehend that someone would attack the Temple itself.

Inside the building, bodies of the dead were still trapped among the debris as Anakin and Ahsoka mounted their investigation. The screams of the injured echoed through the Force, reverberating in Anakin's mind. He had seen more than his share of death and destruction; however, the bombing was a fresh trauma. Skilled Jedi, innocent civilian maintenance workers, and dedicated clone soldiers were killed when the bomb exploded. Soon after, Master Yoda led a somber funeral service, reminding the survivors that they would all pass on into the cosmic Force one day. Despite the many lives lost since the First Battle of Geonosis had plunged the galaxy into war, burying the dead after the vicious attack on the Temple felt very different to memorializing fallen soldiers on the battlefield.

Instead of the relief in uncovering the culprit, Anakin and Ahsoka's investigation into the attack took a sharp turn. From the outset, they suspected that the bombing had not been carried out by Separatist infiltrators or an assassin for hire. The boldness of the strike suggested someone with clear knowledge of the Temple's inner workings, a former ally who had betrayed the Order with the purpose of sending a stark message. The Jedi could no longer ignore the fact that the people weren't just tired of the seemingly endless conflict, they were losing their faith in the Order, in everything the Jedi stood for, and their role in the war. The possibility that a Jedi had played a part in the attack sickened Anakin. He was aware that the Jedi were not above becoming political fanatics, such as Count Dooku or the rogue Jedi General Pong Krell. Their beliefs had made them traitors, enabling them to rationalize atrocities against the Jedi and the Republic.

Thanks to a fiendishly cunning Separatist plot, Anakin's own Padawan Ahsoka was ultimately arrested and accused of planning the bombing. She was charged with manipulating a dedicated civil servant and his wife into doing her bidding, and then murdering them both to cover her tracks. Anakin refused to believe that his gentle student could be capable of such butchery. While he desperately clung to the hope that together they could discover the real culprit, Ahsoka completely lost faith in the Jedi and the Republic. Anakin looked on in dismay as she was expelled from the Jedi Order. A Temple guard roughly snapped the braid of Padawan Silka beads that Ahsoka always wore slung over her head. Skywalker protested in vain as she was stripped of her rank in the Grand Army of the Republic and made to stand trial in a military tribunal. In an instant, the Jedi Council's decree had nullified everything they had worked for and accomplished together. In Anakin's eyes, the Jedi's actions made a mockery of their avowed dedication to justice.

At the subsequent trial, presided over by Palpatine himself, it seemed certain that Ahsoka would be convicted. Anakin decided to take matters into his own hands. In an echo of his wartime interrogations, he violently questioned the bounty hunter Asajj Ventress on the lower levels of the capital planet until he elicited a confession that pointed the finger at another Jedi Padawan, Barriss Offee. It transpired that Barriss had become so disillusioned with the Jedi she was willing to resort to mass murder to expose them for the frauds she now believed them to be, and frame Ahsoka for the crime. In her confession, she denounced the Jedi as the real instigators of the war. But even with her conviction, her actions damaged the reputation of both the Jedi and the Republic. Her allegations spread through Coruscant like ripples in a dark pool, causing many, Anakin included, to believe that neither the Republic nor the Separatists—and certainly not the once-peaceful Jedi—could truly bring an end to the chaos.

Anakin comforted himself with the thought that he alone had never doubted Ahsoka. He had stood by her, defended her, produced the evidence that had acquitted her, and saved her from losing everything she had worked for, just as he had promised he would. However, even this solace was to be denied him: Ahsoka refused to return to the ranks of the Jedi. Having been falsely accused and cast out of the Order, while the Jedi's once-legendary second sight had clearly been dimmed by the dark side, Ahsoka did something few Jedi had dared to do before. Despite Anakin's heartfelt pleas to reconsider and a rare apology from the elders who had wronged her, Ahsoka walked away.

By doing so, Ahsoka accomplished something Anakin Skywalker was too afraid to do himself. Like her, Anakin had also lost faith in the Jedi. He had spurned their strict code and violated their protocols again and again in the name of justice and desire. But he was not strong enough to take a stand and walk away. The Jedi Order had been his life. The Jedi had freed him from slavery and offered him a home. Despite all the reasons he had to follow Ahsoka, abandoning the Jedi felt like a terrible mistake. He owed them too much.

In the end, Yoda had succeeded in teaching the value of letting go of all one feared to lose. Only it was Ahsoka who had mastered the lesson, leaping into the unknown, while Anakin was left with familiar feelings of abandonment.

Chapter 8

Padmé Amidala

Anakin's training of Ahsoka was essentially a test devised by the Jedi to discover if he was truly capable of following their path by calming his turbulent mind and helping an apprentice achieve balance in the Force. When Anakin exhibited what the Jedi thought of as overprotective behavior toward his Padawan, and Ahsoka subsequently rejected the Jedi, it appeared that this was a test that Anakin had resoundingly failed. Without Ahsoka to act as a counterbalance to his passions and fears, his attentions, even more than they had before, focused on Padmé Amidala. He was sure that she, at least, would never forsake him.

Of course, the Jedi had no idea that Anakin was secretly married to Padmé. Had they known, they would have been outraged at his flagrant disregard for Jedi teachings on attachments and the pitfalls of wanting to possess another person.

As soon as the war erupted, Anakin had forgotten all the Jedi's rational arguments concerning the avoidance of romantic entanglements. Having felt isolated for so long—ever since leaving and then losing his mother—Anakin's bond with Padmé felt like finding a welcoming presence at the end of an arduous journey. As Padmé's beloved democracy began to shatter under the weight of civil war, her resolve to reject the bliss they felt in each other's company grew weaker and weaker.

With Padmé at his side, Anakin felt supported and loved in a way he had not truly felt in years. She was a light illuminating the darkness that had surrounded him, filling the void of Shmi's maternal solicitude, bringing warmth and sympathy, as well as physical love. Padmé's belief in Anakin's abilities was unquestioning—unlike the suspicious Jedi, who could not decide if he were the Chosen One or something else entirely. Sometimes Anakin could barely comprehend how someone as accomplished as Padmé Amidala—so resolute and objective in all areas of her life—could love him. But she did.

Padmé accepted Anakin's cybernetic limb as readily as his other less-apparent imperfections. When exposed, its electrostatic fingertips were a fair approximation of the sense of touch; Anakin reserved that part of himself for Padmé alone. She was the one person who could make him feel whole again.

After the First Battle of Geonosis, the couple escaped to Naboo, temporarily casting aside their worries over the future of their forbidden romance, the rules of the Jedi Code, and the impending crisis of war. With R2-D2 and C-3PO the only witnesses, they were married in a secret ceremony by a Naboo holy man. Making their union official in the eyes of the Naboo clergy helped Anakin feel in control of his life, perhaps for the first time. He also relished the secrecy of their marriage, which seemed to make their love safe from prying eyes and sharp tongues.

For a time, Anakin's worries fell away. In Padmé's presence he found it easier than ever to remain in the moment. However, while he basked in his clandestine happiness, to those outside the union, including Obi-Wan Kenobi, Anakin appeared as defiant and willful as ever. To his harshest critics among the Jedi, it may even have seemed that Padmé's presence in Anakin's life had encouraged his ambitious fantasies. Few outsiders realized how deep Anakin's feelings were for Padmé; and those near to the couple kept their suspicions to themselves. Yet from the beginning, the weight of the impropriety had a profound impact on Anakin's relationship to his former teacher. Even more than wanting to open up to Obi-Wan about the truth of his situation, Anakin wished for his master to be the kind of person he *could* tell.

While Anakin thrived in the heat of battle, Padmé pursued diplomatic solutions inside the Galactic Senate, hoping to bring a peaceful end to the bloody conflict. Professional duties often kept them apart. As a result, their marriage was a series of separations, euphoric reunions, and holographic transmissions. The times they spent on different sides of the galaxy—and often in life-threatening situations—intensified their rare moments together.

This is not to suggest that Padmé and Anakin's relationship was without its problems. The stress of their duties, the weight of their secret, and long periods of physical separation strained their marriage. For Anakin, concealing the truth began to turn the ecstasy of his love into yet another decision he'd made in violation of all the Jedi held dear, one more in a growing list of reasons for him to feel ashamed. Padmé also worried about their secret relationship; it seemed to her only a matter of time before they were exposed. Anakin would be cast out of the Jedi and her own reputation would suffer a potentially fatal blow, laying waste her political aspirations.

***

Without a doubt, Anakin and Padmé's secret union had damaging effects regarding the outcome of the war for the Republic. Near the midpoint of the conflict, the Gungan Grand Army captured the Separatists' cyborg leader General Grievous. However, the duplicitous Palpatine, Sith Lord Darth Sidious, instructed his dark-side apprentice Count Dooku to lure Anakin into a trap. With General Skywalker ensnared, Dooku offered Padmé a prisoner exchange she could not refuse: her secret husband's life for General Grievous' freedom. Anakin lived to fight another day, unaware that Padmé had been forced to compromise her ideals, and jeopardize the Republic's chances of victory, to protect her love.

As the Outer Rim Sieges and other far-flung missions kept them separated for weeks—even months—at a time, Anakin's image of his destiny became increasingly focused on Padmé. In her absence, he clung to his longing for her, allowing it to eclipse all other considerations and goals.

In time, Anakin became shockingly possessive of their secret and of Padmé herself. He was convinced that their union was nowhere near as much of a threat to Jedi ideals as the ongoing war, which had forced the peace-loving Jedi to become leaders in battle, in stark violation of their code. Even those seated among the Jedi High Council felt unmoored, uncertain, and uncomfortable. But with no one to confide in, Anakin's anxieties about his marriage and his justifications for it continually gnawed at him.

Anakin's faith in Padmé suffered a grave blow when her work brought her back into contact with the dashingly handsome Senator Rush Clovis, with whom she had once briefly been romantically involved. Padmé, who looked down on Clovis for his past sympathies with the Separatist cause, was disturbed to find that the mere mention of her senatorial colleague's name could incense Anakin almost to the point of madness. It suggested that Anakin had lost his trust in Padmé and her dedication to their marriage and echoed the dissociative break he had suffered in the aftermath of Shmi's demise. Lacking the maturity to conceal or deal with his feelings of jealousy or resentment at Padmé's sudden renewed camaraderie with Clovis, Anakin became convinced that even his beloved was turning away from him.

If Anakin had deliberately wanted to alienate Padmé he could not have picked a better method than demonstrating such furious possessiveness and unfounded suspicion. He demanded that she refuse to have any personal or professional dealings with Clovis. This simply made the former queen of Naboo, who had led her people with understanding and humility, feel like a piece of property. In his greed, Anakin seemed little better than the slave-owning Hutts he professed to despise.

Obi-Wan sensed Anakin's troubled emotional state. In what was perhaps the most open conversation master and apprentice had ever had about the inherent strain of dedicating one's life to the higher calling of the monastic Jedi Order while still being imperfectly human, Kenobi tried to reach his friend as he tinkered at his workbench, surrounded by happy childhood memories—a podracing poster and a model Jedi interceptor among the trinkets of a simpler time. Whenever he was confronted by a problem he couldn't readily fix, Anakin tended to retreat into himself, occupying his mind by working with his hands on some mechanical device. However, fiddling with wires and droid components brought him only superficial distraction from his personal demons.

Kenobi's concern only had the effect of fueling Anakin's present frustrations. Obi-Wan somehow always managed to make Anakin still feel like a Jedi student. His persistent probing caused Anakin's surly facade to crack. Through Anakin's thinly veiled criticisms, mostly chastising Padmé for giving in too easily to her emotions, Obi-Wan began to perceive the real trouble. The Jedi Master tried his best to empathize, offering up his own brief romance with the Duchess of Mandalore, Satine Kryze, as a way of drawing Anakin out.

For years, Kenobi and his apprentice had danced around the issue of Anakin's attraction and affection for Padmé; friendship was all Anakin could ever hope to achieve with her, as long as he wore the robes of a Jedi. Any attempts at more honest teachings on the matter had been derailed by the urgency of the galactic war, but Obi-Wan was sure that getting Anakin to admit to his feelings was the first step in truly working through them. Attachment was forbidden for a Jedi Knight, but the emotions that led there were natural, to be dealt with, not ignored as many in the Jedi Order seemed to prefer. However, fearful of exposing the depth of his defiance of the Jedi Code, Anakin fiercely denied that he and Padmé were anything more than friends.

Anakin's subsequent actions soon revealed the lie to his protestations. Coming upon Clovis in Padmé's apartments—apparently bending the senator backward for a romantic kiss, despite her protests—Anakin went straight for Clovis' throat, reaching through the Force to send him hurtling across the room. Ignoring Padme's desperate pleas for him to stop, Anakin then went to work with his fists, his mechno-hand packing a jaw-rattling punch as he pummeled the man who dared to lay a finger on his wife. It was as if, driven by his basest instincts and desires, Anakin had lost his mind, regressing to a dark, irrational place, where the most primitive part of his psyche could burst forth in a howl of fury. All traces of the sweet little boy he had been when he first met Padmé vanished, and in an instant the years of blissful, yet forbidden, pleasure he had enjoyed with her were swept away by an overwhelming urge to end Clovis' life.

Finally, as if coming out of a trance, Anakin heeded Padmé's desperate cries. He ceased his assault, but could find no adequate explanation for his behavior. It was as if some alien, vengeful creature had emerged from deep within his soul. Anakin wanted to believe it was Padmé's rejection of Clovis, and the traitor's failure to heed her words, that had driven him to such lengths to defend her honor. But he was at a loss, aware that his primal anger could not be justified by Tusken atrocities committed against his poor mother, nor war crimes committed by Separatists. Anakin truly didn't understand what had come over him, and he didn't have the slightest idea how to control it, despite more than a decade of Jedi training.

Anakin's seemingly psychotic episode forced Padmé to take a cold, hard look at their relationship. The foundation of any union is trust, and theirs had eroded beneath the veil of secrecy. She began to recognize that their marriage had been doomed from the beginning; it was built on lies and deception. Anakin had gone too far, and not even Padmé, who had absolved him of his past misdeeds, could stand to see what he had become.

Anakin and Padmé sadly agreed that they should spend some time apart. She no longer felt safe in his presence, a further blow to the fragile ego of one who fancied himself a heroic knight and savior. Anakin apologized profusely to her, but he could no longer hide from the fact that it wasn't his oath to the Jedi or the war that was keeping him from his wife anymore. It was himself. The fragile strands tethering Anakin to the light side of the Force were fraying, and he was drawing closer and closer to the dark side.

Strangely, although Clovis was unable to fully grasp Anakin's reasons for the assault, instead of trying to use the incident against the Jedi, he was content to keep the truth of what had happened to himself. Just as Anakin had difficulty concealing his shame, he could not hide his injuries, but in public he claimed that he'd been beaten by thugs who had fled the scene. Furthermore, he named Anakin, not as his attacker, but as the hero who had helped drive them away. Perhaps he recognized that he and Skywalker were not so different. Beyond their hopeless love for Padmé, Clovis knew what it was to live as a servant, an outcast, and an orphan. He had always felt misunderstood. The Muun people of Scipio had given him a home when his parents were killed, and raised them as his own. But it was hard to find one's place in the galaxy, and inner peace, with such a shaky foundation.

Clovis was subsequently appointed leader of the Banking Clan and the war soon followed to the neutral planet of Scipio. It had become clear that Clovis had been conducting deals with Separatists that would destroy the Republic's economy, and Anakin was hot on his trail. Clovis was in conference with Padmé in his plush office atop Scipio's tallest spire when Anakin burst in. Trying to ward him off, Clovis grabbed a blaster and pointed it at Padmé's head, using her body as a shield. The standoff was interrupted when a vulture droid crashed into the spire, shearing Clovis' office in two. As all three tilted toward a deadly rift below, Anakin found his footing and grabbed onto both Clovis and Padmé just before they would have plummeted to their deaths.

It is impossible to say if Anakin loosened his grip or if Clovis let go— the truth is most likely a combination of the two—but within moments Clovis was no more and Anakin was cradling his traumatized wife in his arms, his violent outburst forgiven and the chill between them forgotten. But Anakin could not erase the images of Padmé's terror—both in response to his aggression and as a target of Clovis' weapon—from his mind. Afterward, he became more fearful than ever of losing control of his emotions and upsetting the delicate balancing act of succeeding as a devoted husband and also a faithful Jedi. He knew that, if he wasn't careful, just one slip could rob him of both his love and his place in the galaxy.

Chapter 9

The Battle of Coruscant

Three years into the conflict, Anakin had made peace with his own belief that sometimes the only way to beat the Separatists was to play them at their own cunning games. Ironically, as the end of the war neared, Anakin came perilously close to becoming the enemy on all fronts.

During the Battle of Yerbana, it almost seemed as if Anakin intended to take on the whole Separatist army himself. He marched toward the enemy, the wind in his hair—his lightsaber hanging carelessly from his belt—and pretended to surrender. He thus drew out the tactical droid in charge, and used the Force to pull the Separatist leader directly toward his ignited lightsaber blade, and behead him. Captain Rex and the rest of Anakin's men then emerged from hiding, flying in on jetpacks to take out the droid army from the skies.

Soon after this incident, much to Anakin's surprise and delight, he received a message from Ahsoka Tano over his ship's holo feed. When Ahsoka walked away from the Jedi Temple, Anakin felt sure they would one day meet again. Ahsoka had left her lightsabers behind and Anakin had made the necessary repairs to the two weapons in the hopes that one day his Padawan would return to their ranks, prepared at long last to accept the Jedi Council's offer and become a Jedi Knight.

However, Ahsoka met her former master's enthusiasm with a

respectful, but cool, response. Her main reason for contacting him was to request Anakin's and Obi-Wan's help in putting an end to the foul reign of Maul on the planet of Mandalore. The warrior once thought defeated in the stymied invasion of Naboo had emerged during the Clone Wars as a formidable opponent no longer allied with the Sith yet bent on taking revenge on Kenobi and making his own way as a crime lord in the galaxy.

Ahsoka's businesslike manner had the effect of making Anakin unsure of himself and unsure of where he stood with his former apprentice. She seemed to be everything the Jedi had willed him to be and everything he had failed to master.

Obi-Wan was adamant that the Jedi Council would have to decide if the Republic should aid the Mandalorians, which meant effectively breaking a centuries-long treaty and drawing them into another war. But before the Council could approve the plan, the Separatist General Grievous launched a daring attack on Coruscant, sending all available Republic troops scrambling to defend the capital. The people of Mandalore needed them if they were to wrest their planet from Maul's tyrannical rule, but so did Supreme Chancellor Palpatine and the citizens who called Coruscant home. Ahsoka was exasperated to find the Jedi putting political gain ahead of humanitarian freedoms.

Anakin faced a dilemma. He wanted to help Palpatine, and fulfill his promise as the Chancellor's defender. But he also didn't want to disappoint Ahsoka, whose poise reminded him of his beloved Padmé, arguing passionately for the rights of her people on the Senate floor.

In the end, Anakin sent half his troops to relieve the Mandalorians, while he led the rest to the heart of the Republic. Anakin returned Ahsoka's lightsabers to her, to show that, to his way of thinking, being a Jedi meant more than a title, more than adhering to a specific set of rules. Whether she rejoined the Order and the Republic or not, Ahsoka remained strong in the Force and the signature weapons of the Jedi, her lightsabers, would help her focus in battle, while she continued to use the mystical energy as her guide. Furthermore, Jedi or not, the lightsabers belonged in Ahsoka's hands, and Anakin knew full well she would need them to face Maul.

***

The Battle of Coruscant proved a pivotal moment in the war, the state of the Republic, and Anakin's allegiance to the light. Anakin and Obi-Wan were soon on a vital mission to rescue Supreme Chancellor Palpatine, who had been snatched by one of the Separatists' top military minds, General Grievous. Even with so much at stake, Anakin felt content behind the controls of a starfighter, pleased to be out-flying Obi-Wan as they pursued Grievous' warship. Anakin privately still felt wronged by the Jedi's reticence to trust him, but in combat, he and Obi-Wan moved as one, synchronized and methodical, as if forming the steps to a brutal ballet. Obi-Wan, there is no question, had trained Anakin well.

Inside the hangar bay of Grievous' ship, R2-D2 traced Palpatine's distress beacon to the observation platform atop a towering spire. When the Jedi reached the spire where he was restrained, instead of encountering Grievous they came face to face with Count Dooku.

Anakin was older and wiser since his first encounter with Dooku on Geonosis, but he was also angrier. During the ensuing fight, Dooku pinned Obi-Wan beneath a balcony. Anakin had to forget Obi-Wan's plight and keep his head clear. He grabbed Dooku's hands and his lightsaber sliced through the Sith Lord's wrists. Dooku's red-bladed weapon sailed through the air and into Anakin's outstretched palm. Anakin held him captive, both blades glowing, one red and one blue, near the flesh of his neck.

It should have been a moment to rejoice. Dooku was defeated and, with him in Republic custody, the Separatists would swiftly falter. If Anakin expected to find his friend the Chancellor crying tears of gratitude at being rescued, he was sorely disappointed. Instead, Palpatine told Anakin to immediately kill Dooku.

At that moment, Dooku seemed to personify everything Anakin had always hated about the war. Without the conniving Count, there would have been no conflict, and the Separatists would have remained a fledgling movement without a unifying leader. For years, Dooku had served as the face of the Separatist regime, and Anakin despised that face, even as it stared up at him in fear, pleading for life. With Palpatine's order still ringing in his ears, Anakin enclosed Dooku's neck with both sabers—one blue, fashioned for justice, the other red, forged in darkness—and lopped off his head.

As soon as the decision was made, the action executed, Anakin felt regret. He was well aware that a Jedi should not strike out of spite or hold vindictive grudges. Killing an unarmed prisoner of war, even one as dangerous as Dooku, was emphatically not the Jedi way. Yet Palpatine—no Jedi, but not yet revealed to be Dooku's Sith Master— seemed gratified by the turn of events. He allayed Anakin's doubts with the usual unwavering support the younger man had come to appreciate. Dooku had once mercilessly cut off Anakin's arm, something he was reminded of every day when he looked down at his mechanical hand. It was only natural, in Palpatine's estimation, to harbor a desire for revenge for such a personal and life-altering attack.

As Anakin released Palpatine's binders, Palpatine once more encouraged him to veer from the path of the Jedi—this time by leaving behind his fallen master. Palpatine reasoned that they would never be able to escape if they were burdened by Obi-Wan's still-unconscious body. However, despite Anakin's devotion to Palpatine, the Chancellor had overstepped the mark. Anakin refused to desert his master and oldest friend.

Obi-Wan came around just before the three were captured and taken before General Grievous. R2-D2 provided a distraction—enabling Anakin and Obi-Wan to reclaim their lightsabers—and master and apprentice joined forces once again. Grievous made a desperate escape through the window of the bridge, and was seemingly blown into the vacuum of space. Anakin and Obi-Wan later learned that he had survived by doubling back and stealing an escape pod.

Meanwhile, the hull of Grievous' craft, which had burst into flames, began to break up. Before it could crash to the ground, Anakin grabbed the controls of what was left of the ship. Drawing on his power in the Force, the superior reflexes that had made him a podracing legend, and with Obi-Wan by his side as copilot, Anakin brought them safely down on Coruscant in a crash-landing.

Eliminating the leader of the Separatists was a decisive achievement, not to mention saving the lives of the Chancellor and Obi-Wan. But as soon as Anakin found himself back on the world that served as the Republic's capital, his attentions and priorities swung in another direction entirely: toward Padmé.

Part I: The Father
The Force, Anakin, and Shmi

Anakin's mother, Shmi Skywalker.

Junk dealer and slaveholder Watto, whose love of gambling would provide Anakin with an escape route from Tatooine.

A young Padmé Amidala in Watto's junk shop on Tatooine.

To help his mother, Anakin built a protocol droid he called C-3PO.

Anakin painstakingly prepared his podracer for the Boonta Eve Classic—a race that would change his life.

Qui-Gon's Promise

The Sith Lord Darth Maul.

Jedi Master Qui-Gon Jinn believed Anakin was the Chosen One of prophecy.

Anakin stands before the Jedi Council.

Two Mentors

Senator Sheev Palpatine, seen during the early years of his time in office.

Jedi Knight Obi-Wan Kenobi.

The Jedi Temple on Coruscant, where Anakin and other Padawans trained to be Jedi.

Love and Loss

Anakin and Padmé enjoying a rare moment together in the lake country of Naboo.

The japor snippet necklace, crafted by Anakin as a boy, and given to Padmé as a gift.

The First Battle of Geonosis

Count Dooku—former Jedi Knight turned to the dark side.

On Geonosis, executions were held for public spectacle in the Petranaki arena.

The Jedi General

Obi-Wan Kenobi and Anakin made a formidable team during the Clone Wars.

Captain Rex fought alongside the Jedi on numerous battlefields during the Clone Wars.

The Separatists' Admiral Trench.

Teachers of the Force

Ahsoka Tano on trial for the bombing of the Jedi Temple.

An ancient mural of the elemental beings of Mortis known as the Daughter (left), the Father (center), and the Son (right).

Obi–Wan Kenobi disguised as assassin Rako Hardeen—a scheme that seriously eroded Anakin's trust in the Jedi Order.

Master Yoda taught Jedi for many generations.

Padmé Amidala

Padmé Amidala, as seen before her secret wedding to Anakin Skywalker on Naboo.

The Battle of Coruscant

General Grievous, commander of the Separatist military and deadly foe of the Jedi.

Anakin crash-lands Grievous' ship the *Invisible Hand* on the surface of Coruscant.

The Offspring

Anakin returned from the Outer Rim Sieges to learn that his wife, Padmé, was pregnant.

"Did You Ever Hear the Tragedy of Darth Plagueis the Wise?"

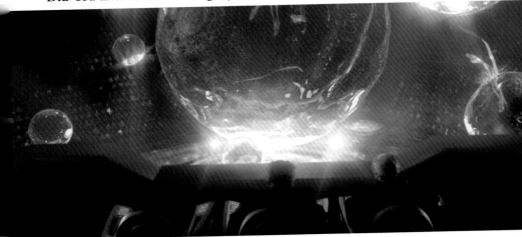

Anakin and Palpatine at the Galaxies Opera House on Coruscant.

Friends and Enemies

Jedi Master Mace Windu, seen during his years as a member of the Jedi Council.

Arise, Lord Vader

Clone Commander Cody receives Order 66—a directive identifying all Jedi as traitors to the Republic.

In his infamous address to the Senate at the end of the Clone Wars, Supreme Chancellor Palpatine gives a speech officially marking the beginning of the Galactic Empire.

Anakin leads the 501st Legion on an assault of the Jedi Temple.

Duel on Mustafar

Mustafar: the scene of Obi-Wan and Anakin's momentous confrontation.

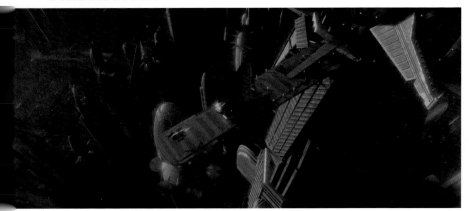

The Grand Republic Medical Facility on Coruscant.

Darth Vader emerges after reconstructive surgery to repair injuries suffered during the duel on Mustafar with Obi-Wan Kenobi.

The Polis Massa outpost, where Padmé Amidala received emergency care.

Padmé lies in state during her funeral, Anakin's japor snippet necklace in her hands.

Chapter 10

The Offspring

Politicians and news outlets alike hailed Anakin as the hero of the hour for smiting Count Dooku and returning the Senate's Supreme Chancellor unscathed after the attack on the Republic's capital. Neither senators nor Jedi suspected that Anakin had in fact been in the presence of the Sith Lord who had orchestrated the war and the actions of Count Dooku, his dark apprentice. They also had no idea that Anakin had killed Count Dooku at the behest of Palpatine, as part of his masterplan. Following Dooku's death, General Grievous rose in rank to lead the entire Separatist Alliance. Grievous was always in charge of the droid army. I'd say Grievous rose in rank to lead the entire Separatist Alliance. He became the Jedi's prime target, if the war was to have a favorable outcome for the Republic.

Dooku's death also meant the Jedi were no closer to unraveling the mystery of the shadowy Sith master who had plagued them for years. The dark side of the Force blunted the Jedi's senses and blinded them to the truth. On more than one occasion Dooku had expounded on the depravity plaguing the Republic. Yet his warnings went unheeded, due in no small part because Dooku's own past made him a most untrustworthy source.

Anakin forgot all these pressing concerns as soon as he was reunited with Padmé. Kissing her with reckless abandon in the promenade of the Senate building, he no longer cared if they were found out. He had had enough of hiding his love from prying eyes or being kept apart from her fighting for the Republic. Nothing mattered to him as much as she did.

Once more the voice of reason, Padmé calmed Anakin down, and with her next breath imparted stunning news: He was about to become a father.

Anakin immediately began to obsess over the ramifications and complications of such a development. Padmé could only conceal her condition for so long, masking her pregnancy under cloaks of fine Naboo velvet. Anyone who had previously suspected a deeper connection between the senator and the Jedi would have more reason than ever to believe that he had cast aside the Jedi's strict Code and consorted with a woman he was clearly hopelessly in love with. And even if he and Padmé managed to maintain their deception, once the child arrived, the Queen of Naboo would relieve Padmé of her post and it would be impossible for Anakin to remain a Jedi—except as an absentee father. For Anakin to allow his child to grow up fatherless while he stood by, cast in the role of caring family friend, was unconscionable. Moreover, a child could hardly be trusted to carry the secret of his or her lineage without disclosing, by a slip of the tongue or betrayal of their feelings—sensed by the Jedi through the Force—to keep the truth quiet for long.

Anakin's Jedi training temporarily helped calm his anxieties, allowing him a moment to embrace what their future might hold. Amid the terrible destruction of the Clone War, they had created life. If he let his worries fall away, if he only focused on himself and Padmé, on their commitment to each other, on the vow they had made on Naboo, he could see her news for what it was: the happiest moment of his life. Padmé had never looked more beautiful to her husband, not even when, as a boy, he mistook her for an angel on the day they first met.

***

Anakin's joy was fleeting. Rapture over Padmé's news was soon replaced by fear. Padmé's transformation into motherhood stirred up emotions he had not felt since leaving Shmi behind more than a decade earlier. Superficially, the two women were very different—a slave and a former queen, one destitute, the other wealthy. One was his abandoned mother, the other the mother of the child he might well have to abandon. History seemed to be repeating itself in ways that Anakin found profoundly disturbing.

Three years prior, Anakin's nightmares had served as a portent of Shmi's death; now Anakin was plagued by visions of the future once more. He should have been at peace, finally sleeping at Padmé's side, but through the Force he saw only staggering loss, a vision of Padmé crying out in pain and pleading for his help, while their child sobbed out of reach. When he told Padmé what he had seen, her worries rested with the baby. She was prepared to give her life to protect her unborn child. Anakin's concerns were chiefly with his wife.

Padmé wanted Anakin to ask their friend Obi-Wan Kenobi for guidance and assistance. But Anakin refused to consider it. Although he and Obi-Wan were like brothers, he could already sense Obi-Wan's judgment if he and Padmé disclosed the depth of their relationship and their news to him. The child was, after all, tangible proof that he had flagrantly disregarded the Jedi's monastic ways. Instead of confiding in Obi-Wan, Anakin sought the council of the oldest, wisest Jedi he knew, as well as the man who had long treated him as a son.

By the time Anakin met Master Yoda in the elder's spartan quarters at the Jedi Temple, a shadow was clouding his mind. The visions of Padmé's death were a torment like no other he had endured, a crack that threatened to open into a chasm. To Yoda, Anakin admitted only the nature of his dream, concealing his secret love.

Yoda had tried and failed to rid Anakin of his tendency to become overly attached to those he cared for. The Jedi Master could see that, despite years of lessons on the importance of remaining in the moment, Anakin's recent vision of the future had paralyzed the young Knight. Yoda was troubled that Anakin still sought to control events, instead of surrendering to the Force and the elements of his life that could not be constrained by his will.

Yoda imparted important wisdom that day, which Anakin heard but did not heed. In Yoda's eyes, seeking control over every major aspect of life was pointless; one would surely lose in the end, confronted with the inevitability that all things must pass. Instead, the master found solace in the acceptance of this hard truth and, for the last time, he asked Anakin to do the same. The future was still in motion, after all, and there was time for Anakin to accept the things he could not change and embrace the time he had with Padmé for what it was: fleeting and ephemeral. Change was the only constant, and death, the Jedi knew, was not the end.

To Anakin's surprise, before he could tell Palpatine about his troubling premonition, the Supreme Chancellor made an extraordinary move. He appointed Anakin to the Jedi Council as his personal representative. Although the Jedi Order had long bent to the Chancellor's will, there was growing unease around Palpatine, who, on account of the war, had remained in office long after the expiration of his term. In that time, he had quietly absorbed more executive powers to all but circumvent the will of the Senate, including control over the banks. According to Palpatine, Anakin would serve as the eyes, ears, and voice of the Republic inside Council chambers, an honor for one so young and the ultimate ascension among the ranks of the Jedi Order: Every member of the Council was an esteemed Jedi Master. Anakin accepted, eager to make Palpatine proud.

Anakin sensed, even before he walked into the storied chambers to join the 12 masters who made up the Council that, despite his prowess as a warrior, his skills with a lightsaber, and his substantial abilities in the Force, the elders would not receive him as an equal. In their eyes, he was still too young and too immature for such a responsibility.

Chapter 11

"Did You Ever Hear the Tragedy of Darth Plagueis the Wise?"

A single day marked a definitive turning point in the life of Anakin Skywalker. Unbeknownst to the 22-year-old father-to-be, his responses to three intense, equally important encounters with the three people he valued most in the galaxy would propel him, decisively, toward his dark destiny.

That day Anakin appeared before the Jedi Council as Palpatine's appointee. The council approved his installation among them with one critical caveat: Anakin would not be promoted to the rank of Jedi Master. The rebuttal felt like an insult and Anakin's rage spread unease through the council chambers. Despite his heroism throughout the conflict, in many ways Anakin was still the same boy delivered to the Jedi too old to be disabused of his tendencies and given to angry outbursts at trifles. The Jedi were becoming skeptical of the prophecy of the Chosen One. It was hard to imagine one so volatile, so partial to particular individuals and outside causes, ever bringing true balance to the Force.

In all the history of the Jedi Order, no Knight had ever ascended to sit on the Council without also earning the rank of master. Then again, in the history of the Order, no Chancellor had intervened in such a way before. Anakin could only see that his unprecedented appointment, given his age, was being met with equally unprecedented dishonor. Once more the Chosen One was cast aside, on the outside looking in.

Anakin soon met with further disappointment. The Jedi Council had decided to manipulate his new assignment to their advantage, frustrating Palpatine's suspected designs to have a pawn among their ranks by turning Anakin into *their* spy.

Anakin was galled by the Jedi's subsequent request—more like an order—which was vouchsafed him by Obi-Wan. It was a devious and underhanded move for a group that pretended to be the epitome of piety, a violation of the Jedi Code he was sworn to serve, that not only pitted him against the Republic, but forced him to betray his mentor and friend. Palpatine had treated him with respect and shepherded his emotional growth ever since he had arrived on Coruscant. It was Palpatine who had often made time for him despite carrying the cares of the entire Galactic Senate on his frail shoulders, listening to his concerns without judgment.

Obi-Wan's assignment locked Anakin into an intense, internal battle between helping his friend, the Chancellor, or his comrades, the Jedi. It was a conundrum for which there was no right answer, at least not one Anakin could see.

Despite his confusion, the irony of his own disregard for the Jedi ways was not lost on Anakin. But in his estimation, loving Padmé and raising their child was a far less dangerous path than the potentially treasonous acts the Jedi Order were asking him to commit.

Once more, Anakin confided in the one person he knew would keep all of his secrets and assuage his fears: Padmé Amidala. He never suspected that Padmé was also seeking to use his new position at the Chancellor's side to her advantage. By the war's end, Padmé was secretly in league with a group of like-minded senators who wished to reform the Republic from within, freeing it from corruption, and preserving the 1,000-year-old democracy for another millennium.

That night, Padmé pleaded with her husband to use his powers of persuasion and his friendship with Palpatine for a good cause. She confessed her fears that the Republic was becoming the very evil that the righteous senators and the pious Jedi had been fighting to destroy. She had come to the startling conclusion that the Senate itself might even be on the wrong side in the war. Padmé was not one to fear standing firm in her beliefs and speaking her mind, even if her opinions were unpopular. The Chancellor had seized control of the banks and was exerting influence over the Jedi Council. He had appointed governors to oversee every star system in the Republic, rendering senators, the supposed voice of the people, little more than powerless figureheads.

The Jedi wanted to make Anakin a spy; Padmé only wanted him to act as a messenger. She begged him to ask Palpatine to stop the fighting and let diplomacy resume. Anakin refused. He would not be forced into playing political games.

Later that evening, Palpatine invited Anakin to join him in his box at the Galaxies Opera House, where the Mon Calamari ballet *Squid Lake* was being performed to dazzling effect. It was a crucial moment for the two men and their heretofore unshakable bond. General Grievous had been tracked to the Utapau system, Anakin learned from his mentor, and capturing or killing Grievous would almost assuredly put an end to the war. However, Palpatine did not share in Anakin's enthusiasm for a speedy resolution for the conflict. He claimed that the Jedi Council wanted to oust him and take control of the Republic.

Palpatine had sprung his trap brilliantly, disclosing this shattering revelation just hours after the Jedi had asked Anakin to spy on his friend. Palpatine's words seemed to give voice to Anakin's innermost thoughts. His emotions opened like a floodgate as he revealed one of his deepest secrets to his longtime confidant: *he* no longer trusted the Jedi. They had ordered him to be dishonest and conniving, the inverse of all they preached.

Palpatine had expertly turned the Jedi's plot against them, casting the light-side users as power-hungry crooks.

The Sith and Jedi were two sides of the same coin, with similar sensitivities to the power of the Force but diametrically opposing viewpoints on how best to harness that awesome energy. The Sith relied on passion for strength, accumulating power for their own devices, while the Jedi extolled emotional control and used power to help those in need. They were selfless and benign, whereas the Sith were selfish and greedy.

Anakin's unwillingness to let go of Padmé, and the child they had conceived, flouted Jedi ways. In truth, he was neither acting as a Sith nor a Jedi would, although veering closer to the former in his conduct. Over years spent patiently grooming Anakin, Palpatine had seduced Anakin and his formidable powers away from the path of the light. He had encouraged Anakin's fiery temper and played on his insecurities. He had offered Anakin belonging and made him feel special. Palpatine could see deep into Anakin's heart. He sensed that Anakin was tortured by visions of Padmé dying. And on this night of all nights, Palpatine spun the young man he had long called "my son" a story: the Tragedy of Darth Plagueis the Wise. The legendary Plagueis was a Force-wielder so powerful that he could create life from midi-chlorians and even prevent death from visiting his loved ones.

Plagueis accumulated so much power that the only thing he feared was losing it. However, he made the fatal misstep of teaching his apprentice everything he knew. To gain all that power for himself alone, Plagueis' apprentice resolved to murder the Sith Lord while he slept. In the end, no amount of power could help Plagueis escape the inevitability of death. His quest for ultimate control had been the root cause of his untimely demise.

Anakin disregarded the moral point of the tale, and instead fixated on a glimmer of hope he found in it. He knew it was dangerous, but he was willing to give anything to discover this mythological power so that Padmé might cheat death. He would willingly lay down his own life, lose their child, and destroy everything else he held dear to save Padmé from his mother's fate—and save himself from enduring a life without her. In exchange for Padmé's life, he was prepared to watch the whole galaxy burn.

Chapter 12

Friends and Enemies

Anakin reported Palpatine's suspicions about Grievous' where-abouts to the Jedi Council, hoping he would be sent to bring the cyborg general to justice. It would be a decisive victory, and the Chosen One, in his estimation, was worthy of it. However, for the delicate matter of capturing or eliminating the Separatists' new military leader, the Jedi Council chose Obi-Wan over the Knight they regarded as little more than Palpatine's puppet. They overruled Palpatine's support for Anakin taking on the assignment, determined to prove the Council could still make its own decisions. Their decree did nothing to lift Anakin's mood, which ever since his return to Coruscant had been both morose and belligerent.

Obi-Wan made his last contact with Anakin's former Padawan, Ahsoka, before he left for Utapau, urging Ahsoka to speak to her former master and discover what was preying on his mind. She never got the chance, occupied as she was with a vital mission on Mandalore. By then, the Jedi Council was starting to suspect that Palpatine was somehow behind the war, orchestrating the conflict to create chaos in the galaxy. But to what end, they still could not see. With Dooku dead by Anakin's hand, the Jedi were robbed of a vital link to unravel this mystery and Ahsoka's quest to capture Maul was considered to be the next best possibility.

Obi-Wan also called on Padmé. He was sure that she was one of the few people the troubled young man trusted and he hoped she could shake him out of his despondency.

Obi-Wan found it hard to shake a sense of finality in his parting with Anakin that day. Clouded though the Force had been for some time, it was as if he sensed this would be the last time he would look into his former Padawan's eyes, the last chance to say things he had left unsaid during their years together.

Obi-Wan was a compassionate and kind soul, but not much given to praising Anakin, aware that the young man was arrogant enough already. His calm, detached manner did not translate into a warm, nurturing presence—he had not been the mentor and the father-figure Anakin had needed. During their time as master and apprentice—and certainly during the war—quiet moments between them had been rare. They parted solemnly, brothers in the Force.

***

That day, Anakin was visited once more by a nightmarish vision of Padmé's death. This time Obi-Wan was perplexingly by her side. It was almost as if Anakin were prematurely grieving the loss of Padmé. In his weary state, he clung ever tighter to the idea of gaining control over his life. His thoughts lingered on Palpatine's words, seduced by all that his mentor's story had implied could be his.

Anakin knew then, with every fiber of his being, that he wasn't the Jedi he was supposed to be. Whether that was the Chosen One or simply a devout practitioner of the Jedi ways, he couldn't say. But he wanted more. He itched for the power Palpatine's tale of the dark side promised—to dominate death itself, a shield to prevent future solitude. He no longer cared about bringing balance to the Force. All his attention was focused on keeping Padmé alive.

Palpatine sensed that Anakin's patience with the Jedi was exhausted and that he was ready to give in to the raw anger that would make him the most powerful pupil Palpatine's alter ego, Darth Sidious, had known in many a year. The next time Anakin visited the Chancellor's office, the Sith Lord was ready to reveal the secrets of the dark side and its alluring powers. Palpatine was, in fact, the apprentice he had alluded to in the Sith legend, the man who murdered his master to claim the unlimited power of the dark side for his own purposes.

For years, Palpatine had expertly probed Anakin's insecurities, learning the intricate pathways of his secret fears. That day, he was ready to give Anakin a place by his side and the promise of becoming something extraordinary, quite unlike the other Jedi. Something even the mighty Jedi would fear.

The Chancellor dismissed the Jedi's dogmatic views as a narrow route to enlightenment. To fully understand the great mystery of the cosmos, Palpatine said that Anakin would have to explore the inverse of the equation, plumb the depths and expose the underbelly of the Force as he knew it. Only then could he be complete in his knowledge and secure the key, not only to conquering death but fulfilling the prophecy of the Chosen One. He claimed that it was impossible to bring balance to the Force while remaining ignorant of its most dangerous aspects.

Palpatine's expertly crafted speech drew Anakin to his side with each new promise. Just as Jedi prohibitions against physical love had made Padmé even more alluring, the forbidden powers of the dark side had an intoxicating effect on the young man who wanted, more than anything, to possess godlike abilities. However Palpatine made a crucial error when he referred to Padmé as Anakin's wife.

Anakin had guarded his betrothal so carefully, and yet Palpatine knew. Angered, Anakin ignited his lightsaber, but Palpatine simply stared Anakin down, daring him to prove all of the worst things he thought about himself by striking down an unarmed man.

At that moment, Anakin realized that Palpatine was the Sith Lord that the Jedi had been searching for. He was the creature who had orchestrated the Clone Wars, implanting his apprentice Count Dooku as the figurehead of the Separatist movement while controlling the

Republic and installing himself as the mouthpiece of the Galactic Senate. Striking Palpatine dead where he stood was not the Jedi way, but Anakin yearned to rid the galaxy of this supremely conniving trickster who had deceived everyone, including the Jedi, for so long. And yet . . . Palpatine was offering him a chance to save Padmé. Paralyzed by indecision, Anakin lowered his weapon, and, following his Jedi teachings, resolved to turn Palpatine over to the Jedi Council.

In the meantime, Obi-Wan had tracked General Grievous to the remote world of Utapau, where, in defense of his own life, he was forced to kill the cyborg warrior. As news of Grievous' death spread, Jedi Master Mace Windu and several Jedi stormed into Palpatine's office to ensure he yielded his emergency powers back to the Senate. Windu was dumbfounded when Anakin revealed Palpatine's secret—that he was in fact Darth Sidious. The powerful and elusive Sith Lord had been among them the whole time playing them for fools. Yet even though Anakin handled Palpatine's arrest honorably, Windu remained skeptical of his loyalty. He ordered Anakin to remain behind while he and other Jedi Masters handled things.

Everything Anakin thought he knew to be true about the Jedi and the Republic was crumbling around him, and even with his superior strength in the Force, he couldn't quell his emotions long enough to untangle the lies that ensnared him. The Jedi had lied, forsaking their own rules to snatch the governing power of the Republic away from the Supreme Chancellor, Palpatine had told him. But Palpatine had lied, too. Clouded by his feelings for his mentor, the kindly man who had welcomed him to Coruscant like a father, Anakin was too confused to perceive the truth and make a decisive move.

So he waited, alone inside the Jedi Council chambers. The thought of losing Padmé still felt like an end to life as he knew it and he did not have the wherewithal to see that his motivations for keeping her safe had little to do with her health, the life of their child, or even her own desires for the future.

Meanwhile, in the Chancellor's office, Palpatine was far from meekly accepting his fate. By the time Anakin arrived on the scene, three of the four Jedi Masters lay dead, cut down by Palpatine's crimson lightsaber blade before it was lost. The Sith Lord's fate was now in Mace Windu's hands alone.

Palpatine had orchestrated so much of Anakin's life to ensure Skywalker would become his apprentice at just the right moment. When Anakin saw Palpatine cowering beneath Windu's purple saber, the time had come to choose. The fate of the galaxy rested on Anakin's decision.

Both men tried to persuade Anakin that the other was the real traitor. Dark lightning emanated from Palpatine's fingertips, ricocheting off Windu's blade to leave Darth Sidious deformed, his placid features replaced by a withered and scarred visage that matched his dark heart. The Jedi had been unfaithful to their own doctrine and become warmongers. The Chancellor had betrayed the Republic, becoming the chief conductor of the Galactic Senate's widespread corruption. Neither was innocent.

Just a few days before, Anakin had found himself standing with his lightsaber ready to end the life of a powerful Sith Lord. Then, Palpatine had urged him to kill Dooku, arguing he was too powerful to live and stand trial. In giving into Palpatine's urgings, Anakin had failed the Jedi Order and been filled with regret. Now Anakin saw that he had a second chance to do things differently—keep to the Jedi way, and ensure Palpatine stood trial for his crimes.

But even as he said the words, Anakin's knew his intentions were not entirely selfless. Palpatine had played him flawlessly. As Mace Windu prepared to land the killing blow and Palpatine begged for his life, Anakin Skywalker severed Mace Windu's saber hand. With the Jedi Master defenseless, Palpatine unleashed a fresh jolt of dark energy, sending Mace Windu plummeting to his death many stories below.

Anakin's legs gave way from the shock of all that had come to pass. He had sacrificed everything he held dear—Padmé being the only exception—denounced the Jedi teachings, assisted in the murder of a Jedi Master, and become the thing he had sworn to fight. Palpatine should have been weakened by his ordeal. Instead, he rose up, stronger than ever, his eyes the sickly yellow of infection, and loomed over Anakin. Such was the power of the dark side, feeding on anguish and fear to become even more powerful.

Anakin Skywalker's spirit was irrevocably broken. No longer bewildered by the choices before him, Anakin understood in that moment with stinging clarity that there was no going back. He had made too many mistakes—ended too many lives—to walk again among the Jedi. Defeated, he made a deal with the dark side: his life, his very soul, and his allegiance as Darth Sidious' apprentice in exchange for the knowledge that would save Padmé's life.

Chapter 13

Arise, Lord Vader

In Anakin, Palpatine's machinations came to fruition with a new apprentice, a dark son, pledging total loyalty and poised to wield more power than his predecessors. Driven to the point of insanity by the complex confusion of emotions and events haunting his life, Anakin knelt before Darth Sidious.

The tragedy of Anakin was not that he was a powerful Jedi who fell to ruin, but that he was a mere mortal—afraid to live, afraid to love, and afraid of death—who believed himself above these frailties and was deceived by a lie. Palpatine had exploited Anakin's weaknesses with deft skill. He spoke to Anakin's deepest desires, while Jedi teachings merely ordered that he repress and somehow move beyond them.

It was not enough for Anakin to claim allegiance to the darkness; his next actions had to be so despicable they would erase all the good he had done during his years as a Jedi Knight. As he pledged to serve Palpatine, embracing the dark side and all it had to offer, Anakin became an instrument of evil.

Palpatine easily convinced Anakin that he had witnessed Mace Windu's attempt to assassinate the Chancellor with his own eyes, instead of being an accomplice in the murder of a Jedi Master. However, the Chancellor's powers of persuasion extended far beyond his manipulations of Anakin Skywalker. His real coup was making the Republic as a whole accept that the Jedi, which, for a millennia, had stood firmly as defenders of peace, were all traitors.

Palpatine's approved narrative would play out on news holos and later in artfully constructed Imperial propaganda: It was a story that cast the Jedi as rebels, on their own quest for domination, a conspiracy of rogues who had used the war for their own ends. This was Palpatine's final act in a cunning campaign of division. He had been sowing discord in the galaxy for years. His apprentices—and there had been several—had aided his plans, manipulating individuals and organizations, from the Trade Federation that had threatened Naboo, to the Separatists, and the Galactic Senate. Without fail, in every instance, Palpatine had exploited their fears, appealed to their desire for power, and provoked them for his own gain.

With Anakin, he had entered the boy's life as a mentor and friend, and cleverly set the young Jedi apart from the Order he was supposed to serve. He had helped to inflate Anakin's ego; buoyed his confidence; and stoked his impulses to acquire, own, and control whatever he wished. In doing so, he had taken the child with a preordained power of the Force like no other and turned him into an agent of disaster of galactic proportions.

Palpatine told his new pupil that he feared the Jedi, in their quest for domination, would kill anyone who stood in their way, including himself, Anakin, and the members of the Senate. Anakin was so broken that he did not even protest for a moment. His new master sent him to eliminate all who remained in the Jedi Temple. Anakin instantly obeyed.

Meanwhile, Palpatine executed Order 66. During the war, Anakin had witnessed a clone trooper named Tup turn on Jedi Master Tiplar, executing her at point blank range amid the chaos of the Battle for Ringo Vinda, and he had understandably demanded answers for the soldier's grotesque betrayal. But Anakin was placated when Palpatine claimed that the clone, along with his brother Fives, had suffered a mental defect brought on by a parasitic infection. Despite Fives' stuttering ramblings of a sweeping deception, a plot against the Jedi that went all the way to the top—to the Chancellor's office—Anakin chose to believe that Tup's defect was a one-off, his friend Palpatine unimpeachable, and Fives sadly teetering on the edge of madness.

To bring an end to the war, the truth was revealed. The protocol activated every clone scattered throughout the galaxy whose brain contained what was supposed to be an inhibitor chip against rogue actions The effects were devastating. On battlefronts across the galaxy, clone troopers turned without warning on their Jedi generals, opening fire and murdering their astonished leaders.

***

The Force moves darkly around one who is about to kill. As he had many times in battle, Anakin marched toward his sworn enemy, but this time like a droid executing its programming.

Holo-vids throughout the Jedi Temple captured the massacre in horrifying detail. Leading a battalion of clone troopers, slaves in Palpatine's scheme, Anakin stormed the hallowed ground where generations of Jedi had been trained in the wonderment of the Force.

Many Jedi were murdered that night. Not even the terrified younglings were spared. Inside the vacant Council chambers, they cowered. By cutting them down, Anakin wasn't just slaughtering the future of the Jedi Order, he was excising the last shreds of his own innocence. Each slice of his lightsaber seemed a sacrifice so that *his* child might survive. And with every Jedi he slayed, Palpatine's hold on Anakin's soul grew ever tighter. What sweeter victory could there be for Sidious than to take control of the Chosen One and turn him into a tool of the Sith, forcing him to exterminate the Jedi and everything they held dear?

Once Anakin had laid waste the Temple, he took his Jedi starfighter to the Mustafar system, where Sidious had sent the surviving Separatist leaders into hiding. As Palpatine had foretold, Anakin's anger and hate made him stronger, and he made quick work of killing the remaining

Trade Federation leaders and all that was left of the Separatist regime. R2-D2 had flown into battle against the same foes numerous times, and so, for the last time, was by his side, a brave and devoted copilot until the end.

With the enemy conquered at last, Supreme Chancellor Palpatine convened the Galactic Senate for his grand finale. Wearing his fresh scars and deformed flesh like a badge of honor, he stood before the elected representatives and, playing the martyr, gave solemn testimony about the Jedi plot that had nearly cost him his life. That day, he made his infamous promise to hunt down all the remaining Jedi and dealt galactic democracy its death blow. Under the guise of renewing stability, Palpatine vowed to dismantle the Republic and reorganize its systems into a new Galactic Empire, with himself installed as its first Emperor. The fearful politicians were so drained by the long and fruitless war, that not only did they not object, they greeted his announcements with delight. Their applause echoed through the vast senatorial chambers to the disgust of the smattering of detractors.

Meanwhile, Obi-Wan and Yoda—who were among the few Jedi to have escaped the reach of Order 66—were confronting the carnage wrought in the Temple.

The twisted bodies of fallen Padawans and younglings, scarred by lightsaber blades, were strewn across the Temple floors. Through the Force, the two Jedi Masters could sense what had come to pass, but Obi-Wan felt compelled to watch the carnage play out. In holo-recordings of the massacre he soon found himself gazing upon the face of his student, Anakin. But this version of Anakin was barely recognizable, possessed with a disturbingly calculated calm. Save for the younglings, who had not yet built their own lightsabers, the Jedi put up a formidable defense down to the last, but were no match for a Sith Lord and a clone battalion bent on their destruction.

With just two known Jedi Masters remaining to take on the Sith, Master Yoda assigned himself the task of confronting Darth Sidious.

He dispatched Obi-Wan to put an end to Darth Vader's brief reign of terror.

Obi-Wan was certain that Padmé was the key to locating Anakin. He soon found his friend, her stomach swollen with the unborn life she carried, and sadly revealed Palpatine's deception, the identity of his new apprentice, and the depth of Anakin's treachery.

The ending of the war should have been a time of happiness for the expectant young mother, but it had brought nothing but agonizing defeat for her political dreams. She realized that neither the Republic nor the Separatists had won the war. They had been little more than fools, squabbling among themselves while Palpatine/Darth Sidious carefully usurped the position and finances he needed to exploit his already impressive executive powers.

On Naboo, she had let her heart rule her head. The chaos of the erupting war had encouraged her to give in to the small comfort of falling in love. Listening to Obi-Wan's revelations convinced Padmé that Anakin was a danger, not only to himself but to all those around him. Despite the life growing in her womb, she had never felt more alone. How could she justify bringing a child into a galaxy in ruins?

Just as Palpatine had divined their union, Obi-Wan's suspicions of Padmé and Anakin's deep connection and commitment were finally confirmed. When she flatly refused to tell Obi-Wan where Anakin was, fearing that information would be fatal to him, he realized what he should have guessed long ago: Anakin was the father of Padmé's child. Ashamed, Padmé refused to confirm or deny the fact.

Chapter 14

Duel on Mustafar

Now in thrall to Palpatine, Anakin Skywalker once more took on a familiar role—one which dominated his earliest years—that of obedient slave. For one who had struggled so much to bend events to his will, suddenly being stripped of all self-determination had an oddly freeing effect on him.

In some corner of Anakin's mind, he managed to persuade himself that his and Palpatine's brutal actions were the justified means to a noble end. However, on the volcanic planet of Mustafar, Anakin had time to reflect. In the calm following the carnage he had wrought in the Jedi Temple, his rage subsided, to be replaced with despair and self-loathing. He had lost count of how many had died upon his blue blade. Anakin mourned the man he had been.

The arrival of Padmé's gleaming silver ship woke him from his gloomy reverie and he rushed to greet her. Padmé was seemingly alone save for C-3PO, no longer backed by a cadre of handmaidens sworn to give their lives for her safety. His mood swung from joy to fury as she informed him of every terrible accusation Obi-Wan had made about his new allegiance to the dark side, and the unspeakable murder of the Jedi children. Just as Palpatine predicted, Obi-Wan had become his enemy. Anakin's mind was so poisoned by Palpatine's insinuations that he could see no other explanation.

The problem with coveting power is that no amount of authority and influence is ever enough. Despite crushing those he believed to be his enemies and taking his seat at the right hand of the newly crowned Emperor, Anakin felt more insecure than ever, terrified of losing everything, just as the Sith legend of Darth Plagueis had warned.

Padmé begged Anakin to join her on Naboo. There, she could have their child and they could live as a family, without interference from the outside world. Retreating to her homeworld was surely their only chance to escape, to salvage their relationship.

For his entire life, Anakin was most comfortable bonded with another, two against the rest of the world. It was how he had been raised, how he had forged his marriage, how he had perceived his union with both his master and his mentor. He had always exalted Padmé above all others. On that day, that meant the newly installed Sith apprentice believed himself even stronger than his devious Sith master and able to overthrow him. Believing that he had singlehandedly brought peace to the Republic, blinded to the demise of the once-great democracy, Anakin now craved dominion over the remade galaxy.

During their courtship, Anakin had once told Padmé that he didn't believe in democracy. Its wheels turned too slowly for him. He hungered for a system where a wise leader could force politicians to agree to solutions to political problems. At the time, she believed that the dictatorship he described was a boyish joke, a sly way of poking fun at her ardent beliefs in public service and the rights of individuals.

On Mustafar, she knew by Anakin's tone and the fire in his eyes that what he was proposing was exactly that kind of tyrannical governance. According to him, everyone and everything in the galaxy needed to be controlled—by him alone.

Something in Padmé broke. Perhaps it was her heart, or simply her ability to continue concocting justifications for Anakin and his mounting transgressions. Fearless and decisive, Padmé refused to follow her husband down the dark path he was so intent on treading. With one final plea, she begged him to stop before it was too late, and return to the light. But Anakin's eyes had drifted from the face of his beloved to rest on a familiar silhouette, backlit in the doorway of the Naboo starship. Obi-Wan Kenobi had stowed away on the ship, anticipating that Padmé would follow her heart and lead him to his quarry: Anakin Skywalker, or, more accurately, Darth Vader.

Concluding that Padmé and Obi-Wan were conspiring against him, Anakin reached out with the Force, seizing his wife by the throat. Padmé was entirely unprepared for the shocking intensity of her husband's wrath. Obi-Wan commanded him to let her go, and, unconscious but still alive, Padmé crumpled to the ground.

Anakin was desperate for someone to blame. He couldn't be angry at Padmé for long, for, in taking on the burden of his child, he had put her on a pedestal as high as the one on which he still kept his dear, departed mother. He couldn't find fault with Palpatine, the mentor who had helped him become more powerful than the Jedi who had long held him back, fearful of his capacity for domination and destruction.

Thus, from Anakin's twisted perspective, all roads led back to Obi-Wan Kenobi. Incapable of being the father figure and teacher Anakin yearned for, Obi-Wan had failed to help Anakin control the instincts that had led him to kneel at the altar of the Sith. To add insult to injury, Obi-Wan had somehow turned his beloved against him.

As one of the last surviving Jedi, Obi-Wan's mere existence was an insult. Just as Count Dooku, in his final moments, had seemed to embody everything Anakin hated about the war, Obi-Wan epitomized everything Anakin sought to eliminate from the galaxy. He was so far beyond the power of reason that he viewed anyone who refused to bow down before the Sith as a bitter enemy.

Darth Sidious, Dark Lord of the Sith, had totally eradicated the good man Obi-Wan had known as Anakin Skywalker. The man who confronted him was something new, an adversary born of the dark side, hellbent on destruction, power hungry, and unrepentant.

The fight pitted an apprentice desperate to keep his meager power against a Jedi Master intent on robbing the Sith of its star pupil: The future of the galaxy hung in the balance. A flurry of sizzling lightsabers harkened back to their days of training at the Jedi Temple. The two diametrically opposed warriors were still somehow in sync at the outset, each attack met with an equally swift defense. Obi-Wan drew on his clarity in battle; Anakin was infused with the frenetic strength of his emotions. The ferocious duel spilled onto the catwalks of the Mustafarian mining facility that rose above the planet's hellish, volcanic landscape. The precarious nature of the planet's surface, much of which was molten lava, added to the intensity and desperation of their combat.

Drunk on dreams of power, Anakin somersaulted toward his waiting opponent. Obi-Wan would have given almost anything for a different outcome, but he felt he had no choice. In one fluid motion, he severed Anakin's legs and his last remaining organic limb. Obi-Wan could not bring himself to deliver the killing blow. Perhaps such an action could have served as both an act of mercy and a means for avoiding the Empire's reign. Sadly collecting his former friend's lightsaber, he walked away, returning to the ship to tend to Anakin's distraught widow. With the help of the dutiful droids C-3PO and R2-D2, they left behind the blackened remains of Anakin Skywalker and the dreadful planet of Mustafar.

Chapter 15

Death and Rebirth

Anakin Skywalker's psyche was cleaved in two as the dark side consumed him. Within the shell of the man he once had been, his new persona—Darth Vader—firmly took hold.

As Vader, he gave himself completely to the darkness, a creature beholden only to primitive needs and desires, obeying and carrying out the directives of his Sith master without concern for their far-reaching ramifications. Uninhibited rage took control of his entire being, blotting out everything the Jedi had once sought to teach him.

The quake in the Force that marked Anakin's decision to join the Sith had been so great that not even former close friends, such as Ahsoka and Obi-Wan could feel his presence. Both of them believed that Anakin was no more. And, in a very real sense, he was gone.

One individual could still feel his presence, however. Attuned to his new apprentice, Darth Sidious felt the young man faltering in battle and rushed to his side. Thanks to his mechanical arm, Anakin managed to pull his body away from the lava river. His lungs were charred, making each intake of breath more excruciating than the last, and his nerve endings were all-but destroyed, the burns penetrating his flesh and muscle to the bone.

Sidious appeared on the embankment of the lava river, a faceless specter concealed in black robes. While clones rushed to retrieve a medical capsule, he knelt over his charge like a father soothing an injured son, and placed one gnarled palm on his forehead. It was the last human touch Anakin would know for many years.

Sidious and Vader returned to Coruscant and the towering Grand Republic Medical Facility bearing the physical scars of their descent into darkness. Droids worked methodically at Palpatine's behest, cleansing Anakin's wounds and fitting new mechanical implants on the raw stubs of his legs and his freshly severed arm. He was encased in a cybernetic suit to support his labored breathing and protect his ravaged flesh from the outside world. As a black mask was lowered over his face, his vision narrowed, limited to what he could see through its red-tinted lenses. A helmet slid over his bald head, and the last shreds of Anakin Skywalker's humanity were hidden beneath layers of scar tissue and apparatus.

As much as the suit was a life-sustaining necessity, enabling Vader to move freely despite his grievous injuries, it was also a prison. It wholly encased him, both a shield and a cage. As his lungs drew in their first ventilated breath, Vader completed his transition into a cyborg of staggering strength, a tool of the Sith content to do the Emperor's bidding.

Yet Darth Vader still yearned for Anakin's beloved. As soon as the procedure was done, he asked about Padmé, his voice now modulated and unrecognizable. Palpatine took great pleasure in delivering the news that he believed would finally cement Darth Vader's destiny. He told Anakin that he had killed his wife while consumed with rage on Mustafar.

During their time together, Anakin had been terrified of losing Padmé. Nearly everything he had done since discovering she was to be the mother of his child was out of a twisted need to prevent death from taking her away from him. To be confronted with the knowledge that she had died by his hand was a staggering betrayal of all the sacrifices he had made.

Padmé's terrified face as she struggled for breath was now the last memory he had of her. In his anguish and disbelief he broke through his medical restraints, anger fueling his brute strength. Totally out of control, he smashed every glass vessel inside the operating theater, and crushed several droids without laying a gloved hand on them. He tossed Palpatine aside like a ragdoll—an outrage he would pay for dearly in the future.

The pain of his loss was unlike anything Anakin had known—far worse than the death of his mother. The bitter knowledge that he was the sole cause of Padmé's demise—not the savior he had aspired to become—filled him with unfathomable fury and regret.

Palpatine gave his pupil one final choice: He could convert his suffering into defiant strength, a will of iron that would ensure entire solar systems would bow before the new Empire. He could secure a place at Palpatine's side and bring all those he encountered under their control. Or he could die. With nothing left to live for, Darth Vader chose to dedicate himself utterly to the dark side.

Meanwhile, on an obscure rocky planetoid called Polis Massa, Obi-Wan delivered the ailing Padmé into the arms of a very different droid doctor. Deep in the Outer Rim, this once-thriving planet had been destroyed by a cataclysm. What remained was fit for little more than mining operations. Its medical center, tucked away far from the center of the galaxy, was perfect for the recently exiled Jedi's purposes.

There, Obi-Wan reunited with Senator Bail Organa and Yoda, looking on solemnly as the droids examined Padmé and discovered that she was carrying twins. Perplexingly, the tests detected nothing physically wrong with her. Nevertheless, her vital signs were fading fast, and they rushed to perform an emergency induction.

Thus, from the shattered union of Padmé and Anakin, a pair of twins brought fresh hope to the galaxy. The older of the two was named Luke by his mother. For the girl, the new mother chose the name Leia. But as soon as they were safely delivered into the world, Padmé began to lose consciousness again. Despite everything he'd done, as her life ebbed away, Padmé Amidala still believed there was good in her husband.

Aboard Bail Organa's Alderaanian cruiser, on a somber mission to return Padmé's body to Naboo, he and the two surviving Jedi weighed their options, a trio of wise advisors shepherding the Skywalker twins. They decided to conceal the birth, making it appear as if Padmé had died while still pregnant. As they had no parents left to care for them, the children were split up in the hopes that the Sith would not find them.

Padmé was duly buried in a ceremony befitting her status as a former queen and politician. Her funeral was attended by her parents, her sister, her handmaidens, and her friends, as well as throngs of onlookers. With the japor snippet Anakin had carved for her long ago on Tatooine clasped between her cold hands, she made her final procession to the grave.

***

Despite his newfound allegiance to the dark side, at the dawn of the Empire, Vader struggled to fulfill his enforcer role with complete conviction. The legacy of Anakin Skywalker, the brave Jedi Knight, loomed large. In at least one of the precious few Jedi holocrons that survived scattered around the galaxy, he was immortalized in his prime, forever young, training the next generation of Jedi younglings on lightsaber forms. Yet there were moments when the seemingly emotionless being beneath the mask of Darth Vader was visited by doubt.

Robbed of his lightsaber on Mustafar, one of Vader's first quests was to secure a new Sith weapon. Traditionally, he would have done so by winning a duel with a Jedi and taking their lightsaber as a trophy, but with the success of Order 66, barely any Jedi remained alive. In the aftermath of the purge, the hilts of the fallen had been collected and ceremonially destroyed. Using his keen understanding of Jedi ways, Vader tracked down a survivor who had taken the Barash vow—among a handful of exiled Jedi seeking penitence. On the river moon of

Al'doleem, Vader confronted the former Jedi Master Kirak Infil'a, a wizened warrior whose scars proved his fighting prowess, and, with some difficulty, succeeded in killing him and taking his weapon.

The kyber crystal that powers a lightsaber is uniquely suited and attuned to its owner. It is a living thing that focuses the energy of the Force, giving the wielder clarity and inner harmony even in battle. Just as Palpatine had turned Anakin, Vader corrupted his new crystal, bleeding the kyber until it glowed red, beating back the visions that danced before him as the Force and the crystal resisted.

For a moment, Vader glimpsed his potential failure, a return to the light. In the vision, he saw what could be if he returned to his Sith master with Master Kirak's blade and used the weapon of the Jedi to strike Sidious down—not out of vengeance but out of contrition. Perhaps then he could have tracked down his friend, Obi-Wan, hoping for absolution, and removed his helmet to expose what was left of the man Kenobi had known as a brother.

But these visions were fleeting. Vader quickly rejected them as false hopes. He was not inclined to ask for forgiveness. The face of Kenobi became a reminder of what the Jedi Master had done to his broken body. There wasn't enough bacta in the galaxy to heal the web of scar tissue, which still burned. Sometimes, even the smallest movement brought a searing reminder of his physical state; pain coursed through what was left of his body, every nerve seemingly on fire. So Vader channeled his wrath until the kyber glowed a magnificent crimson, as fiery as the lava flows that had claimed his flesh.

For those who relished the power of the dark side, pain was the path to domination and Vader suffered to prove himself worthy to stand by Sidious' side. Vader decided that Anakin had been weak. He adopted a stance that would be repeated by Obi-Wan Kenobi among others: Vader had destroyed him. He was convinced that by embracing the Sith, the dark side would come to serve him, not the other way around. But the dark side has an insatiable hunger.

Through his ruthlessness, the assistance of the Inquisitorius—a new breed of Jedi hunters created from the ashes of the Jedi Order—and a penchant for blood sports, Vader built a reputation among the Imperial rank and file as an enforcer not to be crossed. In their shared fascination for attaining immortality and amassing power, Sidious and his apprentice proved a potent pairing.

Despite Vader's proven allegiance, Palpatine never stopped testing his pupil and probing his psychic wounds. He was searching for weaknesses as much as he was aiding Anakin's transition to the darkness.

In time, the Sith master gifted his apprentice Padmé Amidala's Royal Naboo Starship, the same gleaming silver craft that had brought his love to Tatooine and carried her to her death on Mustafar. It was a glaring reminder of all he had lost.

Desiring his own planet to conquer and control, Vader returned to Mustafar and the site of his spiritual demise. He ensured Padmé's pristine craft matched his new reality by burning its mirrored exterior beyond recognition as he hurtled through space. He then established an imposing fortress among Mustafar's churning, molten seas. It was built over an ancient Sith temple and thus a powerful Force locus.

However, making his base at the site of Anakin's humiliating defeat was not enough for Vader. He still had not harnessed the power to negate death nor shook the obsessive tendency to finish Skywalker's quest and bring Padmé back from the grave.

For years after, alone in his castle, save for a few servants, Vader would remain, bathing in bacta to heal his wounds, unable to relieve his physical or mental anguish. He had visions in which he walked on ghostly limbs cutting down the Jedi once more, and finding his beloved. But when he reached out his hand and offered his angelic wife salvation, she rejected him, choosing to slip away out of reach and remain in death's void.

Palpatine continued to mold his new Empire in his likeness—cruel and corrupt. He established his new Imperial Palace upon the Jedi

Temple's sacred ground. This imposing construction was a monument to the downfall of the Jedi, a stark reminder of all the Sith had conquered and destroyed. From his throne, Palpatine and his most trusted cronies continued the laborious work of maintaining order, using their combined knowledge to work in secret on a superweapon they called Project Stardust. Its creation took nearly 20 years. It would come to be known by a simple and well-suited moniker: the Death Star.

Part Two

THE TWINS

Chapter 16

Princess of Alderaan

L eia Organa was a curious child. In her early years, she enjoyed exploring the hidden corners and ancient passages of her family's sprawling castle, yet she never gave much thought to her own genealogy. She had never been told the names of her birth parents, though she was raised secure in the knowledge that she had been adopted, the Organa's child by choice. She knew that she had been orphaned at birth—her biological father killed in one of the last battles of the Clone Wars, and her mother so badly injured in the melee that she had only lived long enough to deliver her baby girl into the world. That was all she knew. And for the most part, this sufficed.

Within days of Padmé Amidala's death, the newborn was adopted into the Royal House of Alderaan, and presented soon after to the people during a Name Day ceremony. Her birth was officially recorded as taking place several months earlier, to avoid any potential suspicions.

For Leia, there was no question that her adopted homeworld of Alderaan, with its serene, snowcapped mountains; glacier lakes; and often-tranquil blue skies, was where she was meant to be. She wasted no time speculating about the mysterious couple who had conceived her. That is not to say that she took her good fortune for granted, but the reality was that she felt so completely loved and cared for by Bail and his wife, Queen Breha, that her actual bloodline seemed of no consequence.

And for many years, only Bail and Breha Organa, as well as the Jedi present at the birth, knew the truth of Leia's lineage.

The Organas had long desired a child of their own, but Queen Breha and Bail's political obligations were a deterrent. Maintaining order, even on their peaceful planet was a complex balancing act; Bail could not afford to be on-world and by her side throughout a pregnancy, nor did Breha wish to temporarily surrender power to ministers who might prove reluctant to concede it once she returned to the throne.

There was also the matter of Breha's health. In her youth, she was seriously injured while traversing Appenza Peak, the tallest mountain on Alderaan, as part of her Challenge of the Body ritual, a rite of passage that every prospective Alderaan monarch had to accomplish. Religious zealots believed that the height of the mountain allowed them to get closer to the Force itself. It was also a favorite site of local myths and fairy tales, which Breha used to whisper to Leia at night to lull her adopted daughter to sleep.

Breha knew the mountain for what it was—equal parts beauty and danger. She had reached the summit and proven her worthiness to become queen, but it had cost her dearly. After the accident, a perilous fall that would have ended her life if not for the intervention of her entourage, her heart and lungs were replaced by pulmonodes. This life-sustaining technology had its limits, and lesser women—and men—have been known to lose their humanity entirely following far less-invasive cybernetic implants. However, Breha grew to appreciate human life more deeply, recognizing that her time was borrowed. Her empathy for her people blossomed. She understood that everyone was battling their own, often hidden, afflictions. As a symbol of her dedication and the honesty, dignity, and compassion with which she wished to govern her realm, Breha refused to conceal her implants with skin grafts. For Leia, it was nearly impossible to think of her mother without picturing the warm glow of the implants' indicator lights emanating from her chest. She had always found it soothing, like a child's night light.

The people of Alderaan welcomed news of an heir to the throne.

Alderaanians accepted adoption easily, publicly celebrating the fact. After all, even those set to inherit the crown by blood were tasked with proving their worth when they turned sixteen. The public looked forward to the day when Leia would have the chance to prove herself a worthy successor to Breha. In time, Leia came to wholeheartedly believe that it was her sacred duty to protect them. "The people [of Alderaan] are my people, and I must save them even if it means my life," she once said with absolute conviction.

Leia strongly reminded Bail of her biological mother, Padmé. He had come to know the young senator well, almost like a sister, during their years of service together. At times, he would look at his adopted daughter and feel as if Padmé's eyes were staring back at him. There had been little time to mourn his dear friend's passing, although the Organas did erect a statue of the former Queen of Naboo at the height of her power in their garden so their daughter—her child—could play beneath its watchful gaze. As a young girl, Leia was known to listen in wonder as Breha told her stories of Padmé Amidala's heroism, using her words to paint a portrait of the valiant young senator and queen who fought for the rights of people across the stars. "Speeches as weapons, ideals as ammunition," Breha would intone. Breha did not explicitly inform Leia that Padmé had been her birth mother, but saw no reason that Leia should not look up to her as a role model. Although Naboo's royalty succeeded by election and Alderaan subscribed to the more ancient practice of dynastic inheritance, the two queens, Padmé and Breha, had quickly become close friends when Padmé paid a visit to Alderaan during her first term in the Senate. They had both understood the burdens and blessings of ruling an entire planet.

On rare occasions, Leia seemed to experience vague memories of her birth mother—even though it seemed impossible—remembering her as a beautiful woman who was also terribly sad. Some would say she simply wished to be Breha's true daughter, so that she might inherit her vibrancy and charisma. With her coils of dark hair and ageless skin,

Breha was at once pleasant and warm, yet confident and commanding. She was born to rule, and Leia worked hard to emulate the qualities that seemed to come so naturally to the queen. By contrast, Leia's light brown hair hung in cascading waves when it was loosened from the plaits she wore in polite company. Even during the day, wisps of hair often escaped, defying the intricate work of her caretaker droid.

Leia often felt anxious and uneasy. In the shadow of the monarchy, it was easy for a young girl to feel overlooked and purely ornamental in the eyes of her mother's loyal subjects.

Bail, who liked to regale his young daughter with tales of adventure from his own escapades during the Clone Wars, was comforted by the knowledge that Leia carried within her some of Padmé's best qualities— fierce determination, sympathy for those less fortunate, and a quick mind. Bail had initially been skeptical about Padmé's youthful earnestness when, at just 18, she first appeared on the floor of the Galactic Senate. However, he soon came to respect her fiery spirit and forthright manner in addressing the most urgent matters of the common people. She gave the voiceless a voice, without concern for political consequences or her own safety. Over their years of service together, Bail came to hold Padmé in the highest esteem, finding common ground as two loyalists who were both staunch advocates for democracy. He could think of no better way to honor his departed friend than by raising her daughter.

As for Leia's paternity, the knowledge that Anakin Skywalker made up half her DNA was, in truth, a worry for the viceroy of Alderaan. He respected the bravery Anakin had shown during the height of the Clone War, but kept close watch over his adopted child's emotional state as she grew up. Leia was not as quick to anger as her father, but Bail knew a mother's stress could be transferred in the womb. He and Breha did their best to stave off the influences of any potentially deleterious "emotional inheritance."

Alderaan bore some physical resemblance to Padmé's homeworld of Naboo, as both were peaceful and resplendent. While rolling green hills and meadows characterized Naboo, Alderaan was famous for its steep, snowy mountain peaks, Appenza being the tallest in the capital, Aldera.

Alderaanians respected the natural wonders of their world, and took care that major public buildings, including the royal palace, blended into the landscape instead of calling attention to themselves. The halls Leia wandered as a child were filled with priceless works of art created in the same fashion—landscape paintings and sculptures that expressed and harnessed the elements of air and water. One air sculpture in particular played a harmonious, otherworldly song that varied with the direction and strength of the wind. To Leia's young mind, it was the song of Alderaan, sung by the planet itself. When a thunderstorm raged over the mountains, Leia was transfixed by the air sculpture's banshee wail, caused by the roaring winds.

The grandeur of royal ceremony called for a throne room and other public spaces befitting the queen and her station, but Bail preferred simpler things. Unless absolutely required to do otherwise, he left the finery to his wife and daughter. He was critical of those who ostentatiously flaunted their wealth, and made sure there were no aurodium-plated refreshers in their royal estate on Alderaan.

The young princess took to the formality of court—by the age of 6, Leia had already met her first king—with natural grace. Thanks to her adoptive parents' guidance she grew up a kind, thoughtful, and independent young woman. She learned to greet each new acquaintance—from Grand Moffs to refugees—with composure. Still, it was a lonely childhood in some respects. Her parents were protective and their status made it difficult to find playmates her own age.

Royalty set Leia apart; it was a privilege that brought with it duty and sacrifice. She had only her fussy droid, WA-2V—who made quick work of the most intricate Alderaanian braids and updos—and her parents as constant companions to confide in. When they were busy with adult concerns, Leia spent much of her time alone in her room, gazing out at the mountains or up at the stars.

To make herself useful, at 14, Leia was granted an internship in her father's senatorial office. Even for a child who had come to see a palace as commonplace, the bustling surface of Coruscant, capital of the Galactic Empire, was greeted with wide-eyed fascination. Bail had known his daughter was bright. He and Breha ensured she had the best tutors on every subject from Republic history to pathfinding. She had also learned combat and survival skills to keep her sharp in the most dire situations, a physical fitness that aided her mental acuity. As Bail's aide, Leia excelled at remembering disparate facts and stitching them together into meaningful data.

The year Leia turned 16, her Day of Demand approached. This ceremony—required of all future queens of Alderaan—called for the young princess to face challenges of the mind, the body, and the heart, to prove she was worthy of ruling their world. Leia chose to climb Appenza Peak in honor of her mother; she joined the Apprentice Legislature in honor of her father; and she spearheaded charity missions to planets in need. Small in stature—in adulthood she would stand just 1.5 meters tall even with perfect posture, her coiled hair and heeled boots giving an illusion of height—Leia quickly learned that she had to use her most commanding voice and stand her ground if she wanted to be taken seriously.

During this time, in her private journals, Leia recounted feeling that her parents were pulling away from her. Her peace of mind was disturbed by new feelings of anxiety as she tried to understand what had changed. Her parents' careers obliged them to attend countless dinner parties and official receptions, but as they became more distant, their eyes glazing over, thoughts seemingly elsewhere even during private family meals, Leia began to rebel. Her defiance did not take the form of late-night parties or secret vices. She simply wished to be seen for what she was—a future monarch, worthy of her parents' time, trust, and respect.

What Leia didn't know was that Bail and Breha were keeping their daughter safe from what would be regarded by the Empire as an act of treason. With Padmé dead and the Republic dissolved, the Organas had stood alongside Mon Mothma as loyalists and continued to quietly accumulate allies and resources in the years that followed the end of the Clone Wars. Theirs was a subdued subversion; they were idealists, seeking subtle solutions to the tyrannical rule that Emperor Palpatine had imposed upon taking his throne. To build a better, safer future for their adopted daughter, the Organas felt they had to keep her in the dark.

Over the course of that year, Leia's obstinacy forced her parents' hands on more than one occasion. Their best attempts to keep her shielded by her own ignorance were consistently foiled by their resourceful daughter. They soon realized that she would do more harm than good blindly pushing forward in pursuit of answers to her various questions.

This became particularly apparent on the planet Wobani, a forlorn Mid Rim world once known for its Imperial detention centers, where Leia mounted a relief effort without her parents' permission. By doing so, she accidentally thwarted months of careful negotiations to resettle the population, many of whom were living in forced-labor camps. Aboard the family's cruiser, the *Tantive IV*, Leia rescued upward of 100 refugees in overt defiance of Imperial protocol, exploiting a loophole in the regulations governing the sector by hiring them as crew. In addition to disrupting plans already in place, Leia's actions invited the hawkish gaze of Grand Moff Wilhuff Tarkin, an ambitious and ruthless man who had rapidly risen to power during the Clone Wars and still clung tightly to Palpatine's trailing robes. When they met for the first time, at the opening ceremony for the Apprentice Legislature, Tarkin had looked upon the princess with disdain.

For Leia's next unsanctioned foray—to the salt-covered planet of Crait—she borrowed the family's yacht, the *Polestar*, and stumbled upon irrefutable proof of Bail's involvement in the rebel cause. Through careful research she had uncovered a mysterious connection between hyperspace routes and a recent attack on an Imperial space station. On Crait, Leia was shocked to find her own father in charge of a band of dissidents, an underground group of rebels who were responsible for the bold strike. This revelation only made Leia more determined to be involved with the family's resistance to what she viewed as the immoral activities of the Imperial elite. However, her parents forbade her from discussing or participating in their efforts.

But Leia would not be denied, and without her parents' protection she continued to endanger her own life as well as the efforts of the fledgling Rebel Alliance.

On Onoam, one of the moons of Naboo, Leia and Queen Dalné worked together to distribute safety equipment to the satellite's miners, unaware that the equipment would inevitably be stolen and sold to benefit the lower ranks of the unscrupulous Imperial leadership. When they discovered what was going on, the princess and the queen paid a visit to the sector's top autocrat, Moff Quarsh Panaka.

During the years of the Republic, Panaka had served Padmé Amidala as her head of security during her reign as queen, and had been privy to the rumors that swirled around the young senator before her death. When Leia walked into his home, a borrowed Naboo gown framing her in a white fanned ruff, he thought he had seen a ghost.

In the formal dress, Leia's striking resemblance to Padmé Amidala made the hardened military man shake so violently he spilled his tea. Although it would be some time before Leia would learn the truth of her heritage, her visit to Panaka that day inadvertently put her in grave danger, as he quickly surmised her parentage. In time, Leia would prove quite capable of rescuing herself, yet in this instance she was undoubtedly abetted by fate. Panaka had recently become a target of another rebel cell, led by the former Onderon rebel leader Saw Gerrera. Moments after Leia and the queen left Panaka, his chalet was obliterated by a bomb that killed the Imperial official. A delay in her departure may have ended her story here. Had he lived even for another few minutes, he would have most likely called on his Emperor to relay his strong suspicions that the daughter of Padmé Amidala lived.

Chapter 17

The Farmer's Nephew

At the same time that Leia was enjoying the privileges of royalty, her twin brother was back in the familial cradle on dusty Tatooine. Having served the Jedi for most of his life, Obi-Wan Kenobi, 38 at the time of their birth, did not regard himself as equipped to become a father. Thus the child, Luke, was placed with his extended family on Tatooine, deposited in the loving arms of Beru and Owen Lars.

When Obi-Wan was first tasked with teaching young Anakin Skywalker, he had resigned himself to being the headstrong boy's guardian, determined to protect his charge even if he left the Order. In similar fashion, Obi-Wan now agreed to watch over Anakin's son, embarking upon self-imposed exile on the arid planet, standing guard against any interference from the Sith. To help cover his tracks, the trusted politician and ally of the Jedi during the war Bail Organa confirmed that Obi-Wan Kenobi was dead.

It had been more than two decades since Anakin Skywalker had lived in nearby Mos Espa as a slave; however, the planet Obi-Wan—who adopted the nickname Ben—found when he arrived with the newborn was largely unchanged. Blistering hot days turned to freezing nights when Tatooine's twin suns dipped below the horizon. Only small patches of the planet's surface were habitable, although some travelers debated the accuracy of such a claim.

Cliegg Lars was one of the pioneers who had settled the great salt flats and made a home there. He had built a formidable structure made up of a series of underground tunnels and connected rooms. This rugged but functional abode, reinforced against the planet's abrasive sandstorms, protected generations of inhabitants. Although the family's moisture farm never proved the profitable venture Cliegg had hoped it would be, their vaporators collected enough potable water to sustain his family and keep their hydroponic garden flourishing.

After Cliegg followed his beloved wife Shmi Skywalker to the grave, the Lars homestead passed to Anakin's stepbrother, Owen Lars and his new bride Beru Whitesun. When the two first met in the town of Anchorhead, Owen saw the same warmth and generosity of spirit in Beru that had drawn his father to Shmi. Had they not been married, Beru might have pursued her other skills in bantha cheese-making and hospitality. A third-generation moisture-farmer herself, Beru understood the value of honest labor and self-reliance in a place where so many things, from the modest clothes they wore to the food on their table, had to be farmed or foraged. Theirs was not an easy life, but they persevered.

Owen and Beru had only met Anakin Skywalker once, when he and Padmé Amidala had come searching for Shmi just before the start of the Clone Wars. The Jedi Knight had left an impression as a wrathful young man, very unlike his mother.

And had it been left to Owen Lars, Luke Skywalker might well have been raised elsewhere. He was initially reluctant to take in Anakin's son, although he grew to care for the boy in his own gruff way. Another mouth to feed was a substantial burden for the struggling farmer, and they were just barely family, and not by blood. Beru, unable to have a child of her own and wishing for a family, convinced her reluctant husband to adopt the son of Skywalker. As soon as Obi-Wan dropped the wriggling baby Luke into her arms, Beru was smitten; she loved the child as if he were her own.

Owen and Beru Lars instilled the value of menial and skilled labor in Luke from an early age. As soon as he was old enough to grasp a hydrospanner in one pudgy hand, Owen set his towheaded nephew to work. His mop of blond hair streaked with sweat, young Luke began to learn how to fix the moisture vaporators dotting the landscape, clean the filters on the garden humidity sensor controls, and perform other essential chores. Luke showed an aptitude for mechanical engineering, learning to keep farm machinery, speeders, and droids working far past their prime with second-hand parts. He seemed to have inherited this ingenuity from his biological father, as well as his quick reflexes and love for hurtling over the terrain in his T-16 skyhopper. His unabashed delight at the helm made it crystal clear he was Anakin Skywalker's son. And, just like his father, Luke hated Tatooine.

In his free time, Luke used whatever he could scrape together from his meager allowance to buy power converters and other parts at the Tosche Station trading post, to make his T-16 even faster. Capable of supersonic speeds that easily outpaced the previous generation of podracers, once the refuge of his biological father, Luke was happiest when he was whipping through Beggar's Canyon in a friendly racing competition with his friends—although those closest to the boy feared he would end up a dark stain on the canyon wall if he wasn't more careful. Beru, in particular, loathed Luke's hobby. But in time, he came to be known among his friends as one of the best bush pilots in the Outer Rim—even if few of them had managed to escape their world long enough to really know.

By his teen years, Luke resolved to turn his penchant for piloting into a career. He hoped to follow in the footsteps of his friend and neighbor Biggs Darklighter, who around this time was receiving training at the Imperial Academy. Neither young man had any love for the Empire and its despotic rule, but they saw an opportunity to break free from the monotony of farm life and were intent on taking it. The Academy, brimming with a degree of formality that Luke detested, nevertheless promised a life of adventure and escape from the limitations of his aunt and uncle's sometimes stifling attitudes and style of life.

One of Luke's less-endearing traits was his habit of dismissing Tatooine as some backwater rock, about as far from the action at the bright center of the universe as it was possible to get. Owen and Beru tried, but failed, to pass down a healthy fear of the unknown and the outside world to their young nephew.

While Leia was content with her adoptive family and situation, Luke remained intrigued by the mystery of his birth parents. Tatooine's magnificent twin suns seemed to beckon him toward the horizon with promises of a completely different life.

***

In the years that Obi-Wan had hid himself in the deserts of Tatooine, repenting the part he had unwittingly played in the fall of the Jedi and the Republic, the galaxy at large seemed to have all but forgotten about the Jedi. Most of those who had some knowledge of them considered the Order to be an ancient, cultlike religion, whose followers were slavishly devoted to some all-powerful energy that had probably never even existed. The Jedi's heroic adventures were dismissed as fantastical stories, the truth becoming more bastardized with each retelling. The Empire was perfectly content to let stories of the Order's exploits gradually die out.

After the Order's fall, Obi-Wan found solace in simplicity. Inside the abandoned hovel he called a home—once the ramshackle abode of a prospecting pioneer who thought Tatooine's sands might conceal riches—Obi-Wan eked out a meager existence beyond the Dune Sea. He learned to fend for himself and subsisted on snake stew and other nutrient-rich foods. He spent his days meditating among the gentle bantha.

Shortly after his arrival on Tatooine, he became known as Old Ben among the children of Mos Eisley and the sprawling surrounding settlements, an eccentric hermit of no import. Kenobi's beard and hair turned gray, the harsh climate and the stress of all he'd endured aging him rapidly. For years, he remained hidden yet cautiously vigilant. He studied the Tusken Raiders and their culture, wishing to understand their brutish nature. And in the stillness he expanded his knowledge of the Force. Before he and Yoda had parted ways, the old Jedi revealed that Obi-Wan's beloved master Qui-Gon Jinn had returned from the netherworld of the Force, manifesting his conscious mind even after death. It took 10 years, but eventually Obi-Wan was able to commune with his dearest friend, resurrected within the cosmic Force. Obi-Wan rarely impinged on Luke's home life, preferring to watch from afar as the child grew into a young man.

When Obi-Wan was 55, nearly two decades into his self-imposed banishment, a young rebel named Ezra Bridger landed on Tatooine, hoping to enlist Kenobi as a powerful ally for the rebellion. Ezra was the same age as Luke—then just 17—and strong in the Force. The dark-side apprentice Maul used Ezra's desire to do good to lure Obi-Wan out of hiding, in order to continue their decades-long feud.

Maul tracked Obi-Wan to an encampment in the shifting sands, where he was sheltering young Bridger after the teenager had passed out from dehydration and delirium. His arrival endangered Luke, and Obi-Wan had no recourse but to silence the beast, lest his knowledge alert Darth Sidious and Darth Vader to the fact of Luke's existence.

Obi-Wan's final blow cut Maul's weapon in two; the blade of Kenobi's saber slicing through Maul's body. Kenobi cradled Maul's head in his dying moments, a compassionate gesture for the adversary who had stalked him most of his life, murdered his master, and set the galaxy on the course that nearly sealed Anakin Skywalker's fate.

Obi-Wan fervently wished to train Luke Skywalker just as he had his father, making up for the mistakes he had made the first time. To that end, he kept Anakin's lightsaber stowed away, an inheritance—Obi-Wan hoped—for Luke one day. Older and wiser, he believed he could make things right in the galaxy by helping the boy reach his full potential. But Owen Lars was adamant that Luke should know nothing of where he came from. For most of his young life, Owen had answered Luke's questions with a concocted story as far from the truth as he could manage, casting Anakin Skywalker as a simple man who had worked as a navigator on some far-off spice freighter before dying in obscurity. Luke knew nothing of his mother, although given Beru's doting nature it's no wonder he paid little mind to thoughts of his real mother.

Owen had even gone so far as to have the tombstones that marked the family graves—his paternal grandparents, an uncle who had died in a landspeeder wreck at the age of 14, and his beloved stepmother, Shmi—buried by sand or removed and repurposed to reinforce part of a wall around the farm. Owen had no wish to forget them, but he did not want Luke becoming fascinated with the past and following in his father's footsteps. His great fear was that the Skywalker genes would one day turn his sweet nephew into a vengeful killer, remembering how Anakin had reacted to his mother's death.

But the boy was strong in the Force. Obi-Wan knew the day would come when he would be old enough to choose his own path. In time, he even came to wonder if perhaps the prophecy had been misread and it was Luke who was truly the Chosen One.

Chapter 18

First Alliances

In the year following her Day of Demand, the then 16-year-old Leia's relationship with her parents became increasingly strained. Due to their secrecy, Leia had no clear evidence to shake her misgivings that their once-noble efforts might have turned deadly. She struggled to reconcile the notion that the people she loved could be complicit in terrorist activities that wounded innocents, even with the aim of securing a safer future for all. There was a partisan element at work within the alliance, an extremist cell that believed such actions were necessary to win the fight. But Leia believed that only made those rebels as bad as the Empire they fought.

During this time Leia threw herself into her new work as a member of the Apprentice Legislature. The training program, a coveted testing ground for young, aspiring politicians, attracted the most ambitious and brightest from around the galaxy to gain valuable hands-on experience in legislation and impactful decision making. Among these like-minded peers, the once-solitary princess began to make friends her own age. The year she turned 16, Leia's two closest allies were an eccentric young woman from Gatalenta named Amilyn Holdo, and her fellow Alderaanian representative Kier Domadi, who became her first love.

Guileless Amilyn had an eerily calm demeanor, and a fascination with breaking the mold, whether she was debating political theory or pathfinding in a dense forest. Instead of allowing her native culture—which favored simplicity and plain dress—to define her, Holdo dyed her hair outrageous shades of neon green and teal blue to match her equally flashy wardrobe, which was filled with dazzling dresses and kaftans trimmed with tinkling bells and glittering tassels. Leia was not immediately taken with this unusual young woman, finding her to be abrasive and showy. But she soon learned to appreciate Amilyn's inherent strength, quick-thinking, and ingenuity. In time, she adopted a more refined, but still distinctive, mode of dress and became one of Leia's most trusted allies and a storied leader in her own right.

Young Kier Domadi was a surprisingly suitable match for the princess. Breha had expected her somewhat headstrong daughter to choose a roguish young man for her first boyfriend, to test her parents' patience. Unlike Leia, who was driven to shine in the Apprentice Legislature as a stepping stone to her own political future, Domadi's interests lay in anthropological and historical study. The Clone Wars had ended before they were born, yet Kier was fascinated by the conflict, spending his free time reenacting and recreating some of the war's most pivotal battles. Kier dreamed of becoming a teacher and lecturer to ensure that the lessons of the past were not forgotten by the next generation.

As their friendship blossomed into something more intimate, Leia allowed Kier to see her at her most vulnerable. It was uncomfortable at first. Leia felt exposed in ways she had only permitted her parents and their serving droids to see. But Kier quickly earned her trust, and to him she revealed many of her innermost thoughts and feelings. Kier was not eager to please just because she was the daughter of the queen. He was honest and respectful, but no sycophant—a welcome departure from some individuals Leia had encountered in her young life. Many of them—too many for Leia's liking—saw her only as the queen's heir, who needed marrying off to continue the line. Like her biological mother, Leia aspired to far greater achievements than marriage and motherhood on their own could provide.

Leia came to trust Kier completely and he, in turn, became her most trusted advisor. Kier alone was adamant that Leia find a way to live for herself, not just in service to her people. Kier alone was permitted to unfurl her intricate braids and see Leia in her unadorned, natural state. And to Kier alone, Leia revealed the depth of her parents' planned treachery against the Empire, as she perceived it.

When she wasn't studying files and formulating points for future debate, Leia and her new friends enjoyed pathfinding classes, learning the value of working together and how to overcome all manner of obstacles. These were important skills for anyone trying to make their way in the galaxy; for Leia they provided a taste of freedom, as well as the foundation of resilience she would need to survive future hardships and life-threatening situations.

Leia studied diplomacy out of necessity, but enjoyed learning piloting and hand-to-hand combat skills for the thrill of self-confidence they brought her. Her father saw her accomplishments through the unique lens of one who had stood on the frontlines with both Anakin and Padmé. Leia soon learned how to headbutt an attacker twice her size and land a punch—although she saw physical violence as a last-ditch resort when all else failed. Leia also reveled in climbing exercises in Alderaan's mountain country. In nature, Leia could be alone and never feel lonely, a part of the living, breathing world around her.

During a pathfinding expedition on Felucia, Leia's adoration for Kier was put to the test when his anchor gave out during a climbing exercise and his field generator—a device that should have broken his fall—was damaged. Perched precariously over a deep gorge, Leia bravely locked her carabiner onto his belt clip, hoping her ropes would hold their combined weight as they swung to safety. Unbeknownst to her, by focusing on her predicament, with one deep breath Leia had tapped into her innate inclination toward the Force. Instead of being afraid, Leia felt centered and calm in a way she never had before. It was as if she had become one with the rocks, sensing the shape of every outcrop and indent on the other side of the gorge. Swinging from a single rope, her body flooded with strength she never knew she possessed, Leia made a graceful, death-defying leap to carry Kier to safety.

This spectacular feat was a defining moment for the young princess and the birth of a conviction that would drive her for the rest of her life. At that moment Leia realized her solemn duty was to save not just citizens of Alderaan, but any being she saw in peril. It was also the day she and Kier shared their first kiss. They enjoyed a brief but tender romance, a footnote in the history of her legendary career that nonetheless had a profound impact on her.

***

Leia's investigations into rebel activity during this time—including spying on one of Bail and Breha's allies making a treacherous deal with a vile Imperial Security Bureau agent—made her a target of some fascination for the Empire's Grand Moff Wilhuff Tarkin. A Republic veteran of the Clone Wars, Tarkin was once so bold as to infiltrate one of her parents' dinner parties, having guessed correctly that it was more than an innocent gathering of friends and like-minded individuals. The Grand Moff was cunning and calculating, applying pressure to the young apprentice legislator in hopes that she would reveal the extent of her parents' treason. But Leia was trained from her earliest days in the art of maintaining an impenetrable and unreadable facade. If she relaxed her features, she appeared aloof and inaccessible. If she focused, she could reduce herself to tears on cue. The stress of the situation, and the months of secrecy and lies, certainly helped her convince him that he had stumbled, not into a den of political espionage, but a simple extramarital affair between Bail and his senatorial collaborator Mon Mothma.

Tarkin was not known for being a kindly man under any circumstances, so when he offered the princess a shoulder to cry on upon their return to Coruscant, she easily saw through him. Tarkin began by testing Leia's allegiance to the Empire, explaining the level of cooperation that would be required of her when she inherited the throne. Through Tarkin's probing, however, Leia discovered that the Empire was plotting an attack on Paucris Major. It was no accident that Tarkin mentioned the exact location where the Organas and the Rebellion were gathering together ships and weaponry. The existence of this armada had been kept secret from Leia, but in that moment she knew that both she and Imperial intelligence had successfully collected the evidence of rebel collusion that her parents had been trying to conceal.

Breha spent long nights working on what would later become the Rebellion's financial records from the relative safety of the palace—to those around her, she was the picture of a hands-on monarch taking an interest in the day-to-day governance of her planet by managing the books. Clever credit shuffling and generous donations from the royal purse helped keep the Rebellion solvent and hidden from regular banking records. Meanwhile, Bail's position within the Senate gave him the freedom of movement to appear at clandestine meetings at the various rebel bases and hubs that by then dotted the galaxy.

Bail was with the rebel armada when Leia alerted her mother and Mon Mothma to the Empire's ruinous intentions. Their public obligations made it impossible for either of the high-ranking women to get away in time to warn him, and they couldn't trust a droid or hazard a transmission. Either could too easily be intercepted, tipping off the Imperials before an evacuation could commence.

That left them one choice: Leia. For months, she had been clamoring to be included in her parents' dealings and, wishing to protect her, they had refused. Through every dinner party and forged transaction, Breha and Bail hoped that if their activities were discovered, Leia's genuine ignorance would shield their child, allowing her to hold up under interrogation better than any training. And yet, Leia had never been content to sit idly by. If her parents were in trouble, Leia wanted to help them. If they were risking their lives, she wished to stand and fight alongside them.

With no one else to deliver the message, Breha reluctantly agreed to send her daughter to warn the fleet and try to save Bail's life. For Leia, it was her first real, sanctioned mission for what would become known as the Rebel Alliance.

***

Amilyn Holdo had already shown readiness, without concern for her own welfare, to help Leia during their pathfinding exercises. Tasked with hiring a ship to get to Paucris undetected, Holdo willingly came to the princess's aid. But on the journey, Leia learned that it would take more than one loyal friend to stave off the Empire's threat.

On a stopover on Pamarthe, a clever distraction in case the Empire were attempting to track their journey, they were waylaid by a storm. Leia began to despair of finding anyone willing to risk their ship and their lives to make the final leg of the trek. Then she spotted a Chalhuddan vessel.

On an earlier mission, the gruff Chalhuddan people had accepted Leia's relief support on the condition that they owed her a favor. That day, she called it in, and it was the first instance that Leia had used her diplomatic training to rally another to her cause and form an alliance.

True to her frank, honest nature, Leia took a moment to explain to the hairy, amphibious Occo Quentto exactly what she was asking. Leia knew it was important for the Chalhuddans to understand the context of the situation and to give their consent freely, before putting their lives in danger. This incident gives a clear indication of the kind of leader that Leia would become: bold yet fair; relying on collaboration and willing participation over decrees and iron-fisted rule; and putting the greater good ahead of her own personal safety.

The Chalhuddans were an honorable species, and they took Leia's briefing in stride. It certainly helped that, despite her noble breeding, she treated them as equals, worthy of respect. They not only agreed to help Leia, they also offered a handful of their own ships to escort her freighter. Their support put the young princess on track to become a unifying leader in her own right.

With Amilyn by her side, Leia was able to get to her father on the *Tantive IV* in time, warn him of the impending Imperial attack, and save the rebel fleet. However, Kier followed her that day and he was killed in the blast that wiped all evidence of the Organas' treasonous armada from existence, save for the ships themselves.

The young man was hailed a hero and buried in a plot in the royal cemetery, a small consolation to his family. In the official account, it was recorded that Kier Domadi had sacrificed himself during a small-craft accident, giving his life so that the Princess of Alderaan could live.

However, it is possible that Kier may have been engaging in espionage, given his close relationship with the princess and access to some of the more damning details of the Organas' quest for freedom from the yoke of the Empire. By all accounts, Kier was loyal above all else to Alderaan. He loved his planet more than he hated the Empire, and was willing to do anything to protect it. He could have arrived at Paucris that day in order to collect evidence of rebel activity as a bargaining chip to ingratiate his homeworld with the Imperial elite, a means to deflect the glare of Imperial scrutiny. If successful, he might well have entrusted that information to Leia, believing that, as next in line to the throne, she would also prioritize the welfare of the people of Alderaan.

The loss of Kier haunted Leia for some time, but she found the strength to carry on. Kier's death cast the work of the Rebellion and its attendant importance and grave risks—in a new light. She was surprised to find that her belief and confidence in the cause had grown. Leia resolved to fight to topple the Empire, and free Alderaan and the galaxy from its dictatorial grip. She also promised herself to avoid future romantic entanglements, until her work was done.

***

At nearly 17, Leia completed her Day of Demand challenges, including climbing Appenza Peak, her mother by her side. Publicly, she proved herself worthy to wear the crown as ruler of Alderaan one day. Privately, she showed herself a valuable ally to her parents and the burgeoning Rebellion at large. Leia's soft brown eyes could radiate innocence before prying Imperial commanders, or pierce the soul of anyone who got in her way or failed to heed her orders. Her youth and slight build enabled her to operate largely unnoticed; potential foes disregarded her as just another princess, who was too preoccupied with hair accessories and the latest in Coruscant high-fashion to pose any serious threat to the Empire.

Promoted to work as a senatorial aide to her father, the teenager exhibited exceptional poise under pressure and excelled at rallying even new acquaintances to her cause. Although she and her family continued to be under surveillance by Tarkin and his minions, Bail taught his daughter how to operate in the open, hiding their activities in plain sight.

The Empire still reigned supreme, its military might easily capable of extinguishing insurgencies. But over the next three years, something miraculous happened. Through countless mercy missions, Leia and others like her came to be seen as beacons of hope among the downtrodden. Under the guise of relief work, Leia was instrumental in helping to get Alderaanian cruisers into the hands of a rebel cell on Lothal, as well as food and other supplies for citizens struggling beneath the Empire's yoke. Moreover, as the Empire tightened its grip on the galaxy, more and more planets and their citizens, began to defy the Emperor's rule, speaking out against unscrupulous regional governors and crime bosses who had become Imperial collaborators. The growing number of dissenting voices was heartened in their defiance by the existence of a princess who was as compassionate as she was glamorous, an intoxicating combination of mystique and kindness. From the Outer Rim Territories to the lower levels of Coruscant, people began to speak out, disgusted with unfair restrictions on exports or increased taxes, emboldened by the actions of Leia, her parents, and their movement.

It was around this time that the core group of like-minded individuals that Bail and Mon Mothma had assembled grew and fragmented;

rebel cells sprang up all across the galaxy. Some fought only for the independence of a single planet or star system. Others held to the lofty goal of freeing the entire galaxy from the Empire, despite the overwhelming odds against success. In the bleakest corners, where farmers were forced from their land and relocated to slums under threat of arrest, bands of rebels helped families stave off starvation, without requiring repayment or sworn allegiance.

Yet even as the freedom fighters gained allies, weapons, and ships, the Emperor's secret plot for total domination churned ever onward. The massive space station known as the Death Star was nearly complete, and the Empire was preparing to unveil its most devastating weapon.

When Leia was 19, Wilhuff Tarkin ordered a test firing over Jedha. This sent shockwaves through the moon, obliterating the Holy City, as well as a cell of rebel extremists. Officially, the Galactic Senate was told that one of the last refuges of the Jedi Knights, the spiritual site of the Guardians and the Whills and the ancient Kyber Temple, had imploded in a mining accident. The incident was simply a test of the Empire's terrifying new superweapon, an awe-inspiring show of strength.

Chapter 19

Obi-Wan and the Call to Adventure

Obi-Wan Kenobi and Bail Organa had agreed to keep the Skywalker twins apart for their own safety, but the fates—and the Force—had other plans. The year the siblings turned 19, the Galactic Civil War erupted in earnest, and the children of Anakin Skywalker and Padmé Amidala were determined to join the fight. While Leia had spent the previous few years becoming a confident leader, Luke still struggled with his desires for freedom. Yet both would attain a near-mythological status in the conflict.

After the attack on Jedha, Mon Mothma and the other architects of the Rebel Alliance were forced to shift their strategy. It had been two years since the senator from Chandrila had resigned her position in the Galactic Senate to dedicate herself to the rebel cause. Broadcast in the stars over Dantooine, her heartfelt call to arms had united citizens desperate to escape the Empire's iron rule and establish rebel cells. The Rebel Alliance founded its base on the fourth moon of Yavin and prepared for battle. The news that the Empire had developed a superweapon capable of total planetary annihilation made all-out war inevitable.

Leia found herself at the forefront as the rebels rushed to secure allies in a last-ditch effort to bring together every powerful friend and capable fighter they could assemble. Bail Organa personally assigned Leia a vital mission: to retrieve the former Jedi Master and storied Clone

Wars general Obi-Wan Kenobi from hiding on Tatooine. When father and daughter parted ways that day, their bond could not have been stronger. Bail was proud of his daughter, and had become less fearful of sending her out into the galaxy, despite the dangers. Leia had earned his trust and become an essential partner in her parents' important work. This fact would provide consolation for the young woman in the years to come, and a source of strength.

As Leia was finishing preparations—dressed in a simple white gown, her long brown hair twisted into two full-moon buns that covered her ears—the Alliance made its first counterstrike in the Battle of Scarif— and forced Leia to change her plans. On the tropical world, a band of spies broke into the Citadel Archive, which held the master blueprints for a number of Imperial weapons and fortresses. Known under the call sign of their ship, *Rogue One*, the entire strike force was massacred. But, before they died, they beamed the blueprint for the Death Star to the *Profundity*. This Mon Calamari cruiser just happened to be where the Organas' ship, the *Tantive IV,* was docked for repairs, and the disk that carried the precious intel was passed from hand-to-hand among desperate soldiers before falling into Leia's grasp.

The theft of these top-secret plans put Imperials at every level on high alert and attracted the attention of the Empire's dreaded enforcer, Darth Vader. Leia was desperate to return to Bail with the plans; however, in orbit of Tatooine, Leia's ship was seized by an Imperial Star Destroyer, which pulled the ship into its hull with a tractor beam. Leia knew that capture was imminent, but she remained calmly defiant, even as the Empire's stormtroopers swarmed aboard her ship.

Bail had taken Anakin and Padmé's droids, R2-D2 and C-3PO, when he adopted Leia and put them to work on his ship under the care of Captain Antilles. As such, they had been a part of Leia's life almost since birth. The protocol droid's mind had been wiped to reset his worldview as if he had always been a part of the Royal House of Alderaan's retinue. If C-3PO had known where he had truly come from—what had become of the maker he praised—it might have fried his circuits. His more level-headed counterpart R2, a veteran in his own right, was far more adept at maintaining discretion. Easily overlooked yet unfailing with rudimentary tasks, precise flight calculations, and matters of espionage, none who looked upon R2's nondescript blue and silver domed head could suspect the secrets he retained. The squat droid had been instrumental in helping Leia collect vital data on the Empire's destructive forces on the planet Chasmeene during her early days spying and amassing evidence for the rebels. As her ship was boarded by Darth Vader himself, she turned to the loyal astromech for help.

Leia recorded an urgent holo-message for Obi-Wan Kenobi, detailing as much as she dared, then transferred the data on the Death Star to the droid's databanks. Leia hoped the Jedi would heed her pleas to finish what she could not: ferrying the plans to her father on Alderaan in order to give the Rebel Alliance a fighting chance against the superweapon. She knew she was an easy target—the Empire had been watching the Organas and their friends for years. Leia had the training, experience, intelligence, and inborn courage, even at such a young age, to devise a plan that, with luck, might enable R2-D2 to gain the safety of an escape pod and thus bring about a rebel victory, even at the cost of her personal defeat.

Dumped on the desolate sands of Tatooine, R2 and his reluctant companion, C-3PO, were captured by a band of beady-eyed Jawa scrappers, who fortuitously sold them to the Lars family. And R2's determination to complete his secret mission led their new master, Luke Skywalker, to Obi-Wan Kenobi. While Luke was cleaning the carbon scoring from his newly acquired astromech, Leia sparked to life in the crystalline blue of a holo-recording, a mysterious guide beckoning him onto a dangerous and unknown path. The Rebellion's all-out war had only just begun, but traders and travelers who passed through Anchorhead had already stoked the young man's fascination with the cause. To Luke, almost *anything* was more interesting than his life on the farm. He was foolhardy, itching for action, and a beautiful rebel fighter dispatching her droid greatly intrigued him.

R2 had always been a wily sort and he used Luke's curiosity to his advantage, claiming his new restraining bolt was short-circuiting his systems and preventing him from playing the message in full. Once freed from the inhibitor, he rolled off into the twin sunsets with Luke on his trail early the next morning. Their journey through the bad-lands attracted a hunting party of Tusken Raiders and Luke was rendered unconscious in the fray. Luckily, Kenobi—who tried to never wander far from the young man—appeared and howled the echoing call of the krayt dragon to scare the Tuskens into hiding. Inside Keno-bi's hut, Luke recovered from his ordeal and took shelter from the heat of the midday suns.

At this time, Luke knew virtually nothing about the Jedi Order and the Force. His uncle had always been brusque when Luke started asking questions. However, in Obi-Wan he found a welcoming presence, some-one who seemed willing to help satisfy his fascination with the past and his curiosity about the galaxy.

In his solitude, Obi-Wan had come to a realization, a phrase he was fond of repeating: "The truth is often what we make of it." Perhaps it was just his own spin on one of his master, Qui-Gon Jinn's, favorite truisms: "Your focus determines your reality." Now in his late fifties, Kenobi was finally beginning to feel like he'd grown out of his youthful foolishness. Nearly as gray-haired and wrinkled as Yoda himself, he had made peace with some of the Jedi Order's folly and come to a reckoning of sorts. In all those years, he had imagined what answers he might give to Luke's curious probing one day.

In the safety of his hut, Obi-Wan told Luke only what he believed the young man needed to know, the most basic facts as he saw them. Their conversation laid the foundation for Luke's initiation into the ways of the Jedi, while Obi-Wan continued to protect him, shielding him from the darkest aspects of his heritage. This was in accordance with ancient

Jedi teaching: disclosing the shocking truth of Luke's parentage—a revelation worthy of a Jedi trial—was best delayed until he became a full-fledged Jedi Knight.

Thus, instead of revealing the truth, that day Kenobi hailed the Jedi Knight Anakin Skywalker as the best star-pilot in the galaxy, a cunning warrior, and a loyal friend. And to win Luke's confidence, Obi-Wan offered his own failure to win the young man's trust; he admitted serving as the master of the future Sith Lord Darth Vader before he turned to evil and became a Jedi hunter. Factually, both statements were true. But he dared not connect the two identities: Obi-Wan simply said that Vader had betrayed and murdered Luke's father. If Luke was the Chosen One, Obi-Wan knew he would have to vanquish Vader to restore balance to the Force.

On this significant occasion, Luke was gifted the single possession that tethered his future to his family's splintered past. That day, Obi-Wan gave him the lightsaber he had taken on the lava banks of Mustafar after his duel with Darth Vader.

Luke was transfixed by this significant inheritance from a man he had often longed to have known. It had been crafted by his father with care, a symbol of his dedication to the Jedi Order and irrefutable proof of his mechanical ingenuity. Of course, Luke was totally unaware that the lightsaber had been used to commit unspeakable atrocities. If the blade could have told its own version of events, Luke would have recoiled in horror. The weapon was like a fairy tale sprung to life. Luke's eyes lit up with wonder when he pressed the switch and ignited the saber, a shaft of blueish light emanating from the hilt with a soothing crackle, buzzing as he swished it cautiously back and forth.

With this gift, Obi-Wan made Luke a proposal that he believed the boy would be powerless to refuse: Obi-Wan offered to train Luke in the ways of the Force. It was as much a response to the duty he felt to help Leia Organa as it was an act of atonement for his failures with Anakin. Given his actions, it is clear that Kenobi intended to end his years of exile and heed Leia's call. Training Luke Skywalker provided him with a new apprentice at a pivotal moment in galactic history. The threat of the Sith and the Empire the Sith had created was too great to ignore. In keeping with other practitioners of the Barash vow, it was time for Obi-Wan to face that threat head on, with or without Luke.

All the young man had ever wanted was to escape his family's humdrum expectations of inheriting the farm and marrying a local girl. Nevertheless, when finally presented with the chance to escape and embark on a totally new course, Luke was not sure if he really wanted to leave the sand pile he called home. The truth was, he was scared. Tatooine was no paradise, but at least he knew his place there. Perhaps he would have grown out of his dislike of the Empire, and become indifferent about matters that didn't immediately concern him. He could have remained, paid his water taxes, met his quotas, minded his own business, and kept his head down. Luke had been raised to believe that the best he could hope for was a quiet life, falling asleep with a full stomach, and enjoying a few harmless activities, like racing through Beggar's Canyon, on the rare occasions when there was no more work to be done. Could Luke have been satisfied with that life? At that moment, he believed it would have to do.

On the day Obi-Wan Kenobi invited Luke Skywalker to become his first Jedi apprentice in nearly two decades, the young man refused outright.

Chapter 20

The Death Star

It was not a long time after Luke first held the Skywalker lightsaber that, worlds apart, Luke and Leia both lost their adopted parents, casualties of the fearful destruction wrought by the Empire. It was the second time a war would make them orphans, and the crucial incident that ultimately thrust the twins together and defined much of the rest of their lives.

Luke returned from his visit with Obi-Wan Kenobi to find ashy smoke billowing from the charred ruins of his home, the husks of each delicate hydroponic plant reduced to blackened stems and shriveled leaves. Empire stormtroopers had tracked the missing droids to the threshold of the Lars homestead and left their signature mark. Near the resting place of Shmi Skywalker's bones, where the imprint of Anakin's trauma and bitter revenge still echoed amid the shifting sands, Luke called out for his family. The act was desperate and careless—if the stormtroopers who murdered his kin had still been nearby, he would have surely been next. But his shouts abruptly ceased when his eyes fell upon the domed entryway that had welcomed generations of farmers home and came to rest on the smoldering remains of his loving aunt and uncle. The image of this senseless carnage was seared into his brain, never to be forgotten—a bitter reminder of how the Empire dealt with matters in dispute.

In contrast to Anakin's grief-fueled massacre of the Tusken Raiders' camp some 20 years prior, Luke's rage paled in comparison to his birth father's capacity for fury. Luke was angry in the aftermath, grief competing with a burning desire for revenge; however, he was more heartbroken over his loss than vindictive. The key difference between father and son in response to similar traumatic events was that whereas Anakin turned his woes inward, assuming a mantel of responsibility that far exceeded any single being's capability, Luke turned his pain into a call to action. The deaths of Beru and Owen Lars would become a driving force, inspiring Luke to devote his life to a higher cause—one that would have nothing to do with moisture farming.

In a significant turnabout, Luke resolved to go to Alderaan and learn the ways of the Force. He would follow what he knew of his father's path, and, with Obi-Wan's help, become a Jedi Knight. He intended to find the beautiful woman who had begged for Kenobi's aid, join up with the rebles and fight bravely against the Empire. That was how Luke intended to seek justice against the regime whose soldiers had butchered his family.

At Mos Eisley spaceport, Obi-Wan hired a freighter to take them to Alderaan. The ship was the *Millennium Falcon*, piloted by a known smuggler named Han Solo and his Wookiee partner, Chewbacca. Known as Chewie to his friends, his people had been aided by the Jedi Master Yoda during the Clone Wars. Although it is unknown if he had met Obi-Wan Kenobi at that time, he recognized the man's lightsaber as the weapon of a Jedi when, in the shadows of Mos Eisley cantina, Kenobi brandished his blue blade in Luke's defense. Obi-Wan's intervention left one Aqualish patron with a stump where his arm had been.

***

At the same time, many parsecs away, in the overbridge of the Death Star, the Empire's second-tier leadership were rejoicing in the technological terror they had constructed. With a radius of 160 kilometers, roughly the size of a small moon, the aptly-named superweapon carried hundreds of thousands of Imperial soldiers prepared to crush anything and anyone in the Empire's way. Their mission: enforcement through terror. Those at the Death Star's controls were utterly dedicated to the Emperor's plans.

When Leia faced Darth Vader on the *Tantive IV*, she was convincingly indignant, relying upon her royal status. Regardless of the Organas' treasonous acts toward the Empire, Leia was by all account a popular senator among the galactic representatives that made up the Imperial Senate. But even if she had been an outcast in political circles, she retained diplomatic immunity. However, her standing only held as long as the Imperial Senate itself remained, and that body had been dissolved by Emperor Palpatine himself in the aftermath of the Empire's demonstration on Scarif of its weapon of mass destruction.

That day, Leia's insults reduced the Sith Lord to little more than an obedient pet tethered to the odious Grand Moff Tarkin, her speech carefully worded to mock Tarkin's pretentious manner of speaking. However, by the time Leia was escorted to the bridge of the space station, she had endured many hours inside a claustrophobic prison cell and undergone brutal interrogation—including an invasive mind probe—and begun to lose some of her composure.

The threat of an execution order, signed by Tarkin himself, made Leia more audacious and reckless. If the Empire was intent on ending her life, she would not give them the satisfaction of seeing her fear. But Tarkin had studied her well. He knew that getting her to crack came down to understanding her nature. He presented her with a choice: Betray the Rebellion by revealing the location of its base, or watch her homeworld perish. Tarkin's error was believing that Leia's youth and lack of experience would allow her emotions to sway her. The princess was intelligent enough to realize that the choice was illusory: Tarkin would never spare the people of Alderaan. Wedged between the glowering Grand Moff and Vader, his masked accomplice, pushed close enough to hear Vader's wheezing breath, Leia was forced to watch as her home was sacrificed in a further demonstration of the Empire's dominance. Leia lunged at Tarkin. It was the only thing she could think to do in the moment, an animalistic instinct to defend her kin. Nevertheless, with a single blast of the Death Star's superlaser, Alderaan was obliterated, reduced to star dust. Kier Domadi's worst fears had come to fruition.

For years after, Leia would contemplate what her parents, her friends, her people had seen in their last moments as the moon-sized Death Star hovered overhead. It was not hard to imagine the sheer panic that must have overtaken the stunned citizens standing in the streets. The image haunted her mind. To bear the burden of the destruction of Alderaan, Leia clung to the knowledge that on that dark day she was not alone in her anger, her hopelessness, and her fear. But she alone had survived. And, for Leia, every battle, every mission, every campaign that followed was dedicated to her parents and the people of Alderaan, to show that they had not died in vain.

In the moments following the destruction of her world, Leia was assailed by a complex mix of emotions. Part of her felt she was to blame for inviting the Empire's withering gaze, although she knew, even as the thought took shape in the fog of her mind that her parents had taken up the cause first. The loss of her parents left her numb. She had never known a world without them. Even as she had struggled for independence, she had always known they were just a holo-call away to help or to listen or simply to reinforce that she was loved. Now, thanks to the Empire's cruelty, all that remained of Bail and Breha Organa was dust and memory. The desire for revenge consumed her, a blind hatred for Tarkin, Vader, and every loyal Imperial soldier who had taken part part in the regime's despicable display of power.

Even in her despair and rage, Leia managed to maintain her self-control, preserve the poise that, in time, would cement her reputation as a staunch leader of the cause. With a colossal effort of will, Leia suppressed her grief and despair at the loss of her parents and her world.

Instead of wallowing in her pain, Leia focused on putting an end to the Empire. This experience would help to inspire her later rallying cry when seeking to encourage distraught and exhausted fighters: "We have no time for our sorrows."

But even Leia was visited by doubt. Lying in her cell afterward, her own death looming, all Leia could hope for was that R2 had reached General Kenobi, and the Death Star plans had enabled rebel tacticians to seek out a potential weakness in the weapon. The alternative—that Kenobi had been killed and R2 destroyed—was too distressing to contemplate. Alderaan had been lost, but, perhaps, the rebel fleet had survived to fight another day. And if the intel was right and the superweapon could be demolished, Alderaan's destruction would not have been in vain. Whether she survived or not, she knew that she had done all she could to ensure the chance of a rebel victory.

***

At the same time that Leia was grappling with her grief, her twin brother was hurtling through hyperspace toward a planet that no longer existed. Luke was oblivious to any disruption, having only just begun to tap into the Force. Obi-Wan, however, was staggered by the powerful aftershock of the Empire's senseless destruction. Through the mystical energy field, Kenobi heard the distant echo of millions of voices howling in terror, only to be cut off in an eerie silence. He felt the tremor, yet could not piece together the source of the destruction until it was too late. Almost as soon as the *Millennium Falcon* had reached its destination of Alderaan—or the point in space where the planet had been—the ship and its crew were pulled into the cold heart of the Death Star.

Darth Vader immediately felt the presence of his old master. While Obi-Wan went to find the power terminal for the tractor beam systems and deactivate them, Vader stalked him, intent on finishing their long-standing duel. Despite his years of existing in the armored shell of Darth Vader, what remained of Anakin Skywalker could not resist the siren song of his former life, a pull to his past out of vengeance and a twisted form of penance.

Meanwhile, Luke joined Chewbacca and Han Solo in an attempt to rescue Princess Leia from her cell, a courageous bid to secure the last surviving member of the royal family and whatever reward her safe return to the rebels might bring. The events that unfolded have become the stuff of legend. But, in truth, Leia was unimpressed the first time she laid eyes on Luke Skywalker. The stormtrooper armor he had donned as a disguise was far too large. He was dwarfed by the helmet in particular, which obscured his vision and made it difficult to land a shot on his intended target. And when he proudly introduced himself, he was so flustered by seeing the princess in the flesh that he forgot that she had no idea who *he* was. It was only when Luke mentioned Ben Kenobi that it dawned on her that her message had reached its target. With no more time to dwell on Alderaan or even her own death sentence, Leia switched in an instant from introspection to a new determination.

Whatever the future held, she knew she was better off taking her chances escaping from the Empire's deadly fortress than wallowing in self-pity and waiting to meet her end. The would-be rebels' courageous infiltration was quickly detected, drawing a battalion of heavily armed stormtroopers to their position. True to form, Leia immediately took control. She grabbed a blaster, demolished a a nearby grating, and led the motley crew into the space station's garbage disposal system. Eventually the group approached the hangar where the *Millennium Falcon* was waiting and ready.

At that point, just outside the hangar bay, Obi-Wan Kenobi was cut off from the others. The sound of Vader's crimson blade greeted him with an ominous hum. In the intervening years between this moment and their last confrontation, Vader had been waiting for another chance to defeat his old master. Despite his own mortal wounds in the life-altering duel on Mustafar, Vader considered Kenobi's survival an insult to his superior strength, tugging at the part of his consciousness that still dared to tread in the shallows of Anakin Skywalker's life before his transformation.

Unlike their previous clash, Vader seemed to morph back into the unsure student he once was, cautiously prodding at Obi-Wan's defenses. Kenobi goaded his former pupil, backing toward the hangar and into view. Meanwhile Leia, eyes focused on the gangway and the freedom it promised, was darting through the curiously vacant hangar bay with Chewbacca and his friend Han Solo. The Imperial soldiers standing guard had abandoned their posts to watch the lightsaber duel. Few among the Empire's ranks had seen such a weapon since the end of the Clone Wars. Those who witnessed a Sith Lord igniting his blade rarely lived to tell of the experience.

For a split second, Obi-Wan glanced away from his opponent to see that Luke Skywalker was watching. For so long Kenobi's job had been to protect Luke from detection, but in a matter of days his purpose had transformed into inspiring the young man to leave his home, to bring Luke to the rebel cause and start him on his journey. He sensed that the Force did not intended for him to teach the son of Skywalker; that task would be left—as Anakin's tutelage should have been—to a more experienced and wise master. Kenobi's role had simply been to give Luke the basic knowledge that would serve as the foundation of his confidence and courage; and Anakin had passed down to his son the inquisitive nature that would spur him on to learn more. Having fulfilled his duty, Obi-Wan centered himself for his final sacrifice as he tilted his lightsaber skyward. To casual onlookers, it would have appeared that he stopped fighting, no longer defending himself against Vader, and allowed the Sith to slice through his flesh. To those attuned to the Force, Kenobi made a calculated sacrifice. Infuriatingly, instead of a seared corpse cleaved in two, all Vader found of the man he had resented for so long was a lightsaber hilt and an empty robe. In what should have been a moment of long-anticipated satisfaction, the defeat of his former master proof that he had finally eclipsed Obi-Wan Kenobi in lightsaber skills, Darth Vader had to face the fact that he had been outwitted.

In his first moments of clarity amid the ether, Kenobi found freedom in leaving behind his aging body. He finally *fully* understood one of Yoda's favorite truisms: "Luminous beings are we. Not this crude matter." The greedy Sith preserved their physical manifestations at all costs, never able to let go of corporeal forms and move beyond to the next plane of existence. Through Qui-Gon, Obi-Wan had learned how to let go of life itself—the ultimate attachment. By contrast, Vader continued to be weighed down by the machinery that kept him suspended in the agony of his darkest hour.

Unfortunately, Luke's understanding of the Force and his own heritage was only just beginning to dawn. To his eyes, the man who had murdered his father had now slaughtered his mentor, destroying the key to unlocking his own abilities in the Force and a man who had been like a kindly uncle, a soothing presence to fill the void left behind by his flesh and blood in the hours after their murder. In the course of a few days, Luke had watched his family and his friend silenced by the Empire's minions, defining his path to seek justice and uphold the values Obi-Wan Kenobi and the Jedi stood for.

With surprising ease, the *Falcon* made its escape and delivered the plans to the home of the Rebel Alliance on Yavin 4, a rainforested moon orbiting the gas giant Yavin. Six had arrived at the Death Star and six departed, but in Obi-Wan's place Leia now sat among and yet apart from the crew. Even disheveled from the ordeal, Leia would have seemed out of place on Han Solo's junk-filled freighter. She felt more at ease upon their arrival at the Massassi Temple, an ancient relic from a forgotten civilization, standing among the lush green landscape and the monuments to the ingenuity of the past. To Luke, the place was a paradise unlike anything he had ever seen—as if his family's moisture farm garden had exploded into breathtaking life.

Unflinchingly, Leia fulfilled her mission. She had no doubt that the

Empire was not far behind. Her arrival on Yavin 4 was a time for action, not a time to grieve. She would shed tears for her unfathomable loss—of her parents, her people, and their world—in private afterward and spend months traversing the galaxy from Sullust to Espirion in search of survivors, seeking Alderaanians who hadn't been on their homeworld that fateful day. But for now, her focus remained fixed on destroying the Empire's vile superweapon, even though she almost certainly knew that, even with the Death Star's destruction, the Rebellion's fight was only just beginning.

Based on old Sith legends dating back several millennia, the Death Star had been created by the Geonosians and refined by the Empire's top scientists. A series of perfectly calibrated kyber crystals amplified eight separate lasers, combining into one pulverizing beam of pure energy. However, one of the scientists, Galen Erso, had deliberately implanted a flaw in the weapon's design. This was cleverly concealed to give anyone who dared to oppose the Empire a chance; a weakness in the creation of an arrogant foe who refused to acknowledge the possibility of such a flaw in its masterwork.

Leia remained behind in the command center, assuming the duties her father would have fulfilled, had he lived. C-3PO was by her side, just as he had served her birth mother and as he would continue to aid the last princess of Alderaan for decades.

Galvanized by all he had witnessed, Luke pledged his service to the Rebel Alliance and climbed into the cockpit of one of the movement's X-wing crafts, with R2-D2 plugged into the ship's astromech socket. He had no idea that R2 had been instrumental in saving his father's life on numerous occasions, especially during their years of flying together during the Clone Wars. But in their brief time as master and droid, Luke had developed an affection for the squat astromech and was even beginning to understand the way his "beeps" and "boops" conveyed a snarky wit and a personality that seemed to go far beyond his programming. As he flew into battle, Luke could almost hear Kenobi's patient and wise voice wishing him well and reminding him to trust his instincts.

Although the Battle of Scarif would come to be seen as the first skirmish of the Galactic Civil War, the Battle of Yavin had a far more profound historical impact on the galaxy and the Skywalker family in particular. With the Death Star looming over the rebel base, this critical clash not only prevented other planets in the galaxy from suffering Alderaan's fate, but preserved the core armada and officers of the Rebel Alliance, who would go on to orchestrate the first several years of the conflict. And in the galaxy at large, it was a significant blow to the Empire's egotistical tyranny, a fearless refusal to allow the might of the Imperial war machine to keep the citizens of the galaxy in line.

As the Red and Gold Squadrons launched their attack, the Empire scrambled its fighters, Vader himself trailing Luke's X-wing, Red Five. Vader had no idea that he was pursuing his own child; all he sensed was that the craft was being piloted by a young man who was strangely strong in the Force. Given his incredibly narrow perspective from beneath Vader's helmet, what was left of Anakin Skywalker could not recognize his own progeny. He saw only a threat that needed to be eliminated.

Many heroic flyers lost their lives in the trench run—Luke's old friend Biggs Darklighter was killed by a blast from Vader's laser canons, with another shot from the Dark Lord frying R2, who could more easily be mended—but the Death Star was ultimately silenced that day. Luke's biological connection to the Force gave him the natural ability, and his years of play racing and target practice gave him the skill. But it was his trust in Kenobi, and Han's intervention that saved him.

Han had, at first, denounced the attempt to destroy the Death Star as a "suicide mission" and refused to get involved; however, he could not abandon a friend in need. The *Falcon* picked off one of Vader's wingmen, sending the other pilot panicking and veering into the Sith Lord's craft, hurling Vader's fighter into space. That cleared the path for Luke to close in on his target: a small thermal exhaust port, no more than two meters in diameter. There was but a glimmer of a chance for a precise hit, which would trigger an explosion in the main reactor; one of his comrades had already tried and failed during the battle. Luke focused on the port, powering down his computer and grasping for the intangible Force that blanketed him and his ship, to fire off two proton torpedoes that blasted through the superweapon's protective ray shield and found their mark. The Death Star exploded in a gigantic fireball. The Empire's monstrous creation was no more.

Soon after, honoring her mother and the customs of her people, as well as the years of dedicated service her parents had given to the Rebel Alliance, Leia presented Medals of Bravery to Luke and Han. Her curtain of hair was braided and piled into a massive bun that added height to her small frame and, attired in a formal gown, she truly looked like the queen she was raised to become. Instead of a planet to rule, Leia had the Rebel Alliance to unite and lead to victory, and the responsibility of helping the leaders find a new location for their base. Instead of the family farm, Luke found new belonging among the rebels and his own spiritual inclination to tend. The Force, like a spectral maternal protector, enveloped the twins, filling Luke and Leia with purpose and propelling them on a journey with an unknown end.

***

Despite the Death Star's destruction, what followed was a dark time for the rebel forces. Driven from their hidden base on Yavin 4, far too exposed after the battle was won, they were pursued by Imperial troops from star system to star system. Meanwhile, Leia pressed the Rebellion's remaining leaders to redouble their efforts, hoping to sap the Empire's overwhelming strength.

Grand Moff Tarkin had presumably perished in the attack on the Death Star. However, Darth Vader had survived. With Kenobi dead, a new fixation began to formulate in his addled mind. While he continued to serve his master, the Emperor, he longed to hunt down the

Force-sensitive pilot who had eluded him. Imperial officers had been vocal in their belief that the superweapon was the ultimate power in the universe, but the rebels' victory suggested—as Vader knew from personal experience—that nothing was more powerful than the Force.

Like father, like son. As the Rebel Alliance continued to work to dismantle Palpatine's Empire, Luke found himself distracted by his desire to understand the Force and also avenge his father and fallen master. While infiltrating a massive Imperial weapons factory on Cymoon 1 Luke came face to face with the emotionless mask of the Sith Lord. It was a dangerous time for young Skywalker. Luke wanted to believe he was equipped to fight Vader, but he was far from ready. The Emperor's enforcer scoffed at the untrained young man, seizing his blue-bladed lightsaber. But as soon as he held it, Vader felt the familiar detail of Anakin Skywalker's craftsmanship. For the first time since the day he had turned to the dark side, he held the weapon of the Jedi Knight he had once been.

The moment's pause was all Luke's rebel friends needed to interrupt what would have likely been a swift end to Luke's quest to become a Jedi. At the controls of a stolen AT-AT walker, Han Solo crashed through the ceiling, disrupting the duel. In the confusion, Luke reclaimed the heirloom blade and escaped. However, the brief interaction further stoked Vader's latest obsession.

Striking Kenobi down had been less satisfying than Vader had hoped, but he believed that if he captured Luke, he could extract all he knew about the Rebel Alliance and train him to become a weapon of the dark side. Vader went back to his home, to the thugs he understood, back to where it all began to find an answer. Only on Tatooine could he find the unscrupulous gang who would do his bidding without alerting the Emperor.

With the aid of the bounty hunter Boba Fett, cloned from the original template used to amass the clone army some 30 years prior, Vader was soon confronted with the startling truth: the son of Anakin

Skywalker lived. He kept this explosive information to himself, refusing to disclose it to the Emperor. But amid the rage he felt, Vader's humanity stirred, a tug of his conscience. Faced with this new reality, Anakin Skywalker would have wanted to protect his son. Vader resisted the urge, his tattered mind reframing the impulse in service to the Empire. In Vader's estimation, if the son of Skywalker could be turned to the dark side, he would be a great asset to the cause. And Vader would no longer be alone.

For the next three years—the same length of time as the Clone Wars, yet only just over half the duration the Galactic Civil War would embroil the galaxy—the rebels fought to rally planets and like-minded citizens to their cause as they searched for a new home base. New allies made themselves known with encouraging frequency, no longer content to turn a blind eye to the Empire's monstrous methods. It had long been understood that the security and safety the Imperial propaganda machine promised was accessible only to those rich enough to pay for protection and willing to bow before the Emperor with unquestioning loyalty, servility more than service. All others were labeled traitors.

Darth Vader had been sired by the dark side, twisted beyond recognition by the traumas of the Clone Wars. But upon reaching adulthood, his children continued the fight, wrestling with the chaos he had helped usher in. In contrast to the Clone Wars, in which armies faced off on various battlefronts, civil disobedience characterized the new conflict. Ordinary people came together for strength.

It is ironic that both Luke and Leia joined up with the Rebel Alliance against the Empire, considering Anakin himself had helped sow some of the first seeds of rebellion during the time of the Clone Wars. On Onderon, Anakin had helped Saw Gerrera and his freedom fighters rally against a Separatist invasion, an intervention to free their planet.

But during the Republic's war with the Separatists, Palpatine's machinations made it impossible for even those embroiled in the conflict to truly understand what was going on. By the time of the Galactic

Civil War, individuals were being inspired by rebel activity to fight the wrongs they plainly saw on their own planets, with Luke and Leia leading the charge, twin figureheads of great potential. For while the governors of so many star systems lived in palatial mansions paid for by Imperial credits, the people of the very same planets were often forced to scavenge for food in a bitter struggle for survival. For these average denizens, the heroics of the Skywalker twins became a rallying cry.

However, with varying degrees of success, the Empire spun the news of the Death Star's destruction as rebel lies and propaganda. After all, they had denied its existence in the first place. But rumors of a weapon of mass destruction, sanctioned by government leadership persisted. The Death Star ripped off the Imperial mask and exposed the Empire for the festering dictatorship it truly was. It would take the rebels years to find their footing and unify a more democratic faction of like-minded star systems, but exposing the Empire's dictatorship was an encouraging start. Whether most citizens believed it to be true or merely expertly crafted counterinformation, the legend of a humble farm boy who flew a tiny starfighter into the heart of the Empire's planet-destroying machine and, against all odds, destroyed Emperor Palpatine's dreaded Death Star, spread far and wide. It marked the beginning of the legend of Luke Skywalker.

Chapter 21

The Princess and the Scoundrel

Han Solo, 13 years Leia's senior, could not have been a more unlikely match for the princess and Rebel Alliance commander. Han was born on Corellia, the core world known for its industrial exports and massive shipyards commandeered by the Imperial military. His father worked on the lines building light freighters similar to the YT-1300 christened the *Millennium Falcon,* the unique ship that would come to define Han's legacy as a smuggler and scoundrel. Oft ridiculed for its shabby appearance—not unlike its owner who always seemed scruffy and disheveled—Han insisted that the ship made up for its superficial shortcomings with speed and dependability. It's little wonder the craft went on to become a symbol of the rebellion itself, underestimated and unimpressive at first sight, yet concealing incontrovertible power within. "She may not look like much," he had once retorted to Luke Skywalker, "but she's got it where it counts."

Whether it was his father who abandoned him or Han who ran away, by his late teens he was essentially an orphan, running scams as part of the White Worm gang. Scrappy and self-sufficient, he learned how to hot-wire speeders and talk his way out of most trouble, his lopsided grin and charm helping to calm—or at least distract—the crime bosses and thugs he ran afoul of. He fancied himself a skilled liar, able to concoct fourteen conflicting stories off the top of his head while grasping for just one believable half-truth to help him out of a bind or buy him time. Cocky and fast-talking, Han walked with a swagger that concealed his insecurities about his troubled upbringing. A stint in the Imperial Navy did nothing to quell those characteristics, but did help him escape his homeworld—with no surname to offer and no family to miss him, a recruiter dubbed him Han Solo. The name stuck; but Han soon found the constrictive nature of service to the Empire was not for him.

By the time Obi-Wan Kenobi hired him for the fateful transport to Alderaan, Han and his faithful friend and copilot, Chewbacca, had been a team for a decade, smuggling to keep their accounts flush with credits and their hunger sated. Han was reluctant to rely on people, but his trust in the Wookiee was total. Theirs was a lifelong bond born in a foul pit—a hole dug into the Mimban mud that reeked of urine, mildew, and decay—and strengthened through a series of gambles and hustles. Part of the success of their partnership was Han and Chewie's mutual respect. In most cases, the Wookiee was content to let Solo take charge, but on the rare instances where they found themselves on his home turf, the smuggler readily deferred to his towering friend. Given Han's rebellious attitude toward any kind of authority, this was no small concession.

Change was the only constant, the *Falcon* their home among the stars. Han fervently believed he could out-fly anyone and outmaneuver even the largest, heavily armed Star Destroyer. At the helm of his ship, he felt invincible. It was the *Falcon* that made the Kessel Run in less than 12 parsecs and survived an escape run through the core of Shu-Torun. He and Chewie savored the freedom that their unique set-up gave them.

Han's main faults were that hated to be told he was wrong, or even that a plan of his, no matter how risky, had a chance of failure; he also viewed showing care and concern for others as a weakness that could be exploited by opponents. As a gambler—his penchant for bending the rules and playing to win had helped him win the *Falcon* from another swindler—Han was no fan of the odds. He would shout angrily at C-3PO whenever the protocol droid gave a well-intentioned—if pessimistic—calculation regarding their survival. In truth, Han knew that he couldn't afford any distractions when his piloting could mean life or death for everyone on his ship.

Han came from nothing, and even with a ship of his own, work to keep him busy, and a fierce warrior by his side, he never forgot it. No amount of money seemed enough to silence the fearful voice that he was just one loss away from returning to the slums, beholden to an oppressive master. He would sooner die than return to that life.

Maybe that was why he initially resented Princess Leia and all she represented. To his way of thinking, a royal personage from any world was bound to be out of touch and condescending. However his preconceptions were almost immediately turned inside out as Leia blasted their way out of the Death Star's detention deck and into the trash compactor. Diving into the muck, her white gown trailing in the cesspool, was the last thing he expected from *any* princess. He bristled as she barked orders and took control of nearly every situation—her training and years of service kicking in like an autopilot setting as soon as trouble arose. And yet, he was drawn to her. Han couldn't help but grin when he discovered that she had a mean left hook, provided he wasn't on the receiving end. Though his partnership with the Rebel Alliance was rewarding, both in credits and the feeling that he was a part of something bigger than himself, it was not entirely dedication to the cause or a hero complex that led him to stay.

Leia did not immediately appreciate Han's ruggedly handsome looks or his snarky sense of humor. At first, he just seemed to be a heartless pirate. Their escape from the Death Star did little to dissuade her from her first impression, but when Han returned to aid the rebels in their fight, his appearance perfectly timed to avoid a crushing defeat, she began to warm to him.

Curiously, Han and Leia were not so dissimilar, after all. Like her first love, Kier Domadi, Han was never in awe of her title. In fact, he rarely missed an opportunity to use her royal status—mockingly deferring to her as he intoned, "Your Worshipfulness!"—as fuel for his sarcastic wit, jokes that made her unsure if he was being friendly or just crude. It chafed at first. *Was she even still a princess without a planet to call home?* she wondered. But over time, Han's derision softened into something she was sure was just his way of showing they were friends. His playful jabs became terms of endearment.

It was difficult for Leia to see beyond Han's emotional armor, carefully constructed over years of disappointments. There had been the heartbreak over his teenage sweetheart Qi'ra, who was swayed by the luxurious side of criminal dealings and ended up second-in-command of the Crimson Dawn syndicate, and some messy business involving a very convincing wedding ruse with the ruthless scoundrel Sana Starros. It was safest to focus his affection on his ship—the *Falcon* couldn't reject him—and Chewie, a friend who had proven he would neither abandon him nor tear his arms out—even when Han occasionally resorted to childish name-calling.

By the time Leia met him, Han was practiced in the art of feigned indifference, but she was convinced she'd seen the real Han Solo when he swooped in to save Luke at the Battle of Yavin. Han's overconfident blustering was just a mask. She wished he wasn't so afraid to allow his other side—the one that cared about people and causes—to show. Leia couldn't entirely fault him for being so self-protective. After all, she had suffered her own heartbreak with Kier's betrayal in her youth and she was perfectly capable of putting on a calm and confident show when inside she felt wrung out, empty, and sick with worry and doubt. Leia perfected her own impenetrable facade over years of royal grooming and political training. Han and Leia had fashioned their own shields for different reasons, but deep down they were just two people trying to mask their fears and protect their vulnerabilities amid the churning tide of war.

And in that war, Leia outranked Han. It wasn't that he wanted to ascend the ranks of the Rebel Alliance and lead his own battalion. He just wasn't used to taking orders from anyone but himself. In the wake of the Battle of Yavin, Han remained committed to the rebel cause for reasons even he couldn't quite fathom. Maybe he was just tired of being on the run. In his many years of cons and illegal jobs for gangsters like Jabba the Hutt, he had only truly escaped his earlier days of serving unscrupulous worms when he allowed the Rebel Alliance to take him in. Maybe it was because he saw something of himself in Luke Sky-walker, a kid who needed protecting. With Obi-Wan dead, Solo took on the mantle of an older brother, willing to risk his life to help the young man who needed a family as much as Han did himself.

Maybe he just had trouble walking away from Leia's radiant smile, the way she transfixed an entire room when she spoke. She could inspire even extremist fighters hellbent on destruction to rethink strategies that would condemn other worlds to Alderaan's fate. Leia never lost the airs of royalty, which to some came off as cold and icy, brusque and blunt, yet she didn't stand on ceremony or demand luxury. She was happiest among a few close allies and friends, who simply called her by her first name.

Han realized, even before Leia herself dared to consider it, that he was falling in love. Even *thinking* of saying the word made him wince. He could not deny the jealousy he felt on Lanz Carpo, a bustling world of nightlife and miscreants, when he saw Leia reunited with an old boyfriend, Dar Champion. On the same mission, Han felt complete contentment when he and Leia pretended to be newlyweds, her slim form leaning into his body.

Over time, their frequent bickering turned into genuine affection, the thin line between love and hate rubbed out by acts of bravery, self-lessness, and kindness. Leia tried to resist his charms—she could see he had a wandering heart and what she craved was stability. But heads and hearts don't always agree. She would not readily admit it, but she liked him *because* he was brave and brash and a little uncouth. There was a thrill to unraveling the mystery of what had made Han a survivor, and

cracking open that tough exterior to find the kindred spirit under-
neath. They had both learned to survive by never showing weakness,
and it felt dangerous to allow another person to see them defenseless
and raw. They were two passionate, intelligent, and independent people
trying to find the space to make room for the other in a life that was
already complicated and stretched thin. "A beautiful disaster," as Leia
called it.

***

With her parents gone, Leia was left to finish what they had started. For
months, then years, rebel cells skulked around the galaxy without a
main base to call home, seeking new allies and smaller, strategic victories against the Empire. Even without the Death Star to menace whole
planets, the Emperor's enforcer Darth Vader and his countless soldiers
still far outnumbered the Rebel Alliance.

There was no clear path to victory, no set rules or guidelines to follow in the lawless galaxy. Her gift for debate only went so far when she
was trying to convince leaders to put their lives, their ships, and their
very planets on the line. There was strength in numbers but also inherent danger; the larger the rebel forces, the more they would attract the
Empire's military might. Trusting new allies could prove risky. Leia
became adept at working with a variety of challenging personalities—
Han, Sana, and the notorious archaeologist Doctor Chelli Aphra among
them, as well as what remained of Saw Gerrera's rebels, some of whom
had survived in the ashes of Jedha—with varying degrees of success.
Saw's partisans, she found, weren't so different from the Empire in their
ruthless methods.

At 20, Leia's experience and knowledge of the galaxy far exceeded
her age, but she still had much to learn, as evidenced by the disastrous
defeat of one of her earliest, most promising alliances. When she first
met Queen Trios of Shu-Torun, who had ascended to the throne after
Darth Vader murdered her father and two elder siblings, she seemed an

obvious ally. On the face of it they had a royal pedigree and a hatred for Vader in common. Trios aided the rebels in the mutiny at Mon Cala, spurred by the murder of their imprisoned King Lee-Char at the hands of the Empire, and helped secure Mon Calamari cruisers for the cause. The victory further imprinted the heroic exploits of the rebels on the public consciousness. Buoyed by this increase in popular support, the rebels were inspired to take tentative steps toward more open combat with the Empire.

Then, over Mako-Ta base, the new rebel fleet was annihilated almost as quickly as it had been assembled, sabotaged by Trios, who alerted the Empire to their position while ensuring the rebels' hyperdrives were offline. In a matter of minutes, half the rebels' cruisers were gone and ninety percent of their fighters were wiped out.

It is astonishing that the rebels did not surrender after suffering such a catastrophic loss, but the surviving revolutionaries at the movement's core refused to let the rebellion die, even as the Empire continued to design larger and more powerful warships. Many Clone War veterans and more experienced fighters were killed in the Mako-Ta ambush. As a result, Leia, Han, and Luke rose up the ranks out of necessity, continuing their work alongside storied heroes like General Hera Syndulla and Admiral Gial Ackbar, whose own traumas from the years of galactic conflict on their homeworlds of Ryloth and Mon Cala, respectively, had turned them into skilled and determined freedom fighters.

Within a year after the Battle of Yavin, Leia was promoted to general, Luke to commander, and Han to colonel—though he would still insist that most simply called him "Captain Solo." Trios' duplicity inspired Leia's own quest for revenge. But it was a testament to the Organas that, even then, Leia aimed to wound the Imperial stronghold of Shu-Torun to gain a tactical advantage, while sparing the lives of those innocents enduring the queen's tyranny. Leia believed a counterattack would slow the Empire's stockpiling of munitions by cutting the main power spike that fueled the infrastructure on the volcanic, ore-rich plane. Leia was ultimately forced to kill Trios in self-defense, and, due to rebel activity beyond Leia's command, Shu-Torun was destroyed.

***

Three years after the Death Star's defeat, the rebels secured a new secret base, settling on the icy world of Hoth, the sixth planet ringed by several moons in a remote system. The first rebel scouts failed to record this frozen world's natural predators—a species of tall, white-furred toothy beasts known as wampas—or the fact that the planet was frequently bombarded by meteorites, making it difficult for scanners to pick up approaching enemy ships.

The rebel settlers created livable conditions on Echo Base by digging far below the surface. Their headquarters was largely hidden from view and made up of a series of twisting ice tunnels. These kept the rebels concealed from Imperial eyes and protected from the harsh climate. The base was held together by little more than scrap wire, second-hand parts, and hope, as Leia was fond of reminding the most hardheaded fighters. Still, it took nearly every resource the rebels had to make it work. The newcomers managed to domesticate the planet's native taun-tauns, whose muscular hind legs and thick pelts were far better adapted to the freezing conditions than the rebels' speeders.

In the ice-slicked hangar bay, Han and Chewbacca finally had the chance to start much-needed repairs to the *Millennium Falcon*. With the benefit of a brief reprieve from the war, at this time Han began to take stock of his own personal obligations and debts, including the price on his head from the notorious gangster Jabba the Hutt.

A run-in with a bounty hunter on Ord Mantell hastened Han's desire to deal with his past, but despite the changing circumstances Han found it difficult to tear himself away from the mission. He was enjoying being part of something bigger than his own petty concerns, robbing one thug to pay another. Plus, his competitive streak wouldn't allow him to admit that anyone—even Luke Skywalker—could possibly be a better pilot than he was or Leia a more adept officer. His ship, such a large part of himself, was a symbol of the rebel spirit. His zest helped keep the ragtag rebels together, while Leia's leadership ensured that the greater good was always put above the needs of any individual fighter. He and Leia made a formidable team.

Darth Vader had made finding Luke Skywalker a personal mission. Sensing Luke's presence in the rebel base, he dispatched General Veers and his men to destroy its meager defenses. Despite the rebels' best efforts, the overwhelming firepower of the Empire's All Terrain Armored Transports or AT-ATs forced General Leia Organa to evacuate the base. The Empire's hulking machines lumbered into battle on four legs and pummel opponents with a mix of brute force and carefully placed blaster fire, all while protecting the Imperial soldiers behind an armored carapace.

In the ensuing Battle of Hoth, the rebels launched a two-pronged defense. On the surface, rebel soldiers with heavy artillery protected the generators that powered the base's protective energy shield amid the ground assault. From the cockpit of a snowspeeder, Luke Skywalker expertly commanded pilots who swooped between the massive limb-like struts of the AT-ATs, deploying tow cables to trip up the imposing tanks. Nearby, an ion cannon disabled the hulking Star Destroyer blockade, keeping a path in the stars above clear for the transports Leia deployed, evacuating the base's crew, essential supplies, and equipment.

Both Skywalker twins were nearly killed in the battle. Luke barely survived being crushed inside his craft and Leia was nearly buried alive in what remained of the icy headquarters. Luckily, Luke dodged the AT-AT's massive foot and managed to evade capture and get to his X-wing, and Leia was escorted to safely by Captain Solo, who ignored the chain of command and ordered the last rebel transport away himself. With Leia and C-3PO safely on board, the *Millennium Falcon* was the last ship to flee from Echo Base, leaving a battalion of snowtroopers and Darth Vader in its slipstream. However, the rebels had been scattered and the very future of the Rebel Alliance was in peril.

Chapter 22

The Last Jedi

The beginning of Luke Skywalker's active duty for the Rebel Alliance wasn't exactly what he'd pictured when he dreamed of leaving Tatooine. He was pleased to be among their top pilots and fighters, and proud of his Death Star-destroying shot that had brought much-needed victory at the Battle of Yavin. While Luke's exploits were being hailed as legendary by those citizens eager for a hero to extol, Luke and Leia found common ground, realizing that, in the eyes of ordinary folk and the rebel leadership alike they were both wrestling with the difficulties of being treated as more important than the rest of the freedom fighters they served alongside. Special treatment often meant additional protection to ensure the Skywalker twins were out of harm's way when they desperately wished to be in the center of the fray. Luke in particular found life on the run, always on the lookout for the next Imperial attack and wondering when—not if—he was going to face Darth Vader once more, took its toll.

The precious few details Luke knew of his father, Anakin Skywalker, loomed large in his mind. Luke was dedicated to the cause, but he was also distracted by his own quest for knowledge of the Force. He longed to be as powerful in battle as his father had been at his peak and as strong in his faith. In some way, he hoped to do him proud by being as loyal a friend as Anakin had apparently been to Ben.

His newfound sense of belonging with the rebels took him across the galaxy, but it was the power of the Force itself that compelled him along his way. On Rodia, Luke obtained a sense of the Jedi's greater impact on the galaxy, including the exploits of Anakin Skywalker, and had the chance to examine the weapon of another Jedi. On the jungle world of Devaron, inside the lost Jedi Temple of Eedit, Luke came to understand why the locals believed the derelict house of worship and meditation was haunted. The voice of Obi-Wan Kenobi filled his head as he communed with the ancient wielders of the Force, and began his training in earnest; however, he was compelled to destroy the entrances to the temple after seeing how the riches and untold treasures within invited opportunist thieves.

Without a teacher to guide him, Obi-Wan Kenobi became an inspirational figure, a conscience he obeyed; however, a specter could not compensate for a flesh-and-blood spiritual guide. Gripped by anger and frustration, Luke returned to Tatooine and searched Kenobi's abandoned hut for clues and *any* scrap of knowledge left behind. He came away with only his mentor's writings from his time in exile and a slight concussion after a battle with a bounty hunter. On a practical level, without a proper teacher, Luke's lightsaber work remained clumsy, suitable for slicing through the belly of an AT-AT yet nowhere near precise enough to do battle with a supremely skilled combatant such as Vader.

Luke had yet to discover his higher calling or understand the Jedi Order's true nature. By the end of his life, Luke would come to understand that, after their annihilation, the Jedi were romanticized and deified. Most of the individuals at the core of the Order were anything but perfect; they were flawed, given to hubris and hypocrisy as much as anyone else.

***

In his later years, Luke would dedicate himself to the study of the Force and the instruction of the next generation, forgoing his own romantic inclinations. However, as a young man, he often found himself bemused by the alluring women he met on his journey. There was Leia, of course. Without understanding their genetic connection, for years the two rebels were bonded by other factors, war orphans and freedom fighters dedicated to the cause. But Leia couldn't entirely grasp Luke's preoccupation with studying the Force. She knew from her father's stories of the Clone Wars that the Jedi were once powerful leaders in battle, but their defeat suggested to her that their abilities were not a magic blaster bolt to be relied upon.

There was Warba Calip: an orphan of Jedha and a street urchin who had never formally trained in the Force. Her knowledge was gleaned from worshipping at the altar of the Guardians of the Whills, studying their devotion to the mystical energy. She mainly used her rudimentary understanding of this energy for thieving and gambling, but she taught Luke the mantra of the Jedha priests: "I am one with the Force, the Force is with me." More than a simple Jedi mind trick or combat skill with his father's lightsaber, the words became the basis of Luke's belief and helped bring calm to his frenetic mind.

And there was Tula Markona and her clan. Luke met Tula while stranded with Han and Leia on the isolated world of Hubin, a planet so cut off from the rest of galaxy there were no transmitters available to alert the Rebel Alliance to their location. Far from civilization as he knew it, Luke glimpsed the ideals and restrictions of the fallen Jedi Order through the lens of the leader of the Markona clan, Thane, and his daughter, who were descendants of a Jedi who had left the Order in pursuit of love.

The Clan of Markona was a self-sufficient community linked not by blood but by choice. They were very much like the Rebel Alliance and the Jedi Order of old, a found family of orphans and warriors united by shared beliefs. Luke and Tula enjoyed a brief romance. And Thane was among the Jedi-hopeful's earliest teachers in hand-to-hand combat, leadership, and galactic history.

But Luke was impatient. While sheltered at the enclave he used his mechanical prowess to create a transmitter that beamed a message to the stars above; tragically it was the Empire that answered. In the skirmish that followed, Thane sacrificed himself so his daughter might live to make better choices and lead his people. Afterward, Luke tried to persuade Tula and her warriors to join the rebel cause, but grief for her dead father had extinguished the brief spark between them. She understood that Luke was not to blame for her father's death—Thane had made a choice. Still, Tula couldn't look at Luke without being reminded that he and his friends had brought disaster and death.

Among the lasting impacts of the encounter, Thane forced Luke to confront the fallout of the Clone Wars without romanticizing the Republic or the Jedi. The older man surmised that those who lived through the war were hard-pressed to define a point in time between the end of the Republic and the Empire. The slow decay of one seamlessly mutated into the other. Through Thane, Luke came to realize that the rise of the Empire was not just down to a single diabolical ruler; it was a collective failure by the people of the galaxy, as much a consequence of widespread apathy as it was of Palpatine's plotting.

***

Luke's natural abilities with the Force and his prowess as a fighter were indelibly linked. Three years into the war, just as the rebels were settling into their new home on Hoth, Luke experienced a vision. Luke had barely survived a wampa attack and, calling upon the Force for strength, used his lightsaber to slash his way out of the beast's lair. Suffering from hypothermia in this freezing wasteland, Luke believed he saw the spectral spirit of his friend Obi-Wan, who instructed him to seek out the Jedi Master Yoda.

Han Solo, who saved the young warrior's life by stuffing his frostbitten body into the still-warm carcass of his dead tauntaun, was highly skeptical of Luke's story. He had long believed the Force was just a "hokey religion" practiced by fanatics and zealots. Most of what he'd seen could just be chalked up to parlor tricks and con jobs, as far as Han was concerned.

But after the Battle of Hoth, when the rebels fled Echo Base to evade the Imperial attack, Luke followed Kenobi's counsel and, using the Force, found his way to the Dagobah system. His sojourn marked the beginning of his formal training to better understand and utilize his innate gift.

Cut off from the greater galaxy, yet in balance with the mystical energy that thrived there, the planet was devoid of cities and technology, yet teemed with life. Time itself seemed to slow down to contemplate the wonders of the Force.

As soon as his X-wing breached Dagobah's atmosphere, Luke's scopes went dead, R2-D2's copilot functions fizzled out, and the ship crash-landed into a bog. The droid, according to his own data records, was nearly swallowed by a scaly beast before he and Luke could make it to the muddy shore. No sooner had the pair arrived than Luke began to doubt the wisdom of his chosen path. He wanted to be a Jedi like his father, but after Kenobi had died he felt utterly lost. Chewing a tasteless ration bar at their dank encampment that night, a fusion furnace to warm his hands and a power cell to help the droid recharge, Luke felt as if he was losing his mind. In his despair, he considered that he could have been hallucinating on Hoth, making his detour to Dagobah a fool's errand that had the potential to permanently separate him from the greater Rebellion. On a more personal level, Luke Skywalker was filled with doubt over whether or not he was strong enough to become a Jedi like his father.

The disruption of Luke's arrival stirred Jedi Master Yoda from hiding, but in truth he had been expecting the young man for some time. After his failure to defeat Darth Sidious and stem the infection of the dark side, Yoda had exiled himself on Dagobah, mourning the hubris that had led to the fall of the Jedi Order and the slaughter of thousands of innocent lives and brave Force practitioners. In his shame, Yoda resolved to never again carry or brandish a lightsaber, and returned to the most basic and humble origins of the Jedi's practice with the Force.

On Dagobah, untouched by civilization, Yoda meditated, communing with the energy surrounding and binding all life. It was as if he was trying to untangle the labyrinthine path of the Jedi by going back to the fundamentals of his faith. Through the Force, Yoda had sensed many things. He had heard the cries of the people of Alderaan as the planet was snuffed out by the evil he had inadvertently helped take hold in the galaxy. He had felt the fateful final meeting of Obi-Wan Kenobi and Darth Vader, and sensed Kenobi's strength and resilience as he became one with the cosmic Force. He had refused to intervene, recognizing the disastrous compromises he had made when dabbling in matters of galactic importance on the Jedi Council and serving as a general in the Clone Wars. Yoda's return to the core tenets of Jedi philosophy would form the basis of Luke's beliefs and attitudes in later years.

But upon their initial meeting, the squat master who dressed in rags and used a mud-packed shelf for a bed fell short of Luke's vast expectations for what he envisioned the Jedi had been and should be. While Yoda no doubt saw his return to simplicity as a monastic penance for all that had been lost, Luke's search was spurred by an insatiable interest in the mythical side of the Jedi's heroics—great warriors whose dashing exploits had kept the Republic at peace for a millennia.

It was a fact that was lost on young Luke in his youthful inexperience, but in his solitude Yoda had learned to face his own fears, to grapple with the failings of the Jedi Order, to laugh in the face of his humiliations and even forgive himself. Despite the rise of Darth Vader, in the years between Anakin's fall and Luke's arrival, Yoda found the strength to carry on, to embrace the past for the lessons his greatest regrets and deepest failures could impart. And when another Skywalker arrived asking to be trained, he could not deny himself—and the galaxy—a chance at redemption: by training the Force-sensitive Luke in the ways of the Jedi. The future was clouded to the point that Yoda knew only that, in order to come to terms with his own potential for good or evil, Luke would have to confront Darth Vader, the man who, unbeknownst to him, had been his father.

If he could have chosen between the two Skywalker twins, he may well have preferred to train Leia Organa in the ways of the Force. Her mind was calmer, her demeanor steady. In her early 20s, she already had the basic temperament required of a Jedi. While Leia tackled matters at hand, her mind puzzling out solutions and creative strategies to best the Empire, Luke's eyes were on the future, yet with no precise aim in view. Leia may have been better prepared and less conflicted to discover the identity of the man inside Vader's shell, having attached no idealism to Anakin Skywalker's heroics or his place in her own ancestry. Leia was so disinterested in the question of her roots, she didn't even care to know her birth father's name.

Leia saw the civil war as a means to a future of equality for all, while Luke simply hungered to be a great warrior. Wars, Yoda well knew, did not make one great. Leia focused on living up to the aspirations of her parents, the people who had raised her. Luke was impatient and reckless, and Yoda could feel in him the guttural growl of the same anger that had plagued his birth father, a hunger not for what was but the intangible idea of what could have been. However it was Luke—not Leia—who crash-landed into his swamp. And it was Luke—not Leia—who came seeking knowledge of the Force. Thus it was Luke whom Yoda agreed to train.

To Luke's eternal embarrassment, when the Jedi Master first appeared before him, without introduction, he mistook the wizened alien—standing at just 66 centimeters tall—for a local imp and pulled out his blaster. Whatever he had imagined in his mind's eye when he first heard the name Yoda, it was not a shriveled green man with long pointy ears and a tuft of white hair. Yoda regarded Luke's defensive response with amusement, and offered his help, leading the young man back to his cramped hut—sized for Yoda alone, not a full-grown human—for a hearty meal of rootleaf stew.

There was something about Yoda, even before Luke realized it *was* Yoda, that filled him with calm. For 800 years, Yoda had taught younglings at the Jedi Temple, bent over his walking stick as age warped his body. But whether he had his lightsaber in hand or simply called upon the Force as his ally, Yoda had proven to generations of students that size was of no consequence when it came to knowledge or strength in the Force. When he first encountered young Anakin Skywalker, he declared that the nine-year-old child was too old to train. At 22, Luke was an adult. Thus, Yoda quickly realized he would have to revise the methods he had used to guide thousands of younglings on the first steps of their Jedi path in order to meet this young man's needs. And there was little time; Yoda could sense it.

With the little master riding upon his shoulders in his backpack, Luke simultaneously trained to strengthen his body and his mind. He ran through the forest, swinging from vines, and building his muscles, his agility improving with each passing day. And as he ran, Yoda whispered in his ear, urgently summarizing years of training and wisdom into the most basic precepts. Quickly and methodically Yoda worked to help Luke understand his deeper connection to the Force and warn him against the perils of the dark side. He was careful not to reveal the truth of what his father, Anakin Skywalker, had become—for Luke had placed Anakin on a sacrosanct pedestal. In his wisdom, Yoda finally understood his own limitations. He hoped that Luke would right the wrongs of the Jedi before him, but he had the humility to understand that he alone was not strong enough to ensure it. It would only be a matter of time before Luke understood the burden of what the galaxy required of him.

Inside a cave suffused with the energy of the dark side, the Force manifested a startling vision. It was Vader, but it wasn't. Luke ignited his lightsaber and adopted an aggressive stance. After just three parries with Vader's red blade, Luke used his father's weapon to cleave off the helmeted head of the Sith Lord. Vader's mask exploded—and revealed Luke's own visage. His own eyes gazed back at him. Luke's vision may be interpreted in different ways, for the Force moves in mysterious ways. Perhaps it was hinting at the truth of Vader's identity or simply warning Luke that giving into anger would condemn him to the same path that had led to Vader's fate . . .

However, Luke's time on Dagobah was mostly devoid of such unusual portents and remarkable incidents; there were but brief breaks in what was otherwise often arduous and tedious work. Only later, when Luke had his own pupils, would he understand the unique frustration of guiding a young unseasoned student convinced that he was wasting his time on apparently pointless exercises, such as stacking stones. Luke was unaware at the time that these simple, repetitive tasks were the very building blocks of all Force-wielders could hope to accomplish. To Luke, learning the fundamentals of the Jedi way while the Empire threatened to extinguish the last light of hope the rebels had been desperately tending seemed a waste of time. The longer he stayed, the more he felt like the experience wasn't grounding him as much as it was keeping him stuck in one place. He was reminded of how his uncle had tried to deter him from ever leaving Tatooine.

Luke's natural strength in the Force was impressive, but insufficient to overcome his own willfulness. As far as he was concerned, the swamp had swallowed his ship and he was stranded on Dagobah. Plagued by doubts, Luke sulked, unable to concentrate on Yoda's teaching. However the little master had a surprise in store for his moody student: Some lessons could only be taught through doing. With one tridactyl hand extended, his eyes closed in quiet concentration, Yoda easily lifted Luke's ship from the swamp, to Luke's astonishment. No matter how much effort one put forth, there was no replacement for faith nor a shortcut to mastery. "Do. Or do not," as Yoda put it. "There is no try."

Belief was essential to victory; so was compassion. Luke would fail at times, Yoda knew, but as long as he kept striving and learned from his mistakes, as long as he woke each day resolved to make better choices than the day before, he would progress on the path of the light. By giving up, surrendering to the dark side, he would be lost, as Vader had been.

These simple truths were more easily grasped by Jedi younglings, whose uncluttered minds were not yet hampered by what could or should be and the emotional baggage of life experience. Luke's adult mind remained unfocused, easily distracted. During one exercise, he was so put off by R2's beeps as he lifted stones and the little Jedi through the power of the Force that he *dropped* Yoda. More significantly, just as Yoda was beginning his lesson on attachments, Luke's attention was disturbed by a vision of the future and his friends suffering.

One could argue that the Jedi Order's complete severing of emotional attachments had actually led to their own demise, a stifling of a natural inclination to the point of ruin. Yet the wisdom that the teaching derived from still held true for Yoda even in exile, exemplified by Luke's angsty abandonment of his quest to become a Jedi, and the fight against the Empire, at the first sign that those he cared for could be hurt as a result.

When Luke glimpsed Han and Leia in danger, he dropped everything—including the crates he was holding with the Force and R2, who had been floating serenely through the air—his control vanishing as his anxiety surged. Like his father, he could not see beyond the people he cared for and his own need to protect them. He didn't care if his rashness toppled the precarious Rebel Alliance and undermined all the sacrifices that had been made. Yoda was blunt about the consequences. Abandoning his training and rushing to save them could mean the difference between life and death for his friends, but would risk destroying everything for which they had fought and suffered.

This was a key difference in the twins' characters: Whenever Leia was faced with a decision, she suppressed her personal feelings. Time and again she proved that she would not betray what her parents and her planet had died to preserve. But Luke's heart ruled his head: With his training incomplete, and the fate of the galaxy hanging in the balance, he left Dagobah, promising to one day return and finish what he'd started.

As his ship departed, Yoda, who surely knew training Luke was a risk, saw history repeating itself. Like Anakin, Luke allowed his personal attachments to get in the way or his spiritual journey, and rushed to put himself in grave danger. At the hands of Darth Vader, a Jedi still so untrained and emotional could be manipulated for evil even as he strived to do good.

Chapter 23

The City in the Clouds

On Cloud City, the tibanna gas mining colony hovering serenely over the planet Bespin, the past caught up with Luke and Leia. In an echo of that freezing night on Hoth, when the base's shield doors were secured with Luke and Han lost somewhere out among the snowdrifts, Leia nearly lost both the man she loved and the brother she had not yet discovered. It tested her own ability to suppress her personal feelings for the benefit of the rebel cause.

While Luke was on his Force pilgrimage on Dagobah, Leia found herself at the mercy of Han Solo's piloting antics, a position that left her exasperated and yet grudgingly appreciative of the man's ingenuity and creative thinking. Despite a faulty motivator on the *Millennium Falcon*'s hyperdrive, Han managed to keep Leia and the rest of the small crew safe from the Empire, avoiding a run-in with three Star Destroyers and navigating a hazardous asteroid field. Unfortunately, despite his best efforts, to Leia's dismay she found herself aboard the *Falcon* when it was swallowed by a sleeping exogorth. But in the face of dismal odds, Han managed to escape from the gullet of this mineral-munching space slug. They finally found respite in the Anoat system, where the *Falcon*'s star maps pointed them in the direction of Han's old friend, Lando Calrissian.

From the moment they landed in Cloud City, there was something about the man that Leia instinctively distrusted. The former smuggler and gambler claimed to have reformed in the years since he and Han had last met, reinventing himself as the administrator of the mining colony. Without knowing the details of Han's past with his peculiar friend—in fact, their dealings had not always been friendly and Lando maintained that Han had cheated him out of his ship in a game of sabacc—behind Lando's smile and fine cape Leia detected a con artist. She had met enough dignitaries and sycophants to suspect that Lando's obvious charm was part of some long game. He reminded her of the unscrupulous politicians she'd encountered in the Galactic Senate, always out for themselves, and the callous Moffs who enslaved their people while they reclined in Imperial-funded luxury.

Leia soon learned that her intuition was painfully accurate. The Empire had arrived before the *Falcon*'s landing gear had even touched down. Although the colony was outside the Mining Guild and Imperial jurisdictions, Lando had cut a deal.

His patience with his own commanders waning, Darth Vader had hired the bounty hunter Boba Fett to do what his army could not: Find Luke Skywalker. By corralling Luke's friends on Cloud City, Vader had baited a trap, one that he soon sprang in the name of the Emperor. Lando claimed he had had no choice in the matter and was simply protecting his people, but Leia knew there was always a choice. Like Kier, Lando chose the people *he* cared for rather than the greater good of the galaxy at large. In Leia's estimation, that made Lando a coward, afraid to stand up to the Empire. And it was fear that had gotten the galaxy into its ideological mess.

With Luke on his way, Vader decided to use Han to test out a new form of brutal imprisonment. Afterward he would turn the smuggler over to Fett as payment for a job well done.

The carbon-freezing facility was a crude chamber built for industrial use. Leia gazed at Han, committing his face to memory, realizing it might be the last time she would ever see him. For once, it was Han who was stoic and calm. In their last moments all together, Chewbacca struggled with a stormtrooper standing guard, and Han—somewhat uncharacteristically concerned for someone other than himself—soothed the Wookiee. Han's courageous demeanor as he was being led to what may as well have been his execution, broke Leia's resolve. She could be strong when she had to be, tough when it was up to her to rally those around her. But Han didn't appear to need her fortitude. With one last kiss, Leia made her feelings known—she had realized for some time that her affection for Han was growing into something romantic—and Han, never good at expressing his emotions verbally, simply replied, "I know." The carbonite-encased brick thudded on the ground. The freezing process had dissolved Han's binders, leaving him frozen, a look of shock imprinted on his features. He was comatose, but still alive. For a second time, Leia had allowed herself to develop romantic feelings only to have her beloved ripped away, a casualty of bitter conflict.

Vader ordered Leia and the rest of Han's friends to be taken to his ship, and placed the facility under Imperial control, terminating the Empire's agreement with Calrissian. Fortunately, Leia's true identity remained hidden from Vader; he was solely, obsessively, focused on capturing Luke, his son, with no thought or even inkling of a second child born from the union of Padmé and Anakin.

Trusting the Empire had been a gamble, and, realizing he'd lost, Lando tried to redeem himself by freeing Chewbacca and Leia, hoping they would also liberate Han. However, Leia was too late to save the man she loved. The bounty hunter Fett spirited Han away and Leia and the others set off in pursuit in the *Falcon*. Thus Luke was left utterly alone to confront his own fate in Cloud City.

***

To his credit, Luke was fearless when he arrived. When he came face to face with Darth Vader inside the carbon-freezing chamber that day, he ignited his lightsaber brashly, full of confidence. But the duel would not be anything as straightforward and easily settled as in the cave on Dagobah.

As they fought, Darth Vader counseled him in the ways of the dark side, trying his best to entice his son to see the world from his perspective. On a metaphysical level, it was as if the dark and the light sides of the Force were holding a debate with Luke in the middle. Yoda had made his arguments for the path of the righteous, but Vader argued for the alluring benefits a life of power and control over others could bring.

The ruckus spilled into the reactor control room with Vader showcasing his strength, tearing pylons from the wall to toss them at Luke. It was as if Vader thought he could prove his superiority by beating Luke down, in the same way Palpatine and the traumas of the war had diminished Anakin's resolve.

Bombarded, bruised, and bloodied, Luke was sucked through a broken window and left dangling precariously from a gantry plank over a yawning reactor shaft. But Luke managed to pull himself back up onto the walkway and slice through the shoulder of the Sith Lord's cybernetic suit, cutting into the flesh of his arm—a jolt of fresh pain. Other than the Emperor's wrath, his own self-hatred, and the existential dread he felt whenever his thoughts turned to Padmé, there had been few in the galaxy that could wound Vader since his rebirth on the Empire's operating table. The fact that Luke not only dared to fight him but managed to land a blow while relentlessly resisting him was infuriating.

Only then did he unleash the full force of his wrath, chopping his blade through the flesh and bone of Luke's saber hand, his weapon—the saber that Anakin had made—swallowed by the gaping shaft below. In Luke's pain, Vader saw an opportunity for his son to realize the true power of his lineage. As Luke dangled from the edge of the gantry, Vader reached for the most potent weapon in his arsenal. He revealed his true identity as the young man's father.

How many times had first Anakin, then Vader, pleaded to be accepted by another? Years of rejection had only served to harden Vader's heart.

But with a malleable child, born of his blood and strong in the Force, Vader saw a lifelong ally and also a shadow of his former self. With his hand held out in invitation to his wounded son, Vader made the same offer he had presented to Padmé shortly before her death. Together, he believed they could unseat Palpatine, restore order to the galaxy, and install their own dynasty of Skywalkers. Father and son. Their natural-born strength in the Force would make them unstoppable.

Denial, rage, and an agonizing regret for all the times he'd wished to know his father and to be more like him, pulsated through the young Jedi apprentice. Vader was sure that joining the dark side was Luke's only recourse, as it had been his own.

But Luke was not his father. An otherworldly feeling of calm settled over him as he made his decision. Instantly weighing the choices between giving in to Vader's demands and sacrificing himself, Luke let go of the walkway, resolved to fall to his death in the abyss below. He refused to share Vader's dismal fate, rejected by those he held dear or giving in to his basest feelings of anger and hate. Death was better than betraying the rebel cause he had fought for, and everything Obi-Wan and Yoda had taught him.

The story of the Skywalkers may well have ended then and there. But Luke did not die that day.

Sucked into an exhaust pipe, he tumbled through the bowels of Cloud City only to be dumped out on the underside of the floating metropolis, dangling from a weather vane.

Luke called out for Ben Kenobi. The Jedi's specter had warned Luke that he would be on his own, yet Luke had still believed that in his moment of need, Ben would materialize in the Force and somehow save the day. When Ben did not answer his cry, Luke instinctively called out to Leia.

In his naivety, Luke may have believed that the Force was a conduit to anyone he hoped to reach. Alternatively, he may have already suspected, on a subconscious level, that Leia was also imbued with a sensitivity to the Force, and that they were indelibly linked in some fashion.

Aboard the *Millennium Falcon,* which had only just made its escape through the orange-hued dusk of Cloud City, Leia heard Luke's call through the Force and quickly weighed her options. Doubling back meant losing Fett's trail and consigning Han to an unknown fate. Yet losing Luke to the Empire was a much graver risk to the Rebel Alliance. She didn't understand the Force, not entirely, but she had seen enough to believe that Luke was somehow essential to the Empire's defeat. She had grown to care deeply for them both. But Leia's primary concern lay with the fate of the galaxy and the Rebellion's best chance of victory would not be well served by her chasing after a smuggler when she could save the commander who had destroyed the Death Star. While R2 made the necessary fixes to restore the ship's hyperdrive, the *Falcon* swooped and scooped up Luke's battered body.

Leia swallowed her grief and took charge, hoping her show of resilience would be enough to keep everyone else going. It was Leia who was the one to tell Luke what had become of Han, in the clutches of the bounty hunter Boba Fett being ferried further and further out of reach. She gracefully took on the role of concerned general and friend, without revealing her own fears in the process. In private, she could let herself feel the depth of her emotions. In front of Luke and the rest of the crew, she remained stoic. More than that, Leia performed her duties as a leader in battle faced with a soldier who had been demoralized, wounded, and beaten. Leia did her best to comfort the injured young man as he voiced his grief over Ben Kenobi's duplicity and his arm, mutilated by a monster who claimed to be his real father.

Among the moisture farmers, such injuries were, if not common, at the very least accepted as the cost of doing business. One slip while unclogging a vaporator or removing the stones from the gears inside a landspeeder's engine compartment, and a Tatooine farmer might spend the rest of their life with a crushed knuckle or face the amputation of an entire limb. But those machines were docile, their programming so simplistic they lacked the sentience of even a basic droid. The machine that had stolen Luke's hand was something far worse. His *father*.

Bacta sprays soothed Luke's cauterized wound. However, no remedy could ease his mind, which lingered on the emotional torment occasioned by Darth Vader's confession. In those moments, Luke felt even more lost and confused than he had on Dagobah. Aboard the *Falcon*, he could feel Vader encroaching upon his mind.

It wasn't entirely corruption Vader sought; it was consideration. The human part of him still longed for his son to join him of his own free will. And that shred of humanity was desperate to find the belonging he had lost with the death of his wife.

For a time, Luke suffered through the tangled mess of his own noble instincts, Vader's insidious proposal of shared power, and Kenobi's evasive story of Anakin's demise.

Luke knew that he couldn't trust anything Vader said and yet, searching his feelings, he was hard-pressed to reject the idea. Mentally exhausted, he searched for answers in the Force. He called out again to Ben, wondering over and over—if Vader spoke the truth—why Ben hadn't revealed the dark secret of his parentage. When Luke tired of calling for Ben Kenobi, he reached through the Force to Master Yoda. He felt certain the Jedi could hear him, sense his pain, maybe even see what had become of him. However, Yoda, too, remained silent.

It was enough to make Luke Skywalker want to quit.

Chapter 24

Unfinished Business

For several months, Han was missing—locked in his carbonite slumber, neither able to fight or flee from his appalling predicament. Leia refused to give up. As she was fond of saying, "Hope is like the sun. If you only believe it when you see it you'll never make it through the night."

During their time apart, Leia threw herself into the primary task at hand—rebuilding the Rebel Alliance. She took over command of the *Millennium Falcon*, commandeering the freighter for the cause. Lando would have taken back *his* ship in an instant, but between Leia's glowering stare and the threat of Chewbacca's muscular paws, he thought it wiser to back down.

Even in those uncertain times, Leia was proud of all the Rebel Alliance had accomplished. But such feelings were tempered by the urgency of the work that remained, the battles yet to be won, the toll of countless fighters lost in the war. Being in charge meant sending soldiers to their deaths, and Leia never grew complacent with the weight of her duty. It was one of the reasons she preferred taking action to giving orders. At least when she was in the heat of the battle, on the frontlines or bringing up the last ship in a dire evacuation, she knew without question that she had taken on the same amount of risk that she asked of her fellow rebels.

Luke faced up to the repercussions of his crippling emotional and physical infirmities—the latter being much easier to mend. The duel with Darth Vader and all it encompassed aged Luke in the time that followed. He emerged a changed man whose relationship to so much of what had become his identity—the memory of his father, the Force, the Jedi—shifted perilously in an instant.

Luke, hero of the Rebellion, struggled. In the aftermath of Vader's traumatic revelation, Luke, no longer blind to what Anakin had become, was forced to comprehend the grave character flaws he could have inherited. His heirloom lightsaber was lost. With the truth of his paternity, he now had a new and debilitating legacy to ponder.

Even Vader, or more accurately the part of him that still whispered the name Anakin Skywalker, felt compelled to search his past for answers.

Soon after the rebels left Bespin, they faced a firefight. With Leia in charge they barreled into the fray, the *Millennium Falcon*'s unmistakable hull drawing its own squadron of TIE fighters away from the larger fight. The ship had become an easily identifiable symbol of the Rebel Alliance spirit. With Leia in command, the Imperial army was even more eager to destroy the ship and silence one of the Empire's most outspoken enemies.

Luke tried his best to help, taking the controls of the belly gun with his good hand. Reaching through the Force, he took control of several enemy TIEs at once, sending them crashing into one another. But instead of elation at the victory—the hole ripped through the Empire's blockade allowed 90 percent of the rebel ships caught in the battle to make the jump to lightspeed—Luke felt shame for what he'd done. And in that shame bloomed a singular rage—not toward Vader or the Empire—but toward the Jedi.

At around the same age Anakin had been when he became the Sith's servant, Luke felt abandoned by the Jedi he had trusted. He was also prey to a nagging fear that, if what Vader had told him was true, then all hope might be lost. If Vader was right, first Ben and then Yoda had *lied*.

And Luke couldn't puzzle out why they would withhold such a momentous truth from him except to manipulate him into doing their bidding. Which brought Luke to a startling conclusion—the Jedi were no better than the Sith. Their intentions may have been noble, but their execution was seriously flawed. The light was no stronger than the darkness, and both could bring a man to ruin. If he couldn't be a Jedi, as Ben had promised, Luke wondered what he *would* become, with his singular combination of Force abilities and unchecked emotions.

A medical droid grafted a mechno-arm onto the stump of Luke's right hand, a lifelike replacement covered with synthetic skin. For a time, Luke retreated into himself, focusing on therapeutic blaster practice to make his mechanical arm truly feel like an extension of himself. Briefly, he cut himself off from the Force altogether.

***

Each of the Skywalkers walked their own lonely path, tethered to the past.

Vader became even more obsessed with locating his son and punishing anyone responsible for concealing the child's existence. He ordered his officers to scour the galaxy for the son of Skywalker, then personally followed up the most promising leads. Instead of the young man, Vader found charlatans who had grown their hair to match Luke's and adopted an astromech partner to make a quick credit.

When the leads ran dry, Vader turned his attention toward the work he had started when he struck down Kenobi: destroying all those who had conspired against him and, in his estimation, made his son too weak to answer the call of his Sith destiny. Accompanied by a squad of death troopers and an Imperial forensics droid, Vader explored his own past.

Vader traced Luke's steps all the way back to the cradle of the Skywalker family: Tatooine. Ironically, this was the first place Luke was recorded as living and the last place Vader had thought to look.

Confronted by his own haunted past, there Vader found no real answers, only pain and rage. His mother's grave had been virtually obliterated by human intervention or drifting sand. Either way, the very event that had set him on his path to the dark side was all-but forgotten by the natural world, a matter of insignificance in its history. And in the Lars home, he imagined, neither Shmi nor Anakin had been mentioned with much enthusiasm, if at all.

In the burned-out shell of the hovel Vader stood over the scorched stone dining slab where Cliegg Lars had admitted defeat and accepted Shmi's death and darkened the door of the garage where Anakin had tried to mend his wounded heart by losing himself in some meaningless task. Vader tried to shrug off the phantasms, but they clung to his black cape, irrefutable tokens of his own past. In his joy over discovering Padmé's pregnancy, Anakin had wanted to be present for his son's life. But it was the Lars family that had nurtured and cared for the child, raising him as their own in the place that Shmi had made her home and that Anakin had decreed as her final resting place.

Vader moved on to Coruscant, to the apartments of the woman who had carried Luke, a place that, as Anakin, he had known intimately. Some 23 years after his last night of fitful sleep in Padmé's chamber, Vader stood among the dust-covered furniture searching for a clue. Palpatine had claimed that Anakin had killed Padmé in his rage, but once Vader knew she had survived long enough to deliver the child, he was determined to discover *who* had seen her die, and to have his revenge.

A transmitter in the home they had shared led him to the jungles of Vendaxa. There he came face to face with Padmé herself—or rather, her ghost. She seemed taller, and older, but she wore the same look of determination, the carefully twisted brown hair, and she spoke with the commanding voice of a queen. Padmé was dead, he told himself furiously: The woman standing before him, hovering in the air as he clasped one hand around her throat through the Force, was not Anakin's bride.

Part II: The Twins
Princess of Alderaan

Breha and Bail Organa of Alderaan
cradle baby Leia, their adopted child.

The Farmer's Nephew

Obi-Wan lived a hermit-like existence
as Old Ben, while, from a distance,
he watched over Luke.

Young Luke Skywalker,
before joining the
Rebel Alliance.

Luke's uncle and aunt, moisture farmers Owen and Beru Lars,
attempted to instill respect for hard work in their adopted son.

One of Luke's jobs
was maintaining
the moisture
vaporators that
surrounded the
Lars homestead.

Obi-Wan and the Call to Adventure

Mon Mothma and Bail Organa: key architects and leaders of the Rebel Alliance.

Princess Leia's hologram message, urging Obi-Wan Kenobi for help.

The Death Star

Destroying the Empire's Death Star superweapon, which obliterated Leia's Alderaan homeworld, made Luke a hero of the Rebellion.

The rebels launched their attack on the Death Star from their base on Yavin 4.

Shabby, but tough and super-fast, the *Millennium Falcon* became a symbol of rebel resistance.

The Princess and the Scoundrel

A portrait of Leia Organa.

Han Solo and Chewbacca—adventuring smugglers who became pillars of the Alliance.

Han Solo and Leia Organa in a quieter moment between the two passionate freedom fighters.

The Last Jedi

The swampy jungles of Dagobah, scene of Luke's arduous training to become a Jedi.

Yoda, as he looked when Luke Skywalker first met him.

The City in the Clouds

Cloud City—the location of the fateful duel between Darth Vader and Luke Skywalker.

Former smuggler Lando Calrissian, seen while he was the Baron Administrator of Cloud City.

Han Solo, imprisoned alive in carbonite.

Darth Vader awaits his quarry in a banquet room on Cloud City.

Unfinished Business

Leia and Luke aboard an Alliance medical frigate after their narrow escape from Darth Vader on Cloud City.

Gangster Jabba the Hutt liked nothing better than seeing his captives suffer.

The Battle of Endor

The Rebel Alliance gathers to learn of a second, more powerful Death Star.

The Ewoks were fiercely opposed to outsiders, but Leia won them over to the rebel cause.

The Ewoks' Bright Tree Village on Endor.

Redemption

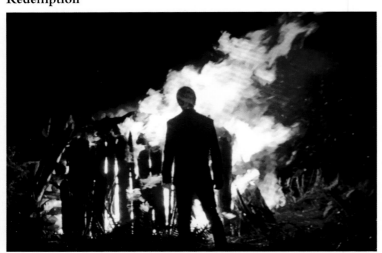

Luke stands in front of Vader's funeral pyre on Endor.

Part III: The Dyad

Heir to Anarchy

Supreme Leader Snoke of the First Order.

The melted remains of Darth Vader's helmet, kept by Kylo Ren.

Darkness Rises

Ben Solo—forbidding and helmeted as Kylo Ren.

Han and Leia embrace during their brief reunion at the Resistance base on D'Qar.

A gathering of First Order soldiers on Starkiller Base, just before the destruction of Hosnian Prime.

And Light to Meet It

Ahch-To: location of the first Jedi temple.

Rey as a scavenger on Jakku.

Luke's failure to train Ben Solo in the ways of the Jedi led him to turn his back on everything he had known.

This Jedi temple mosaic found on Ahch-To represents the duality of the Force.

The Sacrifice of Luke Skywalker

The Skywalker twins share a final moment during the Battle of Crait.

Ben Solo Reborn

A resurrected Palpatine prepares to unleash the Final Order.

Kylo Ren in pursuit of Rey on Pasaana.

A Sith wayfinder: vital to tracking down Emperor Palpatine.

An ancient Sith dagger, found on Pasaana next to the remains of the assassin Ochi of Bestoon.

The wreckage of the second Death Star on the ocean moon of Kef Bir.

Epilogue

On Tatooine, Rey raised her golden lightsaber, looking to the future as proud guardian of the Skywalker legacy.

The Skywalker lightsaber.

It was soon revealed that more than two decades after her death, Padmé's handmaiden Sabé still guarded her friend's home from afar, as if keeping watch for a holy spirit prophesized to return. The handmaidens of Amidala were loyal to the end. Sabé had been the queen's double, a bond unlike any other the young queen and politician had enjoyed. And after Padmé's untimely death, Sabé had come to believe that someone had stolen Padmé away and murdered her. Sabé wanted to avenge both the fallen queen and Anakin Skywalker, unaware that she was already standing before all that remained of Padmé's valiant knight, and believing that Vader had likely killed them both.

In the rolling hills of Theed, the handmaidens who guarded Padmé's tomb prepared for battle. However, for Vader, fighting her servants exposed him to a welter of highly disturbing emotions. A gap in Vader's armor had appeared when he reached for his son's acceptance, but fighting the veritable twin of his dead wife brought forth feelings of almost unbearable regret. Sabé looked most like Padmé, but even the others—who had survived the Naboo invasion, the assassination attempts, and the Clone Wars—all exhibited her poise and determination. They could have passed for her sisters, down to their mannerisms—imprinted when they were just teenage girls in charge of a planet. Although Vader choked Padmé's handmaidens into submission, he could not bring himself to end their lives.

Then he committed a transgression that was low even for Vader: he broke into Padmé's tomb. On a pillow sewn from Naboo silk, he found the japor snippet a besotted young Anakin had carved for a queen—a token to ensure she would remember him. He then cracked open the doors of her crypt. The striking façade of her coffin, carved to match her beautiful face in repose, fully exposed the growing weakness in his heart.

How many nights had he woken next to his bride and seen that face, so calm and serene? So vulnerable yet trusting. Vader reached through the Force to break open the stone sarcophagus, but visions of Padmé in life and in his final embrace—choked by *his* hand—flashed unbidden through his mind. The pain that had fueled him for decades turned into a whimper, replaced by a torrent of grief.

He tried. He failed.

Vader could not bear to look upon the bones of the mother of his son, her decaying flesh surely almost as unrecognizable as his own skin, mottled beneath his helmet. Instead, his droid scanned her remains and located a medical implant that led Vader to his final destination.

Polis Massa had been abandoned, and the maternity ward was in a shambles, but inside a midwifery droid's damaged databanks, Vader found the possible starting point of a new beginning. On a holovid recording, made after the twins were ferried away from their mother, he watched as Padmé beckoned to Obi-Wan with her final breath. Despite all Anakin's mistakes, his betrayal of her and the galaxy, Vader learned that Padmé had used her last moments to declare her undying belief in the righteous heart of Anakin Skywalker. In the words of his long-dead wife, "There's good in him. I know . . ."

Something inside Vader's soul awoke, bleary-eyed: doubt. Vader had allowed himself to wallow in his grief. Instead of feeding the darkness, he began to question his dedication to the Sith. After more than two decades, the conflict within the soul of Anakin Skywalker was reignited by the love of the woman who had refused to believe he was irredeemably damaged.

***

Not long after the incident on Bespin, Lando Calrissian convinced Luke and Leia to return to Cloud City. Leia, least of all the rebels, and Chewbacca a close second, weren't inclined to forget or forgive him for the role he'd played. Nevertheless, the rebel band allowed him to persuade them back to Bespin because it held secrets they needed to unlock: Luke wanted to retrieve his lightsaber; Leia needed to understand the processes underpinning the decarbonization chambers.

When the time came to rescue Han—and she fervently believed that time would come—she did not wish to rely on anyone but herself to finish the job.

Luke returned to the wind tunnel where Vader had severed his hand and his father's lightsaber was lost. There was power in retracing his steps, in reliving the moments of his failure and seeking the lessons that could be gleaned from his defeat. He had no doubts that he and Vader would meet again.

In the trash heap of Cloud City, Luke searched fruitlessly for his heirloom weapon. Eventually, he abandoned all hope of seeing it again; however, he was able to recover his X-wing fighter.

Luke found himself drawn to an alternate path, one that diverged from the challenges immediately facing the rebel cause. He was more determined than ever to discover the mysteries of the Force and become a Jedi, but with an important caveat: He no longer wished to follow in his father's footsteps. He no longer even wished to hold Ben Kenobi in the same esteem, if he were being truthful. He sensed that a different road, all his own, lay before him, leading him to do better than those who had come before him. Through the Force, he felt the first glimmer of knowledge, something beckoning him toward a destiny that was neither tied to the Jedi of the Republic nor bound to his father's wickedness. Leia was sympathetic to Luke's quest, both as a general and a friend, granting permission for him to pursue it, but not everyone was so forgiving of the son of Vader.

The Force beckoned him to the crystalline blue tides of Serelia, where a woman named Verla told Luke the sad truth of the Jedi purge, and of the inquisitors, the Force-wielding Jedi hunters led by Darth Vader.

Neither Jedi nor Sith, just a sentient being with a touch of Force-sensitivity, Verla had been chased across the galaxy, hunted by Vader and his minions. Given Luke's power and Vader's paternity, the young man realized then that Vader would not rest until he had found his son and turned him to the dark side. Like Han Solo and his debts, Luke could not outrun his past. And in his newfound identity, Luke also learned that the galaxy at large—and Verla in particular—would not easily pardon him for the sins committed by his father.

Verla tried—but failed—to drown the young man in a water-filled pit; if not for his faithful droid R2, zapping Luke with a jolt that helped him splutter back to life, she may have succeeded in her revenge. But Luke's response disproved her estimation that he was no better than his father. When given the chance to kill her, Luke spared Verla's life, a small but important step in proving he was not a monster of his father's making and given to revenge.

In compensation, Luke learned of a repository of Jedi relics on the planet Tempes, an ancient Jedi outpost, abandoned long before the shroud of the dark side had fallen and condemned the Jedi Order. The planet's surface was pulverized by electrical storms, but inside the ruin, Luke found the first of many relics and tools that would help him begin to understand the light of the Jedi, as well as their shortcomings.

The lightsaber hilt looked old, a decorative design that was more flamboyant than his first Jedi weapon. Aurodium plating finished the tip, which ignited in a brilliant yellow blade, as luminous as the twin midday suns of Tatooine. To earn the weapon, Luke battled a ghostly version of the Grand Inquisitor, who was standing guard, caught in limbo between resting in his grave or serving the Sith. Luke vanquished him. His laser-sword skills still needed work, but surrounded by the statuary of noble Jedi, Luke felt his resolve rekindle, a sincere belief that the galaxy held people and ideas worth fighting for.

When Luke returned to the rebels, he felt calmer than he had in years. Guided by the blazing light of his new lightsaber, he held the weapon aloft, a beacon of hope and solidarity. Leia insisted on these theatrics. The rebels were on the run, being hunted by the wrathful Empire, and for all she knew their cell was the last one remaining.

Luke's saber, an artifact from the golden age of the Republic, was a symbol of all they hoped to achieve and were willing to die to attain.

***

While Luke had been away, Leia had been dealing with the pressing matters of the civil war, driven by reason—unflinching and with purpose. Leia's young life could be characterized by a series of near-impossible choices. Save her planet or save the rebel cause? Save her parents or save what they fought for? Run after Han or go back for Luke? It was exhausting. But instead of letting herself feel the weight of it, she barreled through the pain and the doubt. It was what her parents had done for years, putting on a brave face while keeping the Rebellion hidden and thriving. Leia never forgot that she'd been left in charge because the Organas, Bail in particular, were made into martyrs. She used her pain to steel her strength. Although Leia never did get used to the salutes and doe-eyed stares from recruits and admirers, she understood honor and the terrible price many families, including her own, had paid as a result of the conflict. Even when the Empire cracked the Rebellion's coded transmissions and jeopardized the cause's future, Leia did not falter. "Bail Organa did not live to see the Empire fall," she told the war-weary rebels who remained, her resolve like a shield to protect them all. "We will."

It was during this time that the rebels explored the galaxy's past to find the key to their future. They devised a plan, Operation Starlight, to reunite their scattered fleet. From the Imperial museum, the rebels brazenly stole the archaic linguistics droid that held the skeleton key for a dead language—Trawak—that formed the basis of a new encrypted code. Over the long months of separation from Han and the rest of the rebels, Leia pieced together a new, safe way to reunite the rebel fleet and lead them to victory.

Operation Starlight was not without its losses and confrontations. A battle with the dead Grand Moff Tarkin's protégé left Leia shaken, even as she tried to maintain a calm front. Leia understood that her most important role in the Alliance was as a symbol of resistance. She risked her life when necessary, but by then had identified the line between bravery and foolishness. However, there were still moments during the Galactic Civil War when Leia saw no other option that to put herself in harm's way, taking a page from the Empire's playbook to willingly bait a trap when it could benefit the rest of the Rebellion. If she were being truthful, Leia preferred to be at the center of the action.

Leia's status as a general gave her access to the most classified information. When Bothan spies discovered evidence that the Empire was constructing a second Death Star superweapon, Leia was in the briefing room for the full report. In the daring gambit known as Operation Yellow Moon, Leia concocted a scheme to distract Imperial operatives from the Rebellion's desperate preparations to amass the forces needed to destabilize the Death Star II: She placed herself at the forefront of what Mon Mothma astutely referred to as "a wild bantha chase." Leia was keenly aware that, to be believable, any ruse needed to have a kernel of truth, so she exploited the fact that the Empire *knew* rebel forces were gathering troops and sympathizers. Leia used their intel to her advantage by embarking on a faux recruiting mission in the Corva Sector. She hoped that Rebel Alliance activity, coupled with the appearance of a wanted fugitive, would be enough to invite Imperial investigation, and distract the Empire from the Rebel Alliance's real work: destabilizing the Death Star II's shield generator on the Moon of Endor in order to destroy the superweapon. Unfortunately, the rebels would later learn that Emperor Palpatine was not ignorant to their grander plan.

The second Death Star symbolized everything Leia and her fellow resistance fighters feared about their enemy. Its construction suggested that the Empire was capable of learning from its mistakes and wealthy enough—in resources, credits, and expendable service people—to build whatever it desired. The second battle station was far larger than its predecessor and, the rebels assumed, free of the fatal flaw that had allowed them to destroy its first incarnation. Even with its jagged, mid-construction outline, the superweapon underlined the futility of everything Leia fought for, what her parents had died for, and what the rebels continued to strive for. Its appearance punctuated one of the general's most pressing concerns about her own organization. Without a base of operations, Leia worried that the fleet's constant motion, small task forces flitting from star system to star system for safety, made the rebels look weak in the eyes of the people that mattered: the citizens who might one day rise up to become allies.

During their years of service together, Luke and Leia formed an attachment to one another that neither had experienced before that time. It was if, before they understood their connection, they could sense a familiar soul. Among Leia's other few friends were heroic fighters and leaders like Evaan Verlaine, an adept pilot and orphan of Alderaan, the reformed Sullustan smuggler Nien Nunb, and the mother of the Rebellion, Mon Mothma with whom she shared a trust born when Leia was still a teenager, when her parents still failed to see her value to the cause.

When Leia found she didn't have to put herself in the line of fire, she relied on a specially trained team known as the Pathfinders, their name a nod to the formative course that had prepared Leia for the demanding physical and mental work of opposing the Empire. A fighter named Kes Dameron and his wife and pilot Shara Bey were among her most trusted operatives. Their young son, Poe, was born during the conflict. Like other children of rebels of his generation, his parents sacrifices would not prevent him from having to continue the fight against their common enemy.

Leia never lost the personal touch that kept the rebel cause distinct from the faceless cruelty of the Imperial way. She keenly understand that *how* they won was as important as victory itself. And when the time was right, she turned her attention back to finding Han Solo. Even with a bounty on his head and a target on his back, despite his loud complaints, Han never abandoned the Rebellion. It was a small comfort to Leia that she had confessed the depth of her feelings to Han before he was frozen and hauled away as a trophy for a crime boss. For several painful months, she didn't know if Han was alive or dead, safely in Jabba's clutches, or murdered for sport. It crossed her mind that he could have been claimed by the gangster only to be jettisoned among the stars, floating like the shipment he'd dropped while on a smuggling job for the Hutt—the source of their longstanding quarrel.

Once the Rebellion's counter maneuvers were under way in what would come to be known as the Battle of Endor, Leia and Luke turned their attentions back to their missing friend. With the help of a wily Force-sensitive pirate of advanced years, Maz Kanata, Leia secured a bounty-hunter's disguise to infiltrate Jabba the Hutt's lair in a three-pronged plan of Luke's creation.

By the time they reached Tatooine, Luke was putting the finishing touches on a new Jedi weapon, a hilt designed in homage to the weapon carried by his friend, Ben Kenobi, with a kyber crystal that glowed emerald green when ignited. The weapon set him apart from his father and his mentor. The saber was a symbol of his growth toward becoming a Jedi Knight.

Luke hid his weapon inside R2-D2, then sent the droids into the crime boss's fortress while Leia secured an audience with the corpulent Hutt, offering Chewbacca as a prisoner and concealing her true identity beneath the helmet of the Ubese scoundrel Boushh, her voice growling through a vocoder.

While Jabba's court slept in a drunken stupor, Leia crept back to where she had seen the carbon block hanging on a wall, and used the information she'd gleaned on Cloud City to free Han. Their reunion was cut short when Solo, still blinded and battling the tremors of carbon sickness, was tossed into a cell with Chewie.

Jabba's reputation as a repugnant and unforgiving crime lord preceded him; even among the Hutts. The clan prided itself on its ability to carry out slavery, debauchery, and illicit dealings of all kinds with impunity, and Jabba was regaled as one of its most fearsome leaders. He savored torturing anyone who wronged him, both as a form of entertainment and a blatant warning to those who dared to cross him. It was not enough for Jabba to incarcerate Leia. He wanted to humiliate her. Leia was forced to don the attire of a servant with a heavy shackle fixed around her neck, tethering her to the Hutt's grubby, slime-slicked hand. The outfit alone was demeaning. Outwardly, she took it in stride and held her head high, but for years to come, Leia would recall the acrid stench of grease and smoke that clung to Jabba's dingy lair, and the weight of her chains. They epitomized all the reasons Leia fought against the Empire, a tangible reminder of the alternative if the rebellion lost.

Not long after it seemed the rebel plot to recue Han had been foiled by Jabba, Luke arrived. His Force powers transfixed the crime boss's majordomo but were ineffective on the Hutt himself. Luke tried to bargain with the gangster, but was instead sent to his dungeon. There he narrowly evaded the hungry maw of a rancor while Leia was made to watch from the safety of the Hutt's throne. In his youth, Luke would have panicked at the sight of this massive voracious beast. But thanks to the calm resourcefulness he had gained during his Jedi training, he was able to slay the monster by crushing it with a heavy gate.

This feat did not earn Luke or his friends a stay of execution, however. Enraged by the Jedi's triumph, Jabba sentenced all but Leia to death by digestion in the belly of the Sarlacc a hungry creature that was mostly teeth and tentacles residing in the Pit of Carkoon.

But as Jabba and his sycophants watched the spectacle unfold from his party barge, the final part of Luke's plan took shape: R2 tossed the Jedi his weapon. Luke and Han put up a fight, and in the chaos, Leia smashed the controls of the Hutt's throne, plunging the room into darkness. In the dim light, the sheer power of Leia's loathing gave her the strength to strangle her revolting captor with her own shackles. Leia was disgusted by the satisfaction she enjoyed in that moment, yet could not deny that it felt good to fight lawlessness with lawlessness, and silence the gangster who had tried to put an end to the rebels.

Some would come to call her "Huttslayer." The legend that arose of her heroic deed, would give many less powerful gangsters and thieves pause before crossing her and rivaled even the starry-eyed tales of Luke Skywalker. Yet it also suggested that even the normally calm and collected Leia Organa could succumb to the spindly hand of the dark side, let her emotions run wild, and enjoy the power of annihilating an enemy.

Chapter 25

The Battle of Endor

The events surrounding what would come to be known as the Battle of Endor would prove critical for both the Rebel Alliance and the Galactic Empire, as well as the individual members of the Skywalker clan.

After four long years on the run, planning strategic attacks on Imperial resources but rarely having the luxury to pause, rest, and reflect, General Leia Organa was looking forward to a time when peace and democratic unity would be restored to the galaxy. However, she was still unsure what form that future would take. She remembered her upbringing on Alderaan as tranquil, but even those happy years were tinged with the understanding that her parents, from the moment they adopted her, had lived in fear of the Empire and its retribution for perceived slights and acts of defiance. The damage and devastation left by the Clone Wars, the fracturing of the Republic that led to the conflict, meant that the galaxy had remained in turmoil for nearly 30 years. Though young—still only 24—and idealistic, Leia realized that the road ahead would be long to rebuild some semblance of security for the many citizens who had only ever known tumult and crisis, herself included.

With Han back among rebel ranks, Leia dared to consider what her own personal destiny might look like as well, beyond her inevitable political duties: It was a foregone conclusion that, given her pedigree and rank she would be among the architects of the New Republic. For the first time in nearly a decade, the princess considered the possibility of a future that would allow her to settle down and raise a child of her own.

Luke Skywalker had completed all but his final Jedi trial— confronting Darth Vader—to set him firmly on course to become the first member of a new Jedi Order in a generation. Even without a master to guide him, Luke had found a way to reconcile himself with the true story and nature of his family.

Just before the pivotal battle, Luke made a brief return visit to Dagobah to keep his promise to Jedi Master Yoda. As the marshy planet came into view, he had a moment to reflect on how much had changed in the year since he'd first traveled there in search of tutelage in the Force and the ways of the Jedi. Luke had walked a solitary path toward understanding what the Jedi Order had once been and his own family's role in its destruction, piecing together what he could from ancient relics and his own intuition. The man who arrived on Dagobah was a very different individual to the frenetic young fighter who had crashed into Yoda's swamp on his first visit.

Luke arrived just in time to find 900-year-old Yoda on his deathbed, moments from breathing his last and transforming into a luminous being through the cosmic Force. However, their final lesson would be crucial for setting Luke upon the path to his true Jedi trial. Years before, Yoda had sent Obi-Wan to destroy Darth Vader at the Sith Lord's inception; now as he lay dying, the Jedi Master instructed Luke to confront Vader and resolve the conflict within himself and the galaxy.

For Luke, his final meeting with Yoda in the flesh forced him to come to terms with the truth of his identity as the son of Vader and his own anger over what he saw as the Jedi's deception. Luke had come to the conclusion that Yoda and his old friend Ben had kept the information about his parentage hidden to ensure that he would kill his father without hesitation. That assessment suggested a degree of manipulation that was totally unacceptable. Luke saw it as a serious moral failure that he had not been given the chance to agree to the task in full knowledge of all it entailed.

But while Yoda confirmed the truth of Vader's confession, he made one critical point of clarification to upend the young man's wounded and skewed perception of the Force-wielder's failings. The Jedi had never intended to keep the knowledge of his paternity from Luke, but had hoped to wait until he was fully trained and could bear the burden. Yoda had believed that only when Luke had completed his training would he be able to shoulder the full responsibility of his destiny. And before he had finished learning the ways of the Force, Luke had fled on his foolhardy quest to evade the future.

Resigned to the fact that Anakin Skywalker lived, but was transformed into the Empire's loyal enforcer and Sith Lord Darth Vader, Luke found his initial feelings of vengeance gave way to compassion. To his surprise, he couldn't hate his father, despite what Darth Vader had become and the ways he'd personally attacked and wounded, not just Luke, but so many across the galaxy. He could not condone Vader's actions, but the complexity of human nature allowed Luke to condemn the Sith and the Empire and still find within himself pity for the man behind the mask. Buried somewhere beneath all the rage and hate festering in Vader's psyche, there still lingered some remnants of the good man he had once been, fighting valiantly to defend his friends and the Republic. Like his birth mother, Luke clung to the hope that good would prevail.

The rebel fleet massed near the planet Sullust as the Battle of Endor commenced. Armed with intel that the Empire was constructing a new Death Star, one even more massive than the first, the rebels sought to avail themselves of a crucial advantage: the space station superweapon was still under construction. Using a two-pronged attack, the Skywalker twins were among members of a strike team deployed to deactivate the weapon's protective shield generator on the planet's surface, while the rest of the rebel fleet prepared to bombard the weapon's main reactor from the skies above.

Newly promoted General Han Solo volunteered to lead the ground forces, posing as the captain of a stolen Imperial shuttle. Even before they had evaded the Imperial blockade, Luke had his first inkling of trouble—he could sense Darth Vader through the Force, a dark presence hovering nearby on the *Executor*, the Empire's command ship. From the bridge of his flagship, Vader could sense his son as well.

Luke initially feared that his presence had endangered the rebel mission, but as Vader and the Emperor had been adamant that the young Jedi must be taken alive, it is equally possible that Vader's recognition that he was aboard the shuttle traveling to Endor actually ensured the strike team safe passage to the moon's surface.

In the calm of the evening before the rebels were due to mount their attack on the Death Star's shield generator, Luke entrusted Leia with the burden of his truth and its implications on her own identity. He knew his next steps were precarious, and he owed Leia his candor in case he failed to return from his personal mission to face the Sith.

Leia was shocked to learn that Vader, a creature of the darkness who had killed so many, was Luke's father. However, she was utterly appalled by Luke's next admission: that Vader had fathered twins, and Leia was Luke's sister.

Feeling the surge of recognition through the Force, Leia immediately accepted Luke as her brother. How often, as a child, had she longed for a playmate, a sibling, another person to understand exactly how she felt? But coupled with her elation was the crushing recognition of the pure malice that was her birth father, hidden behind his angular, emotionless mask yet so often within reach.

For Leia, it wasn't just that Vader embodied the very evil she had fought so long to defeat, a principal leader of the tyrannical organization that had killed her parents and destroyed her planet. It was the fact that Vader himself had tortured her aboard the first Death Star inflicting such agonizing, searing pain that she had wondered, even if for just a moment, if death wouldn't be preferable to endurance. She was sure Vader had sadistically enjoyed inflicting such trauma on her, even though she couldn't see his face. Furthermore, Vader had forced her to witness everyone she had ever loved being wiped out, along with the planet that had been her home. She could still recall the viselike grip of his metal hand on her shoulder.

The list of Vader's subsequent atrocious crimes included savagely maiming Luke on Cloud City, and having Han imprisoned in a block of carbonite that could have well been his coffin, not to mention his deeds during the countless battles between the rebels and the Empire. Leia knew she could not ascribe blame to a single individual for the crimes committed by the Empire, or the casualties the rebellion had endured. But in every instance, Vader seemed to play a crucial role. As much as the Skywalker twins were emblematic of the Rebel Alliance, figureheads of the cause, Darth Vader was the dreaded symbol of the Galactic Empire.

Both Luke and Leia now realized that, in a galaxy at war, Skywalker was pitted against Skywalker. The remnants of their birth father lingered within the life-supporting suit of the dreaded enforcer.

Leia struggled to understand Luke's feeling of compassion for a monster for whom Leia felt only hatred. Somehow, amid all that hate, she would have to begin to come to terms with what it meant to be the offspring of a man capable of such cruelty. Still, the word "father" would only ever conjure the serene smile and crinkled eyes of Bail Organa in Leia's mind.

The shameful secret of their birth would haunt the twins for years after that night on Endor, and cast a pall over the next generation. But for nearly two decades, the only person entrusted to keep their secret was the man Leia trusted as much as Luke—Han Solo.

Unwavering in her dedication to the rebel cause, Leia soldiered on. As she had many times during the war, she pushed aside her personal feelings, debilitating as they could have been, put on a brave face, and completed the mission. And she did it with the full knowledge that her victory could mean her brother's death. Leia knew that Luke's plan to surrender himself to Vader and the Emperor would take him aboard the superweapon the rebels intended to destroy. At the core of the Skywalker twins heroism lay a willingness to give their own lives for the future. Luke was prepared to sacrifice himself for the Empire's defeat; Leia had been prepared to do the same, aboard the first Death Star and numerous times since. So Leia pushed her fearful thoughts aside as she prepared to land the killing blow to the Empire her own father had helped sire.

In the early morning light, as Luke surrendered to Vader and father and son departed for the Death Star, Leia and her team crept toward the Imperial bunker. In their brief time on the moon, Leia had managed to secure the allegiance of a native tribe of aliens called Ewoks. Small but mighty, this relatively unsophisticated species had no truck with intruders on their forest home and had developed ingeniously simple ways to trap their high-tech foes. Using booby traps and spears, they easily captured the rebels. But thanks to Leia's deft negotiating skills, the Ewoks helped the rebels sneak through a secret entrance and prevent an Imperial victory.

Although Leia was injured during the firefight, her team was able to knock out the Death Star's shield generator, giving Lando Calrissian his shot at destroying the superweapon from the helm of the *Millennium Falcon*.

Chapter 26

Redemption

As the rebels fought to destroy the ultimate Imperial war machine in the forests of Endor and the stars above, Luke Skywalker prepared to put forth a remarkable proposal to Vader. Instead of a duel to the death, Luke intended to offer him a way out from the dark side's perverse labyrinth.

At Palpatine's urging, Darth Vader had finally called off his search for Luke Skywalker as the second Death Star neared completion. The Emperor was sure that, just as Anakin's love for Padmé had been the impetus for his transformation to the dark side, Luke's compassion for his father would be the young man's undoing. In one fell swoop, Luke would inherit the legacy of the Sith, or die in defeat, and the Death Star II would silence the pesky freedom fighters for good. Palpatine savored the prospect of a front-row seat for the Empire's final victory and a chance to gain a new, young, even more powerful apprentice.

Luke's surrender that day was a courageous maneuver to penetrate Vader's mask and speak to the remaining shreds of humanity in Anakin Skywalker. Luke insisted on calling his father Anakin. Even though Vader protested that it meant nothing to him, both he and Luke knew that that wasn't so.

Luke then attempted something that no one had dared to do in nearly a quarter century: Luke asked his father to leave the Sith and join him on the side of the righteous. For a man who had known only rejection by his wife, his mentor, his apprentice, and all the others he had cared for besides Palpatine himself, this simple kindness stirred something in Vader. Luke's mother, Padmé, had been the last person to invite him, despite his flaws and misdeeds, to come with her, accepted and absolved of his crimes. She had offered him a way back, but he had been too blinded by power and the allure of the Sith to take it.

Luke was the first person to see past Vader's mask since Padmé. A handful of loyal servants had observed his human features, obscured by bacta or uncovered in his meditation chamber, but none had truly *seen* him. However, unlike Padmé, who had shared a long and loving relationship with Anakin, his son had no reason to offer his father unconditional love. Luke's compassion startled Vader; and Luke could sense the growing conflict in Vader's psyche. Like a wanderer lost in the labyrinth of his own tattered mind, Vader suddenly perceived the first inkling of a way out and dared to believe such a thing was even possible.

Luke's earnest offer struck a chord with Vader, but not in the same manipulative way as the Emperor had employed his mind games. Luke had simply offered his forgiveness.

The entire gambit was predicated on the idea that if Vader were really his father Anakin, hidden in plain sight, masked and unrecognizable, then Luke had to believe would lay down his life rather than allow his own son to die. After all, Vader had refused to end Luke's life on Cymoon I and on Cloud City, when, on both occasions, he could have easily killed him. But he hadn't.

Anakin's mentor, Obi-Wan had protected the child. Anakin's lightsaber had defended the young man. But Anakin himself would have to rise up to save Luke Skywalker's life when faced with the Emperor's wrath.

As we now know, the seeds of doubt had been percolating for some time within Darth Vader's psyche. Yet even after Luke and Vader's brief exchange—which, for a moment, left Vader sad, almost apologetic, exhibiting not the emotions of a Sith Lord born of flame and pain, but of a Jedi finding the strength to begin acknowledging his failures—Vader still believed himself beyond rescue and past the point of redemption.

***

Luke feared that he may have overplayed his hand when he was delivered to the Emperor in binders. It seemed certain that either himself or Vader would have to die. The survivor would serve as Palpatine's apprentice.

At the dawn of the Empire, two Jedi Masters had faced two Sith Lords and lost. It seemed highly improbable that a Jedi still in training could defeat Vader and Palpatine in combat. But though Luke lacked Yoda and Obi-Wan's lightsaber skills, he possessed qualities they had lost sight of when they faced their Sith foes. Luke was not hampered by anger or shame in the Jedi Order or himself. By the time he faced Palpatine and the combined powers of master and apprentice, the key elements that set Luke apart were clarity of purpose and empathy.

Luke looked upon Vader not with hate but with sadness and regret. Faced with the wrinkled visage of the Emperor, the man who had single-handedly orchestrated the Republic's demise and crafted the cruel despotism of the Galactic Empire, Luke was defiant, confident that the rebels would win the day. He even taunted Palpatine for his own overconfidence.

Palpatine was prepared for Luke's show of hubris. He had allowed rebel spies to learn of the existence Death Star II specifically to draw Luke into his clutches.

Meanwhile, the rebel attack run had been abandoned when General Calrissian realized their signals were jammed and the whole thing was a trap. It seemed certain the entire Rebellion would be snuffed out when the battle station was revealed to be fully armed and operational, despite its half-built appearance.

Faced with Palpatine's cunning ingenuity, Luke lost control, taking a few perilous first steps toward the dark side. It seems clear that Palpatine was intent on completing his collection. Maybe he thought Luke would prove even more powerful than his father—younger, less constrained by physical maladies, more malleable, without the indoctrination of years of Jedi training and values. Palpatine taunted Luke, urging him to strike him down, calling him his apprentice, and cackling with delight as Luke's anger flared. In the heat of the moment, Luke forgot Yoda's warning and, pulling his weapon to his palm through the Force, ignited his blade and slashed at the withered leader. Luke gave into aggression, just as his father had so many years before.

To defend his master, Vader deflected Luke's attack. As they battled, Luke perceived the conflict blooming in Vader's heart, but the Sith Lord used Luke's openness against him, exposing his feelings for his friends and Leia in particular. Something in Luke broke as Vader claimed he would turn *Leia* into a puppet of the Sith if Luke resisted. The young man's thoughts had betrayed the secret that had kept the twins safe for more than two decades. Anakin's love for Padmé had sent him spiraling down the path of the dark side; Luke's brotherly love for his sister, only just revealed, nearly caused him to hurtle down the same void.

The savageness of Luke's attack surprised Vader, who was unprepared for Luke's explosive reaction. He pushed Vader backward and forced him into submission, raining a barrage of hacking slashes down on the cowering Sith Lord. Vader tried to defend himself, but one of Luke's blows landed on Vader's wrist, severing the complex system of metal and wiring that allowed him to grip his weapon.

Palpatine recognized the spirit of his prized pupil Anakin reborn in his son. Luke recognized it himself in Vader's defeat. But instead of following his father's brutal descent into darkness, Luke snapped out of his murderous trance, rejecting what he was in danger of becoming.

Luke was not so far gone that he couldn't turn back to the light. He had given into hate, but it did not have to dominate his next decision. So in keeping with the principles of the Jedi, in the face of evil, Luke showed mercy. He lowered his weapon. Luke refused to kill Vader.

Neither Palpatine nor Vader were prepared for this turn of events.

The Emperor naturally saw Luke's refusal to dispatch Vader as weakness and unleashed his dark lightning, sending an agonizing current ripping through Luke's body, the flashes reflecting in the lenses of Vader's mask.

How often had Vader been on the receiving end of Palpatine's wrath during their many years as master and servant? Vader had lost count. Each attack had made him feel more powerless, more helpless, and thus even more a slave to Palpatine's whims. The only way to avoid such persecution was to do his master's bidding. And even when he did so, Vader realized, he was at best rebuilt and at worst replaceable. There was no real trust between him and the Emperor no sense of equality; certainly no love. Palpatine had created him, named him, and controlled him, refusing to allow him any connection to the man he had been, sensing the danger of the humanity Vader had repressed. Any hint of Anakin Skywalker in Vader was met with pain. Vader was made to serve or suffer, the good in him perverted by Palpatine's manipulations. The dark side demanded unquestioning loyalty and servitude, and Vader had done his best to satisfy both requirements. Yet still, Palpatine had treated him as nothing more than a weapon; and for more than twenty years, Vader had submitted, too damaged to defy him.

But Luke, his son, offered clemency and a reprieve from his own depravity. Luke had surrendered himself, faced down the Emperor, and even resisted the dark side's simmering power. He had spared Vader's life when it was his for the taking, and in doing so Luke had paid the price, another Skywalker made to endure Palpatine's tortures.

Vader thought his allegiance to the Sith would make him stronger, but Palpatine was like a creeping disease, infecting everything he touched. The Sith Lord had enforced Vader's loyalty through fear, pain, and cruelty.

Anakin realized he still had the ability to make a choice.

He chose his son.

As Palpatine unleashed crackling jolts of dark lightning upon Luke, Vader seized the Emperor and, fighting through the energy blasts penetrating his cybernetic suit, hurled his master down the Death Star's bottomless reactor shaft.

Soon after, the rebels on the ground disabled the shield generator, and Admiral Ackbar and General Calrissian initiated a second and successful attack run to destroy the second Death Star.

Luke's most powerful weapon against the might of the dark side was his ability to accept things as they were. Instead of denying his father's past, he spoke his name with pride. He was not greedy or possessive, but welcoming, willing to give himself over to Vader, trusting that the man beneath the mask would ultimately do the right thing; and Anakin had delivered, sacrificing himself to save his son and allow the Empire he had helped build to be destroyed.

Luke had refused to become his father, so the father had morphed into something closely resembling his son. And the young man's forgiveness was balm to Anakin's soul. Luke forgave his father for maiming him, for participating in the Empire's evil schemes, for all the death and destruction he had wrought. Luke saw the monster Anakin had become and still he offered salvation. And in seeing that childlike mercy bestowed upon him without qualifiers or requests, the love of his son freely given, Anakin was able to redeem himself. Anakin's heart had condemned him to the dark side in the first place, but, in the end, it also saved him.

The best parts of Anakin and Padmé had prevailed. The father of the Skywalkers had never gained the power to prevent the deaths of those he loved, but in saving Luke and being saved by him, he had tasted the joy of immortality through all that he had passed down to his beloved son.

Anakin was 45 years old when he was finally able to fulfill the ancient Jedi prophecy of the Chosen One. By returning to the light and helping his son vanquish the vile Sith Lord, balance was restored in the Force. By helping his father turn back toward the light, offering him unconditional love, Luke attained what his father, and the entire Jedi Order twisted by the Clone Wars could not achieve. By refusing to fight, to destroy, to let anger eclipse the good in his heart, he had forgiven a monster and revealed a man.

Palpatine's dark energy irreparably damaged the machines that kept

Vader alive. In his final moments, he crumpled beneath the weight of his mechno suit, which was no longer able to assist his breathing. Luke gently removed Vader's helmet to reveal Anakin's pale, disfigured face and found, to his surprise, that Anakin was smiling. At the end of his days in the living Force, Anakin Skywalker was cradled by his son.

The body of the redeemed warrior was given a hero's funeral but his spirit passed on, becoming part of the energy binding the galaxy. And it was Luke who glimpsed Anakin Skywalker's return to the cosmic Force, a vision of Anakin at his best: a young man who was one of the greatest of all Jedi Knights, in harmony with his two greatest teachers, Yoda and Obi-Wan Kenobi.

***

The celebrations did not conclude on Endor. All over the galaxy, thankful populations took to the streets to celebrate the Empire's defeat and the fall of its cruel dictator. On Coruscant, where Palpatine had held court, citizens wound a heavy chain around the neck of his statue and hauled it to the ground. Leia Organa and Han Solo celebrated in a more personal way, by marrying in a private ceremony—a happy conclusion to their courtship beyond their wildest dreams at the height of the conflict.

Yet the chaos of the war continued for another year. The Imperial propaganda machine dispatched categorical denials concerning the outcome of the Battle of Endor, claiming that the rebel attack had failed. Rumors of Palpatine's demise were dismissed or rejected as treasonous. Even holovid footage of the second Death Star's destruction was met by brazen rejections. Fighters on both sides continued to engage, but the Rebel Alliance began to see the fruit of its labors as resistance movements, emboldened by whispers of an end to Palpatine's rule, rose up against local Moffs and crooked leaders. The Battle of Jakku became the last battlefield to become a graveyard and end the bitter five-year conflict.

The building blocks for a new era of peace were slowly moved into place by rebel loyalists, like the architect Mon Mothma, who, having fought the Empire for so many years and survived numerous assassination attempts, was installed as the first Chancellor of the New Republic. She made it her mission to ensure that planets were demilitarized to welcome and ensure a new era of peace.

In time, Leia took her place as a key member of the New Republic's first Senate, a powerful symbol of hope, justice, and democracy. As for Luke, he continued to focus on understanding the power of the Force, buoyed by his success at turning his father back toward the light.

A year after Endor, shortly after the Empire formalized its surrender on the crystal cliffs beneath a tintolive tree on Chandrila, Leia and Han's son was born. Ben Solo ushered in a new generation who, his parents fervently hoped, would know only law and order.

However, while Leia and Han looked forward to a bright future, the past still cast long shadows over the Skywalker family and the galaxy. Even after his death, Palpatine's schemes for galactic domination kept unspooling. In the memory banks of sentinel droids that bore Palpatine's holographic face, a secret contingency plan, devised should his Empire fall, was unleashed. Named Operation: Cinder, its aim was to wreak devastation upon Palpatine's homeworld of Naboo and other key planets. In addition, Palpatine's own genetic line prospered in the shadows, both through the intervention of Kaminoan cloning technology and more natural means.

Graffiti sprang up that claimed that Darth Vader still lived, and a cult known as the Acolytes celebrated his gruesome achievements. They held the dark side in esteem and reverence, and raided the Imperial museum archives for Sith weapons. Some Imperials, temporarily rudderless without their fearsome leader, began to plot a course for a new regime in the Empire's image. Sequestered in the galaxy's Unknown Regions, they waited until the time was right to unleash a new galactic order.

Part Three

THE DYAD

Chapter 27

Son of Solo, Daughter of Darkness

In two generations of Skywalkers there were many pairings: master and apprentice, husband and wife, sister and brother. Anakin and Padmé had been linked by love; Luke and Leia by birth. In the Age of Resistance after the fall of the Empire, a new pairing emerged. It was as if the Force itself were reconciling the reign of the Sith, more than two decades of chaos reaped by Darth Vader and his master, Emperor Palpatine. To make things right, two individuals, born of both bloodlines, would come together, in hopes of finally bringing balance to a divided galaxy.

After their rebellious crusade, Luke and Leia escaped the pull to the dark side, choosing their respective paths wisely. Luke sought balance in his Jedi meditations and the artifacts of eons past, focusing his energy on spiritual study. Leia's equilibrium was founded in service to others, and ensuring that the politicians in power did not manufacture another crisis or unnecessary war on her watch.

Impending motherhood did not dull Leia's sharp mind or her determination to see Bail and Breha Organa's dreams of democracy through to fruition. If anything, the arrival of a new life hastened her need to finish the work her parents had started.

Leia Organa was 24 when she bore Ben at the full-term of pregnancy. With the child's inception, the Force grew stronger in the Skywalker family.

Leia referred to her unborn child as "a little angel." Han affectionately called the baby "a little bandit." Han became a doting husband, watching over his wife when her vitality was sapped by her growing child's needs. When she refused to slow down, his advice to take it easy at least made her pause. However, she hated all the fuss, which increased as her belly expanded. In the last throes of the Galactic Civil War—despite her condition—Leia refused to give up either her military position or her new political career as one of the first senators of the New Republic, which at the time was based on Chandrila. In fact, Leia chafed when anyone referred to her being pregnant as "her condition," irritated that her efficacy as an administrator should be questioned, simply because she was with child.

Leia remained instrumental in the transition of power from the last days of the Empire to the New Republic. However, Han and Luke's attentions were elsewhere. Han had embarked on an urgent quest to find his missing friend, Chewbacca, and help free Kashyyyk from Imperial control, while Luke continued his journey to determine the future of the new Jedi.

The Force remained elusive for Leia. After Endor, she had dabbled in her own exploration of the spiritual Jedi path, with Luke as her patient guide. As Luke's first student, she had even crafted an elegant rose-gold and silver lightsaber hilt for herself. But a horrifying vision through the Force distracted her: a mother's worst fear, the death of her son.

During the nine months she carried him, Leia found the mystical energy spoke to her through the exuberant, restless baby boy within her, sharpening her own sensitivity. Long before he was born, she could sense Ben's wit and intelligence, the intrepid spirit of a fighter—no doubt the perfect blend of his parents, equal parts rebel leader and swaggering smuggler. Yet, coupled with her elation came fears that no parent can fully evade. Amid the instability of the final acts of civil war, Leia was gripped by misgivings over bringing an innocent child, the product of a mother powerless to stem the unrest and a father with an instinct for both fight and flight, into an unstable galaxy,

Leia was plagued by nightmares. In the years following the revelation that she and Luke were the children of the Naboo Queen Padmé Amidala and the Jedi Knight Anakin Skywalker, Leia had come to understand, to some degree, the weight of her family lineage. Through the Force or her own anxious mind, this legacy played out in her dreams. In one, she was alone and dead on an operating table, the mother of two orphaned twins, history repeating itself. Unlike the mystical visions experienced by practitioners of the Jedi way whispering of the future in motion, in the misty fog of half-sleep, she knew without question they were illusions. Still, they haunted her.

Most troubling of all was the vein of darkness Leia felt pulsating through the still-growing boy *in utero*. The knowledge of her heredity and what Anakin Skywalker had become weighed heavily on her thoughts. Luke was content to believe that the monstrous Vader was vanquished when his father was redeemed and turned back to the light, yet Leia did not have the satisfaction of having witnessed his remorse with her own eyes. Her brother eventually convinced her that the shadow she detected was perfectly normal; Leia was not so foolish as to condemn her own son simply because of traits passed down through DNA. Far more important to a child's development, in her estimation, were the influences of those who nurtured the child. Nonetheless, she remained anxious over what she knew to be a troubling undercurrent permeating her family heritage.

During the war, both Luke and Leia had experienced the power their rage could bring them: Leia, in the brute strength she discovered in herself when strangling Jabba the Hutt, and Luke, when, infuriated by the dark side's taunts, he attacked Darth Vader.

Before Ben was born, Leia made the difficult decision to shield her son from the truth of the monstrous Darth Vader's identity until the time was right—just as Bail Organa had kept the full story of Leia's own relation to the Sith Lord from her until she was mature enough to carry the burden.

**

The war ended. Ben Solo arrived. Life, as the Skywalkers knew it, shifted.

Considering the high-profile military and political careers of both of Ben Solo's parents, surprisingly little is known about their child's earliest years, sheltered as he was from the glare of public scrutiny. Ben had his father's pronounced nose and lopsided smile, and his mother's piercing brown eyes. At least that feature, Leia was sure, was inherited from her own birth mother, Padmé Amidala. He had chubby, dimpled hands and a shock of brown hair so dark that it almost seemed black in dim light. He was a cute kid, by most estimations, even if he cried incessantly for much of his infancy. True to his heritage as a Skywalker, he was strong in the Force, an untapped ability that manifested, as it had for two generations, in incredibly quick reflexes, abnormal awareness, and Force-sensitivity. Fortunately, Ben's demonstration of this as a toddler was confined to lifting his favorite stuffed sock Wookiee through the air and into his waiting embrace.

Neither Han nor Leia found the transition from soldiers to husband and wife, parents, and civil servants of the New Republic easy, but they did their best. After five years of terror and triumph, risking her life in battles and secret missions—every minute looking over her shoulder for the next ambush or attack—Leia found domestic life somewhat dull and democratic procedures in the Senate tedious. She believed in what they had fought for and was relieved that the war was over and the Empire dismantled. But for years afterward, Leia had to admit she missed the exhilaration, comraderies, and shared purpose of fighting an enemy.

Balancing the demands of building a democracy from the ground up and caring for her son was taxing even for a person of Leia's resilience and fortitude. Diplomacy sometimes eluded her on mornings when her sleep had been interrupted by Ben's plaintive cries or his sharp toes jabbing her in the ribs. Still, Han marveled at the ease with which Leia seemed able to calm the baby. The infant seemed to instinctively know that his mother would never let any harm befall him, while Han struggled to adapt to his new identity as father. He once quipped: "I smuggle, not snuggle."

While also employing the help of friends and droids, Han and Leia tended to manage the push-and-pull of other demands by taking turns at their apartment to watch over the child. They were present as much as their work and other obligations allowed. Leia recognized that the time she spent away from the boy—exhausting as it was—was still time spent ensuring he had a galaxy to safely grow up in, a benefit she hoped he would recognize in time. Being a parent herself, she came to understand how grueling it must have been for the Organas to raise her, run a planet, aid the Rebellion, and make meaningful contributions to Senate politics.

When he could, Chewbacca was more than happy to spend time with young Ben. The Wookiee could barely believe that his roguish friend Han had settled down and become a father like himself. Leia's motherhood made more sense to Chewie. She had always been a commanding yet compassionate figure in the Rebel Alliance, as quick to give a stern admonishment after an unfortunate incident as she was to celebrate a hard-won victory with a hug and an encouraging smile. After the ordeal on Bespin, Chewie's affections for Han extended in nearly equal measure to the princess. And, of course, the dashing Lando Calrissian, whom Ben called "Unca Wanwo" as he tried to navigate the complexities of adult speech, was more than happy to regale the child with stories of his own daring adventures in the galaxy, his father's smuggling days, and the finer points of living a fabulous life filled with an array of interesting new acquaintances.

When Ben was two years old, the family enlisted the help of a droid, BX-778, adept at both brewing caf and watching over the small boy when his parents were otherwise engaged. The droid's programming was briefly corrupted by a nefarious virus—when Ben was still given to late-night temper tantrums, it nearly slit the toddler's throat. Fortunately, if Ben remembered the incident at all, it remained deep in his subconscious, the stuff of nightmares. Yet it seems possible that it left an emotional scar that influenced his later years.

As he grew, Ben was more often left alone with a droid caretaker. He knew, or at least he was told, that what his parents were doing was important, but in the way that children believe the world revolves around them, he didn't quite believe it.

For Leia, work was senatorial hearings and political banquets. Han, Leia knew, still had a wanderer's heart and she tried her best to understand his need to be in constant motion, especially when his delusions of grandeur and desire to save the galaxy took him away from his family for weeks at a time. When Lando came knocking, demanding Han's help locating a device capable of disseminating a virus that could turn harmless droids—like young Ben's—into killing machines, Leia packed Han's bags for him, recognizing the importance of duty over her own desires.

She made peace with the fact that their union would have to withstand the ambitions of two strong, independent, not entirely compatible people; but their young son undoubtedly felt the rift and found it beyond his comprehension. Leia and Han learned the importance of staying in contact via holo-call. As the years went by, their competing interests forced them to remain apart, sometimes for months at a time, yet they remained devoted to each other.

In time, Han renounced his military rank and turned his attention to the racing circuit, allowing his mechanical skills and prowess as a pilot to inform his career path. He became a respected mentor to hotheaded and daring young pilots, but struggled to find the same ease with his own boy. Han had never really envisioned himself as a parent or guardian. He had no role models to draw on; to him, beating a path through parenthood was like flying blindfolded through an asteroid field and perhaps even *more* deadly. He looked forward to a time when he could show his son how to fix the hyperdrive on the *Millennium Falcon*, or help him procure a ship of his very own. But the quieter moments of nurturing a helpless young child seemed to elude the roguish Solo.

Even before Ben was born, Han allowed himself to daydream about passing along his skills at the helm as well as his mechanical know-how. When his baby son grabbed his aurodium-plated chance cubes, a lucky charm found adorning nearly every ship or vehicle Han had the chance to fly, his pride swelled. But when Ben showed an aptitude as a pilot, Han could not be sure whether that was down to his own genes or the kid's Skywalker blood. Despite being proud of his son's Force-sensitivity, Han could not help but feel pangs of jealousy when the boy decided to follow his uncle, Luke Skywalker, and join his drive to establish a new Jedi Order rather than taking to the simpler, adventurous course of traversing the galaxy with his old man.

***

Rey, born just as Ben Solo was beginning his Jedi training, was ten years his junior; yet the two were indelibly linked by the Force in the form of a dyad. The precise cause and nature of such a thing is shrouded in mystery. Both halves of the Force-centered bond had prodigious strength in the Force, dynastic family lineage, and together, a raw power unseen for generations that had the ability to bring forth life itself. But while Ben's origins were the source of some early consternation, always feeling as if he were being compared to his influential mother or heroic uncle, Rey grew up in isolation and anonymity.

What is known of Rey's early life followed a similar course to Luke Skywalker's own upbringing. She was secreted away on the desert planet of Jakku, to avoid becoming a weapon of the dark side.

Rey was not a Skywalker by blood, yet the young scavenger exemplified many of the Skywalker family's best characteristics. Rey was selfless and independent, surviving on meager rations obtained through barter and trade at the Niima Outpost—named for a Hutt who had once controlled the Goazon Badlands in the barren wasteland. Most of the junk Rey recovered and resold came from abandoned Imperial and Rebel Alliance ships whose jagged hulls were a reminder both of the decline of the Empire and the futility of war. Rey was a skilled pilot, able to navigate the *Millennium Falcon* through a tight spot almost as well as Han Solo himself, as she proved when she stole the ship from a junkyard to escape First Order operatives. She had the same wide-eyed wonder for the galaxy that Leia would have recognized from her own youth. Rey also had a powerful—but very different—connection to the Force.

The influential Skywalkers traced their roots back to the Chosen One of prophecy, but Rey hailed from an altogether different bloodline that meandered through galactic events, exploiting cracks and crevices to favor the Empire with a dark dynasty all its own: Rey was a descendant of the ultimate architect of the Empire, Sheev Palpatine.

Palpatine died, in the normal sense of the word, when his body hit the bottom of the second Death Star's reactor core shaft, moments before the superweapon exploded. But just as the Jedi learned that the living Force could be transformed into the cosmic Force, consciousness that could be reconstituted beyond the grave, the unnatural abilities and macabre obsessions of the Sith allowed Palpatine to be reborn in a clone body of his own creation.

Rey's biological father was the offshoot of Palpatine's genetic research, not precisely a clone but made of cloned tissue and donated cells. His name has been lost to time, as has the reason the young man survived – whether by purpose or neglect. There is no record that the son of Palpatine demonstrated any of the Force abilities that his cruel and powerful father relished. Considering Sheev Palpatine's history, that would have undoubtedly made the boy a disappointment to the man who sired him.

Like Ben, for much of her life Rey had no knowledge of her bloodline. When she was still quite young, her parents sold her to become an indentured servant the same as Shmi and Anakin Skywalker. Rey only remembered her father and mother as shadows. The sensation of feeling loved and cared for remained, but she had no memory of their faces, their names, or the sacrifices they had made to keep her safe. For many years, Rey consoled herself with the thought that, one day, they would return to find her.

Chapter 28

Heir to Anarchy

While Leia was involved with the New Republic's creation, Luke Skywalker continued his spiritual quest. Through ancient relics and cultures he discovered on far-off worlds—entire civilizations made up of beings who touched the Force in ways that transcended the knowledge of the Jedi and the Sith—Luke came to his own understanding of this mystical energy.

A number of years after his first attempt to impart his still-developing knowledge to Leia on the jungle moon of Ajan Kloss, the Jedi Master decided to start his own temple. Luke began his school out of genuine hope for the future of the Jedi Order, a way to resurrect the best of what Yoda and Obi-Wan Kenobi had taught him and instill those core values in the next generation. However, despite Luke's best intentions, his decision set in motion events that would lead to the rise of the First Order and the appearance of Ben Solo's dark alter ego, Kylo Ren.

As Ben neared the age of 10, he was Luke's most prized student. Even without training, it was clear that Ben was gifted in the ways of the Force, a Solo in name but a Skywalker by blood. Leia hoped that Luke's tutelage would keep her son from being tempted by the darkness. But without invitation, the child was visited by an insidious voice. A creature of the dark side calling itself Snoke invaded young Ben's innermost thoughts and, eager to have a friend, he grew to trust—even love—the strange intruder. From his early teens, Ben's inner doubts and fears—of his own abilities, and the power he craved and had yet to attain through the Force—created a fissure that would come to dominate his existence.

The shadow of the darkness loomed large over Ben Solo. On a mission to Elphrona the year he turned 14, while still in the care of his uncle, Ben first encountered the Knights of Ren, a motley crew of dark-side adherents. Inside a Jedi outpost filled with forgotten relics, Luke singlehandedly faced off against the seven knights. He beat them back, defeating them with the Force as his guide and ally. But before they retreated, Ben would recall for years afterward, their leader removed his helmet to reveal both a handsome face and a tantalizing invitation. He offered Luke's young apprentice an alternate course, a path that would allow him to feed on the energy of the natural darkness blooming inside his soul instead of repressing it. Just as Palpatine had first tempted young Anakin Skywalker away from the light, Ren gave Ben Solo the promise of power, if he rejected his Jedi Master.

Ben remained by his uncle's side for nearly a decade after the altercation, and outwardly shrugged off the incident. Yet he never forgot the strange man's face. In addition, the voice of Snoke, a persona of the dark side under the control of a reborn ancient evil, frequently whispered in Ben's ear.

The dark side contained many mysteries, and the boy harbored a grim fascination for it that only Snoke seemed to understand. At times, Luke sensed these flickers of the dark side in his nephew. They grew in frequency as the boy grew to an imposing 1.89 meters in height, a stature emphasized by broad shoulders and a brooding gaze. Although possessing the natural harmony of light and dark that resides in every being, at this time Ben began to exhibit a disturbing penchant for the latter. To make matters worse, the young man was adept at guarding his thoughts and emotions. Still, Luke believed he could help the young man avoid his grandfather's fate, just as he himself had refused to yield to the temptations of the darkness and even assisted Darth Vader in his own vindication.

Luke and Ben traveled the stars, an echo of the life Luke had thought he might lead as a young man leaving Tatooine with his Force teacher, Ben Kenobi. They collected Jedi artifacts, holocrons from bygone eras and strange texts filled with archaic writings. They gathered disciples— young, Force-sensitive beings, adrift, with no way to harness their abilities after the Jedi purge. With a small gathering of like-minded students looking for a spiritual guide and the knowledge of the Jedi of the past, Luke hoped to usher in a new era of enlightenment.

Luke preached patience and balance. He tried to instill the belief that all of his students in the Force were equals. But almost from the first day of his training, Ben believed himself destined for greatness and hampered by worries that he would never measure up to those who had come before him. It's little wonder that Ben would later come to idolize his grandfather Anakin Skywalker, or more accurately his Sith persona, Darth Vader. The other students became his friends, but Ben could not shake the feeling that he was an outcast. Even if they didn't say it out loud, he knew some believed he was the beneficiary of nepotism, a clear favorite, given his relation to their master. In the other students he saw, reflected back at him, his greatest flaws and fears magnified. Feeling ashamed, he vainly sought to quell the persistent insecurities disturbing his peace of mind.

His friend Tai perceived Ben's troubles and the ways he tried to hide them. He counseled Ben to first accept himself, so that others might accept him as he truly was; yet Ben refused to open up about his darkest thoughts and impulses. Another classmate, a human named Voe with gray-blonde hair that made her seem older than her years, struggled to best Solo in everything from lightsaber combat to simple levitation, yet could never quite succeed. Through their friendship, Ben gained a jealous respect for the legendary warriors and Force-users who had come before him. He was ambitious to outdo them, even as he recognized he was fighting figments and shadows for an intangible prize.

Instead of the other students, Ben often felt he was being measured against the generations that came before him, like the wise and powerful Jedi who had trained his teacher, like the esteemed Yoda and Obi-Wan Kenobi, whom he'd never met. It was like trying to beat a ghost at a game of sabacc. The last of the Jedi's old guard had died before his birth, but they meant something to every member of Solo's family. The legacy of the Jedi dominated in the child's psyche.

Obi-Wan Kenobi had fought valiantly in the Clone Wars, and been a friend to Anakin Skywalker. He had heeded his mother's call and given his life to ensure the Death Star plans were ferried to the Rebel Alliance. Moreover, he had been the great Luke Skywalker's first teacher in the ways of the Force.

If Luke worshipped the memory of Kenobi in Ben's estimation, to hear Luke speak of Master Yoda was to witness pure reverence. The Jedi had been regarded as one of the strongest practitioners to ever live, humble and wise, and for Luke he was the ultimate tutor and tester. The basis of his own methods was steeped in Yoda's approach to guiding young minds, passed down from master to apprentice when Luke was himself a young man.

Then there was Luke. Ben Solo could not help but compare himself to his legendary uncle. By the age of 23, Luke Skywalker had helped destroy two Death Stars and redeemed his father. As Ben Solo neared the same milestone, he felt he had accomplished very little and was still nothing more than his uncle's pupil.

***

These events and undercurrents set the stage for Ben's transformation into Kylo Ren. However, the crucial incident that altered both the young man's course and the galaxy itself was the revelation that Darth Vader was his biological grandfather. This disclosure was followed all too soon by a harrowing showdown between Vader's son and his apprentice.

The year Ben Solo turned 23, he remained in his 47-year-old uncle's care, traversing the galaxy on the path to becoming a Jedi. By then, Leia

Organa had enjoyed an impressive two decades of public service in the New Republic Senate. His mother was revered as a war hero and generally regarded as firm but fair. With her still-undimmed beauty and steely stare—the gray hairs peeking through her elegant braids suggested experience and resilience more than age—Leia won respect throughout the capital world of Hosnian Prime, where the New Republic Senate convened, as well as countless planets and species beyond the Inner Rim.

But at this time, in the wider galaxy, the unrest and corruption that had given rise to the Clone Wars and the demise of the Republic were beginning to take hold. Centrists and Populist factions arose, not unlike the Separatists and Loyalists of the past. The historical lessons of the previous 50 years—the rise of the Empire and the Galactic Civil War—were largely ignored. Each new generation took the reins of governance from the one before, and each one made the same inexperienced and disastrous mistakes—decisions that rippled across star systems and embroiled the Republic in conflict. As New Republic leaders struggled to find common ground between themselves, Leia and her colleagues began to detect stirrings of unrest, of wealthy crime bosses and well-armed militias clashing with a democracy founded on the reduction of armaments as a means to a peaceful future.

Recognizing the need for evolving the constitution, after a spate of useless chancellors who were little more than figureheads, Leia, who believed in democracy yet chafed at the grinding gears of government bureaucracy, was the favorite to become a prime candidate for a new position: First Senator. The Centrists—the brightest of whom rejected the Empire's tyranny, but found value in the regime's cornerstone beliefs in strong centralized government—hoped to install their own candidate.

Before the election could get underway, the so-called "Napkin Bombing Incident" ripped apart the Senate building and unleashed a fresh wave of terror, destruction, and uncertainty. Thanks to a hastily scrawled anonymous note—which simply said "Run!"—left on Leia's place setting ahead of a breakfast meeting that day, an evacuation ensured there was no loss of life. The political ramifications of such a brazen attack, however, could not be ignored.

Soon after, Leia's rivals ended her storied career in the political sphere by means of a cruel memento discovered inside her childhood hope chest from Alderaan, which had been in the safekeeping of an Organa relation on Birren. The Centrists unearthed a message that Bail Organa had recorded before his death, disclosing the truth of Leia's biological lineage.

The news that Leia Organa and Luke Skywalker were the offspring of Darth Vader was nearly as explosive as the recent bombing. Overnight, Leia went from an unimpeachable figure to a political pariah. Only a few kind friends remained loyal, risking their own career suicide.

In a galaxy looking for easy answers to complex problems, the Skywalker twins were summarily judged by their biological father's most heinous misdeeds, and convicted in the court of public opinion. Some of their harshest critics suggested that, as the daughter of Vader, Leia could have played both sides of the conflict during the Galactic Civil War, feeding intel to her father even as she pretended to be a leader of the Rebellion. The idea was ludicrous to anyone who had fought along-side the princess and watched as she repeatedly risked her own life to ensure the safety of her troops. Nevertheless, it gained some traction among the most unscrupulous gossips and sensational reporters. Luke's credibility was also tarnished. Doubters even began to question whether he had really fired the shot that destroyed the first Death Star. With a single revelation of the twins' parentage, everything the public thought they knew about the Skywalkers was called into question. Instead of the legacy of Anakin Skywalker, heroic Jedi general, the twins were forced to live in the shadow of Darth Vader, tyrannical Sith enforcer.

The exposé was perfectly timed to destroy Leia's political career and damage her party. In one swift motion, the Centrists rose to power, reshaping the New Republic to their liking. A rival senator whom Leia had come to trust, Ransolm Casterfo, proclaimed the discovery of Leia's parentage on the Senate floor. In Leia's estimation, the least he could have done was respect her privacy and alert her to the information before revealing her darkest secret to the entire galaxy.

Despite Luke's accolades and Leia's years of dedicated service to the Rebel Alliance and democracy, an accident of birth came to define their legacy. To many in the New Republic, nature and bloodline held just as much significance as the choices that a person made to build the life they saw fit, however preposterous that notion may be.

Unfortunately, Ben Solo discovered his own relation to Darth Vader, not via his family, but by holonet news. The revelation felt like a betrayal. Ben, who took after Anakin Skywalker in his powerful Force abilities and hot-headed nature, was crushed by the realization that his parents and his uncle had known the truth for decades yet had not seen fit to share it with him. He was incredulous that he had been left to discover the damning fact along with what felt like everyone else in the known galaxy. And the fact that his family had kept such a dramatic piece of information hidden seemed to justify every dark impulse and feeling of paranoia he'd entertained in his young life.

Too late, Leia recognized her error. Had she felt less shame in the knowledge, and less hatred for Vader himself, perhaps Leia would have answered Ben's questions about his lineage in a more age-appropriate manner. Slowly, she could have unspooled the truth, with Luke's help. Leia, after all, had told her husband the night after she had learned of this bombshell herself, in the elation that followed the victory on Endor. And Han, to his credit, had not allowed it to dissuade him from loving her.

Somehow, Leia and Han never found a time when it seemed right to saddle their son with the knowledge, and explain the nuances of Vader's complex past. Leia sent a tearful and urgent message to Ben after the news broke, but it was too late. The damage had been done.

Although Leia was known for her rational, quick-thinking in the war room, a part of her thought that the dark element of her past might just vanish in time. The possibility was more than mere wishful thinking. Darth Vader's identity was a closely guarded secret for years; of the few who knew, most had taken the fact to their graves, without disclosing it to a single soul. More than two decades after the wrathful Sith Lord's demise, and Anakin's return to the light, Leia had found no biological evidence on file to connect Vader to the Jedi he had been, and thus no irrefutable proof that either she or Luke were his children.

Arguably, Luke should have learned his own lesson about the damage wrought by the disclosure of Vader's identity. The private revelation Vader had made to Luke on Cloud City had shattered the young man's understanding of his own identity and his trust in the Jedi who kept the secret from him. In Ben's case, the disclosure had a similar impact, with the added detriment of making him feel as if nearly everyone in the galaxy was looking at him differently.

In the discord that followed, Ben began to doubt his family and question their plans for him. His anger bloomed, red and hot, giving the more devious elements in the galaxy the perfect opportunity to foster his basest instincts and most primal emotions for their own uses.

The voice calling itself Snoke used Ben's anger to cap off a decade of cunning manipulations. The vein of darkness that Leia had sensed even before Ben was born, and Luke had recognized growing in his student, was stronger than ever before, stoked by Ben's suspicions and every desire he had repressed that ran counter to Jedi teaching. Every cruel thought and savage intention fed into Snoke's doctrine to turn Ben Solo into a tool of the dark side. He whispered promises into the young man's mind, pledging that his guidance, combined with Ben's raw, untamed power would transform him into a figure even greater than Darth Vader himself. Rather than merely competing with the heroes of the past, Ben believed he could rise to eclipse the most feared member of his family. What Snoke omitted was that, for the Sith, power was traditionally attained through great sacrifice. After all, Anakin had lost his wife and his autonomy on the altar of the dark side.

In the early years of Ben's Jedi training, Snoke had warned him that his equal in the Force would one day rise up to match his strength. Only by slaying his equivalent in the light would Ben fulfill his potential, he was told.

One fateful night at the Jedi temple, Luke Skywalker—so sure in his youth that everyone, including Darth Vader himself, could be redeemed through the simple act of choosing to do better, choosing to *be* better— made a critical error that cemented Ben's transition into Kylo Ren.

The story differs depending on the teller.

As Ben Solo saw it, that night he awoke to find his master—his own uncle—standing over him with his lightsaber ignited, prepared to kill him as he dozed. Ben believed Skywalker sensed his power and feared it.

From Luke's perspective, he had realized the mistake of his own arrogance in believing himself strong enough to sire a new Jedi Order and keep the dark side at bay. That night, Luke had done something shameful, an act that in itself was far more invasive than a Jedi should have allowed. While Ben was at his most vulnerable and unguarded, Luke had peered into his slumbering nephew's mind, and glimpsed the encroaching darkness. Interpreting visions of the future is a dangerous gambit. But just as he had on Dagobah during the early days of his tutelage under Yoda, Luke Skywalker saw the shadow of a potential future where the people he loved most were suffering, a flood of destruction and misery.

In a contemptible moment that would replay in his mind for years to come, Luke ignited his lightsaber. For a moment, the darkness in Luke's own psyche flared to life, fanning the gentle flame of fear, and without thought or intention he moved on instinct to eliminate the threat before him. His training took hold to banish the demon, without the conscious realization that doing so would mean ending his nephew's life.

But his base instincts were quickly interrupted by the realization that the light and dark he sensed were dueling parts of Ben Solo's psyche, and Luke put down his weapon. Too late. Ben awoke to see Luke looming over him in an aggressive posture, and grabbed his own lightsaber in self-defense.

Luke would later attest that Snoke had already turned Ben's heart. And for a moment, Luke allowed himself to fall victim to the ever-shifting future he saw unspooling because of Ben Solo's iniquity, an era punctuated by pain, death, and chaos that once again embroiled the galaxy because a member of his bloodline took vengeance.

The incident changed every member of the Skywalker family.

Luke realized he had failed Ben, even before the dormitory around them came tumbling down, imploding with a twitch of Ben's Force-wielding fingers. The last thing Luke saw were the frightened eyes of the child he had sworn to Leia he would always protect. When he regained consciousness, the temple was ablaze and Ben Solo had vanished, believing he had killed his uncle. Many of the temple students died that same night. Meteorological reports subsequently supported a version of events that placed blame for the fire on a freak dry-lightning storm. Ultimately, Luke retreated into exile, ashamed by his failure.

Dismayed by the loss of her son, yet unable to mourn a young man who still lived, Leia thrust herself back into the one outlet still available to her: the military. She was no longer a royal nor a galactic senator, but the Resistance, a new incarnation of the Rebel Alliance her parents had died for, accepted her willingly into their ranks as a general. Her political fall had no impact on her military clout. Even as her son rose in the ranks as the First Order's Supreme Leader's henchman, Leia refused to sit by and allow the galaxy to return to the sins of the past.

Leia chose to fight. Han chose flight, in a literal and figurative sense. He returned to the stars not as a war hero and Resistance fighter but as a captain, pilot, and smuggler. With his friend Chewbacca, he easily fell back into the life he had known before he had ever gotten mixed up with the Skywalker clan.

But for Ben, the incident was life altering.

Chapter 29

Darkness Rises

In the aftermath of the Temple's destruction, rather than continue denying his darkest impulses, Ben Solo allowed them to feed his soul. The Jedi Temple and all it had stood for felt like an obstacle deliberately put in place to keep Ben from achieving his true potential. Snoke's manipulations were all-too evident in Ben's rejection of Jedi ways and willingness to accept the destruction of his innocence. He came to see the family who had raised and loved him as barriers to his own progress to power.

His fall to the dark side, far from being sudden, was more of a slow descent. Over time, Ben's fascination with Vader became a twisted echo of his resentment for a lifetime of comparisons with the icons who had come before him. If he could not live up to the legacy of Leia Organa or Luke Skywalker, he vowed to surpass the anarchy wrought by Darth Vader, and become even more powerful than the famed Sith Lord. The nagging desire for power and control combined with the apparent deceits of the family he had trusted—with inevitable results. With Snoke finally entrenched as his new master, Ben sought out the Knights of Ren on Varnak in the Mid Rim.

The few students who had avoided the carnage pursued Ben Solo seeking justice, believing he was responsible for their Jedi Master's death. They eventually paid with their lives, although none died by Ben's lightsaber blade. A Quarren named Hennix was slaughtered by his own Jedi weapon when he sent it whirling toward Solo, only for it to be deflected. His friend Tai, wise beyond his years, tried to reason with Ben, arguing that his destiny was still undecided and that every path went in two directions. His neck was snapped by the Knights' captain, Ren. Enraged, Ben Solo avenged his friend's death, slaying the mysterious, masked Ren to take his place as leader. Only then did Ben end his former friend Voe's life upon Ren's red blade.

Ben Solo was a Jedi no more.

Adopting the name Kylo Ren, Ben concealed his face beneath a mask and embraced the nickname "Jedi Killer" both in homage to his grandfather and in acceptance of what he had become. In his remade image, he hoped to convince his family and his followers that he had completely done away with Ben Solo, excising his weaknesses and embracing his true birthright among the dominant purveyors of the dark side.

To complete his transformation, Kylo corrupted the kyber crystal that had carried him through his Jedi training. A sacrificial act all its own, in his haste, the crystal bled crimson but also split, resulting in an unstable plasma blade. Ben's Jedi hilt burned out upon its first ignition and had to be refitted with vents to maintain the crystal's volatile nature. Where Vader had killed a Jedi and taken his laser sword to build his own Sith weapon, Kylo Ren simply tried to make his new identity as a servant of darkness fit within the burned-out shell of his Jedi journey. Its duality and irregular nature came to symbolize his own vacillating and doubt-filled heart.

Vader had been alone and without hope. He had believed himself beyond reform. For years, he had instigated a campaign of terror across the stars with no signs of remorse. A student of the light and the dark, in contrast Kylo Ren embodied conflict. His family remained alive and well, despite his turn to evil. Furthermore, unbeknownst to Ben, a being existed beyond his own flesh and blood, who, thanks to the Force was inextricably linked to his own lifeline. Fate would soon bring the Palpatine bloodline and the Skywalker dynasty swerving toward a new collision.

With the exception of the mask of Vader, a melted and warped artifact that came into Ben's possession and served as an altar of sorts and a reminder of his reverence for the man who wore it, Ben considered his family to be traitors to him and his newfound allies in the First Order. This organization, once dismissed as just a fledgling nuisance by the New Republic, had risen to prominence from the ashes of the Empire. Led by Supreme Leader Snoke, its aim was to restore—in the words of its most fanatical followers—order and dominance to the galaxy. Kylo Ren took the organization's quest for domination one step further, following his own mantra to "Let the past die." He came to believe that the only way forward was annihilation: destroying all that had been; a cleansing by fire that would completely remake the galaxy to the First Order's regimented and rigid specifications. And if the past—including the generation that begat him—refused to cooperate, Kylo Ren was prepared to kill whomever stood in his way.

Just as Vader had served Emperor Palpatine, Kylo Ren pledged himself to act as Snoke's enforcer. And yet, just like Vader, Ben Solo was conflicted by his role, perhaps even more so than Vader had been. Anakin turned to the dark side for control, to prevent the demise of his beloved Padmé, but Ben's turn was a reaction to a betrayal, an act of self-defense.

In the years that followed the night of the Jedi temple's destruction, periods of doubt plagued the young man, a secret he feared he would not be able to keep from his master. He knew the perceived insubordination would cost him dearly if discovered. Still, he chose to be guided by the darkness.

Snoke's methods mirrored those of many of the most renowned and infamous Jedi and Sith masters of old. He and his new student traveled the galaxy to complete the young man's training, an echo of Ben Solo's journeys among the stars by Luke Skywalker's side. It was during this time that Snoke administered a series of tests to ensure that Kylo Ren would be molded to obey without question. Through Snoke's teachings, Ren began to believe that his deepest anxieties could be turned into purposeful rage, a destructive power crystalized through the Force itself and a flagrant corruption of Jedi ideals. Ren believed that, in his fury, he gained a kind of control over his wild emotions; however anyone could see that his emotions were in control of him, not the other way around.

Kylo Ren and Snoke traveled to Dagobah, where the imprint of Luke Skywalker still reverberated through the Force from the first days of his training to be a Jedi. Inside the very cave where Luke had once battled a vision of Vader, Ben Solo made the acquaintance of his own demons. He distilled the seething hate he felt for the uncle who had, in his eyes, pretended to care for him then tried to murder him in his sleep, cutting down the Jedi when he apparated into view. But slaughtering the Force-derived image of the last of the Jedi was not enough for Ren. The ethereal form of Leia Organa and Han Solo took shape as if stepping out from inside his addled mind, begging him to renounce the dark side and return to the family that loved him. He hacked at the image of his parents, scarring an ancient tree in the process, but the couple remained somewhere in his peripheral vision, lingering, yet almost out of sight and mind. Disgusted by his own failure to destroy it, he laid waste to the ancient grotto, tearing down every rock and tree through the Force. It was as much a loss of control as a demonstration of his abilities, destroying the natural world and obliterating Dagobah's past in the process. This display of raw power at least pleased his master.

***

For six years, Kylo Ren served Snoke.

Instead of taking over the seated government as Palpatine had managed, the First Order forces took to the battlefield, using their military might to dominate the New Republic and its Resistance, which was led once more by Ben Solo's mother, General Leia Organa. After 21 years of relative harmony in the New Republic, the First Order sought to restore the galaxy to what it saw as the glorious era of the Empire, once again led by a dark side user and a fallen Jedi born of the powerful Skywalker bloodline. And nearly 50 years after the fall of the Jedi Order, Snoke and his apprentice Kylo Ren sought to crush the last vestiges of the Jedi by locating and, once and for all, killing Luke Skywalker. With the last Jedi dead, along with his disciples—save for the corrupted prized pupil Ben Solo—the leaders of the First Order believed they could rule with impunity once more. Eliminating Luke was key to preventing a new Jedi Order from rising up against them. Only in a power vacuum could the dark side be sure to thrive unchecked.

The year Ben Solo turned 29, in its first debilitating act of war, the First Order unleashed a weapon similar in design to the Death Star, yet even more monstrous. Instead of a technological terror roughly the size of a small moon, the new faction used slave labor to hollow out an entire planet's core. Undetected, in the depths of the Unknown Regions, this process took several years. Once fully operational, Starkiller Base could destroy planetary targets in the Republic without warning, silencing opposition in singularly devastating strikes like nothing even survivors of the Galactic Civil War had ever seen. It was a near-perfect weapon of mass destruction. In its first demonstration of dominance, the super-weapon obliterated every planet in the Hosnian system, including Hosnian Prime, at the time the seat of the New Republic government. The First Order then turned their weapon—which was able to harness the limitless potential of dark energy—to send a colossal blast of destructive power halfway across the galaxy toward the Resistance base on D'Qar.

Instead of obliterating the enemy, however, the First Order's new weapon brought Ben Solo's father to his door, leading a mission on behalf of his mother and the Resistance.

While Ben and Han Solo were estranged, Han had fallen back into his old life as a smuggler, traveling among the stars. He convinced himself that he was unfit for marriage or fatherhood. If a Jedi Master, like Luke, and a skillful negotiator, like Leia, couldn't reach the boy, what could he, Han, be expected to do? However, Leia convinced him to try to bring their son home. Leia may never have fully understood Luke's compassion for their father, but she had unconditional love for her son.

Past disappointments and difficulties came rushing back as father and son met at the heart of Starkiller Base, inside the oscillator shaft. Far above their heads, Resistance forces pummeled the planet that day, desperate to destroy the weapon before it could put an end to their rebellion.

On a precarious catwalk, Han bellowed the name of his child, and he knew in that moment, when the young man turned in recognition, and the single word—"Ben!"—reverberated in a primal howl, that Leia's instincts had been correct: their son was not totally lost. Even deep in the bowels of the First Order's prime weapon, Han believed that given the opportunity, Ben would return to the light.

Ben was not as lost as Vader had been on the day Luke helped his father redeem himself. He still answered to his birth name, his *true* name. At Han's behest, Ben removed his mask and revealed his face.

Han's show of compassion contradicted everything Ben had been indoctrinated by Snoke to believe. He thought his family had betrayed and abandoned him, yet it was he who had walked away. Han approached his child with his arms outstretched to show he bore no weapons or ill intentions. Even Ben could see that Han's demeanor suggested that at least some of what he had come to believe was false. Like Luke surrendering himself to Vader, Han surrendered himself to Kylo Ren in a show of remorse and penance for whatever sins Ben Solo believed he had committed as a parent.

Ben felt bewildered and confused. It was as if the fabric of his very being was being torn to shreds from the tension he carried in his heart, the light and the dark battling for his attention and allegiance. He had long believed that both sides had claimed him at his birth, and that constant strain was the source of his agony and fear. By choosing the dark, which he had convinced himself was the stronger, he hoped to alleviate his stress and emerge victorious. But his moral conscience would not stop tugging at him, despite his best efforts to reject it.

When Ben stared down at his lightsaber, the light briefly held sway. The weapon of the Jedi had been mangled to meet the needs of the dark side, a tortured piece of metal that matched the way its owner felt and had come to see himself.

For a fleeting moment it seemed that Kylo Ren would be vanquished and Ben would relinquish his saber, surrender to his father's love, revolt against the First Order, and return home to his parents, the Republic, and the Resistance. After all, the light of the Skywalker line, and the good in the young man's own soul, had as much claim on Ben Solo as the darkness, if not more.

But on that fateful day, as Han Solo touched the hilt of Kylo Ren's lightsaber, and Starkiller Base charged up to full power at the expense of a life-giving star, a sense of creeping doubt made Ben Solo pause. Perhaps he believed that returning to the light was admitting a kind of defeat, that withdrawing into the life that had confused him since he was a child was a cowardly admission of weakness. In the darkness, Ben felt powerful, commanding, undefeated. The seductive pull of superiority through wrath enticed him anew, even as his father gave in to his will. Ben gripped his saber tightly, ignited the blade, and pierced his father's chest.

For an instant, confusion was replaced by relief. As Kylo Ren, he had chosen the path of the mighty. Compassion was weak, and it had gotten Han Solo killed. But the cycle of good and evil, light and dark, is always in motion, always turning. Even before Han Solo's body fell into the abyss, fresh waves of doubt assailed Ben.

In his shock, the former smuggler reached out to caress Ben's cheek. Even in death, Han refused to believe that his child was a lost cause; that small gesture would haunt the young man far more than the act of violence itself. The touch of his father's calloused hand and the terrible truth of what he had done left him weak, wrung out, and miserable.

To add to his emotional injury, Ben was physically wounded in the firefight that ensued, as Chewbacca fired his crossbow blaster at the villain who had killed his friend. The bolt hit true, penetrating the thin armor covering Ren's abdomen, but only grazed his flesh. In more than 200 years as a warrior, Chewbacca was a *very* good shot. Either he missed in his grief or he could not bear, even after witnessing Han's senseless murder, to bring himself to execute what remained of the child he had once held in his arms—when Ben Solo was just a little boy, who needed his Uncle Chewie to protect him.

Chapter 30

And Light to Meet It

When Rey was 19 years old, her connection to the Force flickered into life in a way that entranced and terrified the young woman. Even untrained, she was stronger than she knew. Through the Force or fate, the young woman came into possession of a Resistance droid, called BB-8, that held a secret map to Luke Skywalker, then the focus of Kylo Ren's obsessive search for his former master. Rey and her new friend Finn, a former stormtrooper who had defected from the First Order, escaped from Jakku aboard an old junker—the *Millennium Falcon*. The ship attracted both the wrath of the First Order and the curiosity of the famed smugglers and war heroes Han Solo and Chewbacca.

For a brief time, Rey and Finn found themselves in Han Solo's custody. In Han, Rey found a father figure who shared her love of mechanics and the fastest hunk of junk in the galaxy, which she flew with precision. Rey was like the daughter Han had never had, someone he dared to dream of bringing on as a second mate to help Chewie and himself. She was smart and nimble, which meant she had an easier time folding herself into service compartments than a Wookie, standing at over 2 meters tall, or an aging rogue. In temperament, Rey was quite different to Ben, optimistic instead of brooding, open and inquisitive instead of guarded. She respected Luke Skywalker as a man of legend and myth, just as Han loved the man who had become his family by marriage. But Rey preferred learning marksmanship with a blaster to swinging a blade of light. And unlike Ben, she held Han's reputation as a smuggler in the same kind of esteem that most held the vaunted Jedi Knights of old, a recognition that flattered the older man's ego.

Yet the Force flowed within Rey's blood and it jolted to life with the discovery of the Skywalker lightsaber. Created at the start of the Clone Wars, passed down to Luke and lost on Cloud City along with his hand, severed by Darth Vader's blade, the legacy lightsaber had ended up in the collection of the old pirate Maz Kanata on Takodana. It was part of the wizened raider's treasure, hidden within the walls of her castle. This precious heirloom quite literally called to Rey through the Force, singing to her with stories of the past and the future. When she touched it, her head swirled with visions from her own life, and images she could not place because they belonged not to her but to the saber itself and the Skywalker line. In a few awe-inspiring moments she was privy to fragments of the blade's history, an unfathomable amalgamation of suffering and success. Yet after this first encounter, Rey was reluctant to wield the weapon and frankly frightened by the power that suddenly swelled within her.

Ironically, the only person who could understand what she was going through was Kylo Ren. Caught by the First Order in their quest to find Luke Skywalker, in a holding cell inside Starkiller Base, Rey and Ren finally came face-to-face for the first time. This encounter set the tone for their unique and contorted relationship. Rey was trapped, confined by a restraining rig that kept her immobilized but not docile, yet it was Ren who seemed snared. He wished her to submit to his demands, to give him access to the map to Luke Skywalker that was emblazoned in her mind and accessible through the Force. When she refused, Ren reached into her thoughts to locate his quarry. But by doing so, Rey gained something perhaps even more valuable: access to the mind of Kylo Ren.

That day, he unmasked himself willingly, a gesture that essentially admitted that wearing the mask of Ren was something of an affectation. Ben employed the blank visage to strike fear into the hearts of those he conquered as much as he used it to conceal his face and emotions. Vader's mask had been a means to live, yet Kylo's served only to disguise him. And by connecting his mind with Rey's, he exposed his deepest fears. For two people desperate for belonging, their communication briefly became a twisted form of acceptance.

But that was before Rey watched Kylo Ren murder his father in cold blood. Whatever vulnerability and humanity Rey had sensed within the young man during their first encounter was erased when she saw what he was capable of.

In the aftermath of Kylo's undoing, as the Resistance bombarded the base and day turned to eternal night with the sun extinguished overhead, Rey and Kylo Ren met in the snowy forests of Starkiller, dueling for the heirloom saber. As much as the mask of Vader dominated the destiny of Anakin Skywalker and every tragic family member to come after, the lightsaber he created was a symbol of the best in the Jedi Knight, his children, and his grandson. By all rights, Kylo believed the blue blade belonged to the Skywalker clan and, as the creation of the man who became Darth Vader, it was an object of some obsession for the dark-side acolyte.

As if taking sides through the Force, Rey was able to call the weapon to her hand, stronger than the pull the conflicted and psychically damaged Kylo Ren could muster, even with his own mastery of the Force.

For Kylo, Rey's appearance was a provocation. Her abilities challenged his belief that the light side was weaker than the dark. Without any formal instruction in the Force, she resisted him, even as he growled that she needed training. Kylo Ren promised that he alone held the secrets Rey needed to thrive. Rey had been surviving on her own too long to be trapped by such an obvious lie. She knew there was always another option, even if it remained hidden, despite what dark-side adherents might claim. To emphasize her refusal to join him, Rey fought Ren valiantly and gave him a vicious slash across the face with the coveted blade. Every time he looked in the mirror after their first duel he was forced to consider this disfigurement and the person who had delivered it.

As the Resistance attack on the base reached its climax, the ground itself buckled beneath their feet, cracked, and split apart. There was no victory or defeat that day for the two Force-wielders, simply a stalemate and the realization that their battle would not so easily be decided.

Rey managed to return to the Resistance Base before everyone was forced to evacuate amid the First Order's retaliation. In the calm before the coming storm, she was greeted by the warm embrace of General Leia.

For Leia, unlike her husband, Rey was more than a chosen daughter figure. Rather, she saw the distraught orphan as she viewed the children of Alderaan after its destruction, like so many other refugees she had encountered through her long years on the frontlines.

True to form, Leia found the strength to comfort the young woman, even as she grieved the loss of her own husband. A chasm had opened in the Force the moment Han Solo had died; even before Rey could deliver the news, Leia knew she had been widowed. The daughter of Vader and the granddaughter of Palpatine were united in empathy and grief.

***

Soon after, on the watery world of Ahch-To, a strange and exotic place for a young woman who had spent years toiling on the arid sands of Jakku, Rey went in search of the legendary Luke Skywalker. What she found instead was a mortal man hiding in his shame.

Leia believed that her brother's mythical status as a warrior and Jedi Knight could rally and inspire the Resistance in ways that eluded her. However, after Luke had watched his Jedi Temple burn and his hopes for the future go up in smoke along with it, Luke retreated into exile on the oceanic planet, choosing to sequester himself on an island that had been the site of the first Jedi temple, the birthplace of the venerable faith dedicated to the Force. The remains of the original Jedi temple included a library containing the most precious Jedi teachings and foundational wisdom, all housed inside an ancient uneti tree. For Luke, these books became a daily reminder of his past arrogance and the failures of the Jedi before him, tangible and inescapable relics of a bygone era of peace. Among the ruins of what he called "the last of the Jedi religion," Luke intended to die in anonymity.

Luke's transformation was not unlike the self-imposed exile Yoda and Obi-Wan had endured after the fall of the Jedi Order, although Skywalker took his resignation from the Jedi one step further. Luke's failure to teach and train Ben Solo was so all-consuming that, to complete his disappearance, he cut himself off from the Force, returning to his roots, farming and foraging, fishing in the crystal-blue ocean for food, and milking the thala-sirens as they sat basking on the rocks, teats engorged with refreshing green milk.

Like Ben Solo, Luke rejected his Jedi past. But instead of turning to the darkness, he followed the path that Yoda had taken following the Order's greatest defeat, by retreating to the fundamentals of existence. In those wretched years, the balance he thought he had attained by helping Vader toward redemption seemed worthless, a ruse perpetuated by the dark side's wicked sense of humor. The young man who had thrilled at fighting for the Rebel Alliance and clashing sabers with the Empire's finest was all but erased by the graying old man who had lost the will to hope that peace and justice could ever prevail.

Returning to the land was a form of penance for Luke, for failing Ben, and losing the son of his sister. In the cockpit of the *Millennium Falcon*, which had brought Rey to his hovel, Luke confronted the ghosts of his past soon after the scavenger appeared on his island perplexingly holding his father's lightsaber in her outstretched hand.

For the last of the Jedi, Han's death on Ben's blade seemed to underline his personal failures. Luke mourned the friend and brother-in-law who had saved his skin on more than one occasion. He was so dejected, it seemed to Rey that nothing would convince him to rejoin the fight. But it was R2-D2 who—as he had long ago on Tatooine—showed him the way.

Projected from some dusty old file deep in the recesses of the astromech's memory banks, R2 dredged up the flickering image of the one person who could convince him of his strength, his resilience, and his ability to right even the most hopeless situation: Leia. Ironically, it was the same missive that had helped convince Luke to join the Rebellion, and take his first steps toward becoming a Jedi. His sister—although he had not known their indelible link at the time—had needed him then, and with the First Order gaining strength, she needed him again. And, as her messenger, she had sent Rey, who was eager to be trained by the last of the Jedi Order—the legendary Luke Skywalker—in the hope of understanding herself and finding her own place in the galaxy.

In Rey, Luke saw a second chance to repent the past in a more constructive manner than wallowing alone on an island. In their brief time as master and apprentice, he strived to teach her more than the basics of mastering the Force. His lessons also focused on the wisdom he'd gleaned when his experiment to resurrect the Jedi and the Order itself had failed. From his pulpit inside the temple ruins, Luke Skywalker preached of the evocative mystical energy and the danger for any mere mortal—be they Jedi, Sith, or something else—to believe they could hold sway over it. The Force could be enshrined but it was far too precious, too powerful, to be possessed. It bound all life together; it was not something to be used as a weapon to control the weak and defenseless.

The Force, the energy keeping the two warring sides of every conflict—life and death, violence and peace—in equilibrium, was strong in Rey. Yet Luke recoiled when he saw signs of the untested power he had glimpsed within his nephew. In his estimation, Rey was reckless in her curiosity, potentially destructive in her inexperience, chaotic in her desire to take action and understand herself. He feared she would not be able to resist the pull of the darkness.

The cycle extended to the dyad itself. As Kylo Ren grew stronger and more determined, Rey's connection to the Force grew with it, the two tethered together spiritually and physically, an attachment like none Luke had seen in his travels or his readings.

A metaphysical manifestation of this powerful connection was an ability to communicate regardless of location. Ben and Rey could see one another clearly, even while they were light years apart. At first Rey was gripped with anguish over the unwanted intrusion. She called him "monster," but the word did nothing to wound the young man, who believed it and owned it, finding power in its suggestion of brutishness. However, as their connection strengthened, in a similar fashion to Ben's welcoming of Snoke's prying voice, Rey began to see her enemy as more friend than foe. They related to one another on a level neither had experienced previously, hungry for companionship, belonging, and acceptance. At this time, Ben was beginning to realize that killing his father had not provided the euphoric release he expected nor imbued him with the power he craved. He thought choosing the darkness would complete his transition, yet he was still plagued by doubts.

On the island, in the well of the dark side, Rey faced her own darkness. And it was *Ben* whom she confided in, speaking through the Force about the nothingness, the sheer emptiness she'd felt in the void. As something of an adopted daughter in the Skywalker clan, Rey and Ben's connection evoked the same strange sense of parity that Luke and Leia had experienced before discovering their mysterious birthright. Meanwhile, her reluctant tutor, Luke Skywalker failed to meet the needs of the parental presence Rey sought.

Rey's connection to Ben Solo strengthened as the days passed. Rey's compassion softened her understanding of the man, and she began to enjoy their strange bond that transcended logic, time, and space, to allow them to physically touch over immense distances. In the

Resistance, in the company of Han Solo and Leia Organa, Rey enjoyed the sense of belonging that had always eluded Ben, an irony, given his parentage. Yet together, they had a link forged through the Force, as if its midi-chlorians were conspiring to bring together their powerful lineages.

In those encounters, Rey began to believe that there was still some good in the young man who chose the mask of Kylo Ren, but could not shake his heritage as the son of Solo and heir to the Skywalker legacy. Ben saw something else: a flicker of darkness inherent in Rey's own bloodline, an ally in his pain and his pursuits.

It was this compassion and connection that ultimately led to a rift between teacher and student, Luke and Rey. When Luke discovered her connection to his nephew, he saw the strange alliance as a betrayal and refused to join her on her quest to bring the Jedi back to the Resistance. For her part, Rey became so disillusioned with Luke's shortcomings as a teacher, a view heavily influenced by Kylo Ren's own lens, that she fled the island on a new quest to find Ben Solo.

At the same time, Kylo Ren was beginning to tire of his treatment at the hands of Supreme Leader Snoke. Ren had fought against comparisons to the heroes of the Rebellion, and rejected following in the footsteps of the Jedi. But in time he recognized that Snoke was little more than another master he was beholden to, not a path to freedom. The faces of those he followed changed, but their desire to coerce him into bowing to their whims did not. Even after he had proven himself by slaying Han Solo, Snoke openly berated him, rebuking him as "just a child in a mask." Ben could change his name and forge a new identity behind a fearsome helmet, but Snoke chastised him for the elements of his identity that he could never fully alter: Ben Solo could not escape who he was. Despite Darth Vader's wrath, the legacy of the Skywalkers, in Snoke's bitter estimation, was one of hope, liberation, and fortitude.

In the woods of Starkiller Base, Rey had not hesitated to lash out in her duel with Ren, leaving him scarred. On the dreadnought *Supremacy*, she surrendered to him, hoping that their connection would help the young man accept her help and face his demons. Her arrival heralded an important step for Kylo Ren. In Rey, Ben saw a potential partner to help him break free from the binders of servitude to Snoke, to join forces for a new era under their united command, unencumbered by the mistakes and accolades of previous generations.

Inside Snoke's chambers, the Skywalker saber left carelessly on the arm of his oversized throne, the Supreme Leader's disfigured and wrinkled body sat swaddled in a flowing golden gown. As Kylo Ren's master, he ordered the young man to kill the Jedi apprentice who was, in many ways, his equal. Snoke was confident that Kylo Ren would terminate the young woman, allowing the darkness they revered to consume the galaxy's last ember of hope as he sacrificed his confidante.

But Snoke had made a serious error of judgment. Through the Force, Snoke sensed his pupil's connection to Rey and his resolve, but he could not see that Ren's hate was directed at his master. With a twitch of his fingers, Kylo Ren spun the heirloom laser sword and depressed the ignition switch, skewering Snoke and cutting him cleanly in two, before sending it sailing through the air into Rey's waiting palm. Wordlessly, the dyad went from preparing to fight each other to standing back-to-back. While a battle between the First Order and the Resistance raged among the stars outside, Rey and Ren's combined powers made quick work of Snoke's remaining Praetorian guards, proving the efficacy of their powers working in tandem.

Their unity was shortlived. Rey and Ben had each glimpsed the future they most hoped to see through the distorting lens of their respective desires. In the smoldering ruins of Snoke's rule, Rey believed Ben would join the fight to aid the Resistance, while in Rey, Ben Solo saw an apprentice, a person who understood him completely and was willing to fight at his side.

With his master lying dead on the floor, the shadow of Kylo Ren returned, an ebony pall. Ben's raw emotions took over, turning him into the very thing he had fought against. The doubts that assailed him following Han Solo's demise were replaced by determination. Kylo Ren resolved to take Snoke's place as Supreme Leader. Immediately, he took on the posture of his former master, bellowing at the minions who served him, abusing his military foes through the Force, and chastising his would-be apprentice, prodding at her greatest fears in the same way she had dug at his insecurities during their first encounter.

Literally and figuratively, he reached out to offer Rey his hand, a gesture of partnership and dominance.

For half his life, Ben Solo had been manipulated by the remnants of the Sith elite, and their conniving, destructive ways had indoctrinated him. Leia Organa and her birth mother, Padmé Amidala, were renowned for their diplomacy and poise. But in trying to secure Rey's allegiance, Kylo Ren instead relied on the exploitation of her deepest personal pain. For many lonely years on Jakku, Rey had let herself believe that she had a loving family somewhere out in the galaxy, waiting to return to her. Although she would find that acceptance in the Skywalker clan and her friends in the Resistance, the parents who had given her life were long dead, and furthermore had seemingly abandoned her. With her link to the Palpatine line still shrouded in mystery, both Rey and Kylo Ren believed that despite her skill with a lightsaber and connection to the Force, she lacked the dynastic link that made her suitable for leadership.

Himself an heir to the Skywalker legacy, who would have been a prince if not for the destruction of Alderaan, by comparison Rey's heritage made her a nonentity. Ren then made an even more provoking insinuation: Only through him could she reach her true potential. *He* was the key. Only someone as broken as what remained of Ben Solo could ever give her the empathy she sought.

It was the false binary choice from Starkiller Base all over again, an echo of Darth Vader's desperate attempt at wooing his son to his side. A broken and intense aggressor was claiming there could be only two options: servitude or death.

Despite their connection as a dyad, Ren had no idea who he was dealing with. In Ben's estimation, Rey had no place in the dynastic monarchy *unless* she joined him. However, Rey chose a third option. Despite her disappointment with Luke's inadequacy as a teacher and Ben's insistence on quashing the light within himself, Rey refused to allow their actions and decisions to determine her own fate.

Ben thought she was reaching for his hand, and his mind began to turn to the future and the new order they could mold in the galaxy with their combined powers. Instead, through the Force, she reached for the object that had connected her to her power: the Skywalker lightsaber.

Given their equally matched strengths and everything the saber stood for—the family Ben wanted to eliminate, the discord of the cyclical galactic strife, the Jedi and the Sith they had fought against—Rey and Ben battled over the weapon until it broke in two. United, they may have been unstoppable. But when they fought they were so evenly matched it was an exercise in futility.

Chapter 31

The Sacrifice of Luke Skywalker

With Rey gone, Luke Skywalker may have expected to retreat back into his monotonous routine on Ahch-To, but her appearance and his reignited connection to the Force had upset his uneasy tranquility. Alone once more, the Jedi Master truly believed his failure was complete. Based on what Luke had witnessed, the young woman was powerful in the Force but unruly. Her sympathy for his nephew Ben suggested a level of similarity that frightened him, rather than signaling the compassion that had marked the best of the Jedi before him. In losing Rey, not only had Luke failed to help Ben resist the darkness, he had also failed to keep the grandchild of Palpatine—for he knew her lineage even if she refused to name it—from giving in to her worst impulses. In short, Luke had neither learned from his mistakes nor heeded the warnings of the masters who had come before him.

Once so foolhardy that he imagined taking on the whole of the Empire singlehanded, Luke, older and battle-worn, became convinced that he lacked the strength to help his sister and aid the Resistance against the First Order, even as the band of rebels was being crushed several parsecs away.

In his despair, as a storm brewed over the island, pelting it with rain, the ground trembling with thunder, Luke resolved to burn down the first Temple, beginning with the tree of knowledge and all its ancient tomes. Unbeknownst to him, Rey had already taken the books for her own further study.

That day, the spirit of Master Yoda appeared just as he approached the uneti tree, surveying what had become of his final student in the Force. At 53, Luke still appeared young to the Jedi Master, who had outpaced many human lifespans and lived to be around 900 years old. And he still had much to learn.

Luke hesitated as he approached the library, doubt coloring his determination, his confidence wavering as he considered what it would mean to erase the Jedi from history. For all their failures, in their prime, the Jedi had maintained peace and justice in the galaxy, defended the weak, beaten back corruption . . . With the flick of a finger, Yoda's ethereal spirit seemed to summon the power of the passing storm, bringing a single bolt of lightning crashing down into the heart of the tree and setting it ablaze. And just as quickly as his irritation had set in, Luke forgot his self-pity; he instinctively rushed toward the flames to try to save the sacred Jedi texts inside. His desire to do good, to uphold the values of the Jedi eclipsed his doubt and angst.

In his darkest hour, when he was prepared to destroy all that had come before him, Yoda appeared in the cosmic Force to impart a valuable lesson that Luke, in his despair and consternation, had failed to understand. For nearly 30 years, Skywalker had held the Jedi of old in esteem, striving for a false perfection and ultimately recognizing the folly in their defeat. But he had not applied the same wisdom to his own personal disasters. Instead of learning from his failure to help Ben Solo remain a Jedi, he had retreated to wallow in shame. He had cut himself off rather than help Leia. He had refused to teach Rey, fearing she would only rise up as powerful and damaged as his nephew, ripe for manipulation by the dark side. According to Yoda, the loss of Ben Solo was a lesson, not for the pupil, but his master, a lesson for Luke in conquering his own apprehension and learning from it.

Luke had tried to pass on his knowledge of the Jedi ways but had hoped to avoid their inadequacies. The Sith masters were undoubtedly corrupt but in one aspect they understood the Force in a way that evaded most Jedi: The good in life could never be entirely divorced from the bad, nor the light separated from the dark. The Sith preached knowing all aspects of the Force as a means of harnessing the darkness, but there was an alternate path that allowed even a Jedi to know the most troubling impulses within themselves, stare them down, and make the choice to remain in the light. The two opposing forces would always coexist, regardless of the name given to those seeking knowledge in the spiritual nature of all living things. Success was not a straight path nor an upward climb toward enlightenment. There were backslides and broken ankles to be contended with along the way, and often more disappointments than achievements.

Through Yoda, Luke finally understood that his failure, though it felt all encompassing, did not have to define his legacy or his abilities. Despite the damage wrought by the galaxy-wide revelation that Darth Vader was his father, Luke Skywalker had done far more good than harm in the galaxy.

Luke never left the island. Just as Leia had sent him a messenger asking for help, he sent his own reply with a spectral envoy.

Through the Force he saw the Battle of Crait beginning, the Resistance forces on their knees and cowering behind a massive steel door at an abandoned old post. After fleeing D'Qar, the rebels had dwindled to some 400 individuals spread over three ships; by Crait only a handful remained. Luke recognized the uncertainty; it was Hoth all over again. Instead of holding off their foes, the Resistance could only hope to escape, evade the slaughter, and regroup to fight another day.

Leia and her forces sent out a distress beacon, a call for help that was received but no one came. In a defining moment for a career veteran who had managed to rally entire movements behind her own commitment to hope, Leia's confidence waivered.

Then Luke appeared, as if out of thin air.

Mustering all of his strength, Luke projected himself across space and time to appear in his prime at the base. Unlike the tired old man Rey had found hiding himself away, Luke put his most imposing self forward. For years he had seen the worst in himself, but that day he was once again the formidable Jedi teacher he had been in Ben's youth.

The Resistance general he found was not the hardened and assured version of his sister he remembered. Cornered on Crait, Leia felt certain this battle would be her last. There seemed no point in soldiering on any longer. Even worse than the loss of her planet and her people, that day Leia Organa nearly lost all faith in what she had spent her life fighting for and her conviction to keep going.

Although not a dyad in the Force, the Skywalker twins kept each other in balance. When Leia was morose, Luke was resolute. He was determined that his final act as a Jedi Master would ensure her survival and that of the few remaining freedom fighters. The Skywalker twins said their goodbyes, with no apology for all that had happened in the past left unsaid.

On the battlefield that day, Kylo Ren faced his uncle for the last time. In contrast to his father, who had willingly succumbed to his murderous whims, he found the Jedi much harder to silence. His uncle was not interested in reaching an understanding or pleading for tacit forgiveness. His goal was simple—to keep his fallen nephew distracted long enough for the core of the Resistance to escape the base undetected, trailing the native Vulptices as they fled the path of destruction themselves.

Ben attacked his former master with wild ferocity, perplexed by the old man's assurance. The wild-eyed Supreme Leader could not control his temper; in stark contrast, his opponent calmly dodged every strike.

The Jedi taunted his lost pupil. Luke dared him to end his life and Ben charged at his uncle and lashed out with his unstable blade, landing a hit that should have sliced him at the waist. Yet Luke remained unharmed, and—serene in the knowledge that the Resistance was now safe—allowed his fallen apprentice to understand the latest deception that had ensnared him. Onlookers soon came to find that Kylo Ren had been fighting shadows and ghosts; Luke, seemingly so invincible and indestructible was nothing more than a Force projection, an illusory distraction. Ben believed he was showcasing his abilities, when in reality he was shadowboxing, feeding the spectres of his past, even as he tried to fight them.

On the other side of the underground tunnel, Rey returned to the absolute basics of Jedi training. While Kylo Ren had been blinded to the ways of the light, Rey understood that some of its most tedious tasks—such as learning to lift stones—could mean the difference between life and death when friends were buried beneath the rubble.

Still on his island, alone save for the wildlife and the friendly Caretakers, the humble Lanai women who maintained it, the last of Luke's energy drained from his weakened mortal form as he gazed at the rising sun.

The Jedi was at peace. As his final act, Luke gave his life to protect Leia, and aided the Resistance with the help of his final student. Taking stock of his journey from the sands of Tatooine to his hermitage, Luke had come full circle. He had overcome crippling doubts to join the Rebel Alliance and discovered his place in the galaxy through the Force itself. He had faced the destructive nature of the dark side and dealt with the consequences of his family's place within the evil Empire. In the end he was willing to come out of hiding, overcoming his shame over the part he had played in the creation of Kylo Ren and his failure to prevent the rise of the First Order. He faced the most debilitating aspects of his identity with patience, calm, and understanding.

Luke Skywalker enjoyed a life well lived, not free of mistakes but ultimately absolved of regrets. He surrendered to the Force and became a part of the mystical energy.

It was a noble death and Luke greeted his transformation into the cosmic Force with his eyes on the horizon, an acknowledgment that a new day would dawn with or without him. For Kylo Ren, it was a demoralizing defeat.

***

After the escape from D'Qar, Leia Organa had watched as her own forces—led by Poe Dameron, a young man on whom she hung her hopes for the future of the revolution—were decimated in an ill-advised attack on a First Order dreadnought. Reduced to a handful of ships, the rebels made the jump to hyperspace only to be trailed by a form of tracking technology they had never encountered before.

Kylo Ren was among the fighters bearing down on the last of the Resistance fleet that day, but sensing his mother's presence aboard the flagship *Raddus*, he hesitated to fire. His TIE pilots, however, had no such qualms, and unleashed a torrent of blaster bolts that ripped through the ship, killing many high-ranking Resistance members and jettisoning Leia into the vacuum of space.

Floating amid choking smoke and fiery debris, with all she had fought and sacrificed for over the decades in pieces, Leia nearly gave up. She could have suffocated in space, a peaceful death out among the stars, a hero's demise on the battlefield. But Leia Organa refused to surrender. Even on that desperate day, she summoned her natural-born strength in the Force and pulled herself back into the embrace of the rebel ship and the soothing machines of the medical bay.

While Leia recuperated from her ordeal, her longtime friend and ally Vice Admiral Amilyn Holdo took charge, leading the survivors toward Crait and ultimately sacrificing herself to ensure the smattering of escape vessels made landfall. She and Leia had enjoyed a lifelong friendship, endured two tyrannical uprisings, and overcome numerous obstacles placed in their way by those that had questioned their authority, no doubt judging them by their looks instead of their abilities.

By the time the *Millennium Falcon* escaped from Crait, with just a handful of rebels aboard, Leia had lost Luke, too. Reduced to such a pitiable number, Leia took comfort in those who remained. Although Leia was by then the defacto leader of the movement, she took pride in passing command duties on to the next generation in the same fashion that she had been entrusted to lead while just barely an adult herself. Rather than mourn, the deaths of her brother and countless others reinvigorated Leia to continue her life's work, itself an extension of her parents' greatest hopes and her brother's ultimate sacrifice. Where others among the ragtag crew of survivors saw ruination, Leia saw possibility. The Rebel Alliance had been born out of necessity, to battle the seemingly insurmountable odds against a despotic regime that accumulated its power legally and with the blind support of the Republic. Although Leia would have undoubtedly wished to escape the twin defeats at D'Qar and Crait with most of her forces intact, in the belly of the ship that had once rescued her from the Death Star itself, Leia still had hope.

Every rebellion, from the upheaval on Onderon to Bail Organa's great alliance, had started the same way. Although the most successful grew in mass and might, in their earliest days, every flicker of resistance began with a few likeminded citizens who refused to be cowed by autocratic forces ruling by fear.

The only way Leia Organa would have ever ceased fighting was when she, too, was dead, or when the last Resistance fighter had been silenced by the First Order and no others remained to take their place. To ensure that never came to pass, for six months after the Battle of Crait, Leia rededicated herself to everything she and Luke had fought for together. She turned 54. It was strange to be older than Luke for the first time since birth, when he emerged ahead of her into a damaged world. Back on Ajan Kloss, where Leia had once learned the ways of the Force and considered her own path to becoming a Jedi, she established a new base of operations, a beacon of hope in the wilderness.

Leia watched over the other recruits, Poe and Rey's close friend and ally Finn among them, with a maternal presence. Rejected by her biological son, Leia became a motherly figure to a new generation of rebels.

She took on the mantle of a teacher in the Force, despite never having mastered the Jedi teachings herself. Her life experience and natural inclination toward the mystical energy helped Leia to give Rey the knowledge she craved; and Luke's abandoned training course helped her hone her physical strength and mental acuity.

There, Rey meditated in the Force, calling to those who had come before her for guidance and wisdom. In her quest for companionship and camaraderie within the ranks of the Resistance, she adopted a mantra, "Be with me," as if to summon the spirits of the Jedi past. It was, in fact, the very core of the Resistance's plea to the galaxy at large at the time, an invitation for unity as much as a battle cry.

Rey studied the ancient Jedi texts and mended the Skywalker saber, refurbishing the weapon to once again glow a brilliant blue. During this period, she often spoke to Luke through the Force, even though he didn't answer. She did not call to Ben, truly believing him to be lost to the dark side. She and Finn, the reformed stormtrooper who had helped her to escape Jakku, became close friends and trusted fighters, connected by Force-sensitivity and their shared belief that good must, in the end, defeat evil. She withheld her judgment on Poe Dameron, who always seemed to her to be too self-involved and difficult to truly become one of the next great leaders of the movement. For someone who had survived on necessity for much of her life, the amount of time he spent maintaining his hair suggested a level of narcissism that she had no time for.

Perhaps most importantly, Leia—who knew that, while her son had been born from the mighty Skywalker lineage, Rey was the product of the equally powerful Palpatine ancestry—passed on her own hard-won truth. In their belief in self-determined destiny, the Skywalker twins, the true son and daughter of Darth Vader, believed Rey alone could define her future, regardless of her bloodline. "Never be afraid of who you are," Leia told the young woman. Leia wished that someone had given her the same crucial mentorship, encouraging her to find the strength to face her parentage head-on rather than repressing it. She had been afraid that the hate she felt toward Vader would be turned inward and extend beyond herself to the people she loved, so she had tried to silence it. But demons must be confronted in order to be vanquished; in the shadows they merely gain strength and power over those who wish to banish them but refuse to go to the trouble.

Leia redoubled her efforts to pull together new resources for the war effort and contacted every friendly crowned leader and planetary diplomat who might lend ships, parts, supplies, and people to the cause of eliminating the First Order and freeing the galaxy once more.

In her quieter moments, she wrote to the families of the dead. So many fighters were lost that year that it seemed the task of expressing her condolences would never end, but Leia resisted employing her faithful protocol droid C-3PO to pen such personal correspondence. Leia felt it was her duty to address each and every widow, widower, and orphan, to pay homage to the tremendous loss of their loved ones and the sacrifice that had been made in the name of the war and the survival of the New Republic she had helped build.

Slowly but surely, she and her dedicated forces found new allies. Fighters like Wedge Antilles and Lando Calrissian, veterans and heroes of the Galactic Civil War, courageously came out of retirement to take the helm of whatever craft they could find to command. Leia visited old friends on Ryloth and Mon Cala to ask for assistance in person, then sent envoys in her stead to Minfar, Batuu, and beyond to collect as many other willing souls as she could. When possible, Leia employed a network of spies to infiltrate First Order strongholds and rally Resistance fighters on the ground.

The work during that period was difficult. Every First Order blockade or narrow escape from Supreme Leader Kylo Ren's armies left Leia and the rest of her soldiers on edge. Their numbers were low, along with their spirits, and just one crushing defeat could have easily meant disaster.

However, the legend of Luke Skywalker and the Resistance

gradually ignited the passions of a new generation of freedom fighters and Force-sensitives who saw their hope for a brighter future sparked by the story of the Jedi who had faced down an entire army alone and bested it. It seemed to prove that the light could be more powerful than the darkness, a new chapter in Jedi lore that could inspire hope for years to come.

The tale itself was not exactly a factual account of what had transpired, Leia knew, but it was more effective than any piece of propaganda she herself had seen.

Chapter 32

Ben Solo Reborn

With both of his masters dead, Kylo Ren greeted the year he turned 30 feeling almost invincible. He busied himself with personal quests to secure his power base without allowing himself to be distracted by what he perceived as the last remnants of the Resistance fighting his rule. However, instead of feeling free to pursue a new era in his own image, Kylo Ren could not deny the creeping presence of external forces of darkness still clouding his mind.

In a chilling message relayed across the galaxy, the voice of the dead Emperor Palpatine growled back to life, alerting the New Republic to his presence. "At last the work of generations is complete. The great error is corrected," it stated. "The day of victory is at hand. The day of revenge. The day of the Sith!"

The missive reopened an old wound for the young man who had felt so deeply wronged by the mysteries his family and then his master had kept from him. For the galaxy at large, Palpatine's apparent survival threw the political realm into disarray. For the Skywalker clan, it called into question the truth of what had transpired on the Death Star II. After all, Darth Vader's redemption hinged on the destruction of his Sith master, an act of love to save the life of his son.

Kylo Ren turned his attentions to his quest for power and the tantalizing allure of the darkness, hoping to piece together the secrets of the Sith, thought dead along with the Empire's leader, yet not quite forgotten.

Kylo Ren journeyed to Mustafar, once the retreat of his grandfather Darth Vader. There he cut down the Alazmec cultists, who also revered the dead Sith Lord, and recovered one of two fabled Sith wayfinders. The one he coveted lay amid the ruins of Vader's fortress. It was his personal artifact, a twin to the Emperor's own map to his secret Sith lair. Aboard his modified TIE whisper, the mysterious object guided the Supreme Leader on a course to Exegol in the Unknown Regions.

Luke Skywalker himself had spent some time trying to trace the way to this forgotten planet, steeped in Sith legend and shrouded in mystery. But it was Ren who succeeded, following the beacon to an unlikely source of his personal consternation and the plight of the galaxy at large.

Kylo Ren's journey led him to the Sith throne of the resurrected Emperor Palpatine; or, to be precise, the fleshy remnants of a cloned vessel that had been created for the Imperial king and hastily animated to stave off his demise at Darth Vader's hand.

On Exegol, Ren learned the truth of a lifetime of manipulations and deceit that, unknown to the young man, spanned two generations of his family. For more than half his life, Ben Solo had thought that he was obeying the voice of Snoke, but even the foul creature who led the First Order before Ben destroyed him was little more than a puppet in Palpatine's grand plans. Anakin Skywalker had sought control over life and death, but his grandson Ben evinced a more modern—and feasible— desire to control the galaxy as ruler of a new Empire. To satisfy Ren's hunger for power, Palpatine offered the son of Han Solo leadership of his greatest creation—the Final Order—a fleet of Star Destroyers summoned from the rocky soil and armed with turbolasers. In exchange, at Palpatine's behest, Ren was to kill Rey and conclude Darth Vader's journey by eliminating the last of the Jedi and surmounting the throne to rule as the new Emperor. The true nature of the Sith requires every successful apprentice to strike down their master and take their place. Kylo Ren would have to fulfill his destiny to become the leader of a new Empire, leading the Final Order, by ending Palpatine's decrepit life.

As many of Palpatine's promises had proven over the years, this one was threaded with deception and nuance. It is certain that the mastermind of the Empire and the First Order had no intention of dying at anyone's hand, but fed off the corrupt energy required to mount such a murderous rampage against a skilled and revered mentor.

Kylo Ren rallied the Knights of Ren for a campaign of terror, silencing any star systems that remained defiant in the face of his new regime, murdering traitors who dared to disobey him.

His mask once broken in a fit of rage after some disparaging remark made by Snoke, was reforged by a Sith alchemist called Albrekh. Once repaired, Ren's visage looked more intimidating than ever, reflecting his true nature. Its broken shards accentuated the damage it had received, creating a crimson web that mirrored Ren's own fractured psyche but commanded attention. Behind the mask, Ren reclaimed his dual identity of Supreme Leader and marauder. The helmet didn't sustain his life in a biological sense, but it was his chosen identity as much as Darth Vader's own mask came to define his legacy.

***

The news of the Emperor's apparent resurrection reached the Resistance via a coded message from a First Order spy, a not-altogether-friendly new ally who hated Kylo Ren more than the challenge the freedom fighters presented to the regime. By the time it was decoded, they had less than a day to find Exegol, using Luke Skywalker's old journals as the key.

The journey to the Sith Eternal's enclave was a path to self-discovery for Rey. The coming storm visited her in visions glimpsed through the Force and a smattering of clues that pointed to her past, while signposting the road to her future. For much of that day, Kylo Ren stalked

Rey, like a hunter on the trail of his ultimate prey, always mere steps behind her.

As Rey became more desperate, her capabilities seemed to grow, and the bond between the dyad grew stronger. Rey discovered her hands could harness the power to heal wounded creatures. When she lost control, those same hands were also capable of destroying anyone who stood in her way. Rey could be both a giver of life and a purveyor of death, a power that left her feeling bewildered.

Luke's writings took her and her friends to the Middian system and the planet of Pasaana, where the native Aki-Aki were celebrating their Festival of the Ancestors. The welcoming locals happily shared their culture with Rey, placing a kern-nut necklace around the young fighter's neck.

But the dyad in the Force connecting Rey and Ren also enabled *his* abilities to intensify. Despite the distance and her own attempts to ignore their connection, he reached her, snatched her necklace and, analyzing the naturally derived resources for a clue, tracked her to the peaceful, sandy world.

On Pasaana, Rey's past came roaring back to her in the form of objects invested with their own disturbing associations. She found a ship, the *Bestoon Legacy,* that had ferried her parents away the day she was sold to Unkar Plutt, abandoned in treacherous fields that threatened to swallow her and her friends alive. Rey also came across an ancient dagger etched with Sith runes that promised the location of a second wayfinder. Unknown to Rey, the blade had a dark history: It had been plunged into her own father's guts at the behest of Palpatine himself.

In the desert that day, Kylo Ren and Rey once again clashed in battle. On foot, Rey dismantled Ren's ship with a slash of his grandfather's laser sword—a weapon which held its own dark secrets—then grappled for possession of a departing First Order shuttle, which she mistakenly believed was carrying her captured friend, Chewbacca. Fearing that her and Ren's evenly matched abilities would rend the craft in two, just as they had once destroyed the coveted Skywalker lightsaber hilt, Rey became so enraged that a jolt of dark lightning ripped from her fingertips and pulled the craft from the sky. She paid a high price for her actions, thinking she had caused the noble Wookiee's death at her hand and exposed her own worst impulses for all to see.

The future danced before Rey's eyes. Through the Force, Rey's visions grew darker, the pull of her dormant wickedness inviting her to consider a new path. In one fleeting glimpse, Rey saw not just Ren but also herself, transformed in the darkness, relishing its decadent power, both of them perched on the blackened, claw-like stone throne of the Sith. The only person she entrusted with this information was Finn, who neither recoiled in disgust nor offered false sympathy; he merely looked upon her sadly as tears stung her face.

Time grew short. Rey and her friends infiltrated the *Steadfast* in the skies above Kijimi to rescue Chewbacca. There Rey found herself ensconced in Ren's inner sanctum.

Inside Kylo Ren's private quarters, the mask of Darth Vader greeted Rey, just as the connection between the dyad flashed back to life, easily leading Ren to her quarry on the deck of his ship.

It was there that Ren confronted Rey with the knowledge of her birthright to the throne of the Sith. Although she evaded him once more, the damage was done. Rey was forced to confront the knowledge that Palpatine's destructive blood was coursing through her veins. This was Rey's true identity.

In her despair, she returned to her roots as a scavenger. In the Endor system, on the ocean moon of Kef Bir, Rey braved the sighing and rusting remains of the Empire's second Death Star. The wreckage had come to rest in a watery grave 30 years before, with a few pieces floating to the surface like bloated corpses; however, the Emperor's vault remained intact, a tomb and a treasure chest. Inside, she discovered an enclave as powerful in the dark side of the Force as the well of darkness on

Ahch-To. Rey battled a ghastly dark-side vision that reflected her own face, save for dagger-sharp teeth and a hinged red blade in its hands to escape with her prize—Palpatine's wayfinder, the key to her quest to locate Exegol and put an end to Palpatine's protracted reign.

But Kylo Ren was waiting. No sooner had she recovered her family heirloom than Ren crushed it, leaving only Vader's wayfinder remaining and infuriating Rey beyond reason. In their final battle, amid the roiling seas and the remnants of the once powerful Empire Palpatine had created in his own image, Rey hacked at her enemy's saber, losing strength with every thrust, exhausted by her arduous, fruitless journey. Despite their dyad connection, which had historically left them evenly matched, Kylo Ren gained the upper hand. For a moment, Rey resigned herself to certain death amid the wreckage of the aptly-named space station. At least she would have died battling the darkness rather than succumbing to it—a noble end.

Yet, as he drew his arm back to strike the fatal blow, Kylo Ren paused.

From the safety of Ajan Kloss, Leia had felt the tremor of her son Ben bearing down on Rey, her protégée. Through the Force, Luke summoned her to intervene. It was the mother's last chance to reach her child, to console his fears and convince him that she believed he could still reverse course, reject the hatred he felt and embrace the good within his heart.

Ben had told Rey, "The dark side is in our nature."

And for years, for Ben, the only way to deal with this truth was to surrender to it. To become stronger. To hero-worship Darth Vader without pausing to examine the man he had left behind in assuming the horrifying visage. Kylo Ren was prepared to submit to the dark side's lust for power and to cut off all past connections to the Jedi, and the only family he still possessed: his mother. Yet in that moment, he heard the voice of Leia whispering his name. As if she could see him. As if she still believed there was a way for him to return to the light, despite every foul deed he had committed of his own free will and by Snoke's decree. As if she was welcoming him home.

Ren was so dumbfounded by the sound of his mother's voice he let his weapon fall to the ground. And Rey saw the opening and seized her chance. Grabbing its hilt, she stabbed him through with his own unstable blade.

In their different ways, Rey and Leia defeated Kylo Ren, one giving in to her own darkest impulses and the other sacrificing herself to send one last message of hope to the boy she had carried in her womb.

Leia died to reach her son and Rey became the very thing she herself hated. The weapon of a dark side warrior clasped in her palm, the fire of vengeance burning in her eyes. Rey had won the battle but it didn't feel like a victory.

Kylo Ren crumpled to the ground, the last of the Skywalker line dying by *her* hand. A terrible sense of loneliness crept upon her while the man who was once Ben Solo collapsed in agony, sure that he was going to die. Their eyes locked in recognition for their shared loss of Leia, the maternal presence who had welcomed them both with open arms and unfailing compassion.

Rey couldn't explain why at the time, but just as quickly as she'd landed the fatal stroke, Rey placed her hands upon Ben's abdomen and gave her own life force to heal him.

Healing through the Force is a peculiar thing. Rey transferred her own Force energy to the wounded man at her feet; however, the interaction did more than merely mend a gaping wound. Burned flesh and damaged organs were made whole again, and even the scar on his face disappeared. For the first time in more than a decade, Ben Solo's mind cleared.

Rey had reversed the damage she had wrought and more, yet it could not undo the knowledge of what she had allowed herself to become. To vanquish Kylo Ren, she had given in to her own darkness. To ensure it would not happen again, Rey stole Ren's TIE and hurtled back toward

Ahch-To. She wished to become as small and insignificant as Luke Sky-walker had made himself there, hiding among the ruins of the Jedi who were no more. If she could not trust herself with the abilities the Force imbued her with, she could at least keep others out of harm's way.

***

Ben Solo was left alone with his thoughts on the tumultuous seas of Kef Bir that day, having greeted death and lived to see its cold grip loosened once more. The exact cause of Kylo Ren's defeat is complex. His attach-ment to his mother had remained strong despite her failures in his eyes, and he felt her loss like a punch to the chest. And because of her inter-vention, Rey had bested him in battle; the light overcoming the dark at a terrible cost. The granddaughter of Palpatine had proved her bloodline was stronger than his own. In his eyes, she was more worthy to be the Supreme Leader of the Final Order than he was.

But then by healing him she had emphatically proved she was no villain despite her momentary vindictive lapse. She had weakened her-self so that he might live, knowing that doing so could make him strong enough to finish the battle, leaving Rey dead at his feet instead. There was trust in her action; she had sacrificed part of herself for his wellbe-ing out of unconditional love. And with that show of tenderness and compassion, coupled with grief over losing his mother, Ben Solo found himself stripped of all the aggression he had clung to in order to try to make himself feel strong. Relieved of the malice that had ruled him for so long, he had to face the truth of what he had become.

Ben Solo was forced to consider why he had chosen to follow in Darth Vader's footsteps in the first place. Snoke's—no, Palpatine's—near-constant whisperings had prodded him toward that dark path, despite his futile attempts at resistance. Yet he had made the key deci-sions that led him to Exegol. For the first time since he had stood before his father in the heart of Starkiller Base, Ben felt like there was still a choice to be made.

The image of his father, standing before him, caressing his face and offering him forgiveness came to mind again unbidden. The remorse and crippling sadness he felt was worse than any lightsaber wound. A sob escaped his newly healed chest as he finally mourned the death of his father, and reconciled with the monster he had become. Then, Ben Solo hurled the lightsaber of Kylo Ren into the air, sending the fractured weapon spinning end over end, until it splashed down in the same resting place as the wreckage of the second Death Star. The weapon of the heir to the Empire was laid to rest in the same watery grave as its greatest invention.

Ben Solo was reborn that day, infused with the life force of the dyad and eager to fulfill Rey's wish to join forces against the evil that had tried—and failed—to swallow them both.

Chapter 33

The Last Skywalker

At almost the same time that Ben was grappling with his resurgence in the light, Rey was mourning her own fall to darkness. Perhaps she believed that Leia experiencing the apparent death of her son had been so disruptive it had killed her by robbing her of any chance to see her child redeemed. The shock of his loss, felt through the Force, was more than most mothers could be expected to bear. She had died without knowing that Rey had brought her son back to life

Rey was convinced that the only way to escape truly turning to the dark side and becoming Empress Palpatine was by completely cutting herself off from the Force, as Luke had done, and retreating into the survival mode that had kept her safe for most of her life.

Back on Ahch-To, she set to work burning the ship that had ferried her to its shores, ensuring she could not leave even if she was tempted to try. But when Rey hurled Anakin Skywalker's lightsaber into the flames she was astonished to see the ethereal form of her former master stepping from the wreckage holding the hilt aloft.

In the candid conversation that followed, Luke deterred his former student from attempting her own shameful retreat into fear. Instead, he encouraged her to rise to the challenge of becoming the best of the Jedi—someone powerful in the Force and willing to face their fears, their foes, and their failures. If Rey had rejected Luke's proposal, it would have meant the true end of the Jedi Order and the obliteration of the Resistance. (Truth be told, Rey was far more afraid of losing herself than losing that fight.) Luke, like all good masters, imparted the wisdom to help Rey calm her troubled mind and see things clearly: "Some things," he said, "are stronger than blood."

His words may be interpreted to mean that the dyad itself was more potent than any other Force bond or bloodline; or that Rey's choices as an individual were more indicative of her character than her familial heritage, her own accolades and failure outweighing the successes and failures that came before her. Regardless of Luke's intent, his counsel was enough to set her on the path to defeat her grandfather's decades of degeneracy providing Rey with resources of resilience and strength that would have done Shmi Skywalker herself proud.

Inside the same X-wing fighter that had carried Luke Skywalker to victory over the Empire, and ultimately to the island where he died, Rey took Vader's wayfinder, and two lightsabers—one forged by Anakin, the other by his daughter, Leia—to Exegol to meet her fate head on. Along the way, she beamed her coordinates to her friends at the Resistance base. This beacon from a bygone era brought a sudden resurgence of hope. Those who did not know better swore that it was Luke Skywalker himself coming to the rescue, returned from hiding to save the day at last. And, in a way, it was . . .

While the Resistance fleet charted a course to the Unknown Regions to confront Palpatine's vast navy, Rey ventured alone into the bowels of Palpatine's lair. In the brief time she had spent as a member of the Resistance, just over a year, the freedom fighters had become something of a found family to the once-lowly scavenger; together, in a two-pronged attack, they aimed to vanquish the galactic terror for good.

Palpatine had told Kylo Ren that Rey had to die, but as she stood before the throne of the Sith, the truth of his motives became clear. Unseen voices chanted in the darkness as Palpatine gazed at his prize. Decades before this moment, as the apprentice of Darth Plagueis,

Sidious had murdered his teacher and taken all his knowledge of the Sith for himself. In Rey, he hoped to find a willing accomplice to end his life in his decrepit form and permit his spirit to pass into her. Rey was just 20, young and in excellent physical shape, strong in the Force and skilled with a lightsaber. And while Palpatine's cloned body was dying and weak, his bloodline flowed through Rey, making her a perfect host. With their souls fused inside her flesh—not a dyad but an otherworldly and unnatural homage to their shared DNA—Palpatine aimed to grant himself immortality, control of the Sith, and command over the galaxy once more, rising from the ashes of the Empire to be resurrected stronger than ever before.

But Rey refused to let her hatred of Palpatine and her fears for her friends rule her. The Sith Lord offered yet another apprentice the temptations of the dark side, and Rey spurned his false promises.

She did not face her grandfather alone for long. Ben Solo at the helm of a borrowed TIE fighter, no lightsaber to his name, arrived soon after.

The Knights of Ren, once loyal followers of his every whim, had sought to destroy their former leader in what they believed was his weakened state. In their eyes, he had betrayed them: He had regressed to the young man who had been in awe of Luke Skywalker and fearful of alternative paths for his natural-born abilities.

By healing Ben Solo, Rey had cemented their connection far beyond anything they had already experienced. She could see him on Exegol, in battle, as if he were next to her. She could feel him transformed, confident in his decision to renounce the dark persona of Kylo Ren. And without a word spoken, their thoughts entwined, she raised the Skywalker saber to strike down Palpatine, but instead passed the weapon, through the Force, to her partner in the dyad.

They fought together on Exegol, carrying the lightsabers once owned by Luke Skywalker and Leia Organa, battling back the demons of the dark with the legacy of the Skywalker twins and all they had fought for. Then they came together in physical as well as spiritual forms and turned as if as one, standing united against Palpatine. Two Jedi. One Sith.

Unseen for generations, the power of their pairing was made to serve the Emperor one last time. Siphoning their combined energies to restore his withered body, with strength renewed, Palpatine thrashed Rey and sent Ben Solo hurtling toward a gaping crevasse.

Rey could have given up then and there.

She didn't.

Lying on a cold stone slab, Rey reached for the elusive mantra she had used in her training to summon her strength and the spirits of all those Jedi who had come before her. This time, in her utter defeat and desperation, they answered.

The voices of the Jedi sang through the Force, from beyond the grave, like a chorus of the light. They gave her the strength to keep going, to push away all doubt and the overwhelming feeling that she was facing impossible odds alone.

The Resistance had felt so small after the crushing defeat on Crait, and it had been in number. However, the movement found the will to survive, to rally new allies, to grow stronger. Leia had led the charge. But Leia was dead.

And yet, the Jedi of the past were not truly gone: some of their greatest practitioners continued to exist through the cosmic Force. Even those Jedi who passed on without maintaining such a hold on their individuality lived on through their students, through their teachings and wisdom. They lived on in the memories of those they had helped, loved, and served with. And united, they were stronger than the blood in Rey's veins, and stronger than Palpatine himself, despite his scientific interventions to ensure his immortality.

It was the voice of Rey's master Luke Skywalker that rang in her ears as she struggled to her feet. The Force was her ally. Calling Leia's lightsaber into her waiting hand, Rey regained her ethos and her weapon to battle against the darkness within and without.

The thrum of the lightsaber attracted Palpatine's attention and he unleashed a fresh fusillade of dark lightning at his own grandchild. Calling the Skywalker saber to her hand for balance, two stronger than the one, Rey crossed the blades to beat back Palpatine's attack, sending his own destructive power ricocheting back at him until the man, the throne, and all those who had bowed before them were destroyed.

The exertion drained Rey so completely that she collapsed, eyes wide but unseeing. Through the Force, Finn—only just discovering his own connection to the energy—felt his friend's demise. So, too, did Ben Solo.

By the time he climbed back out of the hole where Palpatine had sent him to die, everything in the cathedral was dust and debris. Rey was dead. There were a number of ways Ben Solo could have chosen to honor her sacrifice. But the last of the Skywalker line saw only one option.

Ben had wasted much of his life to date allowing his pain to consume and control him, while Rey had overcome personal hardships and empathized with his extended family. She had viewed the choices Ben had made with sympathy and compassion and tried to reach out to him, succeeding where his parents had failed. She had understood him better than any other living being. Through their dyad connection, she had healed him, saving a life that was hers for the taking, proving that kindness was more powerful than hate.

Cradling her body, Ben repaid his debt with what little strength he had remaining. He summoned the healing power of his own life force to resurrect Rey, though the effort and the amount of vitality took all of his energy. Just as Rey sacrificed herself to defeat the Sith, Ben sacrificed himself to revive her, an atonement for all the damage he had done to the galaxy that she alone had redeemed.

With a kiss—an acknowledgement of the depth of their connection as much as an observance that finally, in the end, she had been right and Ben Solo had chosen the path of the light—Rey touched Ben's cheek, an echo of his father's caress.

Ben laughed, a pure and unencumbered moment of joy and smiled even as he grew cold. But he was welcomed in death by the Force, an admission of how far he had come. Without regrets, Ben Solo, the last of the legendary Skywalker dynasty, faded away, like the best of the Jedi, ferried to the realm beyond the living by the mother who had given her life to pull him back from the brink of his own destruction.

Epilogue

Over 50 years after Anakin Skywalker fashioned his lightsaber to go to war, the weapon of the Jedi remained in his family.

As a child, the son of Shmi imagined the laser swords of Jedi Knights as something from a book of fables and legends. By the time he had trained to use one, he had come to understand the reality of deflecting enemy fire and protecting himself and the people he loved. But while Anakin's first saber was made for defense, his last was built with battle in mind and saw countless enemies fall dead upon its blade.

As a familial artifact, there is no doubt that this was a weapon linked to unspeakable crimes, cutting down the youngest members of the Jedi Order amid Anakin's fall to the darkness. Yet it was also a symbol of hope and triumph, justice promulgated to restore peace and order.

Lost on the lava shores of Mustafar, Anakin's teacher protected the saber as he watched over Skywalker's son. And when the time was right, Luke Skywalker carried the heirloom weapon in hopes of defeating the Empire. In his hands, it was once more a tool of admirable intentions; however, the saber's resurgence was cut short by Darth Vader's own cunning swordsmanship, and banished to the bowels of Bespin.

In time it was returned to Luke, who wanted no part of it or what it stood for, before becoming the weapon of the Jedi Rey Skywalker. Rey was born of the Palpatine line. The legacy of her family was greed and destruction, but that did not fit the place she chose to inhabit. She was trained by Luke Skywalker and Leia Organa, and accepted as one of their own. Her power was derived through the Force, a resonant frequency all her own. And when it mattered, she finished what Darth

Vader had started and ended Palpatine's dark reign, going against her own kin and her own blood to achieve balance in the Force.

When the battle was won, Rey traveled to Tatooine, to the bombed-out shell of the Lars homestead. She buried the blade forged by Anakin, carried by Luke, alongside the hilt that was fashioned by Leia, entombing the heirloom lightsabers near the sacred place where Shmi Skywalker, the matriarch, had been laid to rest. The sands swallowed what remained of the Skywalker relics.

But as Luke Skywalker once told his sister, Leia, "No one's ever really gone."

With the last of the Skywalker line no more, Rey took on the name to further the cause and built her own gleaming gold lightsaber from parts of the staff she had carried during her years as a lonely orphan, an immaculate fusion of her past and the future she had chosen. A symbol of hope, not an instrument of war.

The Skywalker bloodline ran dry, their heirlooms were buried, and only the stories of heroics and cruelty remained. But Rey Skywalker, empowered by the teachings and familial love and acceptance bestowed upon her, embodied the finest aspects of that lineage. She was brave enough to conquer the worst facets of herself and earned her place as a Skywalker by choice, not by birth.

The Skywalkers were a family thrust into war while grappling with internal strife. And in the dawn of a new era of peace, Rey Skywalker remained to bury their past, and look to the future, to the possibility of teaching a new generation of Jedi and passing on the responsibility of maintaining the balance, between the light and the dark, in the galaxy and inside each one of us.

And in that way, the Skywalker legacy lives on.

Acknowledgements

Telegraphing the story of the Skywalker bloodline has been both daunting and exhilarating. In the real-life tumult of 2020, it was a welcome respite to spend my days with the first family of *Star Wars*.

But this story may never have found its elusive balance if not for the collaborative powerhouse that helped bring it to life and the brilliant minds who came before it to create the raw material from which this tale is forged. My gratitude extends to my amazing and uplifting editors, Alastair Dougall and Brett Rector; the Lucasfilm Story Group, especially Emily Shkoukani and Pablo Hidalgo; the filmmakers, J.J. Abrams and Rian Johnson; and the family of *Star Wars* authors including Claudia Gray, Charles Soule, Jason Fry, and Rae Carson, who have cleared the path with their own storytelling. I could not have done this without the support of Lucasfilm's Mike Siglain, Mickey Capoferri, and Dan Brooks who opened the door to my work on StarWars.com and beyond, nor the patient guidance of Dean Kashner and Jim Sachetti, who took a cocky kid who thought she knew how to write and actually taught her to make a story sing.

"Thank the maker!" George Lucas, who stands alone as the most vital link between the power of imagination and the rich modern mythology that he has gifted us all. He is a testament to what one person can do through the simple act of hope and with the power of tenacity.

My appreciation goes out to my own family, both by blood and by choice: William and Linda Baver, Heather Baver, Michael Andrews, Cynthia Ritter, Megan Varano, and Michael Lester, who has supported me in every crazy idea and far-fetched dream. Thanks to M.J. Mahon

Acknowledgements

and Justin Bolger, the two best work spouses I have ever known, who believed I could write a book long before I did, and my dear friend Phil Szostak who was always willing to lend an ear to my frustrations and elations in the writing process.

Perhaps I am most grateful to you. For choosing this story, for reading these pages, for joining me on a journey to find the humanity, compassion, and understanding of these fictional characters who are neither entirely good nor evil, but something much more relatable. I have been a proud member of the *Star Wars* fan community for most of my life now. Thank you for giving me a place to belong.